HIGHLAND CAPTIVE

Aimil eyed Parlan intently. "I dinnae suppose ye may have changed your mind."

"Nay. I was determined to have ye as soon as I kenned ye werenae a child too young for the having."

Parlan scooped her up in his arms and gently deposited her on the bed. It astounded her that such a large man could move with such silent speed. When he partially covered her body with his own, she shivered slightly. His large, strong body made her feel very small and very fragile, yet she was not really afraid. Instead, she felt the desire she craved to taste eke into her veins.

"Dinnae be afeard of me, sweeting. I mean only to pleasure ye," he whispered, brushing soft kisses over her cheeks.

"Pleasure yourself, ye mean," she grumbled, but felt an odd tingling where his lips touched her skin.

"Aye, but ye as weel, Aimil. Just relax and give yourself over to me."

Books by Hannah Howell

Published by Zebra Books

HIGHLAND CAPTIVE

HANNAH HOWELL

ZEBRA BOOKS
Kensington Publishing Corp.
www.kensingtonbooks.com

ZEBRA BOOKS are published by

Kensington Publishing Corp.
850 Third Avenue
New York, NY 10022

All Kensington titles, imprints, and distributed lines are available
at special quantity discounts for bulk purchases for sales promo-
tion, premiums, fund-raising, educational, or institutional use.

Special book excerpts or customized printings can also be created to fit specific needs. For details, write or phone the office
of the Kensington Special Sales Manager: Attn. Special Sales
Department. Kensington Publishing Corp., 850 Third Avenue,
New York, NY 10022. Phone: 1-800-221-2647.

Zebra and the Z logo Reg. U.S. Pat. & TM Off.

ISBN-13: 978-0-8217-8003-9
ISBN-10: 0-8217-8003-4

Previously published in 1990 by Leisure Books under the title
Elfking's Lady.
First Zebra Mass-Market Paperback Printing: November 2008

10 9 8 7 6 5 4 3 2 1

Printed in the United States of America

Chapter One

Scotland, 1500

Astonishment froze the handsome, young man's face when the sturdy horse he had mounted buckled beneath him, collapsing and sending him tumbling to the ground. For a moment he simply stared at the white stallion nimbly rising. Brushing himself off as he too rose, he glared at the small figure who sat not far away laughing helplessly.

"Brat," he said affectionately, a grin beginning to shape his mouth. "When did ye teach the beast that trick?"

"While ye were tasting the wicked life in Aberdeen, Leith."

Leith grinned as he lay down next to his sister, his arms crossed beneath his head. "Aye, and a hearty taste I had too."

"Wicked, wicked." Aimil sighed, but her aquamarine eyes sparkled with laughter. "What would Aunt Morag say?"

"Please, Lord, that I will never ken," Leith remarked feelingly as he sat up. "We had best be headed back. The day wanes."

"Och, must we? I have seen naught but the inside of that place for the past month."

"'Tis safer, what with the MacGuins raiding again. I shouldnae have let ye persuade me on this jaunt. Not even when ye do look like a wee beggar boy. We might pass unseen, but that stallion of yours would surely catch the eye." He clasped her hand in his and led her toward their horses. "Now tell me about this wedding that all talk about." He saw her pale. "Oho . . . is that the way of it then?"

"Aye. I ken I must, but I cannae abide the thought of it. I dinnae even like Rory Fergueson."

Neither did Leith but he refrained from saying it. "I shall talk to Father."

"I dinnae think it will do any good. This marriage has been set since the cradle. I may be his kin, but he is sore anxious to be rid of me."

There was little to deny for Leith knew it was sadly true. Since the day Aimil had begun to look more like a woman than a child, their father had ignored her. Not only was Leith confused by their father's attitude but his two elder sisters and two younger brothers also were as was most everyone else in the clan. Any attempt to broach the subject with their father, however, met with silence or fury. Now he was about to give Aimil in marriage to a man about whom some very unsavory things were said.

"I will still talk to him. Has he given ye any reason for the marriage?"

"Aye, 'tis time I wed," she replied somewhat bitterly. "And that it was a promise to an old friend."

"That isnae good enough. If ye must wed a man ye dinnae want, father can give you a damn good reason why. Even if it was set while ye still rocked in your cradle."

Aimil smiled at her brother's anger. Leith was much like their father. He could bark orders and expect immediate obedience. Unlike their sire, however, he felt a reason should be given if it was asked for. She knew his anger and determination did not mean that she would be released from marrying

Rory Fergueson, but it was comforting to have an ally. At least he might force their father to better explain the why of it all.

An alliance had been her first thought for though they were far from poor the Mengues were a small clan and were often targeted by the MacGuins. That theory had been dispelled for an alliance already existed as far as she knew. Her sisters', Giorsal's and Jennet's, marriages already attached the Mengues to the MacVerns and the Broths which had greatly added to the Mengues' strength. She did not believe that marrying Rory Fergueson would make any difference at all except to make her life miserable.

Leith felt an urgency to get home and not because it was growing late. He knew that their father was well aware of the man Rory had become. Just as Leith could not understand his father's attitude toward Aimil, the prettiest and most personable of his daughters, so too was he unable to understand how their father could think of marrying her off to such a man. The more Leith thought of his favorite sibling in the hands of Rory Fergueson, the more determined he became to put a stop to the marriage.

Whatever plans Leith may have begun were lost as horsemen bearing the MacGuin colors burst upon the quiet glade. Young Artair MacGuin wondered what young fools had so unwittingly placed themselves in the path of his raiding party's return to its lair. Recognizing the Mengue colors, he thought to impress his elder brother with some captives for ransom. The excellant horseflesh the pair of lads had with them was a prize worth taking as well. His brother had not sanctified Artair's raids but Artair felt sure that such gain would ease whatever anger was aroused by them.

Drawing his sword, Leith stood firmly between Aimil and the MacGuin raiders, pushing her toward her horse. "Flee while ye can. I will try to hold them."

The instant's pause Aimil took while pondering the desertion of her brother cost her dearly. She had barely vaulted onto the back of her steed when a MacGuin was there, trying to seize her reins. He received a small booted foot in the face which sent him flying. She realized it was only a temporary victory for she was surrounded by MacGuins and prevented from making a run for safety. She and her horse put up a valiant battle nonetheless, leaving many a MacGuin and his mount with bruises to remember. The melee seemed to last for hours, but Aimil knew it was only of a few moments' duration. A scowling man ended it swiftly by the judicious wielding of the flat of his sword against her head. As she slumped into unconsciousness, she saw her brother fall beneath a half-dozen MacGuins. The last sound she made was a terrifying scream that Leith was about to be murdered.

The strong smell of horseflesh was her first sensation as she edged back into awareness. She then realized that she was tied to the back of her horse, her face pressed against his sweat-dampened coat. They moved at a ground-covering pace, but her body seemed numb to the abuse. All except her head, she mused with regret, which throbbed with each hoofbeat. She could not see Leith so she could only assume that he was in a similar ignominious position just out of view. The thought that he might be dead was one she forcibly rejected.

The strong keep of the MacGuins came into her limited range of vision, and the horses slowed their pace. Her heart sank for, once inside the gates, it would be nearly impossible to escape. Though no soldier, she easily recognized the strength of the place as a fortress and a prison. There was no doubt in her mind that she and Leith would be ransomed, but even the shortest term of imprisonment made her quake. Was her disguise still intact, she fretted, and, if it was, how long would it remain? She had heard enough to know how she would be treated if these fierce Highland raiders discovered that one of the lads they held was really a lass.

"So, ye be awake. Weel, I will wager all the fight has been ridden out of ye, laddie."

Her eyes closed briefly in relief then she glared at the burly, dark man who was untying her bonds. He looked nothing like a man who would cut a man's heart out without a blink, but she was wiser now. She did not trust so easily, especially not in her own opinions. After all, she had felt that her father's love was secure and she had been proven painfully wrong.

"Here now, there isnae any use in your looking like that, me wee ghillie," the man scolded jovially as he released the last bond holding Aimil, then caught her as she slid helplessly from the broad back of Elfking. "Ye are in no state to carry out the threat in them eyes."

"Put them in the dungeon, Malcolm," Artair ordered coldly.

Still supporting the weakened Aimil, Malcolm frowned. "They be only a pair of lads and nae too healthy ones at the moment."

Artair scowled. "Those lads have sore bruised half my men. Aye, and several good mounts. In the dungeon with them. Leastwise there I willnae have to worry about a close guard until Parlan returns and decides what is to be done with them. Best if he decides the ransom to be asked."

Malcolm continued to frown as he picked Aimil up in his arms, since the lad seemed too groggy to walk. He noted that the other young man needed carrying as well. To put two young boys into the pit, as the dungeon was aptly called, seemed cruel. They were in no condition to be a threat. Prisoners they might be, but Malcolm felt sure the laird would not treat them so callously. He was at the steps of the keep before he realized the huge white stallion was following at his heels, treating any who tried to stop him with lethal viciousness. Malcolm eyed the horse with an astonishment tinged with fear.

"Put me down."

"Ye cannae even stand upright," Malcolm grumbled, uneasily eyeing the huge horse that faced him.

"Then hold me upright. I must speak to Elfking or he will kill to stay with me."

Steadying Aimil, Malcolm was not the only one who watched in near awe as the small boy caressed the stallion's head, crooning, "Nay, Elfking, ye cannae follow. Stay with the men. Stay. We will be here but a wee while. Stay with the men." Aimil felt the thick fog of unconsciousness claiming her again. "I think ye must carry me again, Master Malcolm, if ye would, please."

"It isnae right," Malcolm grumbled a bit later as he watched the door secured over the unconscious prisoners.

"Ye have ever been soft of heart, Malcolm," one of the other men said with no real condemnation.

"Aye, but he is right this time," remarked Lagan Dunmore, a cousin to the laird, who often visited with the MacGuins.

"Right or wrong, Artair's the laird whilst Parlan is away. He said to put the lads in here so here they be staying."

Lagan exchanged a helpless look with Malcolm then sighed. "Weel then, let us pray that Parlan returns soon or there will be naught for the ransoming."

"Aye, only for the burying," Malcolm said heavily before stalking away.

Darkness greeted Aimil when she woke. As she lay trying to come to her senses, she became more aware of her surroundings. There was a pervasive damp, and beneath her hands was cold, moist earth. By the time she spotted the grate over her head, she knew she was in a dungeon, perhaps even an oubliette. She fought the urge to scream for she knew it would be fruitless and she did not want to expose her terror.

Blocking out the feel and knowledge of the myriad of small creatures that no doubt shared the pit, she groped around for Leith. In so small an area it was easy to find him.

He was still unconscious so she settled his head upon her lap, her hands gently searching his form for serious wounds.

"Aimil?" Leith groaned as he tried to sit up only to fall back with an oath.

"I am right here, Leith. Where are ye hurt? I cannae tell by feeling ye, and 'tis too dark to see," she muttered.

"'Tis all right. A few scratches and more bruises than I care to count. Dinnae fash yourself."

She frowned for his voice was weak and strained but, without any light, she could not tell if he was lying. "We have been tossed in a ground dungeon."

He searched out her hand to clasp it comfortingly. "It willnae be for long. We are for ransoming. Father will be quick to buy us free." A shaky laugh escaped him. "They must have been sore impressed with us to lock us up so tightly. We being but a pair of lads."

Knowing that he sought confirmation that her disguise still held, she replied, "Aye. What should I tell them when they ask my name?"

"Tell them ye are Shane. Father will ken what is about and will follow through with the subterfuge. Aye, he will be glad of it."

"He must wonder where we are even now." She sighed, knowing that her father would be sorely worried, if only for Leith.

Just as Lachlan Mengue had noted the absence of his two offspring, word had come that the MacGuins had raided the Ferguesons. He began to fear the worst as the searchers he had hastily dispatched continued to find no sign of Leith or Aimil. Instinct told him that they had been caught. Several places they often rode to could have been in the path of the retreating MacGuin raiding party, a prize easily snatched up.

Only a fool would miss seeing what an easy chance for ransom they presented, and Parlan MacGuin was no fool.

As night faded into another day, Lachlan sat drinking and praying for some word, any word. His heir and his youngest daughter were a loss he was not sure he could bear despite four other children who could have consoled him. In anticipation of a ransom demand, he began to review his purse and his options for supplementing it. Even as yet another day passed with no word, he clung to the thought that they were prisoners. Anyone who even looked as if he might think differently suffered the heat of Lachlan's impressive temper. His children were alive, and he refused to consider anything else unless their lifeless bodies were brought before him to be seen with his own eyes.

Aimil very much feared for her brother's life. His injuries may have been slight but they had been untended. Two days and nights in the cold, damp hole had sapped his strength. He was unconscious more than he was conscious. She was also certain that he was feverish. Meager food once a day and a thin blanket had not helped at all. She could not believe the callousness of the guards who ignored her increasing pleas. Two men had shown some pity, but they were gone. The less compassionate men who had taken their place hinted that that consideration had been the reason the other two were gone from Dubhglenn.

By the time a man arrived with the daily ration of food late on the fourth day, there was no longer any question in Aimil's mind that her brother was feverish. She held him as he ranted, weeping over her inability even to bathe his face. She had slept little during the night, dozing only during the few times her brother was quiet. Her dirty face streaked with tears, she glared at the man who peered down at them.

"Will ye not take him from this rat hole now?"

"I cannae, laddie," the man said with sympathy for the tear-streaked child who stared up at him. "The laird hasnae returned yet. His brother holds this place and he willnae free ye."

"Then he is a fool. He will have naught for ransoming. Even a blind man can see that my brother is feverish. He could easily die."

The man did not have the heart to tell how Artair was indeed blind, blind drunk, and that he had been since the successful raid. There was no hope of reaching the man, of getting him to understand the plight of his captives. None dared to act without word from Artair. To remind him of Parlan's fury if he should return to find a dead youth only gained a beating. There was nothing that could be done until Parlan returned. With a sigh, the man closed the grate, wincing at the stream of abuse that came from the hole. The small boy had a vicious, colorful tongue. The man felt no urge to retalliate, however. He only wished that Artair was there to be verbally lashed for he deserved it.

"How is Artair this eve?" he asked the guard at the head of the stairs that led to the dungeons, emboldened enough by pity for the two boys to consider approaching Artair.

"Sore-headed and drinking to cure it. How fare the lads?"

"If the laird doesnae return in a day or twa, there will be but one laddie in that hole and him with a rightful vengeance to take."

Aimil was a little startled at how vengeful she could feel as she held her brother and wept with frustration and grief. In all the time they had been in the pit, no one had even asked their names so she knew that ransoming was no hope to cling to yet. From things said, she knew her only chance for Leith was if Black Parlan, the much-feared laird of the MacGuins, returned in time. It struck her as funny that she should wish for the return of a man often used by nursemaids as a bogey to scare their charges into obedience. Her laugh had an hysterical note to it, however, so she abruptly stopped.

Clutching Leith whose breathing grew more terrifyingly rasping, she began a slow rocking motion. It was vital that she retain her wits, but she feared that they were beginning to slip. Being held captive in a damp, black hole that was far from fresh of smell was hard to endure. To be kept there to watch her brother slowly die was a torture beyond bearing. At this point, she mused, she would willingly sell her soul to Satan to gain some care for Leith. As she began to pray for the Black Parlan's return, she wondered if she was doing just that.

Catarine Dunmore stretched very much like a contented cat. It had taken a lot of time and work to get the Black Parlan into her bed but it had been worth it. He made all her other lovers seem like fumbling boys or eunuchs. Watching him as he stood staring out the window, she let her gaze greedily roam over his large, muscular frame. She had him now and he would not slip away. A well-earned confidence in her ability led her to believe that one night in her bed would be enough to secure him.

"Come back to bed, Parlan," she purred, licking her lips when he turned, giving her a full view of his endowments.

Eyes so dark brown they were nearly black studied the woman on the bed with little expression. Parlan did not like Catarine but could not deny that she had serviced him very well indeed. There was, however, something repulsive about her insatiable appetite. He cared less about the state of her emotions, but he did not particularly care to be seen as little more than a well-proportioned staff that happened to have a man attached. She could no doubt have done as well with some inanimate object shaped appropriately.

Inwardly, he sighed as he moved toward the bed where she wantonly displayed her indisputable charms. They did nothing for him now that his need had been dulled. Noting the anger that settled upon her lovely face as he reached for his clothes, he began to form his farewell. It had to be phrased carefully for she was attached to his family. If he insulted her in any way, her anger would be formidable and he did not want to be troubled with it. Her kin were anxious to get her wed and that made her a little dangerous.

As he pulled on his trunk hose, he watched her sardonically. She would probably accept an offer to leave his pintle behind, he mused bitterly. After her avaricious attentions, the poor abused fellow would likely be useless for a few days anyway. He smiled to himself at the track his thoughts had taken. Parlan knew he could not really complain. He had succumbed to her invitation solely because he wished use of the skill for which she was so well-noted.

Even six months ago he would have climbed back into her bed, ready for more. Lately, however, he suffered from a malaise of dissatisfaction. Once his initial lust was sated he lost interest in the woman. At but eight and twenty he felt sure his virility was not waning. The problem was not how much he wanted but what he wanted. It was plainly not to be found in the arms of Catarine Dunmore.

"Ye cannae mean to leave now. The night is still young."

"Aye, but the dawn comes early and I begin the long trek back to Dubhglenn then," he murmured without glancing her way.

"Ye truly are leaving?" It was difficult but she managed to keep from screaming the words in anger and frustration.

"I must. I have been gone near to a month and 'tis folly to leave Artair in charge for so long." He frowned, caught up in thoughts of all his brother could do wrong in his absence.

"Surely ye need not fear that he would try to usurp your place."

"Nay, but he plays the role too seriously and with little thought. I have plans afoot and I cannae risk his ruining them."

She knew better than to ask what those plans were. Sitting up, she adjusted her hair so that it did not hide the full curves she knew were attractive to men. It was ending far too soon. She needed more time to entrap him completely. Her family was urging her to take another husband. Parlan MacGuin would suit her fine. She could not catch him by crying over lost virtue or seduction, for her lack of celibacy since her husband's untimely death two years ago was far too well known. There were, however, a number of routes to the marriage bed. Yet each one required time. She could not allow this chance to slip away. Unfortunately, it looked very much as if Parlan was going to yank it away.

"Come, Parlan," she crooned, reaching out to caress his manhood and hiding her anger over his evident disinclination, "what is one more night?"

"Too long," he replied succinctly as he put on his pourpoint and stepped out of her reach. "All is readied for the journey. I cannae forestall it."

Gritting her teeth against the curses she wished to hurl at him, she queried, "When do you plan to return this way?"

Parlan wondered if the woman knew how obvious she was in her ploys. "I cannae say. 'Tis a busy time of the year."

"I must return home soon myself," she lied smoothly. "Mayhaps I could stop at Dubhglenn on my way."

"If ye like." He hoped fervently that she would not as he gave her a light kiss. "Take care, Catarine."

As soon as he was gone, Catarine gave vent to her fury, demolishing her quarters, then keeping her servants busy most of the night restoring it to order. Parlan would not get away so easily with using her like some tavern wench, she vowed.

She would give him time to settle his business then go to stay at his keep. Once there and in his bed, she was certain she would win the game.

Dawn found Parlan on the road and riding hard for Dubhglenn, his keep. Although he partook of the delights of town, he did not like being away from his home. If Artair was older and less rash, he would be sent on some of the necessary trips to town. Unfortunately, Parlan knew Artair would either spend his time soaked in drink and wenching, or make them new enemies they did not need. It saddened him but Artair's unreliability was why Lagan Dunmore was the man most often at Parlan's side. He could only hope that during his absence Artair had done nothing too terrible.

When Parlan finally reached Dubhglenn two days later, he knew immediately upon riding into the bailey that something was not right. The people he met greeted him jovially but with a poorly disguised air of relief. There was also that air of someone waiting to speak but not wishing to be the one to carry tales. Parlan was about to demand explanations when he espied the horse.

Speechless with admiration, he did not even inquire about where the animal had come from, but merely spent long moments studying the fine points of the stallion. The animal was at least a hand taller than his own, very impressive mount. The horse's lines indicated strength as well as speed. The white coat of the beast was startling in its purity. Parlan was ready to test how far the stallion's tense, aggressive stance could be tried when Malcolm and Lagan returned to Dubhglenn. They wasted no time in moving to speak to Parlan.

"Have ye seen this magnificent animal?" enthused Parlan, slowly becoming aware of the men's tension.

"Aye, I have seen him." Malcolm turned to one of the men lurking nearby. "How fare the laddies?"

"Nae too weel. The older one be sickening something fierce and the wee one has condemned the lot of us to seven kinds of hell."

"And weel we deserve them," cried Lagan who got no argument. "Has naught been done? Has no one tended to them?"

"Aye, they be fed and watered regular," protested another man but weakly.

"I gave them extra blankets last eve but I fear the wee one be right when he says they will only be used as a shroud," added the first man.

"Hold!" The silence that immediately met Parlan's bellow was a tense one. "What lads?" he snarled.

"Artair raided the Ferguesons," Lagan explained, knowing that would displease Parlan because it was done without his consent. "As we rode back to Dubhglenn, we chanced upon twa laddies in Mengue colors and seized them."

"How wee are the laddies?"

"One must be nearing twenty, mayhaps a year or twa less," replied Malcolm. "A man by some's reckoning but still a laddie by mine. The other cannae be more than twelve."

"What ransom has been asked?"

"None," Lagan answered reluctantly. "They rot in the pit awaiting your return so that ye can decide upon it."

Malcolm and Lagan followed Parlan as he strode into the keep. Several other men followed hesitantly. When Parlan's request for Artair met with the word that the young man was sleeping off yet another long night of whiskey and women, Parlan's fury was a glory to behold. Usually brave men scattered before him as he made his way to the dungeons where the sound of a soft keening greeted his ears.

The grate was speedily opened, and Parlan looked into the hole, a lantern held inside its depths. He saw a small, slightly-built boy holding a larger one, rocking and weeping softly. The elder boy was evidently dangerously ill. Suddenly the small lad became aware of the intruders and looked up. Even streaked with filth and tears, the small face had a delicate beauty that seemed strange for a boy. It was not even marred when that face was contorted into a snarl of hate and rage. Parlan noted all of that as he struggled to control his ever-growing anger with his brother.

At any other time the dark, imposing face peering down at her would have made Aimil at least hesitant, but she had no thought of caution when she held her dying brother in her arms. "Carrion! Filthy corbies! Ye have come too early to pick at this flesh."

"Get them out of there. Now!" Parlan snarled as he moved back from the pit's opening, his voice clipped with fury.

Chapter Two

For a moment Aimil doubted that she had heard right. It quickly became apparant that the Black Parlan himself was there, biting out commands in a deep voice that barely escaped being a very feral snarl. With her brother's vital needs at the fore of her thoughts, she neither asked nor cared if they meant to free her too. Once Leith was lifted out, she started to sit down again.

"Ye as weel, laddie," Parlan called, failing to keep all his fury at Artair out of his voice despite his efforts to stay calm so as not to frighten the boy.

She slapped away the hands that were offered to assist her, scrambling up the rope by herself. The time spent in a pit in which she could barely lie down had sapped her strength, but she refused to reveal that. In fact, she had practiced some odd exercises several times a day to keep her strength up for Leith's sake. It had served its purpose for she was able to stand without wavering badly. The last thing she wanted was for these men to espy any weakness in her.

"Dinnae touch me, swine," she hissed when, as they began to leave the dungeons, a hand moved to assist her.

Parlan was unused to being spoken to like that but he

quelled an instinctive burst of anger. Later, he would even find amusement in the thought of the seething, somewhat filthy boy. For now he only wanted to ease the dangerous situation Artair had created. Despite the dirt, there was no mistaking the richness of the boys' attire, which meant that they were of a high standing within the Mengue clan. An incident such as this could easily provoke a blood feud that could last for generations. That was the very last thing Parlan wanted or needed.

When they reached a room that could be secured from the outside, the MacGuins hastily attended to Leith who was for the most part, unconscious. Aimil stood out of the way but watched their every move. Even though the tending was late in coming, she could appreciate the speed with which the men stripped Leith, bathed him, and lay him on a clean bed to nurse his wounds. By some miracle the wounds had not yet festered even though they had not healed as much as they should have. There was yet some danger for Leith.

"Your names," Parlan rapped out, no longer worried that his anger would frighten the boy.

Aimil did not quail beneath the man's penetrating, dark gaze. "Shane and Leith Mengue. 'Tis Leith ye have almost murdered."

Swearing colorfully and with admirable diversity, Parlan continued to help in tending young Leith Mengue's wounds. He too saw it as a miracle that the boy's wounds had not festered filling his blood with a deadly poison. Even if the boy lived, which seemed imminently possible now, such harsh treatment of the Mengue heir could provoke the very feud Parlan hoped to avoid. The little Mengue boy certainly looked eager to begin one, he mused.

A man of his times, Parlan did in truth like a good battle or the thrill of a raid. It was the blood feuds he detested, feuds where hate passed from generation to generation, with the initial cause for the feuds becoming distorted, even forgotten.

More often than not, the cause was one where, if it had occurred within the clan, a settlement would have come about quickly between the original antagonists. Instead whole clans tore at each other, killing each other wherever and whenever they were able, using up their resources in a long, bloody, seemingly unending feud. What truly annoyed him was how those feuds so often interfered at a time when unity was desperately needed, such as against an enemy like the English.

His thoughts came to an abrupt halt when Artair stumbled into the room, but Parlan's fury had to wait to be vented.

Aimil recognized the man who had ordered that she and Leith be put into the hole, knew from things said that it was this man who had kept them there, who had drunk and wenched while her brother slowly died. Her delicate hands curled into claws, and she lunged at Artair.

Artair saved his eyes only by a quick raising of his arms. Two men grabbed Aimil before she was able to inflict much damage but it was a few moments before she stopped hurling curses and threats at Artair, and was calm enough to be released. In the confusion the feminine manner of her attack went unnoticed. When she moved to stand by the head of the bed where Leith rested, she was not ready to forgive any MacGuin. But she did note that Artair was getting anything but praise for his actions from Black Parlan. It was clear that he had acted completely of his own accord, something that was clearly an old bone of contention between the two men.

"I see ye found the prisoners," Artair began weakly for Parlan's face was dark with rage.

"I nearly had naught but corpses. Did ye never think that they might be worth more alive?"

"No one told me." Artair's excuses were abruptly cut off by a sound blow from Parlan's broad hand that sent Artair slamming into a wall.

"Ye were already too drunk to heed a word said. Fool! Ye

have done your best to kill Lachlan Mengue's heir. Do ye ken what that would have meant? Do ye ken what that would have brought down about our heads?"

"The Mengues arenae strong enough to beat us," cried Artair only to suffer another blow from his enraged brother.

"Nay, mayhaps not, but they have ties to the MacVerns and the Broths. Aye, and those bastards, the Ferguesons." Pinning Artair to the wall, he snarled, "They also have power in court and could easily bring the king's wrath upon our heads." He released his hold so abruptly that Artair fell to the floor. "Murder it would have been called and murder it would have been. If the king didnae put us to the horn, declare us outlaws, we would still have to deal with four clans at our throats plus God alone kens how many others for t'would be a righteous vengeance."

"I dinnae ken what ye are so angry about," sputtered Artair. "The lad still lives and he will bring a fine ransom."

"Get out!" bellowed Parlan. "Get out before I stuff ye in that accursed hole and forget ye for a week."

There was no hesitation in Artair's obedience to that command. When Parlan was in such a fury, retreat was the better part of valor. After seeing Leith Mengue's precarious state of health, Artair was guiltily aware of his culpability.

Parlan turned his attention to the delicate boy called Shane. "Now we shall get ye cleaned up."

"I dinnae need your help. I can weel clean myself," Aimil snapped. "Aye, and I will do so once I ken that Leith fares weel."

"He willnae fare weel if he is forced to smell ye all the while," growled Parlan, then ordered his men to fetch some fresh bath water.

Aimil started to tell the big man just where he could put his bath water when Leith weakly touched her arm and rasped, "Clean up, brat, before ye fall ill as weel. Ye do stink a bit."

Clasping his hand briefly, she teased in a shaky voice, "Ye were no rose yourself until a wee bit ago."

"I cannae believe I stank quite so foul." His smile faded as he was seized by a violent fit of coughing ending their banter.

Lagan moved to aid Leith in the drinking of a hot, strong broth that had been delivered. Aimil watched her bath prepared and hoped that the MacGuins would accede to her demand for privacy. There was no need of a guard within the room, and the very thought of what could happen if they discovered she was female sent chills up her spine.

"Here be some clean things for ye to don," said Malcolm as he set some clothes upon the bed. "These should fit. I even brought a new bonnet for ye as ye seem right fond of the things." He frowned at the dirty bedraggled bonnet that sat firmly upon her head. "Do ye never take it off?"

She ignored the question, feeling certain that he did not really expect an answer. "Thank ye. How fares Elfking?"

"Weel, though the white Devil lets few near him. Unfriendly beast," Malcolm grumbled.

"That white stallion was yours?" Parlan could not hide his amazement, thinking it far too much horse for a beardless boy.

"Is mine, aye. I raised him from a colt." She could not repress the note of pride in her voice.

"Weel, ye didnae do so weel in curbing his bad tempers. I shall have to work upon that."

"Ye willnae have any time. My father will ransom us soon." Yet again she felt fear, the fear of losing something very dear to her.

"Aye, he will but the horse stays here. I have taken a fancy to him."

"I doubt he will take a fancy to ye. He is a verra discerning animal. Ye cannae keep him here," she said sharply.

Parlan's brows quickly rose. "Child, no one tells me what I can or cannae do."

"I am telling ye naught, merely stating a fact. He willnae take to a new master."

"We shall see. Into the bath."

"Aye, when ye leave. I wish some privacy for my ablutions," she said haughtily, even though her heart pounded so fiercely that it hurt.

His thin lips twitching as he repressed a grin, Parlan drawled, "Your wish is my command." He started toward the door, the other men moving with him. "Whilst m'lord bathes, I shall busy myself by putting my new horse through his paces."

"Going to ride him, are ye?" She made no effort to hide her slow grin, knowing the comeuppance he would soon face.

"Aye." Parlan's gaze narrowed as he paused in the doorway. "I will tell ye how weel we suit."

"Ye do that."

A frown touched Parlan's face as he shut and bolted the door, hearing a soft laugh. "A strange boy."

Even stranger than he could ever imagine, thought Aimil, when she overheard the muttered remark. Once free of prying eyes, she wasted no time in pulling off her soiled clothes. She ached to rid herself of the dirt and stink of her imprisonment.

Leith watched her, amazed at how womanly she had grown since the last time he had seen her naked which, he realized, would have been when she had been only about fourteen and they had gone for a swim together. Using the eyes of a man viewing a woman and not those of a brother seeing his sister, Leith carefully studied Aimil. She was small and lithe but did not lack for curves. Full, high breasts offered all a man could want. A tiny waist led to gently-rounded hips and slim legs that appeared longer than what was accounted for in her height. Her skin had a light honey tone and was without mar. As if that was not enough to stir any man, her every movement was graceful, unknowingly sensual. He was surprised that the MacGuins still thought her a lad.

"Lass, if your ruse is discovered, dinnae fash yourself over me, just run," he said sternly, his order given strength by his fear for her.

Pausing in drying herself, Aimil looked at her brother in surprise. "All right, Leith, if ye think it best."

"Aye. Trust me. 'Tis best." He smiled weakly, knowing she was unaware of her draw for a man, something he knew would only make her appeal stronger.

"I wonder if I can see the stable from here," she mused aloud, and moved toward the window while donning the shirt that had been set out for her.

"'Ware now. Dinnae let them see ye. That hair can be like a beacon at times."

Aimil scowled at the calf-length hair she was rubbing dry. "Aye, cursed mane. Never fear, I can stay to the shadows here."

"Weel?" Leith asked when she sat grinning for a moment but did not say a word. "Can ye see anything?"

Hardly able to talk because of her laughter, Aimil gasped, "Aye, Elfking performed verra weel."

"God's tears, the Black Parlan tipped out of the saddle. How I wish I could have seen that but I am so weak I cannae even scratch my own arse," he muttered, disgusted with his weakness.

"Weel, dinnae expect me to do it for ye."

Leith's chuckle turned into a cough. Aimil dropped the cloth she had been drying her hair with and fetched him a drink of mead. She was helping him to drink it, easing the rasp that forced the cough, when a young, brawny man entered with a meal for the prisoners.

Stunned into immobility, Aimil gaped at the young man who stared at her. She was unaware of her allure as she stood with her damp hair tossled from its drying and her slim shapely figure only barely covered by her shirt.

His gaze was fixed upon the full curve of breasts barely

restrained by the unlaced shirt and he did the first thing that came to mind. He set down the tray and lunged.

A soft expulsion of breath was all the noise Aimil made as she was slammed up against a broad chest. Leith struggled to rise, but she heard him fall back onto the bed, too weak to aid her. Aimil struggled in panic for a moment as her captor ground his mouth onto hers and mauled her body. Then she calmed as she maneuvered her knee between his legs and raised it with as much force as she could. The young man yelled a deafening howl, released her, and bent over to clutch at his abused groin. Aimil made a two-handed fist and brought it down hard on his head, watching in amazement as he crumpled unconscious at her feet. It was the first time she had used the trick and had not expected it to work. She sank down onto the bed to catch her breath.

"I was wondering when ye would recall what I had taught ye," Leith said in a voice that was little more than a hoarse whisper. "Ye must go."

"How can I leave ye when ye are so ill?"

"They willnae harm me. Ye heard how they spoke. They dinnae want a corpse. Try to flee."

Hesitant, Aimil quickly dressed and covered her hair with her bonnet. She crept to the door and opened it a crack. Not peering out, she heard the sounds of voices and footsteps and knew there was little chance of escape that way. She was lucky that the man's hollering had not been heard. As she closed the door and turned to tell Leith that no escape seemed possible, her gaze fell upon the extra linen left to change Leith's bed. Dashing to the window, she thoughtfully measured the distance to the ground then made her decision.

"I will make a linen rope and go out the window."

"The men in the bailey," Leith ventured, fighting to keep his mind clear.

"They willnae be looking to the walls. Rest, Leith. This

short time of sanity and strength show that ye can beat this illness but only if ye rest." She sat on the bed and began to knot her makeshift rope. "We have done such a height before, and this should be strong enough to hold me."

"Aye, ye cannae be above a hundredweight."

"I would rather stay here with ye."

"Ye cannae. That mon showed ye what can happen."

"Black Parlan seemed to want no trouble though."

"He thought us both lads. Aye, that man will nay doubt be punished but only because he tried to take what should be offered to the laird first. Trust me, your only chance lies in escape." He closed his eyes against a wave of weakness. "Are ye nae afraid of rape?"

Aimil shrugged. "'Tis hard to say. I am afraid of being hurt. T'was that which made me panic when this man leapt upon me. I look at rape much as I look at death. There is little I can do about either. Both are somewhat commonplace. I willnae go in search of either nor will I go down without a fight," she said firmly, knowing that her character would make her fight either fate with any means at hand.

Leith grinned weakly as, when the man at her feet began to stir, Aimil calmly knocked him on the head with a heavy candlestick, set the makeshift weapon back by the bed, and returned to knotting the linen all without a pause in her speech.

"'Tis wretched that men must take their pleasure of unwilling women, but they do. 'Tis a fact of life. I cannae fash myself to the bone over facts of life." She tied her rope to the end of the bed and tested its hold. "That should do. Are ye sure I willnae be safe here?"

"Aye, I am sure. The Black Parlan is weel-kenned for his healthy appetite for the lasses."

"Oh. Weel, wish me luck," she murmured and sighed, reluctant to leave him but feeling he was wiser in such matters.

"What will ye do when ye reach the bailey?"

"Whistle for Elfking." She grinned. "If I get down this wall unseen and onto Elfking's back before the men down there move, I will have a verra good chance."

There was no disputing that. Leith knew that few horses existed which could match Elfking for speed. He felt a slight hope rise. She might have a chance of succeeding if all went as she so blithely planned. If Aimil dropped onto Elfking's back and cleared the gates, she had a very good chance indeed. Another advantage would be that Elfking would be carrying a far lighter burden than any steed pursuing him.

Taking a deep breath to steady her sudden flurry of nerves, Aimil lowered herself out of the window. She was not afraid of the descent for she and Leith had come down as great if not greater heights. They had, however, used a proper rope. They had also not been trying to escape an enemy. She saw now that it had proven good practice.

Steadily and slowly, she went down the wall, using her feet against the stone. There was a strong wind, and she grit her teeth as she fought its jostling. Although the wind failed to dislodge her as she neared the end of her descent, it did succeed in stealing the bonnet, which she had forgotten to secure as strongly as she had her first one. To further aggravate her, she discovered she was short of rope. A measuring glance told her she could easily fall onto Elfking's back, however, and, readying herself, she whistled for her mount.

Parlan glared at the horse that had unseated him again. He tried to ignore the badly stifled laughter of the men as he watched the horse rise gracefully and shake the dust from his fine coat. Slowly getting to his feet, Parlan brushed himself off and finally gave a reluctant grin.

"Now I ken what the laddie found so funny." He walked around the animal and studied him as the adversary he was. "The question is how to break him of the trick or, at least, of playing it on me."

"Aye, 'tis a useful trick. Ye would never have to worry about the beast being stolen," jested Lagan.

A soft laugh escaped Parlan as he took Elfking's reins. "Mayhaps if I tempt him with a good run. It has been a long time since he has had one."

Lagan followed Parlan and the horse as did Malcolm and several other curious men. Elfking went along calmly until Parlan tried to lead him through the gates. The horse then stood firmly, refusing to leave the keep, no matter how much he was pulled, pushed, or cursed.

"Curse this stubborn beast to Hades! What ails the fool animal?"

"Mayhaps a touch of the whip will move the beast," suggested one man.

"Nay, I willnae take a whip to the beast and chance marring this fine coat."

Malcolm moved closer to his exasperated laird's side. "I ken the beast be following the laddie's orders."

"How so? The lad isnae here to give any."

"Nay, but, when we brought the lads in, the horse tried to follow me and the wee laddie into the keep. The wee laddie told him to stay."

Shaking his head, Parlan laughed. "And staying is just what he is doing, curse his fine hide."

"Mayhaps ye ought to give up on trying to keep the horse."

"Nay, Lagan. I must think of a way to win the beast to my hand. I may have to get the lad to help," Parlan mused aloud.

"He willnae. T'was plain to see the lad's fond of his horse," protested Malcolm.

"Ye ask the right way and the lad will do it," Parlan said grimly. "He is fond of his brother too."

"Aye, but ye willnae do aught to the lad."

"We ken that, Lagan, but I suspicion the wee laddie willnae be too sure of it. 'Tis no secret that many a dark tale is told about me. Dinnae ye ken that I roast and eat bairns and pick my teeth with their wee bones?" He grinned fleetingly over such nonsense, long since inured to any sting it might have inflicted. "Aye, I willnae do aught to the lad, but that wee laddie can be made to believe I will."

"Seems cruel to deprive a wee lad of his horse," muttered Malcolm.

"In this instance I will gladly live up to my sordid reputation. Malcolm, how can ye ask me to release such a prize? I can sense that the beast has speed and strength. Aye, he has wit as weel. If naught else, think of the stock he will breed. I have several mares already in mind for him to jump."

"Aye." Malcolm moved to take the saddle off the horse's back. "I cannae help but feel for the laddie's loss, though."

"That I can understand for I would feel the loss of such a beast sorely myself. 'Tis a guilt I am willing to live with," he drawled.

Malcolm lifted the saddle from Elfking's back and raised his gaze to the walls of the keep. "Jesu," he breathed, his eyes widening with disbelief.

"God's teeth, Malcolm," Parlan snapped when the saddle fell from Malcolm's hands and barely missed Parlan's foot. "What ails ye? Ye near to broke my foot."

"The wee laddie," Malcolm croaked. "Up there. On the walls."

All eyes followed Malcolm's stunned gaze. The slight figure looked even smaller as it skillfully descended the wall of the keep. There was admiration mixed with the shock for, if asked, several of the men watching would have admitted that they would not have dared such a thing. It was not thought cowardly if a man preferred to keep his feet on or very near to good solid ground.

"Is he mad?" ground out Parlan after a hearty bout of cursing.

"I willnae argue the lad's sanity with ye but I will say 'tis skill that he uses in his lunacy." Lagan nodded when Parlan shot him a brief, piercing look. "Aye, skill. That is no scrambling descent. I have seen the trick of it before. He kens weel how to use both rope and body."

"Aye," Parlan agreed slowly, "that he does. But to escape into a crowded bailey? 'Tis madness."

"We wouldnae have seen him had Malcolm not chanced to look up." Lagan chuckled. "'Tis really quite clever."

"If he doesnae end up splattered upon the ground," Parlan growled. "This is a cursed annoying business. I have one boy sick and near to death and the other trying to kill himself. Mengue will pay dearly for raising such brats."

Lagan laughed. "Weel, we should wander over there to greet the lad when he reaches the ground."

"Oh, aye, I will greet him." His fear for the dangling boy turned to anger as Parlan strode toward the wall.

"It may be the tales ye just mentioned that drive him to such an act," Malcolm suggested quickly as he hurried to keep pace.

Struggling against his anger, Parlan finally nodded as he glanced at Malcolm. "'Tis true. I will keep that in mind whilst I am beating the brat." He looked back toward the small figure gingerly descending the wall just as the wind stole the bonnet the lad wore. "Jesus wept."

Parlan's soft curse was repeated by all around him.

In her haste, Aimil had not only failed to secure her bonnet but her hair as well. It tumbled free in glorious thick waves, the wind catching it and tossling its beauty with abandon. The predominant color was a blond so fair it was silver in color but streaked with shades of gold and red that caught and held every beam of light. What Aimil thought a bane, an unruly mass that could not decide upon a color, Parlan and those with him thought beauty itself.

After shock had released its hold, the first thought that

entered Parlan's mind was that he would like to wrap himself up in that hair which was like silken sunlight. He then wondered if she was old enough to be used in the ways he was thinking of. Her small stature might yet indicate youth. Few mature women he knew could so easily and successfully disguise themselves so. The disappointment he felt when that possibility occurred to him surprised him some. Suddenly he recalled the "lad's" delicate features and swore at himself.

"I should have seen it," he snapped as he again moved toward where Aimil was now hanging some feet short of the ground.

"The lass has come up short. We best hasten before she tries to drop to the ground," suggested Lagan. "She could land afoul and break a bone."

"I am sorely tempted to break a few of her bones. T'was a foolish move for a laddie to make. For a wee lass . . ." He shook his head, stunned by the daring of the girl, even as he guiltily admitted that his reputation, which he had done little to clear, might have driven her to the rash act.

The advance of the men halted as abruptly as Aimil's whistle pierced the air. Parlan sensed what was about to happen, but his shout of warning barely came in time. Men hurled themselves out of the way of an onrushing Elfking who stopped directly beneath the dangling girl. They watched in astonishment while they rose, dusting themselves off, as she neatly lowered herself onto the stallion's back. Her plan of escape was clear to all now.

Aimil recovered quickly from the jolt of dropping onto Elfking's back and grasped the reins. Riding bareback did not trouble her. She did, in fact, prefer it. Exhilaration filled her though she tried to quell it. Freedom was so close she could taste its nectar.

Chapter Three

"Close the gates! Get my cursed horse. Fools! Dinnae bother with a saddle. She will be sitting at Mengue's table before I have even mounted."

If Aimil had not been so afraid that she could yet fail, she would have laughed at the sight of the much-feared Black Parlan bellowing orders and his men scrambling to obey. She knew, however, that what looked like confusion was not. It was only haste, a haste that could rob her of her goal when she was so close to it. With a yell that rivaled any battlecry, she urged Elfking toward the gates that were already being shut against her escape.

Men threw themselves clear of the horse but there was barely enough space to get through when she reached the gates and the men closing them were hurrying to take even that away. She urged Elfking to rear and, as she had expected, the men instinctively shied away from the flailing hooves, allowing her to break clear of the bailey into open ground. The delay had caused Elfking to break stride and she feared it would cost her dearly for she could hear that pursuit had already begun in earnest.

Although he cursed the men at the gate, Parlan did not

blame them for dodging the white stallion. They did at least have the sense to start reopening the gates even as Parlan thundered past them on his black stallion, the purity of the animal's coat marred only by a small patch of white on his nose and a circle of it round his left rear hoof. His horse, Raven, was as yet unmatched in speed, but Parlan sensed he would be pressed to keep pace several lengths behind his quarry. Elfking, with his far lighter burden, fairly flew over the ground. Watching the horse run only increased Parlan's desire to have the mount.

As he watched the girl ride, he recognized her skill, a skill increased by the obvious rapport between rider and horse. With her hair unbound, her lithe shape nearly one with her animal of such grace and speed, there was an air of other worldliness to the pair. Parlan decided that Elfking was a suitable name for the milk-white stallion.

So thought Malcolm and Lagan who followed with a small group of men. They crested a small rise to see Parlan and the girl galloping over an open field. The sight of the black horse with its large dark rider pursuing the white horse with its small fair rider conjured up a vast number of fanciful images. To see two such magnificent animals racing was spellbinding. It would be a close-run race, and both men agreed that they and their horses would not even be in the running.

"We will ne'er catch them."

"Nay, Malcolm, but ye ken that we must follow. Parlan may need aid if he catches her. 'Tis also unwise for him to be abroad alone."

Malcolm followed as Lagan urged the group to ride on, but he grumbled, "Nae sure I want to be about if Parlan loses the race."

Parlan was determined to win but he knew it would be the most difficult race he had ever been involved in. Despite appearances, the girl did not hold all the advantages. The ground was unfamiliar to her and had already stolen some of her lead. He grimly followed and awaited his chance.

Aimil clearly recognized her weaknesses. She had watched her lead eaten away as she faltered to avoid an obstruction, one her pursuer had already adjusted for. One look at him had been all she had needed as it made her think that Satan himself was at her heels and, if rumors about Black Parlan could be believed, he was or at least one of his henchman.

It was not speed, skill, knowledge, nor terrain that ended the race, but something so insignificant that Aimil wondered if fate was playing games with her. She felt the subtle change in Elfking's gait and knew she was lost. Elfking would run until his heart stopped if she asked it of him, but she never would. Neither could she cripple him perhaps to the point where he had to be destroyed. None of the fears that had prompted her attempt to escape were strong enough to make her do that. Weeping silently with frustration, she halted him and dismounted to look at his leg.

The change in Elfking's gait had quickly been seen by Parlan. He cursed, feeling certain that a female would continue to ride an injured animal until the injury was past fixing. Because of that cynical view, he was unprepared for her halt and overshot his quarry. By the time he got his steed under control and turned round, she was sitting on the ground, staring at something in her hand. He dismounted and quietly moved to where she sat by Elfking, who appeared to be suffering only a tender hoof.

"A pebble," she remarked dejectedly. "I would have made it save for this."

"Aye, I think ye might have." He signaled the newly-arrived men to keep her from Elfking.

"'Tis all your fault," she snapped as she surged to her feet and flung the pebble at him.

Flinching as it struck his cheek, he growled, "What in the Devil's name are ye on about? I had naught to do with this."

In too high a temper to care who she was yelling at, Aimil gladly replied. "Men," she said in a voice heavy with disgust. "Aye, and ye most of all. I could have stayed with Leith if it werenae for men, animals that ye are. Aye, ye and your damnable appetites. That is why I had to climb down the keep wall and near crippled Elfking."

"My appetites?" Parlan asked, laughing, his gaze flicking from her face to her finger prodding his chest to punctuate her remarks.

The way she stood berating him amused him as well as stirred his admiration. He could snap her slim lovely neck with one good blow yet she faced him squarely. Her delicate face, with its wide, slightly-tilted, aquamarine eyes, drew his appreciation even when it was flushed with anger. Again he wondered how old she was for there was the promise of passion already visible in her full mouth. Her age suddenly became a question of immediate importance to him. His gaze fell to the pourpoint she wore, but it hid any curves she might have.

"Take your doublet off," he ordered, not giving any thought to how that might sound, but only concerned with discovering her true age.

Aimil gaped then grew even more furious. "Go to hell."

Parlan's amusement fled for he was not accustomed to such resistance or having his wishes denied. "Ye will do as I say, wench."

Being called a wench only increased her fury. "When cows grow wings I will." She swore when he began to see to her compliance himself. "Get your paws off me, ye great hairy brute."

Trying to hold her steady as he unlaced her doublet, and wondering crossly how she could be so slippery, he snapped, "I mean to see how old ye are, brat."

"Ye neednae take my clothes off for that."

"How old are ye then?" His eyes narrowed with suspicion as he watched her face.

She suddenly realized her age could determine how she was treated, and why it was of interest to him. "Twelve."

He grinned, catching her flailing hands by the wrists and securing them behind her with one large hand. "Then ye will-nae care about the loss of this"—he finished unlacing her doublet—"for there will be naught to see." He held her close to stop her squirming as he worked.

Alex, the young man Aimil had knocked out, suddenly came upon the scene. He had come to inside Leith's room when the lass had whistled for Elfking. Although somewhat groggy and loathe to ride a horse, Alex had followed the riders. Guilt over his part in her escape drove him.

"Watch out for the wench's knee," he called out as he dismounted somewhat gingerly.

Aimil squirmed not only to try to escape but to position herself for attack. Much to her annoyance, her previous victim's warning came just in time to save Parlan from the full force of her knee, but he still loosed his grip on her, bending over in an instinctive gesture. But, when she swung her two-handed fist toward his head, he caught her by the wrists before the blow could connect. She suddenly found herself on her back, staring up into a dark face made all the darker by fury. Fleetingly, she noticed that he had positioned himself so that her knee was no longer a viable weapon. He had, in fact, rendered her almost immobile.

When he pulled out his knife, she tensed. There were two things he could do with it. She actually found herself hoping that he meant to cut off the short, padded tunic she had refused to remove, and sighed almost with relief when he did. An affront to her modesty was far easier to bear than a cut throat or pierced heart. The chastity she was struggling to protect seemed minor compared to keeping her life. She did think, however, that he could cease staring so hard.

Parlan was struggling hard not to stare but most of his will had gone to quelling the strong desire to take her there and then. Since she had put the doublet on over her shirt, she had not bothered to lace the shirt thus giving him an almost unobstructed view. His hands itched to flick the shirt open to reveal what he judged might be the most exquisite breasts he had ever seen. One of the things that stopped him was that he had no wish for the men encircling them to share that sight. He intended to be the only one to enjoy the pleasure of viewing her beauty.

"Ye are a weel-formed twelve, lass." He finally tore his gaze from her breasts and looked at her face.

"Oh, verra weel, I was seventeen last Michaelmas. Satisfied?" she snapped.

He leaned down until their faces were very close. "T'will take more than a peek to satisfy my damnable appetites."

She flushed then scowled at his amusement at his barb. What truly bothered her was her awareness of him as a man. His dark, good looks and strong, well-formed body were arousing an uncomfortable interest. There was fear stirred by his suggestion, but she suspected it was no more than any virgin would feel when faced with her first bedding. Her body's indiscriminate desires annoyed her. After all, she had been wooed and left unmoved by many a handsome Lowland gentleman and yet her body had the gall to warm to a barbarous Highlander.

If one overlooked that he was a MacGuin, she mused, as well as the unsavory tales told about him, and studied him simply as a man, there was no denying that he was very fine indeed. His face with its high, wide cheekbones and the modest aquiline cut of his nose gave him a fierce, hawkish look which was far from unattractive. Black brows, gently winged, rose above surprisingly heavily-lashed eyes giving him a saturnine air, an air increased by the darkness of his skin and the midnight black of his long hair. He had to be one of the tallest men she had ever seen, possibly even topping six foot, and was muscular without the lumps or ridges some men developed. The partially-opened shirt and the lack of hose with his kilt let her see that he had a fine layer of hair on his broad chest and a light coat on his long, muscular legs.

He was big and, she grudgingly admitted, beautiful, but she would not let that sway her. Black Parlan was a MacGuin, the laird of that thieving clan, and a Highlander. She knew rumor and tale should not condemn a man, that in the newly-marked century of 1500 men did not, could not, do such things as roast babies and dine upon them, but it could not all be discounted. Behind all gossip and rumor there was usually some hint of truth. There was little doubt in her mind that he certainly did take his pleasure of women freely and with great gusto. It was not all that, however, which would make her fight if he sought to possess her. Instinct told her that she could lose more than her chastity and that terrified her. But she had no intention of revealing her terror.

"Now that ye ken what ye wished to, will ye get off me, ye great ox?" she snapped. "I cannae feel my legs anymore."

"I would be quite glad to feel them for ye." He met her glare with a grin, and his men laughed.

"How verra amusing." His cockiness replaced her fear with annoyance. "Will ye remove your great hulking self before I am crippled for life? What is it?"

Her last question was asked softly and somewhat anxiously for his face had suddenly darkened with anger. Her gaze followed his to her breasts again, but she could see nothing worth such fury only a few bruises from the young man's attack. That the bruises enraged him was made suddenly very clear, and it took Aimil a moment to get over her surprise.

Parlan surged to his feet and softly, too softly, asked her

young attacker, "How did ye ken the way the lass would protect herself?"

Clearly, if a little shakily, the young man replied, "She used it on me when I attacked her."

His words had barely cleared his lips when a blow from Parlan sent him reeling. Scrambling to her feet and clutching her shirt closed, Aimil gasped as the laird of the MacGuins sentenced her would-be ravisher to an alarming number of lashes. Although the young man paled, he made no protest nor did any of the others look surprised. It was evident that the notorious Black Parlan did not tolerate the abuse of women, and did, in fact, consider it a crime worthy of harsh punishment. Aimil decided she would wonder later how that contradicted the image painted of the man. Right now, she felt she had to intervene for it was too harsh a punishment. She had to let it be known how little the man had accomplished.

"Nay, nay," she cried, clutching Parlan's tensed arm. "It wasnae so bad."

"Enjoyed it, did ye?" purred Parlan, angered by her defense of the young man.

"Dinnae be an idiot," she snapped, causing several of Parlan's men to gasp. "I didnae mean that. I meant t'was naught but a kiss and a wee grapple."

"A kiss and a wee grapple wouldnae leave such marks."

"Aye, they would and, even so, t'wasnae all his fault. I was wearing naught but this shirt and that undone. Aye, and my hair was loose. He was expecting twa lads not what he found. T'was but a brief tussle before I knocked him out, and, 'tis true, I bruise easily." She saw the doubt in his eyes and asked, "Did ye mean to mark me just now?"

"Nay," he replied, stiffening with outrage, "I dinnae hold with the rough handling of women. And ye being so wee I thought ye may be but a child."

She bit back an angry retort for his reference to her lack of size and held out her wrists. The marks his hands had left were already livid and clearly delineated. She smiled slightly at his shock.

"As I said, I bruise most easily. 'Tis a fault of the skin. They will fade as quickly and they dinnae hurt. Truth tell, I think the bruises I gifted him with are far worse," she murmured, a faint color tinting her cheeks.

Looking at the awkward stance of the young man, Parlan bit back a grin. "I will let it pass this time, Alex, but if I hear even a whisper of the like occurring again, ye will suffer twofold. I ken ye will be weel reminded for a day or twa of your error. Aye, and for far longer will ye be hearing the jests of the men concerning your defeat at the hands of such a wee lass. T'will do as punishment."

He grasped Aimil by the arm. "We will return to the keep now. Malcolm, ye will lead her stallion." He sighed when Malcolm reached for Elfking only to be greeted by a horsey snarl. "M'lady, wouldst ye be so kind as to direct your beast to follow Malcolm?" he asked with exaggerated politeness.

She obeyed with an equally false politeness then stood embarrassed and angry as he laced her shirt much as if she were a child. On the ride back to the MacGuin keep, she sat before him on Raven and said nothing, disappointed by her failure to escape. But she was also fighting the way her body was reacting to the closeness of his, to his strength and his maleness. When they reached the keep, she dutifully told Elfking to stay and set off to see Leith, but was steered into the hall, sat down, and given some ale.

"Ye are plainly not Shane Mengue so who are ye?" Parlan asked when they were all seated at a table, with food and drink set before them.

"Aimil Siubhan O'Connell Mengue, Lachlan Mengue's youngest daughter."

"Then ye will still fetch a fine ransom. I had feared ye were naught but the lad's woman thus not worth a groat."

He did not have the slightest inclination of letting anyone know there was more to it than economics. Parlan suspected that the restlessness and dissatisfaction he had suffered of late would soon end. It had bothered him to think that this tiny woman was no more than Leith Mengue's whore. Her youth, lack of wedding ring and position indicated that she was very probably a virgin which also pleased him. For once, he not only wanted to be the first, he avidly desired it.

The problem, he mused, would be in getting her into his bed. She was small and delicate but recent incidents had clearly revealed her strength and courage. Seduction might take a long time for he sensed that she had the wit to see through such a ploy and he could not trust his patience. Not only the rules he enforced on his men stopped him from taking her but an absolute loathing of forcing an unwilling woman. To get her into his bed, he needed something to bargain with, a choice to give her that would, hopefully, cause her to come to him with at least a token willingness.

Studying her, he tried to find one particular attribute of hers that could account for his strong desire. Her figure was not without draw, especially her exquisite breasts, yet he had always preferred a fuller shape. Her face was lovely, but he had known many as lovely, even lovelier although her eyes, with their extremely long and dark lashes, he deemed peerless. Delicately arched brows, a small straight nose, and the way her small oval face tapered into a stubborn chin had their appeal but should not cause a man to ache with need as he was.

Suddenly he smiled to himself. He was searching for what could not be seen with the eyes. Although no romantic, he knew it was neither face nor form that caused a man to forsake all other women for one woman or stirred a desire that demanded satisfaction. In the short time he had known her,

Aimil Mengue had revealed several characteristics he had begun to think women no longer possessed. Skill in riding and consideration for her mount came to mind for he was first and foremost a knight, a man of battle who knew how valuable a good horse could be. She had courage amply displayed by her attempt to escape and her refusal to quail before him. He had felt her strength when he had wrestled with her. Her intervention in Alex's case had shown she had a sense of justice. He was eager to discover other facets to her character.

"Will ye send my father the ransom demands now, Sir MacGuin?" she asked, breaking into his musings. "He must be sore worried by now."

"Aye, it must seem as if ye have been swallowed up by the earth itself. My brother should have at least sent your father word that ye were held here. I must assess your value however," he added. He then watched her intently as he said, "There will be enough time before the ransoming is done for ye to turn your horse to my hand."

"Nay, there will never be enough time for that."

"Lass, I intend to have that horse."

"Weel, ye just try but ye will gain no aid from me. Elfking is mine. He was born second in a twin birth and was weak and looked runty. He would have been left to die as such beasts are but I took him. I handfed him the mare's milk his stronger sibling denied him and I raised him. He is mine and there is naught that will change that, not even the great Black Parlan himself," she sneered.

"Ye have a knack for trying a man's patience."

"So it has been said." She watched him as she ate some of her food.

Parlan leaned back in his chair. "So ye willnae help me to win the stallion's favor."

"Nay, I willnae help ye to steal my horse." She thought the way he quirked his brow over one eye an impressive gesture then blushed and stared at her ale when barely-stifled laughter and Parlan's grin told her she had spoken her thoughts aloud.

"Thank ye, mistress."

"Ye are verra welcome," she grumbled with a distinct lack of grace while wondering if she would ever learn to control her tongue.

"Ye do ken that I can keep the beast whether ye do as I ask or not."

"Aye, but t'will gain ye naught. He will come to me as soon as he is able."

"There are ways to secure even that brute."

"But weel secured he will do ye little good as a mount."

"Mayhaps, but he could still be put to stud. I would wager he has weel proven himself in that area."

She thought about lying but knew the man would simply test the truth for himself. "Aye. He hasnae had a miss yet." She could not restrain the impish twinkle that entered her eyes. "Another year or twa of letting Elfking do what comes naturally and I will be a rich woman."

"Ye claim a fee?" Parlan asked in mild surprise.

"Do ye not if a man uses Raven for stud?"

"Aye, but"—he frowned—"payment went to Lachlan, did it not?"

"Nay. Elfking is mine. I take money or one of his offspring. The horse Leith was on is one of Elfking's spawn."

"Whose mare?"

"One of Alaistair MacVern's."

Parlan gave a soft whistle for the man was well known to have prime horseflesh. Then he chuckled to himself. It must have been a sore trial for the stiff-necked Alaistair to deal with a slip of a girl. That he did at all only verified Elfking's worth.

"Then he could weel richen my purse," Parlan observed, and met her glare with a smile.

"Aye, that he could but t'would be a waste to use such a fine horse for naught but that."

"True but who is to say he will never turn to me? Given long enough away from ye and good care at my hands and the bond that ties him to ye could slowly weaken, even break." He took careful note of the fear that briefly flashed in her eyes. "'Tis worth a chance." He let her think on his words for a moment before drawling, "I may be willing to bargain."

Her impulsive start of hope was quelled briefly by the strange glint in his eyes. "What sort of bargain?"

Leaning forward, he murmured, "Ye or your horse."

Aimil frowned in confusion, wondering why the other men at the table were suddenly so quiet. "I dinnae understand."

A slow smile touched his face as he traced the gentle curve of her face with one long finger. "Nay, ye truly dinnae. 'Tis astounding. I want your horse. I also want ye." He smiled a little more when she blushed. "I willnae steal your horse if ye come to my bed."

The outraged refusal she knew she should make immediately did not come forth. "I must speak to Leith."

He sat back with a nod and signaled Malcolm to take her to her brother. "I will have my answer this night, Aimil."

She paused in the doorway to look back at him with all the icy hauteur of a duchess despite her tangled hair and odd attire. "Sir, I dinnae recall giving ye leave to address me so familiarly." She turned sharply on her heel and left before he could reply.

When Parlan had stopped chuckling, Lagan ventured, "So ye ask her to choose one stallion or another."

Parlan frowned, wondering why being termed a stallion should bother him. "Aye, in a manner of speaking."

"Why dinnae ye just seduce her? For such a stud as ye, t'would be easy or so says your reputation with the ladies."

"I dinnae think she would be an easy one to seduce and I havenae the patience to wait long for her."

Lagan's brows rose sharply in a gesture of surprise. "If ye are that hungry for a wench . . ."

"I am not that hungry for a wench. Leastwise, I shouldnae be after Catarine wrung me dry but twa days past." He grinned when Lagan laughed. "Nay, I am hungry for Aimil Siubhan O'Connell Mengue and I mean to have her."

"Even if she doesnae come to your bed this night?"

"Aye. I will simply find another way."

"I think ye also mean to try for the stallion as weel."

"Aye. I said I wouldnae steal it. I didnae say I wouldnae try to win the beast over."

"Parlan, ye are surely destined for hell."

"Aye. Nay doubt, but I mean to have a taste of heaven first."

Chapter Four

"He said what?"

Aimil looked at her brother, thinking how much a warm, dry bed and food had restored him. He was as weak as a baby and the fever still lurked in his blood, but she no longer feared he would die. She did think, however, that he was close to bursting a blood vessel in reaction to the bargain Parlan had offered her. Leith seemed ready to start spouting all sorts of male nonsense about honor and duty to name. It was going to be very difficult to tell him her decision.

"If I come to his bed, he willnae steal Elfking from me. 'Tis his ransom for my horse."

Leith noticed the way she could not meet his eyes, busying herself with disrobing to her shift and performing her ablutions. "Ye mean to meet his price." She began to brush her hair. "Answer me, Aimil."

"Aye, I mean to meet his price."

"Ye would sell yourself to him for the sake of a horse?"

"I would sell myself for Elfking. He isnae just a horse to me. Please, try to understand." She wondered if he would guess that it was not for Elfking alone that she had decided to accept Parlan's deal.

He sighed, regretting his harsh words. "I do understand. I ken weel what Elfking means to ye but what of honor?"

"Honor." She set down the brush and turned to look at her brother. "Honor says I should cling to my chastity, save it for my husband who will be Rory Fergueson, a man I dinnae even like. Elfking is but a horse yet he is worth ten of Rory. Where is the honor in losing the best while clinging to something for the worst?"

"If t'was for my sake, t'would be understood but not to save a horse."

"Those who ken me weel ken that there is a difference between ye in my heart. To save ye, I would give up Elfking. To save something Rory Fergueson will tear from me in but a blinking and with nary a thought to me, I willnae do. I cannae. I dinnae want to."

He closed his eyes for he knew there was no argument to sway her. Having made it clear he did not want murder on his hands, Parlan MacGuin had searched and found the only other weakness Aimil really had. When Leith opened his eyes, Aimil had donned her shirt and stood by his bed, looking at him anxiously, tears streaking her pale face.

"Will ye turn from me, Leith?"

Lifting the bedcovers slightly, he patted the space beside him. She hastily filled it, huddling next to him and resting her cheek upon his chest. When his arm, heavy with weakness, curled around her shoulders, she closed her eyes with relief. Although she had no intention of turning from her decision, she had feared what it would cost her in her relationship with her brother.

"Brat, I think ye could whore yourself bowlegged and I would still love ye." He smiled weakly when she gave a watery giggle. "God, if only I wasnae so weak," he cursed. "I have been a poor protector for ye."

"Nay. Odds have been against us from the start. Ye cannae

fight a whole clan. Even if you were in full health, ye wouldnae be able to help me, Leith. If ye tried to put a stop to things, they would simply lock ye out of the way."

"Aye, I fear what ye say is true. Are ye afraid, sweeting? He is a man about whom many a dark tale is told."

"'Tis odd but nay." She told him of the incident concerning Alex. "Ye see? The fearsome Black Parlan doesnae hold with the abuse of women. I cannae say the same for Rory Fergueson." She noticed that Leith could not either but was not really surprised. "What is the worst that can happen to me?"

"Why, ye will be dishonored and," Leith paused, blinked and continued slowly, "possibly unweddable."

"That isnae a verra great loss to my mind." She decided to be honest. "I hope for that, pray for it. Aye, I act partly with that firmly in mind. Ye never can tell. I may even enjoy myself. 'Tis said he is a great lover."

"'Tis hard to ken if they mean his skill or the size of his staff," Leith muttered. "I heard some ladies, if ye can term them such, their morals being loose, speaking about the Black Parlan last time I was at court." He frowned as he recalled that conversation.

"What did they say about him?" she pressed when he had been quiet long enough to try her curiosity.

"That he is verra weel built. The wenches put it a wee bit less delicately. Called him quite the stallion."

"Oh." Aimil frowned. "Do ye mean that he could hurt me? I mean hurt me simply by doing what is natural?"

"Nay, lass. If what ye said is true, that he doesnae hold with the abuse of women, then he will be careful with ye for he will ken that ye are untouched. A woman's body can shape itself to fit most any man. 'Tis not the size of the horse that matters but the ride it gives."

"I think, nay, I truly feel that it willnae be so bad. In truth" — she took a deep breath to brace herself for her confession—

"my body has already taken notice of his good looks and fine form. To be plain, I desire him greatly. Would it be so verra bad if I took the pleasure with him that I ken weel Rory Fergueson willnae give me? Is it wrong to do something to please myself before I must sacrifice so much to please others?"

"Nay," he replied. "Ye deserve some pleasure and I fear ye have the right of it when ye say Rory will give ye none. I only wish it could be done without shaming ye. The rules are set firm, and the Black Parlan kens weel that he forces ye to shame yourself by making this bargain. For that, I will kill the man when I get the chance."

Aimil shivered. She hated the coldness in her brother's voice. Nevertheless, she offered no argument. Parlan MacGuin would have dishonored her whether she had been given a choice or not. She did not see it as dishonor but others would. Because of that, Leith would feel he was honorbound to make the man pay dearly. That she chose to go to Parlan made no difference.

Malcolm entered at that instant after a soft rap upon the door. "The laird wants his answer now, lass."

She sat up slowly. "Does he now? Weel, mayhaps he can wait a bit more. Could give the big ox some much needed humility."

"It isnae wise to make the laird wait," Malcolm said as he barely restrained a grin, "nor to try his patience."

"He sore tries mine," she grumbled, rising to don her hose. "I dinnae ken what he needs me for. Surely a lusty wench with more flesh upon her bones would serve him better. I think the fool's great size doesnae extend to his brain." The last thing she wished to reveal was how Parlan's desire for her thrilled her even as it puzzled her.

Looking at Leith, Malcolm received only a crooked grin. The girl plainly did not see how appealing she was to a man. Malcolm wondered if her total lack of vanity was part of her draw for Parlan. The laird had certainly known his fair share of vain women.

Answering Leith's signal, Malcolm edged closer to the bed while Aimil continued to ready herself.

"Can ye nae talk the man out of this? She is a maid of good birth and doesnae deserve the shame he will bring her." While Leith sympathized with Aimil's reasons, he could not resist trying to stop her, even if obtusely.

"I tried but 'tisnae any use. The laird has the heat on him. Aye, I have ne'er seen it so strong. He will have her before she leaves here. This bargain is only to make the having come sooner for he feels she wouldnae be verra easy to seduce though 'tis a skill he has refined weel."

"Nay, she would laugh at sweet words and warm looks. She sees them as foolishness and falseness."

"So they ofttimes are. He willnae hurt her. Even though he sometimes doesnae like the woman, he treats her gently. He doesnae hold with treating the lasses rough. Ye ken as weel as I do that many another man would have tossed her down and had at her before now, hostage for ransom or not. 'Tis seen as a right, a right won by capture."

"Aye, 'tis true, but I will still kill Parlan for the shame he deals her."

"Ye can try. Aye, he kens ye will when ye get all your strength back. It matters not. As I said, he has the heat upon him."

Deciding she had dawdled enough, Aimil moved to take her leave of her brother. Malcolm went to wait by the door, allowing the siblings a moment of privacy. She bent to kiss Leith on the cheek, glad to feel that, although still a touch warm, he had already lost most of the searing heat of fever.

"Dinnae fash yourself," she murmured. "If it is too big, I will lop a bit off." She smiled with relief when he chuckled softly.

"I willnae worry. My mind is set upon making him pay for this. 'Tis all I can do for now. I am not one to fret over that which cannae be changed." He patted her hand. "Have no hesitation about coming to me to talk if ye feel the need to. Ye ken that there is little ye cannae talk of with me."

Leith watched her go with Malcolm and sighed. He had meant what he had said. To lie there seething would be an exercise in futility, and he was not a man to indulge in that. He would save his anger for when he was well and free. Then he would put his anger into action. Although he was sure he would be awake all night wondering how Aimil fared in the hands of their captor, if she would find the pleasure she sought or only abuse and shame, his body ruled, forcing him into the healing folds of a deep sleep.

It was not easy for Aimil to quell her nervousness when Malcolm left her alone with Parlan. She may have chosen to come to him, but what she now faced was new, unknown, therefore frightening. As she sought to restore her calm, she studied his quarters. Heavy drapes kept out the chill, and a large fire aided while also controlling the damp that too often plagued a keep. The furnishings were simple but strongly hewn. Rich carpets kept the cold from one's feet. The focal point of the room was the massive oak bed, high and enclosed with rich velvet hangings, drawn back at the moment. It was somewhat barbaric in appearance.

Quickly she turned her gaze to the man who leaned against a bed post with an indolence she knew was false. He wore a heavy robe and, she suspected, little else. The lingering wetness of his long hair told her he had recently bathed. She did not know whether to be flattered by his efforts on her behalf or piqued that he was so confident that she would come to him.

"I had begun to wonder if ye had decided to gift me with your horse."

"When pigs crow the coming day."

He grinned. "Have ye made a close study of all that is impossible?"

Shrugging, she eyed him intently. "I dinnae suppose ye may have changed your mind."

"Nay. I was determined to have ye as soon as I kenned ye werenae a child too young for the having."

Inwardly, she sighed with relief. "Leith will kill ye for this."

"I would think less of him if he didnae try. 'Tis the reason I will try not to kill him when he makes the attempt."

Even though she suspected his confidence in his ability was well-founded, his arrogance annoyed her. "He could weel kill ye."

"That is a chance. A slim one though."

"I think ye have far too high an opinion of yourself."

Her last word ended on a squeak as he scooped her up in his arms and gently deposited her on the bed. It astounded her that such a large man could move with such silent speed. When he partially covered her body with his own, she shivered slightly. His large, strong body made her feel very small and very fragile, yet she was not really afraid. Instead, she felt the desire she craved to taste eke into her veins.

"Dinnae be afeard of me, sweeting. I mean only to pleasure ye," he whispered, brushing soft kisses over her cheeks.

"Pleasure yourself, ye mean," she grumbled, but felt an odd tingling where his lips touched her skin.

"Aye, but ye as weel, Aimil. Just relax and give yourself over to me."

"I will give ye naught." She hoped he believed her protests for she had no wish to let him know she was there for reasons other than his bargain.

"Oh, ye will, Aimil Mengue." He trailed kisses down her nose to her mouth. "Aye, ye will."

When his lips brushed and nibbled at hers, she almost sighed. It was very nice, conjuring up a pleasant warmth within her.

Soon her mouth itched for something more, and she felt her hands creeping to his broad shoulders. When his tongue probed for entry, her eyes flew open in surprise for she was unsure of what he was doing.

"Part your lips for me, sweeting. I crave the honey of your mouth."

"There is none there. My teeth are rotted and oozing."

Parlan laughed softly. "Such a liar ye are, Aimil Mengue. Part your lips."

Another shiver tore through her when his tongue eased between her lips to caress the inside of her mouth. Each kiss grew hungrier. He paused briefly between each, letting her catch her breath while teasing her slim throat with gentle kisses. She burrowed her hands into his thick hair even as her body arched, seeking his. The slow warmth that had begun in her started to grow. Tender noises of pleasure escaped her as she succumbed to the heady persuasion of his kisses. The sudden removal of her shift broke through the fog he had created in her mind.

"Nay," she protested in a soft, husky voice, trying to cover her breasts with her oddly limp arms, embarrassment dimming her growing passion.

"Aye," he growled as he gently tugged her arms away to gaze at her breasts with ill-concealed hunger. "So lovely."

Her body bucked slightly when his tongue flickered over each taut nipple. Pure white heat shot straight to her loins. As his hands cupped and fondled the soft flesh, his kisses touching their every curve, she returned her hands to his hair. She pressed his head closer when his mouth closed over one hard, aching tip to draw upon it slowly. A litany of pleasure's sounds escaped her throat, but she was too caught up in delight to restrain them. She ran her hands over the warm skin of his back. The way he groaned and trembled slightly only heightened her pleasure. She was glad when he tore off his robe for now she could touch even more of him.

As he heatedly spread kisses over her satiny midriff, Parlan reveled in her response. She was fire beneath his hands, far more than he had dared hope for. When he began to remove her hose, his hands touched the warm silken skin of her thighs and before he bent to kiss her there, he found that he had barely skimmed the surface of her passion.

Aimil nearly flew off the bed when he touched her bare legs. Parlan took quick advantage of her sensitivity there, his hands and lips moving over her greedily, leaving no spot upon her long, slim legs untouched. The pleasure grew so intense Aimil thought he would kill her with it. His large calloused hands both caressed her legs and held them steady so that he could kiss her, lick her, and nibble her. When he finally made his slow way up her body, his hand slipping between her thighs, Aimil was too frenzied to do more than twitch when he touched her so intimately.

Feeling that faint sign of rejection, Parlan lifted his head from her breasts only to hear her make a sound much like a purr and to see her open for his touch. "God, so lovely. Ye are melting for me." He moved his mouth greedily over her breasts as he stroked her and probed her secrets. "Aye, lass," he groaned against her throat, "let your sweetness flow. I mean to taste it soon. Nae this night but soon."

"Please, please," she moaned, having no idea for what she begged but only certain that he could give her what her body now craved.

"I must hurt ye the first time but t'will pass," he rasped as he readied himself to possess her.

She did not really hear him but moved her hips against his in a way that made him shudder. He took her with one hard thrust in the hope that quicker was better. Feeling the shield of her innocence rend before his charge, he savored the proof that he was the first, even as he flinched in sympathy with the pain he had caused her.

Aimil shuddered beneath the onslaught, but the sharp pain was gone as quickly as it had come. All she could think of was that there was more. She moved her hands to his taut buttocks as her legs clasped him tightly, urging him to move with both actions.

"Oh," she sighed, her whole body shuddering with delight as he moved with slow, measured strokes. "So fine. 'Tis so nice."

"Nice? Sweet Mary, 'tis heaven. Move with me, sweeting. Aye," he gasped when she parried his next thrust. "That is the way of it." He encircled her hips with his arm to press her closer as he brushed fevered kisses over her face. "Aye, take it all. Take me in deep, lassie. God, 'tis sweet."

After kissing her hungrily, he watched her as his motions grew fiercer. He was barely able to appreciate the way her body convulsed with her release when his own seized him. A hoarse cry of exultation escaped him as he drove deeply within her to spill his seed, a gift of passion that her body accepted with trembling greed. She continued to shake and to squirm slightly with lingering pleasure after he collapsed upon her. Parlan found her subtle movements arousing, despite how sated he felt.

Aimil felt as if she drifted down from the clouds slowly and was amazed that she was still alive. That something extraordinary had happened was evident by her furious heartbeat and her gasping breaths. Her whole body tingled, yet she felt heavy and langorous. It had been all she had hoped for and more. She realized once was not enough. Since her maidenhead was now lost, she decided it would matter little if he did it again. She found herself hoping that he would.

Easing himself away from her slightly, Parlan grinned at her. "There now, didnae I say I would give ye pleasure?"

It struck her that he looked very much like a small boy who

had found the bean in the twelfth-night cake. She felt sure that his experience with women allowed him to know exactly what he had stirred in her. Aimil sincerely doubted she was the only one to gain such pleasure in his arms. There was no way she was going to pronounce him bean-king and add to his already lofty opinion of himself, not when he was supposed to think her there solely because of their bargain. She gazed at her fingernails with an air of boredom.

"I have never suffered such a lack of entertainment in all my short life," she drawled.

Parlan roared with laughter, not in the least insulted for he knew of the pleasure he had given her. He held her close as he laughed, and she soon joined in for it was a contagious sound. Aimil also knew that she had not fooled him.

As their laughter died away, she was seized by a feeling of deep exhaustion. A great deal had happened to her in the past twenty-four hours, indeed, in the last week. Her body had clearly decided that, if she did not have enough sense to rest, it would take the decision out of her hands.

Parlan sensed the sudden laxness in her and raised himself up on his elbows to look at her with a crooked grin, knowing she needed to rest but wanting her again. "Are ye betrothed, Aimil?" he asked, feeling a strong need to know if some man had a claim to her.

She tried to open her eyes to look at him but gave up. "Since the cradle. I am to be wed at summer's end."

"To whom?"

"To Rory Fergueson. I am going to sleep now."

The quickness with which she fell asleep momentarily surprised Parlan out of his reaction to the name of her betrothed. He nudged her but got no reaction. She lay sprawled on her back much as if she had been felled by a blow. Shaking his head and grinning, he lay back down to think about her betrothal for a moment, the feelings his surprise had briefly quelled rushing to the fore.

If there was one man in the world he could truly say he hated, it was Rory Fergueson. The man had no redeeming qualities at all. He had no proof but he was sure that Rory was responsible for the brutal way Parlan's cousin Morna, had died. Rory Fergueson was vicious, sly, a liar, and a cheat. Each time the MacGuins had raided the Ferguesons, Parlan had hoped to find Rory within his sword's reach, but the man had always eluded him. Fondling the lush hair tangled around Aimil's face, Parlan knew he could not let her fall into that man's hands. Getting up, he donned his robe and strode off to Leith Mengue's chambers.

Leith glared at the man who had awakened him and had just come from taking Aimil's virtue. "What do ye want?"

"Is Aimil betrothed to Rory Fergueson?"

"Aye, since the cradle," Leith answered, curious over the agitation he sensed in the larger man, "though I had forgotten the matter until the day we were captured. The wedding plans were being set and that caused me to recall the arrangement."

"Doesnae Lachlan ken the sort of man Rory Fergueson is?"

"I cannae think he hasnae heard the rumors. 'Tis an old arrangement that cannae be broken because of rumor. Of course," he added coldly, "Rory might weel break the betrothal now that ye have stolen Aimil's honor. Few men want to wed another's leavings."

"Stolen her honor I may have, laddie, but I havenae hurt her in the doing of it. Rory Fergueson will kill her."

The charge was made with such conviction that all of Leith's thoughts of Parlan's crimes fled. "Do ye have proof to back your charge?"

"Nay, curse it. Five years back he and my cousin Morna, were lovers. She thought he would wed her, told me of her hopes, for she had been a virgin when he had taken her. Then her hopes changed. She became afeard of the man though she wouldnae tell me why. When she told me she was ending the affair, I was pleased for I had never liked it, but she wasnae a verra comely lass and I felt she ought to have her moment."

"What happened?" Leith prodded when Parlan fell into a brooding silence.

"The next morn she was found dead. If it wasnae for the ring and dress she wore, we wouldnae have kenned who she was she was beaten so badly. She had been used so harshly the women who treated her said she was torn up inside. I have no proof but each thing I have learned of the man since then tells me t'was him, and I have studied him verra closely. The man has left a long, bloodied trail of women who are too afraid to speak against him or who are dead, leaving no proof 'tis Rory doing the killing. The beast covers his tracks weel. I must have proof and then I can cut him down wherever and whenever I find him."

Leith did not question Parlan's conviction of Rory's guilt. "All I can do is speak to my father. He is the law."

"It isnae enough."

"What ye have done this night just might be." Leith did not really want to think that Parlan might have done Aimil a favor.

"Nay. T'will depend upon how badly Rory wants her or what is to be gained through the marriage."

"I cannae give ye an answer to either of those."

Parlan swore and ran his hand through his hair, unable to conceal his agitation. "I cannae allow this marriage."

"Ye cannae allow it?" Leith glared at the man. "Ye are a MacGuin nae a Mengue. 'Tisnae your place to allow or to disallow."

"Aye, but 'tis I who hold her now."

"She is to be ransomed. T'was said ye would send word to my father on the morrow."

"Ransoming can be a difficult business," Parlan drawled, quickly putting together a plan. "A lot of haggling may need doing. Could take a verra long time."

"Rory may wait." Leith found himself uncomfortably allied with Parlan to stop Aimil's marriage to Rory.

"Aye, and he might weel expose himself as the depraved bastard he is. Surely your father would stop the marriage then?"

"I cannae say," Leith reluctantly admitted. "Since she first showed signs of womanhood, he has been blind to her existence. I was meaning to speak to him on the marriage, but your brother captured Aimil and me. Rory's uncle, James, and my father were like brothers. They both wanted the families joined in marriage. James died twa years back naming Rory as his heir. That could make my father all the firmer in his decision."

"God, a promise to a dear friend now dead. They are the hardest to change. Does Aimil favor Rory?" Parlan asked.

"Nay, she says she doesnae even like him. T'was why I meant to speak to my father. The way things stand between Aimil and my father, however, it could make him push all the harder for the marriage." Leith spoke with weariness weighting his voice for he did not have the strength to wrestle with such problems.

"Why? What did the girl do to turn Lachlan against her?"

"She grew up. Aye, ye may weel look puzzled but there isnae any other explanation. She was his favorite. He took the pair of us everywhere. Then, one night she wore a new gown that revealed her budding woman's figure and he has turned a cold side to her ever since. None of us kens why, and my father offers no answers."

"There must be a way," Parlan growled as he started toward the door.

"Weel, I will be verra glad to hear of it if ye find it."

"If there isnae another way, I will wed the cursed wench myself," he snapped, and left abruptly, leaving Leith staring after him in stunned surprise.

Chapter Five

Lagan entered Parlan's chambers after a terse "Enter" had answered his knock. He shut the door and looked at the bed with raised brows for Aimil still slept there. It was rare that a woman was in Parlan's bed come the morning. Parlan would take his fill of the woman and then sleep alone. It was a habit Lagan could not recall the man breaking before without having had too much drink. Lagan leaned against the bed post and eyed Parlan who was shaving.

"Shouldnae ye at least give the poor lass a pillow for her head?"

Drying off his face, Parlan strode to the side of the bed. "I have put her head on a pillow three times, but she moves off it."

"Strange she didnae wake when ye did so."

"I think the bed could collapse about her and she would sleep through it. I even put her shirt on after I awoke and she never even blinked."

"Sure she still lives?" Lagan teased.

Parlan grinned. "Aye, though I did wonder at first. Never seen a person sleep so sound. Only able to rouse her once during the night"—he ignored Lagan's mockingly sympathetic noise—"and she was certainly with me in body but, after she fell asleep again so quickly and so deeply, I began to think she never really woke up. I will be curious to see if she remembers the incident."

"Ye dinnae think something ails her, do ye?"

"I never thought on that. I will ask her brother," Parlan said even as he strode from the room.

While he was gone, Lagan studied the girl. She was flat on her back with her legs and arms flung out. Her long fingers were lightly curled toward her upturned palms in a soft child-like gesture. Nearly obscured by her mass of hair which seemed to fill each empty space on the bed, her face was turned sideways. Lagan had reached the decision that she really was quite lovely when Parlan returned.

"When he could stop laughing, Leith said she does this when she has overworked herself."

"Ah. Weel, she certainly had a busy day yesterday. I have never seen a woman sleep in such a position."

"Nay?" Parlan frowned in thought. "I have never noticed."

"Ye need to sleep with them to notice how they sleep," Lagan drawled. "Once ye are done ye send them on their way."

Not really sure why he had not done the same with Aimil, Parlan made no comment. "Weel? What is odd about the way she sleeps?"

"Aside from the fact that she looks as if she was dealt a sound blow to the jaw? Women tend to sleep on their sides, curled up a wee bit."

Shrugging, Parlan began to dress, murmuring, "She is betrothed."

"I am little surprised by that news. Are ye saying there will be an enraged fiancé coming to face you?"

"Nay, I doubt this man will come to face me though I would sore like it if he did. She is to wed Rory Fergueson at summer's end."

Lagan whistled softly, aware of Parlan's hatred for the man. "Pity. He will break the spirit of the lass."

"That bastard will break more than that. He will kill her in the end. I cannae let that happen. Aye"—he held up a hand when Lagan began to speak—"I ken the problems. Her brother and I chewed them over verra weel last night."

"I would have thought all that lad would wish to say to ye is how and when he is going to kill ye."

"Aye, but he is a practical lad and nae hotheaded. He also cares for his sister and doesnae want this marriage. For that goal, we have formed an alliance. I have given much thought on how to make the ransoming take a long time. I shall ask for coin, only coin and a lot of it."

"There is a fair shortage of that. Aye, it could take a long time, a verra long time for it to be gathered. During which time?"

"I cannae be sure. T'will give the lad time to speak with his father and Rory Fergueson time to expose himself for the beast that he is."

"Depending on how strongly he wants the girl or the marriage he could come after ye."

"God's teeth, I hope he does, but the man is a low coward. He scampers into a hole at the first scent of danger. He kens that I willnae risk outlawry by killing him without just cause." He looked down at the sleeping Aimil. "I cannae knowingly hand him a lass, not when I ken what he does to them."

"I feel the same, Parlan, but ye arenae her laird and ye cannae hold her forever. She is a Mengue."

"I have no real quarrel with the Mengues. Weel, not until now." He flashed a grin at Lagan who laughed and shook his head. "I could mend that and keep her from Rory Fergueson at the same time," he continued slowly. "I could wed the lass."

"Dinnae tell me ye love the lass?"

"Nay, but, at least thus far, I like her and there hasnae been a woman I could say that about for more years than I care to ponder. She is of good family and nae hard to look upon. She was a virgin. I will have Old Meg take note of it before I decide to take that route. I will have none question it."

"It seems a drastic step to take."

"I must wed someday and I have met no other I even wanted to consider. I am eight and twenty, and many another my age has been wed a few years with a family started. In truth, the decision may already be made for I may have already begun my family."

"Jesu," Lagan whispered, shocked, for Parlan had always been as careful as a man could be in preventing such a thing. "I am not sure that was verra wise," he ventured after a moment.

"I wasnae concerned with wisdom. Nay, I didnae have a thought in my head save to go the full length. 'Tis another reason the idea of wedding her came into my head. For months now I have found little pleasure with the ladies and wenches."

"But ye found it here?"

"Aye. Tenfold. I will wait though to see if it wanes."

"It could be that she was untouched. Being the first can make a man feel verra possessive."

"I ken that. 'Tis another reason I will wait to see. I am not so old I must rush to wed and I willnae tie myself to a lass who neither interests me nor pleasures me. I will suffer no empty marriage. Have ye seen Artair?" he asked, abruptly changing the subject.

"Aye, I saw his back as he rode out of the gates with three men for escort."

"Do ye ken where he hies to?"

"Aberdeen. I think he means to hole up there until he feels your temper has cooled."

"'Tis best. Curse it, I have failed with that lad."

"Nay, he has failed by his own doing. He is but twenty. He may yet get set upon a straighter course. Many a youth has seemed lost only to turn to the better as age sharpens their wits. The lady stirs."

Aimil's eyes opened suddenly giving both men a start. She was not awake yet, however. The heaviness of her exhaustion still clouded her mind and weighted her limbs. She looked about in sleepy confusion.

"What are ye doing in my chambers?" she demanded in a voice husky with sleep.

"These are my chambers," Parlan corrected with a soft laugh.

Rubbing the sleep from her eyes in a childlike gesture, she looked around again. "Oh. What am I doing in your chambers?"

"Ah, how quickly they forget," Parlan mourned, casting a laughing glance at a grinning Lagan.

Bright color flooded her cheeks as memories of the night rushed into her mind. "'Tis easy to forget the little things in life."

Lagan clamped a hand over his mouth but it did not stifle all of his laughter, and Parlan sighed. "Ye wound me sorely, mistress."

"I doubt much can pierce that thick hide," she grumbled, then grimaced over the small discomfort her introduction to passion had left her with. "T'would it be possible for me to have a bath?"

Parlan astutely guessed the cause of her grimace. "Aye, I will have Old Meg see to it and to restoking the fire in here."

"There is no need of a fire here. I will be in Leith's chambers."

"If ye are, I will drag ye, tub and all, right back here. These are your chambers now." He started out the door.

"Ye ask a high price for my horse."

"'Tis a fine steed." He saw her open her mouth to speak. "I wouldnae if I were ye. I havenae broken my fast yet and ye must ken how short a man's temper can be when his belly is empty."

"She has a quick and sharp tongue," observed Lagan as he followed Parlan to the hall where they would find some hearty fare. "That is a lass who will do little stroking of a man's vanity."

"Aye. I wouldnae like to feel the lash of that tongue when it is unleashed by anger or hate."

"Ye dinnae think she feels either now? She has a verra good reason to feel both."

"True but she doesnae. I offered her a choice in all this. She cannae blame me for the choice she took."

"To give herself to save her horse." Lagan shook his head. "'Tis an odd thing for a woman to do."

"Grown men have wept like bairns over their steeds. We never find that a puzzle. She raised that brute by hand. There isnae any denying the bond between them. And I ken there is none who claims her heart so there was little to hold her back in that way, no man she feared to hurt or to lose. Howbeit, I do have a strong feeling that there was far more behind her decision. In truth, I cannae help but wonder how much this betrothal prompted her choice."

As Aimil watched her bath being prepared, she thought about her betrothal to Rory Fergueson and the duty she owed him. She wondered where her guilt was as well as her shame. Being a fallen woman was not affecting her very much. She knew the reason for that was her betrothal. Although the chance that it might be ended because of what she had done was slim, it was something to be considered. Then too, she had honestly enjoyed herself and she knew she never would with Rory.

"Weel? Are ye going to use it or stare at it?"

Grinning, Aimil got into the bath. Old Meg reminded her of Annie at home. Both, rail thin and sharp of tongue, were past their prime, although it was difficult to guess how far past. She wondered if such women were common features of keeps.

"Ah, so ye were a virgin," muttered Old Meg as she and two young maids took the linen from the bed.

Concentrating on washing her legs and cursing her blushes, Aimil snapped, "What matter if I was?"

"Ye never can tell. Nay, ye never can tell, lassie. Ye remember to do as I told ye," Old Meg growled at the maids.

The younger, less comely of the two maids looked at Aimil. "Did ye really do this to keep a horse?"

"Some men have killed for less," Aimil replied, determined to cling to that story even if people did think her mad. "I simply lie back, closed my eyes, and thought on king and country."

She had to choke down a giggle over the astounded looks upon the maids' faces. Old Meg eyed her narrowly, and Aimil suspected that there was as little chance of fooling the woman as there was Annie. Suddenly, the buxom, pretty maid flounced to the edge of the tub, her hands on her well-rounded hips and her eyes glinting with maliciousness. Aimil wondered idly how many times Parlan had used the maid.

"Are ye expecting us to believe that ye lay with the Black Parlan and thought on the king?" she sneered.

"There are one or twa of us that can keep more than one thought in her head at a time." Aimil smiled sweetly at the woman.

"Let us get out o' here, Jeanne," urged the other maid when Jeanne swelled with fury.

Old Meg cackled merrily and made no attempt to interfere. She had been Parlan's nurse and was interested in the girl. Only the finest would do for the man she still called her lad. He could not be happy with any weak-willed girl.

"Mayhaps 'tis best if ye keep your mind on the king. T'would never do for ye to take a fancy to the Black Parlan.

He has no use for some Lowland slut and will send ye off as soon as your cur of a father begs the ransom."

Aimil moved so quickly that Jeanne had no chance to avoid retribution. Aimil might have ignored the slur upon herself but she would not allow an insult to her father to go unreprimanded. Jeanne's screeches were cut off by the water when Aimil pushed the girl's head under.

Parlan stopped abruptly in his advance toward Leith's chambers when he heard a scream come from his own chambers. It ended quickly, but he still decided it warranted checking. Parlan burst into the room, gaped at the sight of the well-endowed Jeanne bent over the tub, arms and legs flailing, and then hastily yanked her free of Aimil's hold.

With equal haste Aimil covered her breasts with her arms and sank a little deeper into the soapy water. Old Meg tittered over the sight of a gasping, dripping Jeanne as did Lagan who hovered inside the door. The other little maid clearly wished she was someplace else. Aimil sympathized for she found herself wishing the same but decided to hide her embarrassment with haughty bravado.

"What the Devil is going on here?" Parlan demanded, cursing softly when he saw that he was now wet.

"I lost my soap and she was helping me find it." Aimil tried to ignore Lagan who fell into a fit of laughter.

"She tried to drown me," screeched Jeanne.

"Nonsense," snapped Aimil. "If ye had kept your big mouth shut when ye went under, ye wouldnae be in such a state."

"Aimil." Parlan's voice was a growl of warning as he restrained a furious Jeanne and with a firm grip held the other maid's arm. "Ilka, tell me what happened here."

Reluctantly, Ilka obeyed the command, shrinking a little when Parlan's face darkened with anger. "Then ye came in."

"Since ye cannae keep a civil tongue around your betters, Jeanne, I suggest ye keep to the kitchens." He spoke coldly to the maid then turned to Aimil as Jeanne stormed away. "Ye must learn to hold your temper."

"Coming from ye that advice lacks a wee bit," she drawled. "Now, may I have some privacy for my bath?"

"But of course, m'lady." He bowed mockingly. "Just try to restrain the urge to drown my serving wenches."

"If I must, I must," she sighed, and waited for the door to close after him before she began to bathe again.

"Ilka, ye make the bed afresh." Old Meg looked at Aimil. "I cannae think of what to get ye for clothes. There hasnae been a lady here, save serving wenches and crofters' wives, for a score of years. They wouldnae have anything to suit ye even if they had it to spare."

"It doesnae matter. Most all here have seen me dressed as a lad. It willnae shock them if I continue so."

"Aye, 'tis how it must be for now, but I may yet come round with an idea. T'would be best if ye were dressed as the lass ye are."

Shrugging, Aimil continued to bathe. When her father had started to ignore her existence, she had done as she had pleased. One of the things that had pleased her was to ride dressed as a lad. She did in truth find it far more comfortable than female attire. To have to wear it was no hardship in her mind. She only hoped that Leith did not see it as a further insult that needed avenging.

Leith feared his family was facing dire hardship as he reacted in horror over Parlan's exorbitant ransom demands. "T'will leave us naught."

"Do ye think your father will pay it?"

"He will try to whittle ye down, as he should. This demand is far beyond reason."

"Aye, I thought so but nae too far beyond, so it should be taken seriously."

Frowning in confusion, Leith muttered, "I dinnae ken what ye are about."

"I dinnae want this much. 'Tis not my way to leave a man in rags. I expect him to haggle and I will be stubborn, slow to come down. If he accepts it or a still too high cost, t'will take him a fair while to raise it in coin. Time is what this is all about. I but try to buy time. A man should pay a goodly fee when he was foolish to let his kin be caught." He ignored Leith's scowl. "Howbeit, I wouldnae pay this much for my own mother."

A reluctant laugh escaped Leith, but then he grew serious. "I hope that time will solve the problem."

"It has to. Time is important no matter what and this game will buy that. I but hope that your father doesnae see that we play a game or we shall quickly be robbed of that time."

Lachlan Mengue felt that time weighed far too heavily upon his hands. Even his ability to believe that his children still lived had begun to waver. No word and no sighting of them had weakened his confidence in their continued existence.

His family had gathered close to him to lend their quiet strength. Both married daughters, their husbands at their sides, had come home to be with him. All they could do was wait with him for either a ransom demand or, as they all silently feared, the discovery of the bodies. Waiting put a strain on the nerves, however, and the arrival of Rory Fergueson helped little.

Tall, strong, and almost too handsome, Rory Fergueson had little taste for waiting. When it concerned the possible loss of Aimil Mengue, he had no taste for it at all. It was not only her handsome dowry he saw slipping away but the chance to possess Aimil, to dominate her and to avenge an old slight that had festered for many years. He faced Lachlan, trying to force the older man to act.

"Curse it, man, the only solution is to ride against the MacGuins. 'Tis past time that thieving clan was put to the sword."

"We arenae sure they have the pair," Lachlan reminded the man. "No word or ransom demand has come."

"They make ye wait so ye will pay quicker and without question. 'Tis an old game."

"And one I havenae heard of the Black Parlan playing," the redheaded Iain MacVern growled.

"The man is the Devil himself and we all ken it. He would play any game if it suited him. He raided me the verra day Aimil and Leith disappeared. What more proof is needed?"

"T'was Artair who raided ye from what I heard," James Broth drawled in his deep gravelly voice. "The Black Parlan was away."

"Aye," agreed Jennet Mengue Broth, her light blue eyes shining with the sudden hope she felt. "That may be why we have heard naught. Artair could await his brother and laird's return before any ransom is asked. Could that not be the how of it, Father?"

Lachlan nodded slowly. "Aye, could be the way of it. He may fear to ask the wrong amount and so leaves it for Parlan to decide."

Jennet watched how Rory Fergueson reacted and felt certain that the man was grinding his teeth. "His call to ride against the MacGuins would carry more force if he were to ride at the fore of the force," she murmured to her husband, James.

James hid a smile over the dry sarcasm in his wife's voice. Rory Fergueson was well known never to leave himself open to charges of cowardice yet was overly fond of his own skin, never really turning from a fight but keeping himself well out of any danger. If there was an attack made on the MacGuin, Rory would be there but well to the rear until the worst was over.

Giorsal, Lachlan's firstborn, also watched Rory. He repelled her despite his beauty of face and form. She was not very close to her youngest sister but the thought of Aimil wed to such a man brought tears to her eyes. If that was to be Aimil's fate, then it might be best if the girl was dead. Giorsal suddenly clasped Iain's hand, fervently glad that such a good man had been chosen for her. For all her sulkiness when the match had been set, and her disappointment in his ruddy, plain looks and gruff character, he was good to her and the two children they had been blessed with. She looked back over nearly five years of a peaceful, secure home life with a faithful, kind man and suddenly realized she had been a shrew. Sweet words and fine looks mattered little. She had what was important.

"Here now," Iain blustered, blushing fiercely when his usually undemonstrative wife kissed his cheek, slipped her arms around his waist, and hugged him. "Are ye ailing?" he whispered, his hazel eyes moving nervously as he assured himself that they were unnoticed for now.

"Nay, I just felt I must let ye ken how verra glad I am that ye were chosen for me," she replied as she pulled away.

"Humph, weel, 'tis about time ye kenned how lucky ye are," he mumbled, but the light that flared in his eyes told her that he was more than pleased with her words. "Here, ye best heed this. Rory makes another try. The man is hot for us to spill blood for him."

She nodded, but her gaze rested upon the hand Iain still held close to his thigh. Gently, she placed her other hand on top of their clasped ones and then turned her mind to Rory and his ranting. Iain's reaction to her words had told her how willingly he would accept such displays. She realized that she had never really given him any soft words, and had expected them from him with no promise of return. For five years she had given him little more than congenial indifference. She hoped it was not too late to change all that.

"I am to judge from that exchange that ye willnae ride against the MacGuins?"

"Nay, Rory, I willnae. If they have Leith and Aimil, I cannae risk their lives and, if they dinnae, I willnae attack without cause."

"And what do ye think is happening while ye sit and wait?" growled Rory. "We cannae guess what Leith may be suffering but I think we all ken how the Black Parlan will treat a comely female captive."

"If ye are concerned about the chastity of your bride, ye can be released from the betrothal, Rory," Lachlan said, stiffening with anger.

Grabbing his cloak and striding to the door, Rory snapped, "Nay, I willnae withdraw but, if she is a maiden no longer, someone will pay."

As soon as he had left, Jennet stumbled to her feet. "I hope the Black Parlan does take Aimil to his bed."

"Jennet!" her husband snapped in an attempt to halt her reckless words.

"Nay, I will say it. From what I have heard said, the Black Parlan kens weel how to please a woman, something Rory Fergueson doesnae even care to do. If the Black Parlan has bedded Aimil, at least she will have had a taste of what could be between a man and a woman before she is consigned to a life of hell on earth." Jennet hurried from the room, followed quickly by an apologetic James.

Later, as Giorsal lay in her husband's bed, trying not to giggle over his hesitation in undressing, she said, "I agree with Jennet."

"Aye?" Iain was far more concerned with why his wife had suddenly decided to share a chamber.

"Aye. Rory will bring Aimil only pain." She hid a grin at the cautious way he slid into bed, an expression that grew more difficult to hide when she snuggled up to him and he blushed. "There are some verra dark things said of the man. I have tried to speak to Father of them but he says he willnae listen to rumor. Mayhaps Rory will yet back out of the betrothal."

"'Tis possible. A man doesnae want to wed a woman dishonored." He tentatively moved his hands over her well-rounded backside.

"There is something in Rory Fergueson that frightens me. Aye, makes me shudder until my teeth click. T'was when I realized that poor Aimil would be wife to that man that I finally opened my eyes and looked at ye, Iain. I have been a cold, heartless shrew, the greatest of blind fools. Nay, I ken how I have been," she cried when he murmured a protest and she pressed her face against his hairy chest. "I will make it up to you, Iain."

Over his repentent wife's head, Iain grinned. He had no intention of telling her that he had no real complaint, had only occasionally wished for a little more fire in her and a return of the love he had always felt for her. As he put her new softness to a very practical use, he found the fire and new hope for the love he wanted. With her heart and mind free of regrets and self-pity, Giorsal responded to his lovemaking in a way that left them both dazed. As he fell asleep with a complacent smile upon his face, Iain wondered fleetingly if all the sisters held such passion. If they did, he doubted the Black Parlan would be in any rush to release Aimil.

Parlan MacGuin yawned and rested his head comfortably upon the breasts of the small woman sprawled in sleep at his side. He hoped that what flared between them would not fade. It was much too good to lose. As sleep took him, he acknowledged to himself that he was also determined that Rory Fergueson would die before he ever touched Aimil.

Chapter Six

Lachlan Mengue read the words before him yet again, unable to shake free of his disbelief. After his first elated relief over the proof that his children were alive, he had begun to comprehend the outrageous demand for their safe return. It would impoverish him. He doubted that even a king could meet such a ransom. Furthermore, it would take weeks to raise only half of it. To his way of thinking, it was thievery of the lowest sort.

"The man must be mad!" he roared, not for the first time. "I cannae meet this."

"Will ye send an offer by messenger?" asked Iain.

"Nay, I will go to the rogue myself. I cannae believe that this is any more than a cruel joke."

"At least we ken now that Leith and Aimil are alive and weel," said Jennet as she eased her very pregnant body into a seat.

"I will see the proof of that with my own eyes before I even begin to bargain."

The messenger from Dubhglenn found himself leading a size-able party back to his laird. Giorsal rode beside her husband, having insisted on going along with an uncharacteristic stubbornness. Since the party traveled under a flag of truce, the men had finally, if grudgingly, complied. Rory Fergueson was noticeably absent although, as Aimil's betrothed, he had been informed of the venture. Giorsal was glad of it for she did not trust Rory to follow the rules of bloodless negotiation.

Due to a slow start, and having waited fruitlessly for Aimil's betrothed, they had to camp out. Giorsal found the whole matter adventurous and cheerfully readied the interior of her husband's tent, but Iain was not particularly cheerful when he joined her.

"What troubles ye, Iain?" she asked as she folded the clothes he shed.

"'Tis no problem really. A puzzle. Aye, love, 'tis a puzzle." He failed to notice her start of surprise over his casual endearment.

"What is a puzzle?" she asked as he joined her in the bed she had made upon the ground, leaving the two small cots in case it rained.

"For the last four or five years your father has been cold to Aimil, his heart hardening to the girl who had been his favorite."

"Aye, t'was verra odd. We have ne'er kenned why." She let her hand wander over the well-muscled frame of her husband, a body she now took the time to discover and to appreciate. "She was sore hurt by his defection, especially when there seemed to be no reason for it. Leith is closest to her now."

"Weel, I cannae say why but I think the man's a fraud. I think Aimil is still verra dear to his heart."

"Then why turn from her? It doesnae make any sense." Tentatively, she moved her hand where it had never been before.

All thought fled from Iain's mind save for the intimate touch of his wife's hand and, hoping it was the right reply, he gasped, "Nay?"

Stifling a giggle that was more from delight than amusement

over her husband's reaction to her touch, she bent her head to kiss his chest. "I believe I must look into the situation more closely."

"Giorsal? Have ye been drinking?" Iain asked as he pushed her onto her back, but he did not bother to wait for an answer.

Parlan did not even ask Aimil if she had been imbibing. He could tell that she had already had more than enough to drink from the moment he had entered the room. She, Lagan, and Leith were playing a rowdy game of dice, betting vast sums of nonexistent money and drinking freely. It was evident that neither her brother nor Lagan, who was supposed to be her guard, were paying much heed to how much she drank. He grinned as he sat down next to Aimil on Leith's bed for Lagan had just wagered Stirling Castle and lost it to Aimil.

"Ye make a poor guard, Lagan. Letting the wench drink and indulge in gambling." Parlan shook his head with a false air of dismay. "Did ye nae think to watch how much she drank?"

"Aye." Lagan grinned. "But it hasnae dimmed her luck at all." He laughed along with the others. "She has the Devil's own luck."

"'Tis an easy game," Aimil remarked, and reached for the ale only to have Parlan intercept her. "I wasnae done."

Setting her tankard on the table near Leith's bed, Parlan used the hold he had on her wrist to tug her to her feet. "Aye, ye were."

"Has anyone ever told ye that ye are a tyrant, Parlan MacGuin?" she inquired with a false sweetness as he towed her to the door.

"Aye. Say good sleep to your brother." He paused in the doorway.

"I wasnae ready to say good sleep, but if I must . . ."

"Ye must." He started to draw her out of the room.

"Good sleep, Leith. And ye, Lagan," she cried as Parlan shut the door after them, muffling the replies sent her way. "Ye are a verra rude man. Uncivilized," she grumbled as she was hastened toward his chambers.

"I am nae feeling verra polite just now." He shut and bolted the door to his chambers.

"Why not?" she asked as she sat on his bed, finding her boots harder to remove than they had ever been before.

Already stripped to his braies, a short undergarment, Parlan moved to help her undress. "Ye are fou, lass. Verra drunk indeed."

"Nay. Weel, mayhaps a wee bit. I am not verra good with the drink though I have never got ill from it."

She made a noise much like a deep-throated purr when his mouth covered hers, the swift deep probes of his tongue hinting at his hunger for her. It was a hunger she readily returned, the drink making her bold in her passion.

The way her small hands caressed him drove Parlan beyond control. He was barely able to finish undressing them without tearing their clothes. His possession of her was swift, but she met and returned his ferocity. The culmination of their desire left them both somnolent, unable to move, except for Parlan's pulling the covers over them. It was awhile before he even had the strength to talk and by then Aimil was half asleep.

"Lass, are ye wanting to wed Rory Fergueson?" He felt himself tense, waiting for her reply.

Aimil was past any subterfuge and opened her eyes to gaze at him sleepily. "Nay. He is too pretty."

"Too pretty? 'Tis a strange thing to say. A lass often wishes a husband who is fair to look upon."

"Nay. He is too pretty. He is so perfect in face and form that he nearly frightens me. Then there are his eyes."

"What about his eyes?"

"They are like a snake's. When I meet his gaze, I feel as if an adder watches me, waiting for the right moment to strike. The color is a verra pale one and flat, and he doesnae blink verra much which only makes it worse."

Rolling onto his back, Parlan pulled her against his chest. "Aye, I think ye have the truth of it. Like a snake's."

Her eyes closing as sleep overtook her, Aimil said, "It will be hard to be wife to a man I dinnae even like."

"I promise ye, lass, ye willnae have to," he swore as he looked down upon her sleeping face.

That small lovely face was still tucked nicely against his broad chest when Parlan woke in the morning. Her arm encircled his trim waist, and one of her legs was flung over his. Parlan decided that she was a very nice little bundle to wake up to. Alternating his gaze between her face and his hand, he stroked her soft curves, enjoying the way her passion slowly grew.

He traced the gentle curve of her backside and the slim line of her leg, feeling her squirm slightly as she and her passion awoke together. He had always at least tried to give the women he had used some pleasure but never had their enjoyment been such a source of pleasure for him. His actions had been prompted by courtesy and a need to be sure his lust met more than tolerance. It intoxicated him to feel and to see Aimil's body come alive for him.

"Oh, Parlan," she whispered as he turned them onto their sides and slid his hand between her thighs.

"Such a lovely warm good morn," he growled against her breast before greedily taking a hard tip into his mouth.

"'Tis morning?" she gasped, shocked despite her intensifying passion. "We cannae do this now."

"Nay?" He grinned at her as he positioned her leg over his waist and swiftly entered her. "It seems we are."

It was a moment before she could find the breath to speak. "'Tis light. Ye are supposed to do this in the dark."

"Ah, lass, there is a lot ye have to learn," he murmured before he stopped any further talk with a kiss.

The culmination of their passion came swiftly and simultaneously. Still caught in the lingering tremors, Parlan rolled onto his back, holding them snugly joined. He still did not release her when they had regained their senses.

"I think ye have forgotten something," she murmured suddenly, realizing that they were staying joined for a long time.

"Nay, I havenae," he replied, holding her firmly when she moved to separate them. "Stay a wee bit, lass."

Rubbing her cheek against the crisp hair on his chest, she murmured, "What does it feel like?"

He was not sure of how to answer her, not only because her question startled him, but he had never spoken of his feelings and had no ready words to describe them. His policy had always been one of a polite but hasty exit after taking his pleasure.

"'Tis hard to say, lass. Lovely doesnae say enough." He gave a soft growl when she moved sensuously. "Ye shouldnae do that."

"I think I can tell why." She was surprised to feel him becoming aroused.

"Oh, God's tears," he cursed when a rap came at the door. "Nay, dinnae move." He held her close as he called, "What is it?"

"'Tis Lachlan Mengue," Lagan replied. "The man has set up camp outside the gates and is demanding to speak with you."

"My father," Aimil muttered in shock and tried to wriggle free of Parlan's hold but only succeeded in arousing them both.

"Tell him I must break my fast first. If he has not yet done so, he is welcome to join me," Parlan bellowed to Lagan.

"Leave go," hissed Aimil as she tried to ignore her desire to stay where she was.

"Lagan's gone," he growled, neatly rolling over so that she was pinned beneath him.

"I cannae carry on like this with my father so close at hand," she whispered, even as she was stirred by his gentle rhythm.

"I will muffle your cries." He grinned over her look of outrage then bent his head, his mouth moving eagerly to her breasts.

The tart rejoinder she intended to make never emerged. Her nails dug into his hips as she tried to urge him on. He soon gave her what she cried for, bringing their union to a swift yet highly satisfying conclusion.

She scowled at his broad back as he rose to dress. He had every right to look the contented male. She never put up much resistance. In fact, she enjoyed herself so much that she never felt any inclination to say no. What truly bothered her was the problem of facing her father without looking like she had done exactly what she had just finished doing. She was sure she radiated sexual satisfaction. Something that gave one such pleasure had to leave its mark. She may have chosen to be where she was, but she did not want her father guessing that.

"Out of the bed, wench. There is your father to face this fine morn."

"Nay, I cannae." She rolled over and buried her face in a pillow.

Yanking the covers off her, he resisted the temptation to show his appreciation of her lovely back, and gave her a sharp slap on her pretty backside. "Ye can and ye will. I wish to show him clearly that at least one of his offspring is hale and hearty."

Gathering the covers around her, she sat up and glared at him. "Ye dinnae understand."

"Aye, I do but ye are wrong, lassie. He willnae guess. He may wonder, but he will never ken for certain unless ye tell him."

His words still ran through her head after he had left, making it clear that she had better appear in the hall before too long. If she did not look guilty, she suspected her father would not be able to tell that she had lost her innocence, or, worse, had enjoyed losing it. After all, she mused, as she took one last look at herself in the mirror, there was no evident outward change in her appearance.

As she headed down to the hall, she shook her head. It was foolish to worry. There was no retrieving what had been lost. In truth, her father took so little notice of her that she doubted he would notice the change in her even if it was branded on her forehead.

When she heard her father's deep voice, she edged into the hall, standing by the door to look at him. A large man, he was nearly as tall as the Black Parlan, and broad of shoulder. There was white mixed with his thick blond hair but he was still youthful of figure and face despite his four and forty years. The signs that life had dealt a little harshly with him were on his face. His well-cut, handsome features were drawn with lines that nothing could erase, and a sadness lingered in his blue eyes.

She adored her father, and the ache of his rejection never left her. Not only fear of his discovering she had shared Parlan's bed had made her want to avoid him. She avoided him as a matter of course for it hurt too much when he ignored her. The pain was less if she stayed out of his way. Unfortunately, that was something she could not explain to Parlan.

Parlan watched her as she stared at her father. She reminded him of a starving child viewing a feast being devoured by others who offered not even the scraps. It was a situation that escaped his understanding. Too often a parent was burdened with an unloving child yet this man turned his back on one who adored him. Parlan grimaced over the twinge of jealousy that assailed him.

He watched Lachlan Mengue closely when Aimil approached the table, reluctantly obeying his signal to join them. When she came into Lachlan's view, there was an instant brightening in the man's blue eyes but it was quickly veiled. A man did not try to bury his affection for his child unless there was a good reason. Parlan was determined to discover that reason.

"Hello, Father," Aimil whispered as she sat down next to Parlan. "I am sorry for this trouble."

"So ye should be. I am told that Leith heals weel?" He seemed blind to the color that surged into her cheeks.

"Aye." She swallowed her hurt over his attitude. "He nears full health with admirable speed. He is well cared for."

After those few words, Lachlan proceeded to ignore her. She struggled to eat, to act as if it did not matter. A glimpse of a fleeting look of pity in Lagan's brown eyes told her that she was not fooling anybody, and her food was hard to swallow. A few minutes later, she could stand it no longer and rose to leave, wincing when everyone's attention turned to her. Parlan eased the moment some by nodding slightly and signaling Lagan to go with her. Without a glance at her father, she hurried out of the hall.

"Ye ask far too large a ransom," Lachlan said as soon as the last bite of food had been swallowed. "Ye dinnae hold the king, ye ken."

"I hold your heir and youngest daughter," Parlan reminded him, his voice soft but firm.

"I have other sons. Two. I wouldnae be left without an heir. Rory Fergueson can find himself another bride as weel."

Parlan ached to speak on that marriage but knew that the time was not right. He and Lachlan dickered over the price, Parlan staying icily calm and Lachlan fighting to keep his temper. Even though Parlan sympathized, he did not ease his stance. He had to drag the business out for as long as possible.

"At such a cost I can only buy one of my bairns back. I willnae have the coin for the other for months."

"Then ye best choose which one ye mean to leave in my

care." Parlan intended to erect another obstacle if the man chose to free Aimil.

"T'will be my firstborn, my heir. He must take precedence. I will need some time to gather the coin."

"'Tis as weel. The boy is best off where he is for a while longer."

"I dinnae like leaving my daughter in your hands. She is a fair wee lass."

"Your daughter will suffer no hurt at my hands or my men's. Do ye wish to see your son?"

As Parlan had hoped, Lachlan did not press the issue of Aimil. The man was in a precarious position. No matter what Lachlan suspected he could not make accusations. If he offended Parlan, he lost too much. Parlan could see that the situation sorely annoyed the man, annoyed him to the point of fury.

"Didnae ye have any gowns for the lass to wear?" Lachlan burst out as they left the hall.

"Nay. She was found in lad's clothes. Aye, we thought her a lad, your son Shane, until she was climbing down my walls and her cap was taken by the wind. We dressed her in the best we had. Feel welcome to send clothes for her of your own choosing."

"All she owns now is her trousseau," grumbled Lachlan. "I cannae send that. 'Tis held for her marriage."

When they entered Leith's chambers, Parlan was not surprised to find Aimil there. He had guessed that she would seek out one who loved her to ease the sting of her father's apparent indifference. The warmth with which Lachlan greeted his son was salt in Aimil's wound that even Parlan felt. He was sorely tempted to strike the older man. All that stayed his hand was the sure feeling that Lachlan did not feel as he acted, that some deep reason drove him to act as he did.

Aimil tried to lose herself in the shadows of the room.

Slowly, she edged toward the door. That her actions were not unseen was attested to by Lagan being only a step away no matter how many steps she took toward the door. So too did she sense Parlan watching her. Neither mattered to her. All she was interested in was getting away from her father's coldness.

"Ye will be coming home soon, son," remarked Lachlan, his gaze assuring him that the youth was regaining his health.

"The ransom is too high," Leith protested, wondering if Parlan's plan had failed or, worse, if he had been a fool to listen to Parlan and to trust him.

"Aye, but I have talked him down a bit." Lachlan moved to look out the window. "I am also paying only part of it."

"Which part?" Leith whispered, yet dreading the answer for he suspected it would hurt Aimil.

"Yours."

For a moment Aimil did not believe what she had heard. "Am I not to be ransomed?"

"Not now. The cost is too high." Lachlan kept his back to her.

"When?" she asked in a small voice, not afraid to stay with Parlan but deeply hurt by her father's actions.

"I dinnae ken."

Knowing she was going to cry, she bolted from the room. Blinded to the startled looks that came her way, she raced through the keep and headed for the stables. She collapsed on the hay near Elfking and wept.

Her father had ignored her for years, but this was worse. To leave her in the hands of her captors was a blatant indication of how little she mattered to him. He could not know how she was treated. Even if he did, he was not so blind that he did not see the threat to her chastity, to the honor of the Mengue name. It was plain to see that he cared nothing for her, not even that she carried his name.

"Ye are a hard bastard," Lagan growled before the door had even shut behind Aimil.

"Enough, Lagan. Follow the girl. Be sure she is all right." Parlan stared at Lachlan after Lagan had left. "He is right, for all that."

"I havenae the funds to ransom both of them. The heir is more important than the youngest daughter." Lachlan eyed the Black Parlan with little friendliness. "Ye wouldnae take my word that the money will come and let me take both away now."

"There is no doubt in my mind that your word is good, but I want the coin in my hand before I release either of them."

"Aye, so I thought. I will bring the money for the lad in a fortnight. I cannae say yet when I will buy back the girl." He paused at the door. "I trust her in your care. She must not come to harm."

"I have said that the girl willnae be hurt whilst she is in my care."

"Curse his eyes," Leith hissed after his father had left.

"All is not as it seems," Parlan said. "The man does care for the girl."

Leith stared at Parlan as if he had lost all his senses. "How can ye think that after what he has just done? The choice to be made was not the heir over the maid but the maid first for she is most at risk."

"I saw his face when she first came into his sight. Something else holds him back from revealing his love. There is a reason for the way he acts. I intend to find out what it is. I ken it isnae a simple one. Rest, Leith," he said as he too left the room.

Parlan found Lagan and Malcolm lurking outside the stables. "Where has the lass fled to?"

"She is inside with that beast of hers," replied Malcolm. "We werenae sure whether to leave her be."

"I will see to her. See if our guests have any needs. They intend to leave come the dawn. Also, see that I am left alone with her."

* * *

Aimil knew he was there even before he sat down and took her into his arms. It did not seem strange to seek comfort in the arms of the Black Parlan who was her captor and should have been her enemy. He was a strong solid haven, one that she needed.

Parlan lay back on the straw with her held firmly in his arms. It puzzled him that he should feel such a strong need to ease her pain. Even stranger was that her pain seemed to be his. He was sharing it whether he wanted to or not.

"Ye are fair close to drowning me, lassie," he grumbled, hoping that he could tease her out of her grief.

"I dinnae cry verra much." She sniffed loudly as she fought to control her tears. "'Tis a weak thing to do."

"Och, weel, ye have a good reason for them. There isnae any faulting ye for this. Are ye afraid to stay here?" he murmured.

"Nay. Not now, that is. That could change if ye start roaring and stomping about," she said, and smiled against his chest.

Rolling so that she was beneath him, he feigned a glare when he saw her impish, if trembling, grin. She was the first woman to indulge in teasing with him, and it delighted him. He was not sure why but many assumed his nature to be as dark as his visage.

"Roaring and stomping, is it, wench?" he growled, and nuzzled her neck in a way that made her giggle.

Suddenly, she grew serious. "Ye would think that he would fret over the honor of his name. He doesnae seem to worry about what ye might do, which ye have already done, but he doesnae ken that ye have. But he doesnae seem to care that ye might do what ye have already done."

It was difficult but Parlan managed to keep from laughing. "Am I to understand that great jumble of words?" He did laugh when she frowned, rethought her words and then laughed. "He does care, lass. He had me give my word that I wouldnae hurt ye."

For a moment she looked at him frowning slightly as she thought over his words then she shook her head. "That was verra sneaky of ye, Parlan MacGuin."

"Aye, it was." He grinned when she laughed at his air of immense satisfaction. "Have I hurt you, little one?"

"Nay, not in body though I ought to be sick with shame for becoming your whore."

"Ye are not my whore. Ye are my lover. Dinnae frown, 'tis-nac the same at all." He unlaced her jerkin then began on her shirt.

"I dinnae understand how ye can think that but it matters not. If I must lay beneath a man, I would far rather it was ye than Rory."

He pushed open her shirt, finding the tips of her full, high breasts already taut and calling for his touch. "Ye will never lie beneath Rory Fergueson."

"I must. I am to be his wife. Oh," she sighed with pleasure when his mouth latched hungrily onto a breast. "We cannae do this here."

"Ye are always saying we cannae and I must show ye that we can." He lifted his head to stare at her. "Ye willnae be wed to Rory."

"How can ye stop it?"

"I can and I will. Now, hush, and let me show ye what else we can do though ye will say we cannae."

Chapter Seven

"I cannae believe it," gasped Giorsal, her gaze fixed with disbelieving accusation upon her father. "How could ye do it?"

"The ransom is high, lass. I cannae pay it all. Not now. 'Tis necessary to make a choice. My heir takes precedence."

"But to leave her in that man's hands for so long. Ye ken what could happen, if not by force then by seduction."

"Aye, I ken," Lachlan growled, the long day and trying decisions taking their toll on his patience. "I ken that he will bed her. She is a comely wee lass that many a man has ached for. Mayhaps he will even fill her belly with his bairn. I wonder how fair Rory will like that? There is naught I can do about it, Giorsal. Naught. So leave it be, for sweet Mary's sake. Leave me be. 'Tis done and cannae be changed. Aye," he muttered, his gaze looking distant and unfocused, "it cannae be changed but mayhaps what was to be will be."

Giorsal left confused and angry. Her father's claim that his heir was more important in this instance did not ring true. She sought out her husband to complain even though she knew he could do little to change matters. Just as she found him, her attention was suddenly diverted for the Black Parlan himself strode into their camp.

She could only stare in awe at the tall, dark man flanked by four men who would have been equally impressive on their own but were overshadowed by the Black Parlan. Magnificent was a word that sprang quickly to mind. So did large and overpowering and Giorsal felt afraid for her little sister. Such a man could crush the small Aimil with no effort at all. When his obsidian gaze settled upon her, she shivered but not only with fear for Aimil. Even she, so newly awakened to the delights of the marriage bed, felt the man's sensual draw. Giorsal doubted that, even if her strong-willed, young sister wanted to, Aimil could resist that pull for very long.

Recognizing Iain MacVern from one meeting at court a few years ago, Parlan greeted him with reserved cordiality. He noticed the look that came from the well-rounded blond woman's eyes but did not respond with his usual calculated flirtation. With Aimil in his bed, he found that he had little interest in other women. He was doubly glad for that when she was introduced as Aimil's sister Giorsal.

Lachlan appeared even as the pleasantries were ending and Parlan was about to ask for him. "What do ye want now?"

"I have come to invite ye and your family to dine at my table this eve," Parlan replied quite pleasantly, unperturbed by Lachlan's crossness.

"Will Aimil be there?" asked Giorsal, thinking that the man's voice was as dangerous to a woman as his looks.

"Aye. Aimil isnae confined verra tightly. She has free access to all within the walls of Dubhglenn. Do ye join me or nae?"

"Aye, we will be there." Lachlan then bid Parlan a curt farewell and strode back to his tent.

"The man is oppressed by many worries as ye ken weel," Iain offered in apology for Lachlan's rudeness. "He must be excused."

"For this, aye." Thinking of Aimil's pain, Parlan's expression hardened slightly. "For other things, nay, not until I ken the reasons."

"What did he mean by that?" Giorsal asked after Parlan had left.

"I cannae be sure. I think he refers to Lachlan's coldness to his daughter. Aimil may have revealed how it pains her."

"He should think more on how he could hurt Aimil. She is such a wee lass and he is . . . he is . . ."

"Such a great lad?" Iain finished with a grin, which widened when Giorsal blushed.

"'Tisnae a matter of jest. 'Tisnae just his size I speak of either, but him. I mean, he is so much a man. Even I kenned it."

"I noticed," Iain drawled. "Dinnae scowl. I ken what ye mean but I think ye are as fooled as many by Aimil's delicacy of looks. Aye, she is a wee lass and comely enough even for the likes of the Black Parlan. She is also made of steel. She can be as tough as Lachlan. The Black Parlan willnae find her bending to his will easily. Nay, nor petting his vanity as so many women have done."

Although Parlan enjoyed the way Aimil did not quail before him, at the moment he was viewing her with a distinct lack of amusement. He saw her refusal to dine with her father as pigheadedness. Parlan did not feel that avoiding unpleasantness was the way to solve anything. Despite that, he did admire the way she met his growing annoyance squarely. Too few did.

"Ye will come down, lassie, even if I must drag ye down by the hair and tie ye to a seat."

Aimil glared at him, unaware that she was doing anything

unusual by not cowering before his displeasure. "Ye wouldnae dare."

"Try me," he purred.

She did not think that would be a very good idea but refused to go down without a fight. "I cannae sit before my family and act as if naught has changed. That is a lie too large for me to play out. Someone will say something that will set me to blushing and they will ken weel what has happened."

"Ye worry over naught." He started out of the door. "Ye best be at that table when the serving begins."

She stuck her tongue out as the door shut behind him. It was an ill-timed gesture for he quickly reopened the door to look at her again, catching her childish response to his command. Hastily, she drew her face into the lines of sweet innocence, refusing to be embarrassed.

"Ye have ten minutes," he growled, but lost his stern expression as soon as he was out of her sight. "Little witch," he murmured, laughing as he started down to the hall where his guests were gathering.

Cross but resigned to her fate, Aimil finished getting ready. She still wore boy's clothing but she had an extensive wardrobe of them. The red and black outfit she wore suited her very well she decided, smiling faintly over her touch of vanity. Brushing her hair and securing it with a red ribbon, she squared her slim shoulders and started toward the hall. She was determined not to reveal anything to anyone. If her family discovered that she was no longer a maid, it would not be from her. Taking a deep breath in a last effort to strengthen her resolve, she marched into the hall.

"She looks quite elegant," murmured Iain as Aimil approached them.

Even though she agreed, Giorsal made a scolding noise. "'Tis not right for her to dress so. There is no need to make a scandal of her." She moved to greet Aimil, giving her a hug and a kiss. "How fare ye, sister? Is all weel? Ye have come to no harm?"

Pleased with her calm, Aimil smiled. "I am verra fine. I am always watched but not too obtrusively. I have stayed at far worse places."

"The Black Parlan hasnae hurt ye?"

Meeting her sister's worried gaze directly and proud of her control, Aimil replied, "Nay, not at all." She then scowled at Parlan, who met her look with a smile. "Although he is an arrogant, impossible man who thinks far too much of himself," she said loudly enough for him to hear.

Giorsal's eyes widened at this daring and widened even more when Parlan stepped closer, kissed Aimil's hand, and murmured, "Such a tart tongue for such a honied mouth. The sweetness of your face is indeed deceptive, love. Come and sit down."

Ignoring that the seating might have been arranged, Giorsal hastily took the seat next to Aimil, who was placed upon Parlan's left and across from their father. There was an air between Aimil and Parlan that disturbed Giorsal. She hoped that by being near them during the meal she could dispel that uneasiness, perhaps see that she had misread matters.

Shrugging, Iain sat at her side across from Lagan who was placed between Lachlan at Parlan's right and James Broth. "I think ye have mucked about with the seating arrangements, dearling," he remarked calmly.

"I dinnae care. I intend to watch this pair verra closely. They dinnae act as captor and captive should. She talks to him much as she does to Leith, Calum, or Shane," Giorsal whispered in awe.

Iain chuckled. "Aye, Aimil always did have spirit. Always faced a man square no matter how he blustered and roared."

"I think they are lovers already."

"T'wouldnae surprise me, love. The Black Parlan is weel

kenned to have a healthy appetite for a comely lass, and Aimil is that."

"How can ye be so calm? Ye are her kin through marriage, and I ken weel that ye have always been fond of her."

"Love, look about you. This is a male household. Aimil is a captive, clear and simple. Mayhaps she already occupies Parlan's bed, and, if 'tis so, I sorely feel for her loss of honor, but better that than to be left unprotected. If she is his lover, none will touch her. She could weel be safer in the Black Parlan's bed than out of it. She shows no signs of being ill-treated, and that is what matters most. Leave it be for now. Her honor, if lost, can be avenged later."

"Aye," she agreed but hating it. "Does my father nae see it, or is he holding his tongue because he thinks as ye do?"

For a moment Iain studied Lachlan. "I cannae say. 'Tis odd but I get the feeling he plays a deep game. Dinnac ask me what though."

As the meal dragged on, Giorsal began to share her husband's feeling. Even Lachlan could not ignore the attitude that existed between Parlan and Aimil yet he seemed to be doing just that. Parlan made no attempt to act coolly toward Aimil, to disguise the heat of his glances, and Aimil simply did not know how to.

"And why is Aimil's husband-to-be not amongst your numbers?" Parlan asked as soon as the covers on the dishes of food were removed and more drink set out.

"He was verra busy," Lachlan replied offhandedly. "As ye ken weel, there was some recent damage to be repaired."

"What happens if ye dinnae ransom Aimil by summer's end, the time set for the wedding?"

"Then t'will be set for another time. The man will wait for his bride. He has waited years, a few added months willnae matter."

* * *

As Rory Fergueson watched his man carry out a young maid who had suffered badly at his hands, Rory thought of Aimil. The way matters were being handled it could be months before she was freed. Thinking of Aimil with the Black Parlan had made his lust even crueler than usual. The young maid would be a long time recovering from her spell in his bed.

"Ye near killed that lass," groused Geordie, a burly, sour-faced man who was the closest thing Rory had to a friend.

"What care I?" snarled Rory as he flung himself into a chair and snatched at the drink Geordie held out to him.

"Ye will care weel enough if word of how ye treat the lasses reaches Lachlan Mengue's sharp ears."

"Do ye think he is deaf to what is already whispered about me?"

"Nay, but 'tis rumors yet. If ye keep cluttering up Scotland with dead and battered lasses, he may soon have fact."

"Aye, ye are right. I must tread warily. I lost my head. I must not supply the rumormongers with fact. All I could think on was Aimil in the Black Parlan's hands."

Geordie hid a grimace. He had no doubts about how Parlan MacGuin would use such a fair captive. The bride Rory had waited so long for would not come to her marriage bed a virgin. Even though Rory only meant to use the girl for vengeance, he had wanted her to be untouched.

When Rory suddenly demanded another wench, Geordie protested. Rory had spent all his time drinking and wenching since Aimil's capture. Geordie knew that Rory hung upon the very brink of madness and began to fear that thoughts of the Black Parlan enjoying Aimil would push him over the edge. Only when Rory promised that Geordie could stay to insure that Rory was in control of himself did Geordie fetch a girl. He came back with a lusty wench, buxom and full of avarice, who was quite capable of handling two men.

Rory lay sprawled on the bed, drinking and watching Geordie

gain his pleasure even as the whore pleasured Rory. Though his body reacted in all the appropriate ways, his mind was on Aimil. He would have her, share her with Geordie, and humiliate her. He would break her in spirit, mind, and body before he took her life. Thinking on how he would abuse her increased his current pleasure. Aimil Mengue would crawl and beg for an end to her life before he was through with her.

Aimil suddenly shivered. She tried to tell herself that it was cold in the hall, but she knew she lied. The chill had come from deep within her. All she could think, despite her efforts to shake the image, to resist superstitious fancy, was that some dark, foreboding shadow had briefly covered her soul, that some evil had reached out to touch her with its icy fingers. It took all her willpower not to cry out her fear.

"Are ye ailing, Aimil?" Giorsal murmured. "Ye have gone verra white."

"A goose walked over my grave, 'tis all."

"Dinnae say such things." Giorsal shivered. "Come, let us go for a walk outside, away from all this talk of old battles. 'Tis most like the tales of blood and death that have turned your humor dark."

Lagan trailed them as they went out into the bailey. He did not stay on their heels for there were many eyes to watch them besides his own. Giorsal was glad that she and Aimil would be able to talk freely as they strolled arm in arm.

"How fares Jennet? She must be far along with child now."

"Aye, Aimil. The bairn should make his or her appearance at any time. She fares weel though 'tis tired she is." She looked closely at Aimil. "I will ask it again. How fare ye, Aimil? Ye cannae tell me the man's nae touched ye. I have eyes."

"Do ye think Papa has seen it?" Aimil asked in sudden panic, not even attempting to deny anything to Giorsal.

"Nay, it seems not. I think I wouldnae have seen aught save that, weel"—Giorsal blushed—"Iain and I are much closer now."

"Oh? How did this come about?"

"Ye mean ye kenned there was a fault in my marriage?"

"Nay, not a fault, just nae a loving or a close bond."

"And that is nae a fault?" Giorsal drawled. "I didnae want to wed Iain. I thought him a plain, rough man. I held that feeling since the day we were wed. Now, I didnae deny him or betray him, but I gave him little. T'was after ye were taken. I took a close look at the man ye were going to have to wed and I opened my eyes and looked at my own man. 'Tis a fool I have been. For all my coolness, the man has never strayed, and for all he is rough, he has never been cruel. Weel, I said a few sweet words and put myself in his bed where I belonged instead of making the man come asking and 'tis love I have found now."

"T'was there all the time, Giorsal."

"I ken that now, but my eyes were long turned inward, seeing only my disappointment and that the choice wasnae my own."

Aimil hugged her sister. "I am verra happy for you. Aye, and for Iain. He is a good man. A lot of his roughness is only shyness."

"Aye, I see that now. 'Tis to my shame that my wee sister saw it before I did. Now, tell me of ye and the Black Parlan."

"Are ye going to insist upon it?" Aimil discovered that she really did wish to discuss Parlan with her sister.

"Aye, verra firmly. He hasnae hurt ye, has he?"

"Nay, he hasnae. He wanted Elfking and gave me a choice. If I came to his bed, he wouldnae take my horse. I have shocked you."

"A bit." She shook her head. "To do thus for a horse. 'Tis

not a thing I can understand, but I am little surprised that ye did it."

"Weel, I think the rogue tricked me, but it matters little. I will shock ye more by saying I enjoy being in his bed, that I didnae put myself there for Elfking alone. I tried but I could-nae feel guilty or ashamed. All I could think on was that I am to be wed to Rory Fergueson."

"So why not take pleasure while ye can, where ye can."

"Aye. I grasped it with both hands. Of course, Parlan says I willnae wed Rory though he doesnae say why he is so against it or how he could stop the marriage."

"If he does, ye must tell me. 'Tis sore eager I would be to hear it. He is such a big man," she added, frowning.

"Oh, aye, he is," Aimil agreed meaningfully, then giggled when Giorsal gasped and blushed.

"Wretched, wretched girl. I didnae mean that." She frowned. "I cannae fault ye for what ye do but tread warily, Aimil. The Black Parlan looks to be a man to make a lass lose her head. Ye cannae have any more than ye have right now and to long for more will bring ye naught but pain."

"I ken that weel, Giorsal. Dinnae fash yourself." Aimil wished she could put more confidence into her words.

"Ye said ye think he tricked you. How so?"

"He has been wooing Elfking, winning the stallion's favor. He doesnae even try to hide it, the rogue."

"But he said he wouldnae take your horse. I cannae believe he is a man who would break his word. That is one thing he has never been accused of."

"He isnae. He said he wouldnae steal my horse. He never promised not to try and coax Elfking into his stables. Sneaky man. I suspicioned what was afoot fairly quickly, but I kenned it for sure this morn. I feared Papa didnae care about my honor when he said my ransom must wait, but Parlan said the man had cared. He said Papa had made him swear not to hurt me which Parlan did so Papa's suspicions were lulled. A sneaky man is Parlan MacGuin and fair proud of it he is too."

Wiping tears of laughter from her eyes, Giorsal said, "He doesnae sound the bloodthirsty beast he is rumored to be."

"Och, he isnae." She told Giorsal the tale of her near escape. "He does have a sore hot temper though 'tis mostly roar and stomp."

For the remainder of their walk, Giorsal prompted Aimil to talk of Parlan. Aimil left her sister, thinking that she had eased all of Giorsal's qualms but, in truth, she had increased them. When leaving for their camp, Giorsal found herself alone with Parlan for a brief moment. She glared up at the large man clearly startling him with her ferocity.

"Dinnae ye hurt Aimil," she hissed.

"As I told your father—" he began.

"I ken what ye told Papa, ye sneaky man. Dinnae play that game with me. I am little concerned with her virtue or her body. 'Tis her heart that I speak of, and if ye leave a bruise there, 'tis fair sorry ye will be, Parlan MacGuin."

"What was that all about?" Lagan asked as the Mengue party left.

"The lady's motherly instincts have been roused by the plight of her wee sister. She has warned me nae to hurt Aimil."

"Och, ye would never hurt a woman."

"She wasnae meaning in body but in heart. She fears I may win the lass's love with my charming manner."

Lagan chuckled as they headed back into the hall, but then he grew serious. "And what if ye did?"

"Did what?" Parlan asked absently, his mind on bed and Aimil's lithe body.

"Win her love. Ye have had many a lass's heart tossed at your feet. Aimil Mengue might do the same."

"Nay, Aimil will never toss her heart at my feet for me to

kick about as I please. She would place it in my hands and expect fair treatment."

"And what if she does just that?"

"If I marry her, t'would be a verra good thing, would it not? A marriage goes smoother if the lass gives her heart with her vows."

"Still thinking on marrying her, are ye?"

"Aye. As I have said, I am of an age to wed, to get on with the business of a family, and she still looks the best choice." He grinned at Lagan as he started toward his chambers. "That would do to soothe Giorsal MacVern's ruffled feathers."

Giorsal was still fretting over the state of Aimil's heart when Iain entered their tent and prepared for bed. She briefly contemplated the possibility that Parlan meant to wed Aimil but decided that that was the last thing that would happen. Parlan MacQuin did not look like a man who would choose marriage over the freedom of a bachelor.

As Iain undressed, he watched his wife pace the tent until his curiosity became too strong to contain. "What has ye in such a state, loving?"

"They are lovers, Iain."

"Aye, ye had already guessed that. I thought ye had decided not to let it wear upon your mind."

"Aye, I had but that was before I had discovered how she feels about the man. If she doesnae love him now, she is verra close to it."

"Ah." Iain removed his shirt to wash up.

"Ah? Ah? Is that all ye have to say about it?" she exclaimed even as she fetched him a cloth to dry off with.

"Sweeting, ye cannae do anything about it. There is no directing the heart. It will go where it pleases."

Giorsal lay down, burying her face in her arms. "She will be sore hurt and she will still have to wed Rory Fergueson."

"Aye." He lay down on his side and rubbed his hand soothingly over her back. "Still, the lass will have kenned the sweetness of love and carry some verra fine memories. I think if ye set the problem before her she wouldnae alter the direction she has chosen to walk. She is a practical lass and she willnae let herself forget she is tied to Rory. 'Tis possible she is trying for all she can get before she must wed."

"'Tis what she said." Giorsal turned her head to look at her husband. "She also said that Parlan says she willnae wed Rory Fergueson."

"Oh? Does he say how he hopes to stop the wedding or why?"

"Nay, he willnae give her reasons for wanting it stopped nor say how he will stop it. He just says she willnae wed Rory, that he willnae let it happen."

"Weel, for all the trouble he has caused us, I respect the man. I think that if anyone can stop it, he can and I think too that if he willnae say why, he has a verra good reason for that as weel."

Parlan felt the reason he kept silent about his dislike for Rory Fergueson was justified later that night when Aimil woke from a nightmare, trembling with fear. Reluctantly she told him what had caused her terror, and Fergueson had played a major role in her dreams. To tell her all he knew of the man her father had promised her to would only add to the fear she already had of Fergueson. If she knew the truth about Fergueson, she would probably never sleep peacefully again.

"I wonder if it started with that chill I felt?" she mused as she clung to Parlan's solid warmth.

"What chill, little one?" He fought down a rising passion for he knew it was a time to soothe not to seduce.

"At the meal's end, I felt a chill seep through me, go straight to the bone. Such strange thoughts entered my head."

Holding her tighter he asked, "What thoughts, Aimil? Come, talking of them could ease your fears."

"I kept thinking that some foreboding shadow had briefly blocked my sun. So too did I think that something evil had reached out to touch me with its cruel, icy fingers." She shivered and pressed her face against his chest. "I cannae shake the feeling that something bad awaits me, that out there is something or someone who seeks to hurt me. I saw my mother in my dreams."

"Aye?" He tried to shake the feeling that she was suffering some premonition and had not merely had a bad dream.

Aimil nodded. "She was all bloody, Parlan, and she was pointing at Rory. I cannae think why I should dream such a thing."

"There isnae any explaining a night's terror, lass. Ye are safe here. Think only on that. I willnae let harm come to ye and I mean to keep ye out of Rory Fergueson's hands. Remember that. He willnae get ye. I mean to stop that marriage."

She peeked up at his face. "Why are ye so set against this marriage? I am naught to ye." She found that it hurt to admit to it.

"Weel"—he kissed her forehead—"I wouldnae say naught. Dinnae ask me to explain, lass. Just trust me. Trust me."

Snuggling up to him, she sighed sleepily and closed her eyes. "I do that, Parlan. Aye, I trust ye."

He smiled down at her and wondered why her words should make him burst with pride and happiness.

Chapter Eight

"Ye cannae mean it?"

"Aye, I do. I am staying here."

Lachlan scowled at his eldest son's determined face. This was something he had not foreseen. Leith had always been close to Aimil. It was evident that that feeling still existed, was now driving him to remain in the enemy's camp. Lachlan could see no reason for it, however.

"The lass will come to no harm. I have the Black Parlan's word on it."

"So have I but stay I will. She may have need of someone who isnae a MacGuin at some time, and I mean to be here if she does."

"'Tis good of ye to think on her needs, but the Black Parlan may have an objection or twa."

"He wouldnae send a sick lad out into nature's cruelty." Leith lay back in his bed, looking suitably frail.

"Ye do that verra weel," Lachlan drawled, pulling a grin from Leith, "but I wouldnae hope on it fooling the Black Parlan."

* * *

The Mengue heir's performance did not fool Parlan for a moment, but he let Leith think that it had. He understood Leith's motives and had no objections to the youth's staying. That Leith might still wish to kill him did not trouble him at all. Leith would not stoop to murder but demand a fair fight, face to face with witnesses. Parlan even suspected that Leith was not so hot upon avenging his sister's honor as he had been, although he made no attempt to guess the youth's reasons for his change of heart.

Leith was relieved that he could stay. He suspected that to hurt Parlan MacGuin would be to hurt Aimil. If nothing else, she was far too happy for a woman who was supposedly being used and plunged into shame, even for one who had chosen such a course. So too did he sense something in her looks and actions when Parlan was around. He dared not guess at Parlan's feelings except that the man did not treat Aimil as if she were naught but a convenience for the relief of his lusts. The whole matter needed a great deal more observation which was one of the main reasons he wished to stay at Dubhglenn.

"Weel, ye got your way. Ye are staying. I dinnae believe ye really fooled him though," Lachlan said after Parlan had left them alone again.

"It matters not. As ye say, I got what I wanted."

"If ye are thinking to slip free with Aimil and save me coin, I wouldnae hope too strongly for success."

"I wouldnae. He keeps a subtle but close and effective guard."

"Ye arenae thinking on killing him, are ye?"

"Why should I be?" Leith briefly feared that his father had guessed what was between Aimil and Parlan which could lead to more trouble than any of them needed at the moment.

"I dinnae ken. Ye may have a reason or twa or think ye do. Dinnae try it."

"'Tis not without some skill I am."

"Och, I ken it. Ye are a fine swordsmon. Unless luck rides with ye, however, I dinnae think ye would win in a fight with him."

"Thank ye for your confidence in me."

"Dinnae get stiff on me. 'Tis a wise man who kens his opponent's skill, whether it be equal, more or less."

"And ye feel that Parlan's skill is greater than mine."

"Aye, 'tis. I think, or so rumor tells me, 'tis the best in the kingdom. He also has nine years on ye, more strength and more practice. Ye think hard on the worth of your grievance before ye take up sword against him. It should be nothing less than something ye are willing to die for."

"Fair enough." Leith finally recognized that his father was not belittling his skill merely recognizing the greatness of Parlan's.

"Weel, I think ye are mad to stay, but Aimil will most like be pleased."

When Aimil heard that Leith was remaining at Dubhglenn, she was ecstatic. As soon as her father had left, she raced to Leith's chambers. He laughed and scolded as she smothered him with grateful kisses. She felt there would come a time when she had need of someone who was not a MacGuin. Even though he was voluntarily staying in the midst of the enemy camp, so to speak, she had no fears for his safety.

"Ye are still a prisoner in a way."

"I ken it. They will watch me closely and never arm me for I may, nay, must try to take ye from here when the chance for it comes."

"Aye. Parlan will think on what he would do if he were ye and act accordingly."

"Have ye never wondered why we have seen naught of the man ye are to wed?"

"Nay, not much. Did our father give any reason for Rory's absence?"

"Nary a one. They have told him of each move, but he fails

to journey here. It would seem your betrothed is loath to face the Black Parlan."

"Parlan hates him. He would like to see him dead. I am certain of it. Rory mayhaps kens that and he has always been fond of his own skin."

"Ye feel sure Parlan hates Rory, verra sure?"

"Aye. 'Tis there to hear in the way he speaks the man's name. I dinnae ken why though. Do ye?"

Leith shook his head. He hated to lie to Aimil but he did not want to reveal to her just how black Rory was. At the moment she only objected to the marriage intended for her. He did not wish to give her reason to be terrified. So too he still hoped to stop the wedding, and there was no sense in frightening her over a thing that was not to be. Neither could he tell her that to stop the marriage was one reason he lingered at Dubhglenn. Meeting her smile, he silently hoped Parlan could prevent it as he had stated he would.

Leith's ransom had been easier for Lachlan to get than Parlan had hoped. He now feared that the time he needed to end the marriage plans for Aimil was not to be given to him. Rory continued to be careful and a careful man took time to catch. Frowning over that problem, Parlan let Lagan into his chambers.

"Artair's back."

"Where?"

"In his chambers readying himself to dine."

"Hoping to slip past me and avoid my anger."

"Still angry with him?"

"Nay. S'truth, I am more weary of him and his ways."

"That may be for the best. A man with his ways cannae be shouted or coaxed out of them. He can only pull himself out."

"So ye think I should leave him in his mire and let him crawl out on his own, if and when he has a mind to."

"Aye, though it sounds hard, he being your brother and only near kin. Howbeit, ye cannae tell how such a one thinks. If ye coddle them, they may think ye are weak and flaunt their vices. If ye scold and bellow, they may grow to resent ye, even hate ye. Seems to me that the safest course to follow is to leave him be. He kens weel that ye disapprove. Leave it at that. Then he can only blame himself for what he is."

"Or blame me for not caring . . ."

Lagan grimaced. "Aye, there is that chance. Sometimes such ones blame others no matter what."

"Weel, 'tis a thought. I havenae got anywhere with him with any other ploy. He wallows in drink and tempts the pox at every turn." Parlan suddenly smiled slightly. "Will he be surprised to see how the wee lad he caught has changed! Now why do ye frown?"

"Artair caught the pair."

"Aye," Parlan murmured, then asked carefully, "what matter that?"

"They were his booty. He may feel he has a right to the enjoying of it."

"Then he will be quickly enlightened. In fact, let us search him out and see that he is told how matters stand here before he even meets Aimil."

Aimil made her way to the hall from the lower floor's privies, glad that Lagan was not about. He was a nice man, but it got tiresome to have him forever at her heels, infringing upon her privacy. As she neared the end of a dim hallway, she came face to face with the man who had captured her and Leith. Suddenly she found herself wishing that Lagan was dogging her heels. Artair made her very nervous.

"Weel, where have ye come from, me pretty? Now, dinnae run away. Why the lad's clothes?"

To her dismay, Artair was not as drunk as she had first thought. He nimbly caught her when she tried to dash past him. With equal agility, he pinned her against the wall in such a way that she feared it would be impossible to use the means of defense Leith had taught her. She wondered if Artair had met with the trick before.

She noted that he was much akin to Parlan in looks, being tall, darkly handsome and well-built but that was his only resemblance. Aimil was amazed at how clearly his features were stamped with his weaknesses. Even as she thought on that, she frantically sought a way out of her dilemma, finally grabbing at the one thing she felt sure would work to stop him.

"I belong to Parlan," she cried as she tried to twist away from the hand that traced her curves.

"Oh ho, do ye now? Where did he find you?" His eyes suddenly widened then narrowed as he looked her over. "By God's santy," he breathed. "Ye are the Mengue lad. I must have been weel in my cups that day not to see it." He took off her bonnet and roughly mussed her neatly tied back hair. "Weel, ye are my prize then. Parlan will see that."

"Nay," she gasped, trying to avoid the kiss he tried to press upon her mouth. "I am Parlan's." She could not believe that assertion was not enough to stop Artair.

He ignored her, his gaze fixed upon the thick waves of bright hair he had freed. "B'Gad, that is lovely. Be still, wench," he growled. "I brought ye here so ye are my prize. I willnae trouble or waste time asking Parlan about it."

A soft cry escaped her when he roughly grabbed her by the throat, his fingers gripping her jaw so that she could not turn her head. Her stomach rolled when he slammed his mouth against hers. Try as she would, she could not get her leg between his to cripple him briefly with a blow to the groin and then, hopefully, escape. Instead, she sank her teeth through his lip, filling her mouth with the warm, salty taste of his blood and nearly making herself ill.

He jerked away from her with a bellow of pain, blood streaming down his chin. Even as she broke free of his loosened grip, he grasped her by the arm and backhanded her across the face, hard enough to send her sprawling. She tried to gather her dazed wits to scramble out of his reach, but he caught her up by the front of her pourpoint and slapped her again. Aimil thought, a little wildly, that Artair clearly did not adhere to his brother's ways. Groggily, she lay watching as he reached for her a third time, spitting curses her ringing ears could not understand, only to hear a roar of fury and see Artair flung aside like a bundle of rags.

She was not really surprised to see Parlan. She had recognized the roar. What did surprise her was the extent of the fury her pain-blurred gaze could see in him. That Artair could see it too was revealed by the stark terror on his face.

The only clear thought in her head was to stop something terrible from occurring between the brothers. If Parlan only meant to beat Artair, she would not care. However, Parlan's blind rage did not make her confident that he would know when to stop. With a cry, she forced her aching body to move and flung herself at him, clasping her arms tightly around his neck and wrapping her legs around his waist. She hoped that, if only because of the time it would take him to dislodge her, a little sanity would soon prevail.

Parlan instinctively put his arms around her, but it was awhile before he could unclench his fists. His breath came in harsh gasps, and he briefly squeezed his eyes shut as he fought the red haze that had encircled his mind the instant he had seen Artair strike Aimil. The first clear thought he had was that he had come very close to trying to kill his own brother. In a cold, flat voice he ordered twenty lashes for Artair.

"Parlan," gasped Artair as Lagan grabbed him by the arms and pinned them behind him.

"Now. Quickly. Before I change my mind and banish him instead."

Peering at Artair, Aimil noticed that he was ghost-white as Lagan dragged him away. "Parlan . . ."

"Say nothing."

She pressed her lips together and buried her face in his neck as he strode to their chambers. She stayed silent as cold cloths were applied to her face in hopes of keeping the swelling down and lessening the bruises. Even through the meal they ate in their chambers, she said not a word.

Plenty of words swirled in her mind, but she bit them back. Not only was she unsure of what to say but Parlan looked too cold and too remote to make her brave speech. She feared she had failed miserably in stopping something terrible from happening between the brothers. Along with that fear was the deeper one that he would blame her for the trouble. It would be unfair for she had done nothing to tempt Artair, but that did not mean that Parlan might not think she had or that Artair might not claim she had.

When Lagan arrived, she retreated to the bed to sit huddled amongst the pillows. He sent her a brief look of sympathy, and her fears eased a little. If he did not blame her for what had occurred, then perhaps Parlan would not either.

"Is it done?"

"Aye, Parlan. Old Meg's tending him."

Parlan nodded curtly then moved to stare out the window into the moonlit bailey. Lagan gave Aimil an encouraging smile. He thought that she looked very much like a frightened child awaiting punishment. With one last glance at Parlan's stiff back, he slipped from the room and headed straight for Artair's chambers.

"Where's Parlan? Doesnae he mean to come and gloat?" Artair rasped when Lagan strode in.

Glancing at the marks upon Artair's back, Lagan realized that Malcolm had not held back at all. "Ye are a fool, Artair."

"What did I do save to try for a wee bit of pleasure?"

"It looked to me as if ye were planning to beat her senseless. Is that your idea of pleasure?"

"Nay." Artair's gaze flinched away from Lagan's for he was ashamed of his lack of control. "She bit clean through my lip."

"Your mouth shouldnae have been anywhere near hers. She is Parlan's."

"Isnae she one of the Mengue pair? I caught them. By rights she should be my prize."

"She is in Parlan's bed. That gives him rights. She isnae there as a prize either. They made a bargain."

"Weel, what matter that? He had no right to have this done to me."

Artair sounded very much like a sulky, little boy, and Lagan shook his head in a gesture of disgust. "Ye got the same he would have given anyone else who tried to do what you did."

"I am not just anyone else. I am his brother, his heir."

"Ye are a drunkard and a foolish boy. Nay, dinnae whine and act wounded or insulted. Ye should be at his side, not me."

"He doesnae want me there," Artair groused with a whine to his voice, despite Lagan's warning.

"Nay, he doesnae for he cannae trust ye to do as ye should or even to be sober enough to try. There isnae room for tolerance or second chances when lives are at stake as they so often are. He cannae risk it."

"He never gave me a chance."

"By the time ye were old enough to be of any use, ye had tasted the pleasures of flesh and drink and were wallowing in them."

"What has that to do with all this?"

"More than I dare to hope ye would understand. If ye werenae so sodden with drink or trying to avoid the scold ye ken ye deserve by running to the fleshpots, ye would ken what goes on here. Ye would ken that that lass is Lachlan Mengue's youngest daughter not some lowborn wench or whore. Ye would ken what it would mean if she was hurt. Ye would ken she was to be wed to Rory Fergueson and ye would ken how hard your brother is trying to stop that and why." Lagan strode to the door, fed up with trying to talk sense into his young cousin. "Ye would ken as weel that, with each passing day, the wee lass ye were slapping about and planning to rape draws nearer to becoming the mistress of Dubhglenn." He slammed the door after him, leaving Artair stunned and full of questions.

Lagan found Malcolm in the hall. Getting a tankard of ale, he sat down opposite the man. He recalled that he had had nothing to eat yet but, at that moment, was not particularly hungry.

"Ye didnae hold back on the lash."

"Nay, I didnae. He deserved every stroke and nae just for trying to hurt that poor, wee lass." Malcolm shook his head. "I must say, I am surprised that the laird ordered it done. I have often thought him too soft on Artair."

"Ye wouldnae if ye had been there. He was close to killing the boy."

"What stayed his hand?"

"'Tis hard to beat a man to death when there is a woman clinging to ye. It was enough to make him pause and clear his head some. I ken that is why Aimil did it. Then he offered Artair the lashes or banishment."

"Jesu," whispered Malcolm. "'Tis not just a lusting he suffers then."

"Nay. God alone kens what it is he does feel. Especially right now. He hasnae said a word. The poor lass sits there wondering if she will be blamed but doesnae speak. 'Tis a strange mood gripping him. I left him staring out the window."

"Heartsore most like. Artair be a brother to bring it on. I fear Parlan blames himself for what his brother is."

Searching his memory, Parlan could not find where he had gone wrong with Artair. Neither could he see where he would have or could have acted differently. Yet, somehow, he had to have stepped wrong, he was sure of it. He did not want to believe that it was bad blood. Then there would be no change in Artair, perhaps only a worsening of his character. It would mean Artair was doomed and that saddened him.

He was sure that he could no longer effect a change in his brother. The events of the night had surely marked an end to what meager relationship had existed between them. It would be a long time before he could view his brother without anger. He knew it was not only because Artair had abused a woman, something Parlan loathed, but that he had done it to Aimil.

Slowly, he turned to look at Aimil then smiled faintly. She sat huddled against the pillows fighting sleep. He realized that his actions since the incident might have left her worried, even afraid, for she could easily think that he blamed her. Moving to the bed, he gently laid her down and began to remove her boots.

"Time ye were abed, sweeting." He frowned when she just stared at him.

Aimil tried to read his cool expression. He did not appear to be angry with her even though anger still lurked in him. Unable to discern his mood or his thoughts, she decided to keep quiet as he had ordered her to do earlier. She wanted nothing she said or did to exacerbate the situation, to increase his anger at his brother or at herself.

"Ye can talk now," he murmured in an attempt to tease her, an attempt weakened by his troubled mood.

"I am so verra sorry," she whispered, immobilized by weariness and nerves as he finished undressing her.

Prompting her beneath the covers, he sat at her side and traced the bruises forming on her neck and face with his finger. "Ye have naught to be sorry for, little one." He stood up and undressed. "Ye had naught to do with it. I saw that. I but wish that I had arrived sooner."

"He was angry, Parlan. I bit clean through his lip. It must have hurt some."

"I suspicion it did." Parlan smiled slightly as he slid into bed beside her. "One knock would have answered for that, dearling. He was set to beat ye senseless and weel ye ken it. There is no excuse for that. So too does he ken my ruling on such matters."

"Shouldnae ye go and see him now?" she ventured as he tugged her into his arms and she cuddled up to him.

"Nay. There is still an anger in me, a violence. I might weel do what ye stopped me from doing earlier—kill him."

"Nay. Ye wouldnae. He is your brother."

"Nay? Then why did ye stop me?"

"Weel, I feared ye might come close to it so angry ye were. I didnae want ye to do something ye would sore regret later when the anger had left ye and your senses had returned."

"I dinnae think the anger will ever leave. Inside I rage at Artair and at myself."

"Why at yourself?"

"I have failed with him."

Tightening her hold on him, she shook her head. Parlan smiled faintly and ran his hands through her hair. It was comforting in a way to have someone believe in his abilities. With this problem, however, there was a spot that no comforting could reach. It touched him too deeply.

"Some people are just weak, Parlan. There is naught anyone can do. A person cannae always ken what prods them to act as they do. They can only help themselves for only they ken the why of it, if there is any why at all."

"So Lagan claims."

"Weel, he is right."

As he was about to give his opinion on that, a rap came at the door. He smiled when Aimil dove beneath the covers as he bade the visitor to enter. It did not surprise him to see Leith enter.

"Should ye be out of bed, sickly as ye are and all?" he drawled.

Ignoring that, Leith asked, "How is Aimil?"

"I am fine," she replied, her voice muffled by the covers she hid beneath.

"Shy before me?"

Easing out from the covers, she murmured, "Weel, ye have never seen me abed with a man before." Seeing his fleeting grin fade as he saw her bruised face, she hurriedly said, "It looks worse than it feels."

"I wish ye didnae bruise so badly, so easily. 'Tis hard to ken how sorely ye are hurt."

"He slapped her but twice before I stopped him."

Nodding for he had heard of the punishment Parlan had meted out to his brother, Leith said, "Weel, I but wished to see how ye fared, Aimil. I best be back to my bed." He looked appropriately languid as he withdrew, saying, "I still tire so verra easily."

When his chuckling ceased, Parlan sighed. "That is what I wish Artair to be."

"He is still young. He could change."

"The way he goes on he could die before he alters. Ah weel, 'tis out of my hands. Go to sleep, loving. Ye need to rest your bruises and I hold too much anger to try loving ye. I darenst try. I might hurt ye myself."

She cuddled close to him and let sleep grasp hold of her.

There was nothing she could do. If the trouble was to be sorted out at all, it had to be done between Artair and Parlan.

For long hours into the night, Parlan stroked her hair and stared at the ceiling. Failure and disappointment left a bitter taste in his mouth. He also found them hard things to accept. Resting his cheek against Aimil's hair, he fleetingly acknowledged that his reaction to what Artair had done had been extreme because of who Artair had done it to. He decided to wait a few days before attempting to see Artair, and with that decision made, he finally went to sleep.

Chapter Nine

"What do ye think, Leith?"

Leith studied his sister carefully. The outfit she wore was odd but not unattractive. Someone's tartan supplied a slim skirt. She still wore a man's shirt but that was partially hidden by a sleeveless jerkin, laced tightly in place to make a fitted bodice. Her figure was almost as nicely displayed as it had been in the boy's attire, more so in fact for her full breasts were delineated.

"'Tis oddly pretty if that makes sense. T'will do verra weel until Father finally sends some gowns for ye. Ready then?"

"What about my hair? I couldnae find anyone to help me put it up." She frowned into the mirror, noting with relief that her bruises were completely gone at last.

"I can do it. Dinnae look so doubtful. I used to play with our mother's, aye and our sisters' even, and am a fair hand at it."

When he was done, she was suitably impressed. It was nothing elaborate but was well done and neat. The sedate style managed to make her outfit a bit more respectful than the ragamuffin air she had carried. She smiled her gratitude at Leith as he took her by the arm and they started on their way to the hall.

As they reached the bottom of the stairs, there was sudden confusion. As Parlan spotted Aimil, smiled and headed toward her, a woman strode into the hall. She was lovely and carried herself with the dignity of visiting royalty.

All complimentary thoughts concerning the woman fled Aimil's mind an instant later. The woman became the lowest of creatures when she stopped Parlan's move toward the stairs by hurling herself into his arms and giving him a lengthy kiss that went far beyond a polite greeting. Aimil had to summon all of her will power not to fly at the woman and tear her from Parlan.

It was then that she had a revelation that caused her to pale. She was in love with the Black Parlan. That was the only explanation for the white-hot fury she felt toward a woman she did not know and for the agony it caused Aimil to watch Parlan embrace the woman. Suddenly she wanted to run away. It would be hell to face everyone so soon after such a discovery. She feared it would be read in her every look and gesture, and it was the last thing she wished Parlan to know.

Parlan gently, but firmly, released himself from Catarine's grip. She was the last person he wanted to see. He had hoped that she would not honor her threat to visit. It was a bit late to wish he had not succumbed to her wiles that once, but wish it he did—wholeheartedly—especially when he glanced up to see Aimil looking at him in cold-eyed dislike.

Holding out a hand to Aimil and keeping his gaze fixed upon her, he said, "I would like ye to meet a guest of mine, Catarine."

Reluctantly and prodded by Leith, Aimil went to Parlan, letting him take her by the hand. The woman obviously felt she had a right to arrive unannounced at Parlan's doorstep and to kiss him so intimately. Aimil was not anxious to get mixed up with this. She wished she was back at Leith's side.

Leith watched his sister closely. He did not like flinging her into the reach of the she-wolf clinging to Parlan, especially when he had a good idea of the revelation that had sapped all the color from Aimil's face. Nevertheless, it would not be wise for Aimil to back away. Not only should she fight for the man she loved but to allow herself to be nudged aside too easily would cause her to lose her protected place within the MacGuin keep. She was, after all, only a captive, one whose ransom was slow in coming.

"Catarine, I would like ye to meet Aimil Mengue and her brother Leith. Catarine Dunmore, Lagan's cousin."

"Surely I am more than that," she purred, although her gaze was fixed coldly upon Aimil.

"Are you?" Parlan hooked Aimil's arm through his. "We prepare to dine. Do ye wish to clean up first, Catarine?"

Aimil could see that the subtle snub enraged the woman. When Catarine allowed herself to be escorted to a room, Aimil was sure it was more to cool down and replan her strategy than to wash. As she let Parlan lead her to a seat next to him, Aimil also felt sure that it would prove to be a long, tense evening. She wished fervently that she could find a good excuse to leave.

Despite his best efforts, Parlan got little more than monosyllabic replies from Aimil. He wanted to talk to her about Catarine even if he was unsure of what to say, but the time and the place were all wrong. On the other hand, it delighted him to have this indication that her feelings might consist of far more than passion. He realized suddenly how much he wanted that to be true.

When Catarine entered, she was less than pleased to find that Malcolm sat on one side of Parlan and Aimil on the other. While she washed, she had questioned the maid assigned to her and found out exactly what Aimil Mengue's position was. She had every intention of altering it. The girl could remain a captive treated as a guest, but she would do it out of Parlan's bed.

The moment Parlan was distracted, deep in discussion with Malcolm, Catarine looked at Aimil. "Is it truly a lack of ransom that keeps ye here, Mistress Mengue?" She felt Leith tense at her side, saw Lagan do likewise, and felt she had aimed her dart well.

"My father has paid Leith's ransom. It was verra large. He needs time to raise mine," Aimil replied coolly.

"Of course. And does your father ken how weel ye are enjoying your stay?"

"He kens that I have come to no harm." Aimil struggled to keep a firm hold upon her rising temper. "The MacGuin hospitality is unsurpassed."

"Definitely unsurpassed." Catarine cast an easily read glance at Parlan. "Tell me, are the men so large in the Lowlands?"

The way in which Catarine said the word "large" told all at the table that she referred to one particular part of Parlan's anatomy. Parlan was not deaf to the conversation around him although he had let it be thought he was. Yet again he resented the referral to him as a stud. He waited for Aimil's reply.

Aimil sensed that Catarine meant far more than she said but was not sure what. One possibility came to mind, but it was beyond her comprehension that anyone would speak so over a meal and within the hearing of the very one referred to. It also seemed to her that women would be drawn to Parlan as a total man. His attraction was as much in his character as in his appearance.

"Weel, aye, he is verra tall," she replied in all innocence, frowning when there was a sudden epidemic of coughing.

Catarine stared at Aimil as if she were dimwitted. "Ye are either verra innocent or verra dim of mind. I wasnae referring to his height."

Frowning even more, Aimil said, "He isnae too broad. I have seen men wider of shoulder."

This time the laughter was not suppressed, and Aimil realized that she had missed something. After a moment's thought, she hit upon the only other thing the woman could possibly mean, the very insinuation she had discarded earlier. She gaped and blushed deep red.

"Ye cannae mean that. We are having our meal. 'Tisnae any time to speak of such things."

Catarine thought that highlighting Aimil's naivete would lessen the girl's attraction for Parlan who was a man of the world, one who would undoubtedly find such sweet innocence tedious. "I think 'tis a most suitable time," she purred, running her tongue over her lips with a lewd meaning that all the men gathered understood.

That Catarine's meaning was lost on Aimil was clear to Parlan. His lovemaking had been varied but not as much as it could have been. He had curbed several inclinations out of respect for her innocence.

This time Aimil quickly guessed that the woman was playing games with her words. Using the pouring of a fresh tankard of wine as a cover, she leaned closer to Lagan. Before she made any response, she wished to be sure she understood.

"My mind has come up with a verra unsuitable meaning for her words. Can I be right?"

"I dinnae doubt it. Catarine is a whore, Aimil, and doesnae seem to ken any manners. Pay her no heed." He glared at his cousin. "Ye grow crude, cousin."

"And ye suddenly grow righteous, cousin. 'Tis late in life for the child to be so protected."

Aimil grit her teeth and said softly to Lagan, "If she calls me a child again, I willnae be responsible for my actions."

Parlan gave up the pretense of talking to Malcolm. He knew all too well how sensitive Aimil was about her stature, about being seen as a child. Seeing the glint in her eyes, he waited with ill-disguised glee for Catarine to prod that sore once again. It was the one thing certain to make Aimil lose control.

"I ken that Parlan favors youth but he is near to robbing from the cradle with a wee lass such as ye are."

"That does it," Aimil hissed as she surged to her feet.

She picked up the nearest plate of a sweet made of fruit and cream. Before Catarine guessed what was happening, Aimil tossed it at the woman. Her aim was true, and Catarine's screech was well-smothered by the sugary concoction. The curses the woman spat were covered by the laughter that roared around the table.

It was not so amusing to Aimil, even when Lagan dragged his sputtering cousin off to be cleaned up. She had been insulted by being called a child and she had reacted to that insult as a child would have. Embarrassed by her behavior, she hastily sat down.

"Och, lassie, that showed a verra fine aim," Malcolm said with a big grin.

"Tsk, tsk," clucked Parlan, his eyes alight with laughter. "Ye must learn to control that temper."

Her embarrassment fled and she glared at Parlan. "Ye arenae able to say a great deal about that."

"Ye havenae seen me hurling the food about."

Deciding it was not safe to banter words with him, Aimil lapsed into silence. She had to give Catarine credit for not giving up easily when the woman returned attired in an even fancier gown. Aimil decided that she would not let her temper slip again no matter how the woman pressed her. She would bear all with the dignity of an adult and a lady.

It was not an easy vow to keep. Catarine seemed bent on becoming permanently attached to Parlan even though she had to reach across Malcolm to touch him. When Malcolm excused himself to take his turn at guard, Catarine quickly took his place at the table. After that, it was all Aimil could do to stop herself from lopping off the woman's hands with the carving knife. The constant touching quickly became subtle then not-so subtle groping. Aimil's jealousy ate away at her, exasperating the temper she sought to control. When Catarine's hand disappeared beneath the table, Aimil's patience gave out even though she restrained the urge to inflict extreme violence on the woman.

"Lost something, have ye?" she asked brightly, and peered under the table to see Catarine moving her hand between Parlan's legs. "Allow me to help you," she purred, and reached for Parlan.

As he was extracting Catarine's hand, Parlan felt Aimil's slim fingers give him a painful pinch. Leaping back with a shouted curse, he nearly unseated himself. Rubbing his abused parts, he glared at her.

"What the Devil did ye do that for?" he growled over the badly-stifled laughter of the men at the table.

"Oh, I do beg your pardon," Aimil said primly. "I thought it was her finger."

Catarine gasped in horror, her wide eyes fixed upon Parlan awaiting a show of his legendary temper. Parlan sat torn between amusement and anger. The realization that Aimil was showing definite signs of jealousy pushed amusement to the fore by increasing his good humor in one sudden leap. He burst out laughing, freeing his men's laughter. Catarine sat silent, detesting Aimil Mengue.

A few moments later Aimil decided she had had enough of both wine and company. She quietly excused herself and headed to bed. When she hesitated outside of Parlan's chambers and glanced toward Leith's, she knew Lagan was near. She hesitantly took one step toward Leith's chambers, and Lagan matched it.

"I wouldnae if I were ye," he drawled.

"Weel, I have no wish to find myself with three in a bed."

"Ye willnae. He has no desire for the woman."

"He did once. I may not catch all that is said but I am nae blind," she groused.

"Aye, once. He is sore regretting that now. Catarine is after a husband, and she isnae one for a man to wed. She is a whore." He opened the door to Parlan's chambers and gently pushed her inside. "Get in where ye belong, lassie. I am of no mind to hunt ye down later and 'tis certain that I will be made to if ye arenae in that bed."

She did not argue any further. Stripping off her clothes, she washed and then brushed out her hair. Crawling into the huge bed she had shared with Parlan for all these weeks, she wished she felt as sure as Lagan that she belonged there. All she could do was wait for Parlan and pray that he arrived alone.

Parlan found it difficult to extract himself from Catarine with any amount of politeness. Even when he excused himself to retire for the night, she stayed close to him. Exasperated, he stopped before his chamber door to scowl at her.

"Ye were shown your chambers, Catarine. Mine are quite full at the moment."

"How can ye speak to me so after all we shared?" Catarine cried, and flung her arms around his neck.

Aimil tensed for his answer, her body leaning toward the door.

"We shared an hour or two of hearty lust, something ye have shared with many. There wasnae any more than that."

"Mayhaps, but ye cannae even share that with that child ye cater to now."

Giving into an indisputably childish impulse, Aimil stuck her tongue out at the door.

"Let me show ye, remind ye, of how a woman can please ye."

From the sounds coming through the door, Aimil decided it was best that she could not see what was going on. She held a pillow over her head so that she could not hear it either. Stoutly, she told herself that it was not worth crying about.

"I have tried to be polite but ye can push a man too far, Catarine," Parlan growled as he pushed her away. "There is naught ye can do to turn me away from what waits in my bed. Find yourself some other man to feast upon."

After she had flounced away, Parlan entered his chambers. "Why have ye got that over your head?"

"So I cannae hear ye and Catarine Dunmore slobbering over each other," Aimil snapped.

He grinned as he strode to the bed and peeked under the pillow. "I will wash off the slobber, shall I?"

"Humph. Can ye wash away the paw marks as weel?" She knew she sounded like a jealous shrew but could not help it.

A soft laugh escaped him as he stripped off his clothes, the signs of her jealousy putting him into a very good humor. "'Tis the pinch mark that has me sore worried."

"Being such a large man, I am surprised ye felt it." She cursed softly when he only laughed again.

After a moment of sulking, she tossed aside the pillow and sat up. He stood naked before the wash bowl, drying himself after his brief scrubbing. He really was a remarkably fine-looking man, and Aimil could understand what drove Catarine. What troubled her, what truly worried her, was what had driven Parlan to Catarine.

"Parlan?" she asked tentatively as he extinguished the candles save the one by their bed.

"Aye, lass?" He slid beneath the covers and pulled her into his arms.

Glad for the dim light for she was already blushing fiercely, Aimil asked, "When she said that dinner was a verra suitable time for talking about, weel, that, did she mean what I think she meant? Did she really, weel, with her mouth?"

"Aye. 'Tis why I went to her."

"Oh. Ye like to be kissed there?"

"Aye. I kenned that she had a talent for that and sought her out or, rather, gave into her ploys. It wasnae verra good. Catarine leaves a man feeling as if he has been eaten alive, as if he is naught but a staff. She served me weel the once, but I wasnae eager for more."

Suddenly Catarine was no longer a threat. He talked of her as if she were no more than some utensil. Aimil knew that he always seemed to want more from her. That was one thing she was certain of. What Catarine had shared with Parlan had been brief and unimportant.

"Do ye really like to be kissed there?" she whispered as his mouth touched her throat.

His hands cupped her breasts, and he felt his usual delight in her nipples that needed no prompting to harden. "Aye. What man wouldnae?"

"Then why havenae ye asked it of me? Is it a whore's trick?"

"Nay," he replied slowly, "though 'tis often only a whore a man can get to do it for him."

"I will do it if ye wish." She felt a shudder tear through him.

"Why?" he rasped, his body already taut from aching with anticipation.

"Weel, ye do so much to me, 'tis only fair to do something to ye. Ye give me pleasure. I should give ye some."

It was not exactly what he had hoped to hear her say but he was in no state to argue. "Then kiss me, little one."

When he turned onto his back, she hesitantly began her journey. Instinct told her that a slow approach would please him more. She edged her way down his body, letting her lips and tongue caress the taut flesh of his chest and abdomen. His body trembled slightly and that sign of his pleasure increased her own. So too did his husky words of approval and verbal exclamations of his delight.

Upon reaching her final goal, the cry that broke from his lips at her mere touch emboldened her. She tried many ways to increase his very evident pleasure, using her lips, tongue, and hands. When his hips rose up slightly off the bed, instinct told her how to answer his silent plea, and his reactions told her that her instinct had again been right.

"Oh, my God," he groaned when the moist heat of her mouth surrounded him. "Aye, loving, that be the way of it. 'Tis so good. Sweet heaven, but 'tis good. 'Tis a sweet, sweet pleasure ye give me, little one."

He writhed beneath her ministrations until he knew his control was slipping. Grasping her beneath her arms, he pulled her up his body and set her upon him. After but an instant she was in control, his prompting no longer needed. The fact that she had been readied for him, that pleasuring him had evidently aroused her own passions, sent his desire to new heights.

The shivers of her release had barely begun when he held her snug against him, his hips bucking with the force of his own. When she nestled against him with delight, he pulled her tightly into his arms. For a long time they clung to each other, trembling from the force of their passions and weak from the sating of them.

Although he finally eased the embrace slightly, he still held her against him. He had never experienced such pleasure. Even the way she could stir him past control was a sort of pleasure. With each night he spent in her arms, even when they had not made love, he became more certain that he would be a fool to let her go.

His happiness with her, both in and out of bed, had not

faded. The boredom he had so often experienced was not there, not even envisionable. Even when she infuriated him, he never thought of being rid of her. The same things that could set his temper off were part of what fascinated him. It was undoubtedly time to stop playing games with ransom demands.

Not being of a romantic turn of mind, love did not enter his calculations although he sorely wanted her to love him. He liked her and he trusted her. There was no doubt in his mind that he could be happy with her and proud of her. He wanted her to bear his children and to be at his side to see them grow and have their own families. That, in his mind, settled the matter.

"Aimil," he asked softly even as he wondered what prompted him to, "what is it that ye like about me?"

"Assuming that I did like ye?" she teased.

"Aye, assuming that. What is it about my looks that ye like the most?" Although he silently scolded himself for his foolishness he tensed for her reply.

"Weel . . ." She frowned in thought as she lifted her head to look at him and tried to think of an answer that would not expose her feelings for him. "Your eyes. I like your eyes. I never kenned that black could have so many shades, one for each emotion when ye arenae making them flat and unreadable. Aye, ye have verra fine eyes."

"Why, thank ye, Aimil." He felt genuinely flattered. "Anything else?"

"Pleading for compliments, are ye? Weel, your hands. I like your hands." She lifted one of his hands to her mouth and kissed his palm. "They are strong, calloused from work and holding a sword, but can be verra gentle. They could crush me but they never even try to." She noted that, although he looked pleased, he also looked quizzical. "What did ye think I would say?"

"My staff." He grimaced slightly when she looked at him as if his wits had gone begging.

"Why should I choose that? Every mon has one of those. As Leith says, ''Tis not the steed but the ride that matters.' A large horse doesnae always give a good ride. When ye asked me to say what I liked, I looked for what made ye different from other men." She suddenly grinned at him. "Mayhaps if ye had smiled more, the women would have looked at your face and not your breeches."

Laughing quietly, he rolled them over so that she was beneath him. "Are ye saying that ye care not about my endowments?"

"Nay. I daresay this wouldnae be quite so much fun without it." She laughed with him as her hand slid down to discover him ready and eager again. "Though, I must say, your appetite threatens to wear it down to a stub."

"I will take my chances, witch," he growled against her breast. "I think I must raise your ransom."

"If it goes any higher my father willnae be able to pay it and take me home," she pointed out in an increasingly husky voice.

"Exactly." He slowly drew the hard tip of her breast into his mouth, delighting in her soft cry of pleasure.

When their passion had spent itself, he lay with his head against her breast. Aimil smoothed her hand over his broad back and her cheek rested against his thick hair. It was hard for her to recall a time when she had not shared his bed. She did not even try to.

Now she began to mull over her recent revelation. It brought her both happiness and sorrow. There was an indisputable pleasure in loving someone. She did not need experience to know that was why their lovemaking was so good. That she loved the man who held her and possessed her and helped her reach those high levels of desire and satisfaction. Aimil was confident of that. It also kept her wanting more.

She wondered if love was what had kept guilt and shame away. It had been there from the start, had simply been too new to recognize. She had so easily accepted his absurd bargain because the seed of love had already been planted and had begun to grow within her.

The sadness came from the fact that he did not share her love. He desired her, and she did not think it was vanity that made her so certain that he liked her as a person. It was not love, however. He gave passion and friendship while she gave him her soul. It was not the fairest of trades and not one to make any woman happy. Unrequited love was all the poets claimed it was she decided.

Her real pain stemmed from the knowledge that it must end. Once her ransom was paid, she would be sent home, home to marry Rory Fergueson. She could not believe that Parlan could stop that as he claimed he could. Holding Parlan a little tighter and smiling when he murmured her name in his sleep, she stoutly vowed not to think of what was to be but only of what she was enjoying at the moment. She would wallow in her love without a thought to the morrow.

Chapter Ten

"Elfking is a verra smart horse."

"He is a verra contrary beast." Parlan, leaning against the fence watching Aimil feed the stallion an apple, fought a smile as he added provocatively, "Just like his mistress."

"Because he willnae let ye woo him doesnae mean he is contrary."

"Ah, ye have caught me." He made no attempt to deny her accusation, saw no reason to do so.

"Aye, though I was slow to do so. I said, 'Nay, Parlan wouldnae be so sly.' Then ye said that sly thing to my father."

"Sly am I?"

"Aye, a bit. Verra clever with words ye are. What ye say is the truth and lulls a person, stopping their questions, but 'tis not the whole truth."

"Here I am thinking I am being charming and gallant, wooing ye and your beast and ye call me sly."

She sent him a mock glare, struggling not to laugh at his crestfallen expression. "Give it up. Dinnae ye have aught to do this day aside from pestering me?"

"Aye. Actually, I do. I must leave for the Dunmore keep soon."

"Ye are taking Catarine home?" She tried hard to appear casually interested.

"Nay. She claims she needs time to ready herself before she travels to the court at Stirling."

He could not hide his smile at the annoyed expression Aimil could not disguise. It pleased him to see the hint of jealousy and possessiveness in her. He knew there was more to it than that, however. Catarine was annoying. If she was any but a Dunmore and his sense of hospitality any less, she would have been tossed out on her ear a long time ago. Instead, she lingered, accosting him at every turn and filling Aimil's ears with poison, making far too much out of one evening of lust. It was fortunate that Aimil did not let jealousy turn her shrewish. He hoped it would not take Catarine much longer to realize that she could not gain her obvious objective of replacing Aimil in his bed and to see that he had absolutely no interest in her. Aimil might have the strength to tolerate the woman, but he was rapidly losing all patience.

"I will be gone twa days, mayhaps three."

Pleased by the expression of distress that fleetingly passed over Aimil's face, he idly wondered if she knew how easily read she was. She could shutter her expression, but more often than not, not fast enough. He had quickly learned to keep his gaze trained upon her face when he said anything, for in that first brief instant was the chance to glimpse her real reaction to whatever he had said.

"I see." She told herself that she was glad he would be gone for a while and did not believe a word of it.

Quietly drawing nearer to her, he mused, "Aye, there will be talking, dealing, drinking . . ."

"Wenching," she muttered.

"Nay," he said softly, and kissed her ear, meeting her start of surprise and resultant scowl with a smile. "None for me. I must give the poor, wee fellow a rest. Ye are so greedy." He sighed. "I fear t'will be worn out before its time."

"I am greedy?" she squawked, turning to look at him in outrage.

Moving so that she was caught between him and Elfking, who now tolerated Parlan completely, even if the horse still did not let Parlan ride him, he drawled, "Weel, mayhaps I am nae so temperate meself. Of course, ye being such a comely lass . . ."

"What are ye after?"

"Now, lass, just because I try to speak sweet words to ye and to cuddle some . . ."

"It isnae that exactly, but there is an air of wheedling about ye."

He grinned, not the least bit disturbed by her suspicions, but then said quietly, "I have a fierce desire to ride Elfking to the Dunmores. I am thinking I would look verra fine and impressive arriving on such a mount."

"Ye look verra fine and impressive riding on Raven."

"Aye, but they are used to the sight."

She rolled her eyes in disgust over his lack of modesty, but he grinned. Even while indulging in that nonsense, she was thinking hard. He would look impressive upon Elfking, his darkness a perfect foil for Elfking's pure white form. It would be a sight the Dunmores would not soon forget. Unfortunately, despite her efforts not to be suspicious, she could not believe that his only motive.

"Is that your only reason?"

"Ye wound me with your mistrust."

"I doubt that. Ye have been working verra hard to woo Elfking away from me. Dinnae try to deny it. This may be but another ploy."

"Nay, 'tis not that."

"Ye really wish to be grand-looking before the Dunmores?"

"Aye. It never hurts to have your allies see ye as a wee bit bigger than life."

He watched her frown in thought as she stroked Elfking's neck. A twinge of guilt assailed him for, although he had not lied, he had not been completely truthful, just as she had accused him. Advancing his cause to win the horse was ever there but did not prompt his request. He would be gone, out of her bed. Without the bonds of passion holding her, she could well try to slip away. There was a far less chance of her attempting escape if she would have to do it without her precious horse. Inwardly, he grimaced recognizing that increasingly, he found himself jealous of the animal's place in her affections.

Aimil stroked her mount and tried to order her thoughts. No matter what Parlan's reason for wanting to ride Elfking, once he was on the mount's back, she suspected it would be hard to remove him. She was sure he knew that once Elfking was made to accept him as a rider there could be no going back. The horse could not be made to understand that something was only temporary. To let Parlan ride Elfking could well be the first and irrevocable step to giving him the horse.

She realized suddenly that that no longer troubled her. Elfking was important but no longer all important. What would make Parlan happy was dear to her. As she turned to look at Parlan, she wondered a little nervously if he would read all that was behind her gesture. He would know as well as she did that once she bade Elfking to let him ride, she was, in most respects, giving him her horse, her most prized possession. It was a gesture that could mean a lot or could be rash. Although she did not want him to think her foolish, she decided that, under the circumstances, it would be better than having him guess the state of her heart.

"Aye, ye can ride Elfking to the Dunmores."

Parlan struggled not to embrace her heartily so exultant did her gesture make him feel. She might be unaware of what lay behind her act. Too exuberant a reaction could be seen as a triumphant display for getting nearer to possessing the horse not her heart. That was not an impression he wished to give her so he simply smiled.

"How do we go about this then?"

"We must ride together first."

Tossing her up on the horse's back, he said, "Let us be off then."

"Ye are verra eager," she drawled as he carefully mounted behind her.

"What man wouldnae be over the chance to ride such a magnificent beast and"—he nuzzled her neck making her giggle—"with such a bonnie lass to wrap his arms about."

"Humph. Ye are verra sweet of tongue when ye get your way." As they rode out of the gate, she cast him a sly glance. "I may be luring ye to a lonely spot where I plan to stick a dirk between your ribs and then be off."

"Malcolm wouldnae stand for it."

Looking in the direction he indicated, she saw Malcolm and Lagan trailing a discreet distance behind. "They truly dinnae think I would ever do such a thing, do they?" She was a little offended at that sign of mistrust.

"Nay, but there are some about who would sore like to."

"Husbands most like."

"Ye do see me as a rogue."

"Are ye not then?"

"Nae as great a one as ye think, I am certain. Are we on an old woman's ride then, little one?"

"Ah, ye want some speed, do ye? Then ye shall have it."

He laughed as she spurred Elfking into a gallop. As he rode with her, he was acutely aware of her skill, of how at one she was with her mount. He doubted that there were many other women who could ride as well as she. It was something he deeply admired.

So too did he deeply admire the horse they rode. His guilt

over his ploys to gain her stallion would have been greater except that he grew more certain each day that Aimil would remain at Dubhglenn. It would be a sharing of her horse that he acquired, not full possession. He grew as eager to make Aimil a permanent part of Dubhglenn as he had been to make Elfking a permanent part of his stables.

The ride was short for she did not want to tire Elfking. It was a relatively long ride to the Dunmores. So too was she certain that Parlan would wish to experience Elfking's full potential while he held the reins. She reined in at a small clearing.

"Here is as good a place as any for your maiden ride."

"Are ye sure he willnae toss me to the ground?" he asked as she slowly dismounted.

"Nay. This is how I got him to allow Leith upon his back. To get him to toss Leith, I must order him to do it. 'Tis a way to discourage strangers. If ye had mounted alone, ye would have found yourself sprawled in the dirt but because I have let ye on with me then left ye on, Elfking willnae object to ye. Weel, go on then. Ride away."

Hearing the reluctance in her voice, he smiled. He bent down, grasped her chin, and pressed a brief kiss to her slightly pouting mouth. Then, because he could no longer wait to take his first ride, he spurred Elfking on, leaving Aimil behind.

Aimil stood watching them disappear and sighed. He did look magnificent upon Elfking. They were two strong yet graceful male animals. She simply wished she did not feel as if she was always giving but never gaining. Forcing away such depressing thoughts, she smiled at Lagan and Malcolm as they rode up to her. She wished that they did not look so sympathetic. It made her fear that her feelings were all too easily read.

"We willnae have to go and find where your beast has tossed him, will we?"

"Nay, Malcolm." She smiled a little. "Ye may have to search him out to remind him that he has work to do though."

Parlan had to remind himself sharply of the plans he had made. Reluctantly he reined in, sitting and gazing around at his lands briefly before returning. He also savored the feeling of sitting astride one of the finest pieces of horseflesh he had ever seen.

"She isnae slow of wit, Elfking. She kens what she has done. I just wonder if she kens the why of it."

He continued to think about that as he returned to collect her. They rode back to Dubhglenn in relative silence. He then shooed her away so that he could see to Elfking's rubdown and order the preparations for his journey. It did not really surprise him to see Malcolm lingering for the man had never approved of his plans to gain the stallion.

"So ye finally got your arse on the back of her horse."

"Aye, Malcolm. I mean to ride him to the Dunmores."

"Ye will make a fine show."

"We will that."

"She has given ye a verra fine gift."

"She has. 'Tisnae a gift though but a sharing."

"Ye dinnae mean to keep the beast in your own stables?"

"Aye, I do, but I mean to keep his mistress in my own private stable as weel."

"So ye have decided that, have ye?"

"I think I would be a great fool to let this one slip away."

"Weel, I wouldnae be saying so," Malcolm drawled, slowly grinning.

"Mayhaps not, but ye have been thinking on it. Nay, the thought entered my head that first night and hasnae faded, only grown to a conviction. She will make a fine lady of Dubhglenn. I will see to that when I return from the Dunmores."

"Are ye taking that bitch, Catarine, with ye?"

"She willnae go. She claims she prepares to return to Stirling."

Malcolm made a sound of scornful disbelief. "She means to fill the wee lass's head with poison about ye."

"Aye, I ken it. She has been trying that since she got here. I cannae toss her out though. 'Tis my hope that Aimil will trust in all I have said on the matter and recall where I have spent all my nights despite Catarine's lavish invitations. T'will come to a test of trust. Keep a close eye upon the Mengues."

"I cannae stop twa lasses from fighting."

Parlan laughed. "Nay, my thoughts veered without warning. Watch for an attempt to escape."

"Ye think she will try?"

"On her own, mayhaps not. I should like to think she would be reluctant to leave me. So too will I have her prized Elfking. Howbeit, her brother lingers here and may spur her on. He cannae ken what I have decided. The plan he and I first talked of has taken too long to work, and I cannae blame him if he thinks I play him for a fool."

"To take her home is to take her to Rory Fergueson. He willnae do that."

"He will no doubt have many a plan to keep her out of Rory's grasp. He may even think to bestir me in some way."

"So why dinnae ye tell him how ye be thinking?"

"I have no time to do it right now. Just keep a verra close eye on the pair. They are canny brats," he muttered as he strode out of the stables and headed for his chambers within the keep.

Aimil watched Parlan pack and tried to act as if she did not care that he was leaving. It was not an easy pose to hold. The only good she could find in it all was that Catarine was not going with him, but then she wished heartily that Catarine was going somewhere.

He had jested about having no need for wenching but that was no calming vow of fidelity. There was no reason for him to give her such a thing as she was but a captive for ransom who was convenient to serve his needs. Since she doubted that the Dunmore keep was without women, there would assuredly be ones there offering to warm his bed. There were no doubt past lovers there eagerly awaiting his return. She could not confidently envision him refusing a willing woman and that hurt.

"Ye are looking a wee bit dowie. Going to miss me?" Parlan sat down on the bed at her side.

"I am merely fretting over Elfking. He has never gone anywhere without me," she huffed.

"Weel . . ." He grinned as he pushed her down onto the bed, gently pinning her beneath him. "I think I best leave ye something to remember me by."

"Ye cannae mean to do that now?"

"Och, lassie, ye are always saying I cannae and I must show ye that I can."

Aimil forced a scowl to her face as she struggled back into her clothes. "Ye are a rogue, Parlan MacGuin."

"Aye, I ken it." He laughed and neatly avoided her attempt to hit him. "Thought ye ought to have a proper fareweel."

"That was far from proper. Who goes with ye?" she asked, not truly interested but feeling a need to keep talking.

They kept talking until he was mounted upon Elfking and ready to ride out. Parlan knew it would have soothed her troubled feelings a great deal if he would tell her how tempted he was to take her with him. He resisted the temptation, however, for that could easily cause more trouble than it solved. Until he openly declared otherwise, she was a prisoner for ransom and should stay at Dubhglenn.

Before all, he gently kissed her farewell. He knew she would not understand what the gesture meant to the ones watching. If there was a man at Dubhglenn who thought to take advantage of Parlan's absence, he would now think again. Parlan would not take such a public and fond farewell of a woman who was no more to him than a prisoner for ransom and a convenient vessel for his lusts.

As he rode away, he told himself not to take it to heart if she did try to escape. She had no reason to believe that she was anything more than a prisoner no matter how well-treated she was. Even Leith, despite the discussions they had had, could not be sure that Parlan could or even would do as he had said he would. Leith could well think it his duty to free Aimil and end any further extortion of his father. It would be easy enough for Leith to make Aimil see it as her duty too. Until she was offered more than a place in his bed, it was her duty for she certainly had no cause to feel that she owed him any fealty or even that he wished it of her.

Suddenly he wished he was back at Dubhglenn and not forced to visit the Dunmores. Parlan saw that he might well have erred in waiting so long to decide what he wished to do about Aimil. For once he might have been too cautious.

Although he tried not to recognize that there was a chance that she and Leith could escape, he knew they were clever enough to succeed in such a venture. He would then have to find a way to get her back. A direct approach would gain him nothing for she was still promised to Rory Fergueson until that man either revealed his true self to Lachlan Mengue or repudiated Aimil. Parlan realized that by being so wary, he could well have let himself in for a great deal of trouble.

He also recognized that he could do nothing about it until he returned from the Dunmores, a visit he was now intending to make as short as possible. It was suddenly imperative to settle things between himself and Aimil. As soon as he returned to Dubhglenn, he would arrange an appropriate setting and let her know that she was no longer simply his prisoner and lover.

An uncustomary sense of nervousness, almost uncertainty, came over him. Even the fact that he was riding to the Dunmores on Elfking did not banish the unease he felt. For the first time in his life, he was planning to offer a woman more than a brief time of pleasure. Parlan wryly admitted that it was not going to be as cut and dried a matter as he had thought. Now that he had made the decision, he easily forsaw complications. Telling himself not to look for trouble did not really stop him from doing it.

Riding into the Dunmore keep on Elfking caused all the excitement he could have wished for. He found himself wishing that Aimil was at his side, she on Elfking and he on Raven. There was no doubt in his mind that such a sight would have impressed the Dunmores as much if not more. He was determined to show them such a sight on his next visit, a visit to introduce the mistress of Dubhglenn.

Being careful not to cause offense, Parlan nonetheless made it clear that he was making only a short stop. He used the situation concerning the Mengues as a reason for the haste he displayed. Since the value of such captives was recognized without explanation, the excuse served him well.

Several women made it clear that they would be more than willing to fill his bed, but he paid them no heed even though a few of them had pleasured him well enough during past visits. He found himself feeling slightly ashamed of his past. It occurred to him that he had been greedy and without restraint. Wincing inwardly, he wondered if there would be any place he could take Aimil where there would not be some woman or women whom he had bedded. He had enjoyed far more than his share and was suddenly not very proud of it.

Lying in his bed, he found that he missed Aimil. For nearly four months they had shared a bed. He now found that he hated sleeping alone. Even when they had slept back to back, not wrapped in each other's arms, it had been comforting to know that he had only to turn over and to reach out to find

warmth, loving, or simply someone to talk to. He decided a
bed without Aimil was something he would do his best to
avoid in the future. He wondered, even hoped it was so, if
Aimil found an empty bed as distressing as he did.

Aimil sighed with heartfelt despair as she crawled into
Parlan's large bed. Even if she did not love him, it would have
been nearly impossible to find someone able to fill his place.
The absence of a man like Parlan made for a very empty bed.

She could not help but wonder if the bed he now slept in was
as empty as hers. It was hard to think he would refuse a bed
partner, and she had no doubt that there would be some available. His appetite was far too large to go hungry voluntarily.

Cursing, she turned onto her stomach and forced her eyes
shut. It might have been easier to fool herself into thinking
that he would be faithful if she did not have Catarine's poison
seared into her mind. What confidence she had gained was
consistently eroded by Catarine's venomous words despite all
her efforts to ignore the woman. A little spitefully she wished
Catarine joy of her own empty bed. The woman seemed to be
the sort who would find an empty bed too much of a depriva-
tion to endure for long.

"He hasnae been to see me since he ordered the flogging,"
Artair groused as he watched the scantily-clad Catarine move
to the window.

"Ye erred in touching his precious Aimil," Catarine snarled.
"B'Gad, I am fair sick of that child. 'Tis her innocence he
likes. That is all."

Artair did not think so but was wise enough not to say it. He
was healed enough to be eager for a woman, and Catarine's
presence in his chambers plus her alluring attire indicated she

would be willing to accommodate him. It would not be wise to raise her ire. Her particular skills in bed were well known, and he intended to do nothing that would stop her from giving him a sample. In Catarine's case he knew that Parlan would not have any objections to Artair's tasting what Parlan had already enjoyed and had so firmly and clearly set aside.

"Weel, she will soon be back with her kin and wed to Rory Fergueson. They are betrothed."

"Parlan means to stop that wedding."

"So I heard, but I cannae see how he means to do it. She isnae a MacGuin he can rule and order about," Artair countered.

"Nay, but neither is she kept under lock and key," Catarine said slowly, her look thoughtful as she turned to face Artair.

Distracted by his own inner discord, Artair was not at first aware of the air of plotting Catarine exuded. "Nay, she isnae. In a lot of ways she is near to a guest."

"That could be ended at any time," she mused aloud. Nearing the bed and thinking that, although he was young and not the man his brother was, Artair was not one to be tossed aside especially when she was so hungry for a man.

"What do ye mean?"

"Just that Parlan has never been one for constancy," she said as she sat on the bed.

He did not believe her. Even as she leaned toward him and he eagerly met her kiss, he finally sensed her plotting. Her animosity toward Aimil was no secret. That she would plot against the girl was entirely possible.

Despite his own troubled and confused feelings concerning Parlan, Artair could not shake his loyalty to Parlan who was not only his brother but his laird. It was now painfully clear to him that Aimil Mengue was more to Parlan than a wench to tussle with. As he debated whether he should speak of his suspicions to Parlan upon his return, Catarine's skilled hand reached between his thighs and put the matter out of his head.

Chapter Eleven

"Loving, I can understand why you would like to stay." Leith looked at his crestfallen sister with honest sympathy.

"Aye, there are the reasons ye are thinking on but there is also Rory."

Leith sighed and sat down beside Aimil on Parlan's bed. He was torn two ways. Parlan was a man of his word yet nothing seemed to be getting done. Time passed without sight or word of Rory while his father struggled to fulfill ransom demands that Parlan swore had only been made to gain time. And Aimil was falling more in love with a man who made no visible effort to make her any more than his bed-warmer. If nothing else, perhaps if Aimil was taken from him, Parlan would decide he wanted her back—as his wife. It was past time to make some decisive move and escape was all Leith could think of.

"I will do all I can to keep ye from being wed to him."

"But is all ye can enough?"

"That I do not ken, but I swear upon our mother's grave he will never have ye, Aimil. I will help ye flee and hide ye if all else fails. I will try all else first but I will do even that if I must."

"Oh, Leith, that would put ye against our father."

"In this I am already set against him. 'Tis time to cease being silent about it and take action."

"Parlan said he would stop the wedding."

"Aye, and I want to believe him. I do believe that he means to, but what can he do? What has he done? Each day that passes brings the ransom closer to being paid in full. He swore to me that the ransom was made so weighty so that he could have time to stop the marriage."

Although that surprised her, Aimil added softly, "Yet the marriage is still planned and the ransom gathered." She shook her head. "Nay, I cannae believe that he plays us for fools. He is an honest man."

"So I believe, dearling, yet I cannae let Father hand the man a purse that will leave us paupers because I cannae face the fact that I could be wrong. There are times, Aimil, when trust becomes a risk too great to take, and I begin to think 'tis one of those times. Ye could be wrong. Feelings for the man could blind ye," he added softly.

She rose from where she sat on the bed and agitatedly paced the room. "Aye, they could. I think ye have guessed more than I wish ye to. Yet, as those feelings may blind me, they also make me sicken at the thought of wedding Rory Fergueson."

"I swear to you, sweeting, ye will never wed Rory."

"'Tis our duty to try to escape," she murmured, hoping that by repeating that she could convince herself of it.

"Aye, because of the ransom and because of what he is doing to ye. There is no honor for ye in this arrangement. If he would but offer to wed ye . . ." he began.

"I will wed no man for honor's sake."

"Ah, loving, many is the man that speaks of honor but is wedding a woman because he wishes to."

"Mayhaps." She sighed. "I cannae stay only because I wish to."

"Nay. Because ye are his captive, there are many who will pay little heed to the bedding of ye. If ye stay of your own will, ye are agreeing to the arrangement and that is when all will think ye but a whore, or most all."

"I ken it." Her mind cringed at the very thought of it. "When do we leave?"

"This night. I wished to go last eve but I needed to be certain of the best place to slip away through. It took longer than I had thought. 'Tis a weel-guarded place. Even the place I have found is watched but nae as keenly as others. Also, less time is needed to go from one place of cover to another then out beyond the walls."

"What time do we try this then?"

"After the evening meal. We will retire as always and, as soon as the place quiets for the night, we will be gone."

She smiled when he kissed her cheek, but her smile faded quickly when he left. Leaving was the very last thing she wanted to do. All of Leith's reasoning was perfectly sound There was no arguing with it yet she desperately wished that there was. Once she was back home, Parlan would never get near her again. She could not even feel sure that he would try.

There was also the possibility that, if he did hold some feelings for her, her escape would hurt him. He would probably understand what drove her to it, but emotions could be irrational things. She knew that all too well. No matter how solid her reasoning, there was no ignoring the fact that she was escaping not only Dubhglenn but his bed. She did not relish delivering that dart. She could almost wish that he held no more feelings for her than a healthy lust.

Shaking her head, she sought to disperse such thoughts. She needed to convince herself of the need to escape, of the rightness of the action. To view the unpleasant even painful side of it all would weaken her and she needed strength.

It proved difficult to keep up a facade of normality during the evening meal. Aimil found herself almost glad of Catarine's presence and her continued acrimonious talk. It kept her thoughts from dwelling on how soon she would be gone from Dubhglenn and Parlan. So too did it give others a reason for her less than cheerful mood. They no doubt felt that she was simply angry with or tired of Catarine.

As she waited for Leith in Parlan's room after they had retired, Aimil thought on Catarine and wished she had not. The woman would heartily welcome a vacancy in Parlan's bed. Aimil did not feel confident that since she had left him of her own free will, Parlan would suffer an empty bed. She felt sick over the thought of him with other women, especially Catarine. It was enough to make her determination waver, but then Leith arrived.

"Ready, love?" he murmured, his gaze soft with understanding as he recognized her distress.

"If we must." She sighed.

Grasping her gently by the shoulders, he said, "We must try, Aimil. If the man cares for ye, he will come for ye."

"I am betrothed to Rory." She did not really want to cherish too many hopes concerning Parlan for it would only hurt her more when they came to nothing.

"Then Parlan will end that betrothal as he said he would. He can do that be we at Dubhglenn or at home."

She nodded and allowed herself to be led from the room. It was tempting to look back but she resisted. Now was the time to look ahead and to concentrate upon the business of escaping. Memories and regrets could come later. She was sure that she would find herself heavily ladened with both when she finally gave them free rein.

Moving through the shadowed halls of Dubhglenn, she was a little surprised at the laxity of the guard. Soon after that, she grew insulted. It appeared that the men felt Parlan had her well and firmly shackled to the bed. That a woman would try to escape the Black Parlan's arms was a possibility they plainly considered a remote one. In what she knew was a rather contrary and perverse way, she decided she was going to enjoy proving them all wrong.

Slipping out of a little-used door into the bailey, she and Leith pressed their backs to the wall, taking full advantage of the shadows while they surveyed the strength of the guard. Here she noted that it was far more in evidence even though the men's attentions were mostly turned away from the keep. She realized that slipping through the keep had been the easy part of their plan.

"Where do we head, Leith?"

"To the stables, loving. Between the wall of the stables and the curtain wall is a small space, barely enough for us to slide into. There is a small door in the curtain wall there. Getting to the stables from here will be difficult, but it can be done. When I cry 'now,' ye are to bolt over the open ground toward the curtain wall. Flat against it, ye will see the space."

Aimil felt her heart quicken with tense excitement. She held no fear for she felt sure that Parlan's men would not harm her or Leith although there could be a few bruises forthcoming in their recapture. Despite her regrets and her desire to stay, there was a thrill in the thought of eluding Parlan's men and escaping such a well-secured keep as Dubhglenn. She wished a successful escape did not mean an end to all she had shared with Parlan.

When Leith hissed the signal, she moved with no hesitation. She had seen that he watched for that brief moment when the two guards who could have spotted them had their attention elsewhere. That meant not only stealth was needed of her but speed, and she produced all she could as she silently raced across the open space to the stables.

Upon reaching the high stone wall beyond the stables, she clung to the cool stone and the safety of its shadows. It took a moment for her to espy the space Leith had spoken of. The shadows and its narrowness made it nearly invisible. Still clinging to the wall, she slid into the space, releasing her breath in a soft expulsion of relief when no outcry was made. She had made it without being discovered. Now she tensely waited for Leith to do the same.

Her tension, accumulating as she waited for her brother, was released in a soft squeak when he finally reached her side. There had been no warning of his approach by sight or by sound. One minute she had been alone, in the next he was there. It took her several deep breaths before she quieted the furious pounding of her heart. Despite that, she felt proud of his skill.

"Where is this doorway, Leith?" she hissed, eager to continue now that she had committed herself to the plan.

"Slide along some and ye shall feel it."

It was several feet before her hand left stone and touched wood. "A bolthole, do ye think?"

"Aye. T'was weel concealed with debris and there is but a wee walkway of rock between it and the loch that guards this side of Dubhglenn. A boat may have been tethered below or near. There is none now, but I cannae think any who fled by this route meant to swim the loch. It has been long forgotten, I believe."

"It could be a weak spot if 'tis forgotten, a way for enemies to gain Dubhglenn."

"We will send your love word of it when we are safe away. I have no plans to make use of such a thing. Open the door, sweeting. By staying close to the wall, we can work our way round to the front whence comes another difficult part. There is a large open space between the walls of Dubhglenn and any cover. We shall have to bolt across and hope that some clouds arise to dim what light there is."

She forced herself to open the door. It required all her

strength, and she pressed her body against it. Leith kept a grip on her in case she stumbled for there was no room for a misstep outside the door. She could easily be plunged into the loch. As she slowly worked the door open, she fought the urge to end the escape, to give into the temptation to return to Parlan's bed and await his return.

Parlan scowled when Elfking hesitated in his steady pace toward Dubhglenn's gates. He had little patience for dealing with the spirited animal's vagaries. Although he could not stop himself, he felt foolish for driving his men so hard just so that he could reach Dubhglenn and a tiny lady one night earlier than planned. That the men suspected what pushed him only annoyed him more. Cursing when Elfking sought to turn toward the loch, he struggled to keep the horse on the road. Finally, he decided that he would waste less time if he allowed the animal his way for the moment.

"Ride on ahead," he ordered his men. "This fool beast has a fancy to see the loch and willnae be dissuaded. I have decided that, this time, t'will be easier to let him have his way."

"I will ride with ye," murmured one burly man as he moved out of the group to ride at Parlan's side.

Rolling his eyes in exasperation, Parlan nodded curtly. It would be unfair to take his ill temper out on the man. Iain felt he was only doing his duty in insuring that his laird was well-guarded even so close to Dubhglenn's walls. Although Parlan did his best not to gather too many enemies, he had enough to warrant the concern.

A frown touched Parlan's face as he allowed Elfking the freedom to go where he wished. The animal's ears twitched, and his nose worked much as if he were a hound on the scent. Parlan's curiosity began to outweigh his annoyance. He thought now that the horse was not simply being contrary.

As the horse picked his way over the increasingly rocky ground, Parlan mused upon what had brought him hieing back to Dubhglenn. He honestly admitted that it was not only physical need. There was no doubt about his eagerness to bed Aimil again, but he was also eager to see her. He wanted to hear her laugh, to see her smile, and simply to talk to her. It was a source of some wonder to him to discover how thoroughly he missed her as a person and not just as a body that gave him pleasure.

When Elfking's steps faltered, Parlan dismounted. Something drew the horse to a place the animal would not usually go, and Parlan wanted to see what it was. He drew his sword and heard Iain do likewise. Although he could not fathom why the animal would approach danger so doggedly, there was always the chance that it was a threat the horse had scented, and it would be wise to be prepared for it.

"We run out of land," Iain muttered when they reached the edge of the loch.

"Aye, but the beast wishes to move on yet even he balks at trying to walk the wee spit of land between the walls of Dubhglenn and the waters of the loch." Handing Elfking's reins to Iain, Parlan ordered, "Hold him here. I will go along and see what draws the fool animal."

He smiled grimly as he heard Iain's soft mutter. The man did not like being left behind where his sword could prove useless. Parlan knew that Malcolm would have been far less reticent in his disapproval. Parlan also decided that he had better speak to Aimil about what tricks she had taught her mount so that he would not be caught by surprise by the horse's actions again.

"Did ye think to try this door?" panted Aimil as she struggled in her battle to open the thick oaken portal.

"I nudged it and it gave. Do ye wish me to take a turn?"

"Nay, for if ye stumbled, I would never be able to hold ye and ye would end in the loch. I am near to having it open enough."

"We but need a space to slip through and we being so slim it doesnae have to be a verra big space. 'Tis not enough as yet?"

"Nay. An inch or twa more will do it though.'Tis noisy," she hissed when the hinges groaned, strained by use after so long.

"I should have thought to grease them." He waited with her to see if any alarm was raised. "'Tis not as loud as we think," he murmured a few moments later. "Try again. Mayhaps the noise doesnae carry beyond this spot. Come, loving," he urged when she continued to hesitate. "There is always the chance that someone may look into our chambers and see that we are gone. We cannae hesitate now." When she pushed the door and again the screech of little-used hinges rent the air, he cursed softly then said, "Ignore it and continue."

"But, Leith," she protested, sure that the noise would be audible to a guard.

"There is no other way nor is there any other time for us. If we are caught now rather than later, so be it, but let us not hesitate simply because of the risk of capture. Push."

Parlan pressed himself against the cold stone wall. He was not sure what he had heard but something had alerted him. Listening tensely, he waited for either a movement or a sound. A soft whicker from Elfking told him that whatever had drawn the horse to the spot was still there.

His searching gaze suddenly fixed upon an irregularity in the line of the wall. Although he was not well-acquainted with this side of Dubhglenn, he felt sure that there should not be a length equal to a man's height jutting out from the wall. Even as he stared at it, a soft noise reached his ears, and he was certain it had come from that spot.

Carefully he edged toward it. As he watched, he detected a faint movement accompanied by the faint squeak of something akin to rusted hinges. Suddenly he knew what he saw. Some long-forgotten exit was there, and someone was trying to open it. Someone had found an old doorway in the walls of Dubhglenn and was struggling to put it to use.

He was assailed with an odd mixture of emotion as he moved even nearer. There were only two people in Dubhglenn who would need to leave it so stealthily. Angrily he wondered how they had managed to get so close to succeeding. They were supposed to be closely watched yet no one had apparently noticed their absence.

Catarine hesitated as she passed Leith's chambers. The youth had been cold to her, quite insulting in his attitude. That stirred her to fury, but she suddenly recognized his possible usefulness. He was very close to Aimil. The girl listened to him, and he had a great deal of influence with her. Catarine realized that she could find the way to drive Aimil away either by using him directly or by the use of some information she managed to glean from him. That he had shown her little warmth was something she felt sure she could change.

Opening his door, she slipped inside only to halt and stare blankly at the empty bed. It took her a moment to realize what had happened. Hurrying down the hall, she flung open the door to Parlan's chambers. When she saw that bed was also empty, she began to smile. Leith had convinced his sister to escape. Considering the time that had passed since the pair had retired and the lack of any outcry, there was a very good chance that they had succeeded, and Catarine's smile widened.

A sudden stir in the keep prompted her to leave Parlan's room quickly and shut the door. If she was caught there, she would be asked why she had raised no alarm. She listened tensely, but there was no outcry simply a sudden bustling, an increase in activity. Her smile widened again as she understood the meaning of it. Parlan was returning. Laughing softly, she hurried to greet him, planning to let him see that she held no grudge and was more than willing to assuage whatever sense of insult Aimil's flight had inflicted.

"'Tis nearly open enough, Leith," Aimil gasped as she paused to rest a moment.

"I should have tested it more. We waste precious time struggling here."

"Are we to give up then?" she asked with weak hopefulness.

A light smile touched Parlan's face. He stood near enough to hear the faint whispers and knew his suspicions were correct. Aimil and Leith were attempting to escape Dubhglenn. Reluctantly, he admitted that it hurt to think she would wish to leave though he understood the reasons behind the escape did not need to be personal ones. The reluctance he heard in her voice was some balm to that hurt. She did what she felt she had to, not necessarily as she wished to.

"Aimil." Leith sighed. "Now isnae the time to argue that again. We do as we must."

Aimil pondered crossly that duty was a tiresome thing. She would much rather follow her heart which told her to stop breaking her back on the door and go back to Parlan's chambers. Her heart did not care what people thought if she chose to stay in Parlan's bed or if he did impoverish her father with his demands for ransoms. Unfortunately, the demands of pride and duty were proving as strong as her heart's desires.

"'Tis that I dinnae like losing Elfking," she muttered, and

was disgusted with herself for mouthing such a lie, one that was so easy to see through.

"Of course," drawled Leith. "I err in thinking 'tis the other stallion ye crave to see return."

"Dinnae call him a stallion."

The twinge Parlan had felt when she had spoken of Elfking passed. He knew she loved her horse and that she would feel regret for having to leave him behind. Her defense of Parlan, however, indicated otherwise. It at least revealed that she was not without some feeling, enough to make her object when she thought a slur had been made about him.

"Many call him so. 'Tisnae an insult for a man."

"I shouldnae like to be compared to a beast not even one as fine as Elfking," she gritted as she pushed against the door. "There is more to the man than that. I thought ye kenned it."

"I do."

"Yet we try to flee." She knew the length of time it was taking to break free of Dubhglenn was why she faltered.

"I told ye the why of it. Even if we dinnae succeed, mayhaps t'will spur him to confide the plans he speaks of or to show us some results." Leith released his hold upon her to test the opening of the door. "Nearly there."

At that instant, Aimil gave a push that utilized all her waning strength. She suddenly realized that it was not only a lack of use that made the door hard to open but the fact that it rubbed against the ground. Her efforts had finally caused it to clear that obstruction and made the door suddenly jerk open. She fruitlessly tried to maintain her balance but fell to the ground.

For an instant she hung at the edge of the small rocky walkway. She frantically tried to gain a hold that would stop her from falling into the cold, fierce waters of the loch but failed. With a soft cry, she plunged into the cold waters. She fought to regain the surface, but her clothing pulled her down.

Fear gripped her when she discovered that she might lack the strength to save herself, having seriously depleted it in trying to open the door. She struggled against the paralyzing effects of terror as fiercely as she fought to remove the clothes that worked to hold her beneath the water. The fear began to win as she failed to remove her clothes in time. For a moment she tasted sheer terror, then blacked out.

"Aimil," Leith cried, staring in horror at the black waters that had swallowed her.

He hurried to tug off his heavy boots only to find a sword thrust toward him from out of the dark. Stunned though he was, he recognized the large form that dove cleanly into the water after Aimil. Another man suddenly appeared at his side, and together they tensely waited for Parlan to reappear.

Parlan fought a gnawing panic as he dove after Aimil. She had been fully and warmly dressed which would act as an anchor. So too there was little light beneath the water to aid him in his frantic search. When he located her, her limpness frightened him. He fleetingly noted that she had tried to lessen the weight that pulled her down but suspected that she had lacked the strength.

Four hands reached out to aid him when he broke the surface of the water, but he ordered Iain and Leith to a wider spot where they would not be so dangerously hindered by the lack of room. Once he got Aimil upon the bank, he worked to free her of the water she had swallowed. He joined Leith in softly thanking God when Aimil spewed out the cold water and spluttered briefly awake. Curtly refusing any assistance, he carried her to Elfking then into Dubhglenn where he intended her to stay.

Chapter Twelve

It was a moment before Catarine noticed the bundle that Parlan carried. She halted abruptly in her advance toward him to glare at the limp, dripping Aimil. Briefly hope flared that the girl was dead but that was killed when the girl groaned. After Parlan turned Aimil over to Old Meg's care and ordered Leith escorted to his chambers, Catarine followed him into the hall, watching him hungrily as he changed into dry clothes even as she plotted another way to be rid of Aimil.

"I told ye to watch them carefully, Malcolm," Parlan growled.

Malcolm took the rebuke as his due. He could have placed extra guards upon the Mengues but had not. Even a long-forgotten doorway would not have aided them had he done so. It was an oversight and he acknowledged it.

"How did ye come across them?" he asked Parlan.

"That horse sniffed her out. He forced me to that point. 'Tis weel that he did. Fool lass could have drowned." Parlan downed almost a full tankard of ale that was served to him. "Where did that door come from? Did none ken it was there?"

"I think not. The stables have been there since your father's father's time."

"Come the morn I want it sealed. Now, I will go speak to that fool lad."

After glancing at an avidly listening Catarine, Malcolm suggested softly, so that she could not overhear, "Ye didnae tell the lad your plans at all. I ken he trusts ye but he darenst, nay, not when the ransom is still collected and ye still bed his sister as ye will."

Parlan ran a hand through his damp hair. "Ye are right, Malcolm. I will say what is needed. Tomorrow. I am too weary to do it right this night. How promises the weather on the morrow?" he asked Angus, a man reknowned for his forecasting skill.

"Bodes well. Sun, clear skies, and warmth. A rare summer's day."

"Good. Maggie, ye will see that food is readied. I dine in the sun tomorrow at noon with Aimil." He winked at Malcolm. "I ken just the spot. The Banshee's Well copse. Now, to speak to Leith."

Catarine did not care to think on what such special arrangements could mean. She crept out of the hall and sought out one of her men-at-arms. Ordering him to leave with two horses giving the excuse of readying matters for her journey to Stirling, she told him to wait for her just beyond sight of Dubhglenn. He had barely cleared the gate when she was at the door Leith and Aimil had tried to escape through. Luck was with her, and moments later she was riding toward one who would certainly aid her in her quest of ridding Dubhglenn of Aimil Mengue.

"Who?" muttered Rory when Catarine was announced.

"Catarine Dunmore," growled Geordie. "She says she has a bargain to set before ye."

"Show her in then."

"I have little time," Catarine began immediately upon entering the room. "I must be back at Dubhglenn before the morn."

"Then tell me what ye wish. I cannae think what bargain we can strike however."

"I can give ye Aimil Mengue." Catarine nodded with satisfaction when Rory tensed with interest and she quickly told him of the plan she had devised.

"And what do ye gain?"

"Parlan. I want him. Alive," she hastened to add. "A bargain?"

"A bargain. Where will they be and when?"

"I mean it," she said after they had made their final plans and she prepared to go. "I want Parlan alive. Do as ye will with that girl but leave Parlan to me."

"Of course. My word upon it." A smile eased over Rory's face after Catarine left, and he turned to Geordie. "Ten of our best marksmen are to be ready to ride on the morrow. I will get my bride back and I will see the Black Parlan dead."

Leith tried very hard not to feel like an errant child as he faced Parlan. He was, however, uncomfortably aware of the fact that he had been allowed to stay at Dubhglenn on Parlan's good graces. His attempt to escape with Aimil was akin to an insult to that hospitality. Leith hoped he would not be sent from Dubhglenn as a result.

"How fares Aimil?" he asked quickly, thinking to divert Parlan.

"Fine. She sleeps. She will most likely sleep through the night."

Inwardly, Leith winced. That was a circumstance that would not improve Parlan's mood at all. He watched the man warily.

"How did you find the door?" Parlan demanded.

"I was kicking a ball around, and it went back there. I then explored its suitability as an escape route."

"It didnae prove too suitable, did it? Aimil was nearly drowned."

"Aye," Leith rasped, "I ken it, and the guilt lies heavy on me for I pressed her into leaving."

"I told ye I wasnae taking all the ransom."

"Ye did yet ye still let it be gathered."

"Because I have naught on that hellhound Rory yet. If I give ye your sister back, she will be wed to the man, and if this ransom game ends, I have no rights to hold her. She is only my captive and all hold I have flees when the ransom is paid."

"The ransom my father sweats to gather for ye."

"It willnae break him to gather it. In truth, he will learn something. He will learn who his true friends are."

Leith suspected that there was a great deal of truth to that so did not bother to argue but went directly to the next point of contention. "And as my father learns who his friends are, ye continue to bed my sister as ye will."

"She and I made a bargain."

"Aye, months ago. That cursed horse has been ransomed ten times over."

"'Tis a fine mount."

"Dinnae play with me, MacGuin. I have been more than patient but I cannae sit by any longer and let ye make a whore of my sister. 'Tis no longer a matter of using a hostage. It has gone far beyond that."

"Aye, it has."

"Then ye mean to put her from your bed?"

"Nay, I mean to wed her if she will agree." He smiled faintly at Leith's surprise which the younger man made no effort to hide. "On the morrow, if the weather is fine and if she doesnae sicken from her swim, I will take her for a wee ride and talk to her."

"What of Rory? God's teeth, what of my father?"

"I care not. They willnae be able to do verra much about it after a priest has done the vows. Mayhaps t'will even drive Rory to act. T'will depend upon how badly he wants Aimil. Mayhaps it willnae be enough to bring him to sword point with me, though, by God's bones, I wish it would be. I have long ached to come to sword point with him."

"As have many another but Rory guards himself verra weel. Enough of him. I care not for the swine. There is still my father to consider. Ye cannae up and wed his daughter with nary a word to him. 'Tisnae done."

"Then I shall break with tradition. Heed me, Leith. Aimil stays in my bed. Does she stay there wed or unwed?"

"Wed, curse ye." Leith spoke rather mildly for he knew Parlan was the one Aimil wanted. "T'will brew a mighty storm though."

"I have faced down one or twa in my time. I will speak to you again after I have had my say with your sister."

Parlan left before Leith could think of any further objections. He hoped Leith would continue to be persuaded. It would not make an auspicious beginning to his marriage if he had to lock the younger man up until the priest had finished wedding him and Aimil, he mused.

His thoughts were abruptly interrupted when Artair suddenly stopped in front of him. Parlan met his brother's nervous gaze with coolness. Anger over what Artair had done to Aimil still lingered. He was not sure he was quite ready to forgive, if that was what Artair sought.

"I have come to apologize for what I did to your woman."

"'Tisnae really me ye must apologize to."

"Aye, 'tis. Weel, and the lass too. See, she told me she was yours, but I paid her no heed. I shouldnae have tried to take what was, is, yours. That wasnae right and I ken it."

"Nay, it wasnae right but 'tisnae the real wrong ye did.

'Tisnae right to reach for another man's lass but, if she proves willing, weel, so is the game played. She wasnae willing though, Artair. There is your wrong. Ye didnae heed her nay. Ye hit her."

"She bit clean through my lip," Artair said in his defense, but it lacked strength and he knew it.

"So ye cuffed her one. I still wouldnae have been pleased, but that I could have understood. 'Tis a man's nature to strike out at what strikes him. But ye hit her again and meant to keep on hitting her. That was your other wrong, Artair.

"Being a man and one who can fight weel with sword and fist, if ye are sober, ye are stronger than a lass. 'Tisnae right to turn that against her. 'Tisnae right to take what a lass doesnae want to give. I ken many think me a soft fool for such beliefs, but I dinnae think it has weakened me. Nay, nor has my bed been empty too often because I choose to wait for a willing lass. Ye cannae just grab as ye will. Woo it, seduce it, or pay for it, but dinnae beat it out of a wench."

He stared at Artair, but his brother was neither speaking nor returning his gaze. Parlan began to wonder if any of what he had said had been heeded. It was a gain of sorts that Artair had even attempted to apologize, but Parlan knew it meant nothing if Artair did not really mean it nor had learned anything from the whole business. His hopes lifted when Artair finally looked at him for shame was clearly written upon his face. For the moment at least, Artair understood that he had been wrong.

"I dinnae ken what possesses me at times."

"Drink, laddie. 'Tis a Devil no man can let get a hold upon him. There is a brutal side to a man, 'tis what lets us pick up a sword and hie to battle. Aye, even enjoy it. What a man has to learn is when to let the beast free and when to rein him in. No man can do it when drink clouds his mind. Ye must learn to control the drink and not let it rule ye."

"Aye, I ken it. Might I speak to Aimil now?"

"Nay, not now. The fool lass nearly drowned herself. She needs to rest. On the morrow." He started to move toward his chambers.

"Parlan?"

Stopping to glance back at Artair, Parlan asked, "There is more ye have to say?"

"Aye. Do ye mean to wed Aimil Mengue? I have heard talk of it."

"Then ye have heard right. Aye, I mean to speak to her of it on the morrow. I shouldnae have hesitated as long as I did. If I had spoken up when first I had decided on it, I wouldnae have been fishing her out of the loch for she wouldnae have tried to run." *Or, at least*, he mused with an inner grimace as his confidence wavered, *I dinnae think so*. "Do ye object?" he asked coolly when Artair frowned.

"Nay, though I will say that I am a wee bit surprised. I never thought of ye as a man to don the yoke of marriage."

"With Aimil I dinnae feel as if t'would be donning a yoke and that, mayhaps, is the best reason to wed her."

"Aye, mayhaps. For your sake, I hope it never feels so. The why nor even the wisdom of it isnae why I mention it." He nervously cleared his throat and ran a hand through his hair. "I have been with Catarine or, shall we say, she has been with me."

"Take warning, Artair, she is a sly wench and she seeks a husband but would make a man a verra poor wife."

"I ken that she seeks a husband, but she wants the laird not the heir. She seeks ye, Parlan."

"Aye, she has made that clear enough though she thinks not. I have made it clear that I am not interested in aught she has to offer. Dinnae fash yourself. I ken the games her sort plays and they willnae work with me."

"That much I am sure of. I wouldnae waste the time of either of us by speaking on it if that was all I suspected. Aye, she plots but it isnae against ye, I think. She plots against Aimil."

"How so?"

"She didnae really say, and I fear I paid little heed until, weel, later. She distracted me."

"She is skilled at that."

"Aye, verra skilled. Still, I did sense that she plots against Aimil. She wishes Aimil gone. I but thought ye should ken it."

"'Tis good to ken it. I thank ye for speaking on it. I will be certain to look more closely, to keep an eye upon the slut. I begin to think 'tis far past time for the wench to be gone. She takes sore advantage of our hospitality. If there is more ye want from her, best ye gain it now, Artair. I will seek my chambers now for t'was a long ride home. Aye, and the swim I took wearied me some."

"I hope Aimil fares weel. Good sleep, Parlan."

"And to ye, Artair."

With a slight frown, Parlan watched Artair walk away. There seemed to be a change in his brother, but Parlan dared not let himself hope. He had done so in the past and tasted disappointment too often. It would take awhile before his wariness disappeared.

Striding into his chambers, he found Old Meg dozing in a chair by his bed. It pleased him to see that the woman had personally taken over Aimil's care. Gently he roused the woman, smiling faintly over her sleepy grumbling as she woke and stood up.

"How fares the lass?" He stood by the bed and studied the restlessly sleeping Aimil. "Do ye think she will sicken at all?"

"Nay, she be too hale a wee lass to be felled by a wee cold swim. There be no hint of fever."

"Her sleep is an uneasy one."

"Nay doubt the lass be troubled with the memory of them dark waters."

"Has she roused at all yet?"

"Enough to grumble that she didnae need to be tended like some wee bairn. I paid her temper no heed."

Parlan laughed softly as he escorted Old Meg to the door. "She would no doubt have been verra surprised had ye done elsewise. Get your rest, Meg. I pray I willnae have need of ye again this night."

"I dinnae think ye will, laddie. Good sleep to ye."

After the woman left, he got ready for bed. He kept a close watch upon a continually restless Aimil as he undressed and washed. It did seem that her sleep was troubled, and he hoped she had been badly frightened. A good scare was often the mother of caution, and he felt it would not hurt if Aimil had a little more of that. He would find it comforting if she did.

It still pinched at him that she had tried to leave him, even if Leith had had to prod her. He had thought her more than content in his bed. While he knew that she desired him, he found himself wondering if the passion they shared was as strong in her as it was in him. While he craved it, she might simply enjoy it. All the reasons Leith had given for trying to escape were very sound and easily understood, but they were not strengthening his confidence as he wished they would.

Cursing as he snuffed the candles, he told himself not to be a fool. Her trying to escape was perfectly understandable and no real indication of how she felt. It had been a matter of choosing honor and duty over a man who offered her nothing more than passion. By remaining silent about his plans, he had given her no choice. To stay when escape was possible was to be marked as his whore, and Aimil had far too much pride to allow that to happen.

Carefully, he eased into bed. He ached to make love to her but knew there would be none of that. Even if she woke, she would still be suffering from the effects of her near drowning. Recalling how he had felt when the same had occurred to him in his youth, he knew that she would be feeling little inclined even to try for a taste of passion, and he did not want her unless she could share his pleasure. He could wait until the morrow when she would be recovered and more responsive as well as more receptive. When he gently tugged her into his arms and she nestled near him, he decided that the morrow was going to seem very slow in coming.

As Parlan was about to give into the tempting pull of sleep, Aimil began to thrash about. He quickly got a firm grip on her to still her flailing arms. From her movements he guessed that she was reliving her near drowning in her dreams. As he held her, he called to her, trying to pull her from her nightmare. He decided that he did not like to see her so afraid, even in her dreams.

Aimil fought the pull of the waters. She desperately needed air but dared not breathe knowing that the cold, dark waters would fill her if she did. Something held her firmly and she fought its grip, but nothing she did seemed to break it. Then breaking through the choking terror she felt was a deep, soothing voice. She saw Parlan and reached for him, certain he would save her. Slowly, she felt herself pulled from the depths. With a gasping cry, she opened her eyes and met Parlan's gaze.

For a moment she felt swamped with confusion. She was not wet and neither was he. Although her throat was sore and her chest hurt, she felt no need to spew out any water. Then she realized that she was warm, dry, and in Parlan's bed. An instant later she recalled all that had happened, the nearly tragic end to her attempt to leave the man who now held her.

"T'was but a dream."

"Aye, lass." He eased his hold on her.

"I thought I was drowning."

"Ye nearly did."

"Aye, I remember that now. Wheesht, I dinnae fell verra weel."

"Nay, I suspicion ye dinnae but t'will pass quick enough."

She sensed a sternness in him and eyed him warily. What surprise she felt over his presence faded quickly as she faintly recalled him crouched over her while her body violently rejected all the water she had swallowed. It occurred to her that he must have been the one to pull her from the water. Although he did not look very receptive to gratitude, she knew she ought to thank him. He had obviously saved her life and probably at no small risk to his own, something that made her feel uncomfortably guilty.

"I owe ye my life."

"Aye, ye do."

"Weel, I thank ye for it."

"If it means aught to ye, mayhaps ye shouldnae risk it so carelessly."

There was anger in his voice, and her initial reaction of chagrin quickly changed to annoyance. She decided that he had no right to get cross with her. If not for him, she would not even be at Dubhglenn. If not for him, she would still be a maid and not concerned with people thinking her a whore. He was the one with all the grand plans that did not seem to be working so that it began to look as if he could not be trusted. And if his plans were working, he was not telling her and Leith about it which was nearly as bad.

"'Tis all your fault."

"My fault?" Taken aback, he was torn between amusement over her belligerence and an urge to shake her.

"Aye, right from the beginning. Weel, mayhaps not exactly right from the start for t'was Artair who made the raid and caught us, but ye didnae send us home. Then ye speak of all these plans that seem clever yet naught happens save that my father still pays."

"Dinnae ye trust me?"

"Aye, I trust ye and Leith does too, but, as he said, there

comes a time when ye must ask yourself if 'tis wise to set still and be trusting, if ye have been wrong and act upon what ye see and not what ye feel. We both feel that ye can be trusted, but we see naught happening save that my father still struggles to collect the ransom and I," she said, sighing, "and I still share your bed. We both ken that the bargain made for Elf-king has long since been fulfilled."

He smoothed away the lines caused by her frown with his fingers. "And ye are no longer happy to share my bed?"

"Aye, but therein is some of the trouble. Cannae ye see that? As Leith said, my being here is accepted as part of my being a hostage, but when I make no attempt to escape, especially when the chance arises, then I become naught but a whore in all eyes." She looked at him closely, hoping he would understand for she had never wanted to deliver any insult. "I couldnae do that to my family."

"Nay, ye couldnae. Weel, ye have now soothed all that worry for ye have tried to escape, something all can attest to. Aye, and ye nearly killed yourself in the doing of it." For a moment he thought about speaking of marriage now but decided he would stay to his original plan. "So, now ye can stay right where ye are and I mean to see that ye do."

She thought that sounded arrogant but was feeling too weary to take him to task about it. With an inner sigh, she also admitted to herself that, if he wanted her to stay in his bed, she really had no objections. It was where she really wanted to be. While he gave her only passion when she ached for so much more, there was still more joy than sorrow to be found in the arrangement. Neither did he ever leave her feeling no better than a whore. She was not quite certain of what he felt for her and continuously feared that his feelings would change, that he would eventually discard her. However, she was sure that she was more than a mere bedmate with whom he sated whatever lust he felt. As long as he allowed her to, she would stay and try for more, try to win his love.

"Go to sleep, loving," he ordered gently. "Ye need your rest. Get a lot and on the morrow ye will feel better."

"I hope so," she murmured, and yawned widely. "I can still taste the water of the loch. Aye, still feel as if it fills me."

"T'will fade."

Suddenly recalling that he had been gone for a while and realizing that he was making no move to make love to her, she forced her heavy eyelids to open to peer at him. "Isnae there anything ye want? Ye have been gone a wee while."

"Aye, I have." He smiled faintly and lightly kissed her. "And, aye, there is something I want but it can wait until ye are rested."

"If ye are sure," she said even as she closed her eyes again and started to let sleep conquer her. "Seems verra tolerant of ye when ye are such a greedy rogue."

"Aye, 'tis and ye will no doubt pay for it on the morrow."

He smiled when she laughed softly and then almost immediately fell asleep. Although it had been a nightmare that had made her wake, he had had a lot of his fears about her health eased by that short time of coherency. So too had her words softened the sting her attempt to escape had inflicted. She had not said much more than Leith had, yet seeing it all from her side had aided his understanding. Knowing that she still wished to share his bed and that in her heart she still trusted him was going to make what he planned to say on the morrow a little easier.

Chapter Thirteen

"Where are we going?"

Swinging her up onto Elfking's back, Parlan smiled sweetly at Aimil. "'Tis a surprise, lass. Dinnae ye like surprises?"

Frowning as she watched him mount his horse, she grumbled, "Not particularly and even less when I consider who means to spring it on me."

"Ye wound me, loving. Come, arenae ye a wee bit curious? Let your curiosity lead you."

"Curiosity can lead one into a great deal of difficulty," she intoned a little piously, eyeing him with suspicion.

He laughed and spurred his mount foreward. After a brief hesitation Aimil cursed and followed him. His cheerful mood and the air of a mischievous boy that he carried drew her. She was curious. She simply hated to admit it especially when it made him grin so.

Deciding to ignore him, she turned all her attention to riding. It was something she had not been able to indulge in as freely as she had been accustomed to since coming to Dubhglenn. She was determined to enjoy the freedom, false though it might be, and the unusually fine weather, a sunny day the like of which came along too rarely.

When they finally reined in, Parlan indicating that they were to stop and dismount, Aimil looked around in interest. There was a wild, somewhat desolate beauty to the spot he had chosen. She wondered why he had chosen it and again found herself wondering what he was up to, why he needed to get her alone. It was then that she realized just how alone they were.

"Ye have left your guard behind?" she asked in surprise as he drew her toward the blanket he had spread out upon the ground.

"Weel, I wished to spend some time alone with ye, and I cannae rightly do that with them stomping about, now can I?"

She was about to remark upon that when she heard what sounded like a soft wail, the cry of a woman. Giving a gasp, she flung herself into Parlan's arms. Her fright ebbed quickly when she saw that he was grinning.

"Didnae ye hear that?" She tensed, listening closely. "There it is again. What is it, Parlan?"

"'Tis the banshee."

Meeting his grin with a stern frown, she drawled, "Ye jest with me, but look at my face. Even a man of your wit can see that I dinnae find it verra humorous." She frowned even more when he chuckled and kissed her downcast mouth.

Standing up, he pulled her up after him and started toward a ravine. "Come, my sour-tongued wench. I will show ye." He stopped near a hole about a foot away from the edge of the ravine, holding her back when she would have stepped closer. "Careful, sweeting. It may be unsafe. The hole might have been made because the roof of a cave has collapsed. That moaning is made by the wind. There must be a second hole in the wall of the ravine somewhere. The wind sweeps through, and, lo, ye hear the wail of the banshee of Banshee Well. She calls to those foolish enough to walk without heeding where they step."

Aimil shivered as the sound came again. "I ken 'tis naught but the wind but 'tis a verra mournful sound."

"Aye. When I would come here as a lad, I often made up some wild tales to explain it. 'Tis a sound that near begs to be more than just the wind. I had myself lowered into it once and found naught, but felt the wind and with each stirring of it came that sound. It doesnae sound so ghostly from inside either."

"Was there a cave there?" she asked as he drew her back to the blanket.

"There was a small hole and a lot of rubble. Mayhaps I would have found something had I taken the time to clean out the rubble, but I was only after discovering the source of the moaning. I was past the age where caves were of any interest to me."

"Is the hole verra deep?"

"Deep enough so that ye could break your neck if ye took a tumble down it." He began to unpack the basket he had brought along.

Her eyes widening as she saw what he set out, she asked, "Ye mean for us to dine here?"

"Aye. 'Tis a fine way to spend a beautiful day. I have even brought us some wine. We shall drink and eat and loll about in the sun like idle royalty. Have ye never dined in the sun?" She shook her head knowing he did not refer to the sometimes rough and rushed meals taken while traveling. "Then this shall be something new for you. Come, enjoy."

She did and, as they ate and drank, her enjoyment grew. Parlan was in high spirits and kept her laughing with his teasing and nonsense. It was not until they had finished the food that she began to suspect there was more to the trip than food and sun. She half-lay in his arms, sipping wine, and recognized the look that was slowly altering his expression.

"I begin to think ye have been sly again, Parlan MacGuin," she drawled but made no move to leave his hold.

"Sly, am I?" He took her cup and tossed it aside then pushed her onto her back. "I thought I was being most clear about what I want." He began to unlace the jerkin she wore. "Ye needed but one look to guess it."

She attempted to stop him from removing her jerkin but even she recognized it as half-hearted resistance. "We are outside and the sun is shining."

"Aye, and I think ye will look beautiful in the sun's light."

"Ye cannae mean to do it here?"

"Ye do favor saying that, sweeting. Aye, and I do favor showing ye that we can."

He halted her other protests with kisses. When Aimil grasped at sanity long enough to recall that they were outside beneath a very bright sun, she was already naked. Parlan crouched over her, staring at her with eyes black with passion, and quickly shed his own clothes. Despite the fact that she ached for him, she felt the heat of modesty stain her cheeks.

"I was right, dearling." Once free of his clothes, he eased himself on top of her. "Ye do look fine lying naked in the sun."

"'Tis a scandal," she whispered, and arched toward him when his mouth found her breast.

"Och, lass, it does a body good to have a touch of scandal in his life."

It was beyond her to argue with that outrageous opinion. She was too consumed by the desire he awakened in her to form a coherent sentence. All thought and concern about where she was faded as the passion they shared became her world. Shock briefly broke her free of desire's grip when his mouth moved that small distance from her inner thigh to touch the silken curls adorning her womanhood. Her embarrassed protest was short-lived as his hoarse love words and kisses drove her beyond thought.

He ignored her cries for him when she neared her crest. She had barely recovered from her intense release when he employed all his skill to renew her desire. Although he wanted to enjoy the way she was so wild and free when caught in passion's grip, he finally had to answer his own need. He entered her, his passion too strong to control, but she met his fierceness equally and tirelessly. When he felt her inner tremors begin, he thrust more deeply and cried out as his own release tore through him. Collapsing upon her and holding her close, he savored the way her trembling body greedily accepted his seed.

Aimil lay very still, listening to the man sprawled half-atop her breathe. She was certain they had both fallen asleep after their wild lovemaking but was not certain as to how long they might have slept. Looking at the sun would give her some idea of time but that meant she would have to open her eyes and she did not really want to face the man she sensed was awake and watching her. With wakefulness had come the recollection of their unrestrained lovemaking in the bright sunlight, and she was feeling somewhat embarrassed. Knowing she was still naked did not help ease it.

Parlan smiled as he saw her eyelids flicker. He suspected that her reluctance to let him know that she was awake was due to embarrassment. It was growing late, however, and he could not allow her the luxury of hiding for much longer. There was another reason he hesitated and that was because he thought her glorious lying beneath the sun, none of her beauty hidden from his sight. Once he forced her to move, she would quickly put her clothes back on.

"Aimil," he finally called softly, "I ken ye are awake."

"Nay, I am fast asleep."

"Keeping your eyes shut doesnae change the fact that I can see all your charms."

She wondered if she could hit him if she swung toward the sound of his voice then decided that it was not worth the effort for he would undoubtedly block her blow with ease. "Aye, but I cannae see ye seeing it."

"How sensible of ye." He easily caught her by the wrist when she blindly swung one small fist at him then tugged her into his arms. "Are ye embarrassed, loving?"

"Nay, why should I be embarrassed?" She wondered if he knew how stupid a question that was. "I am only rolling about outside with my arse bared to the sun like some hedgerow whore. Why should I find that embarrassing?"

"Weel, if I now tossed ye a wee coin, patted that lovely arse, and strolled off, then ye might have a right to feel like some hedgerow whore but ye have naught to fash yourself about. Unless, of course, ye think 'tis true that the sun can burn tender skin." He laughed when she suddenly covered her backside with her hands.

"Ye are a wretched, wretched man, Parlan MacGuin," she grumbled as she pushed free of his arms and began to dress quickly. "Ye have no care for a lass's sensibilities. Just because ye are accustomed to rolling about here, there, and God kens where."

"Actually," he interrupted even as he dressed with a little more leisure, "while I cannae say for certain that I have never been with a lass out in the air, I cannae recall having such a sweet time of it or planning it so carefully."

"Ye planned to seduce me out here where all can see?"

"Weel, I didnae notice many folk hereabouts but, aye, I did." When she finished dressing, he reached out to grasp her by the hand. "Lass, dinnae taint a free and beautiful moment with regrets and worries. Ye found pleasure. Where is the harm?"

"Ye dinnae understand. 'Tisnae where we did it but, weel, the way we carried on." She sighed as words failed her.

"Ah." He kissed her palm. "Look at me, Aimil. Come, look at me, for I want to be sure ye listen to me."

Although she blushed, she finally met his gaze. "I ken ye

dinnae treat me like a whore, but I cannae help but feel that I act one at times."

"Nay, dearling, ye never do. Wheesht, lass, ye enjoy it and 'twas a rare whore who does. She seeks coin not pleasure, and she doesnae often get to choose her man but must lie down with the one who has the coin. Neither do ye lie down for any man like Catarine does, to feed vanity or a hunger that must have many men and often to be satisfied. Nor do ye do it to make gain in some manner, again like Catarine who is always plotting to catch a rich husband between her greedy thighs. Those are the things that make a woman a whore.

"As far as how we have acted here, t'was but our giving into our passion which runs hot and fine, and, only for each other. Neither am I given to strange ways or fancies. If I enjoy it and ye enjoy it, who can say 'tis wrong?"

"None really if t'was even their business to do so." She smiled crookedly. "'Tis just all so new."

"Weel, I hope it always will be in some ways." He smiled when she looked confused, then he sat up straighter. "Now, there is one other thing we must talk on." He hesitated, frowning at his hand which lay palm down upon the ground.

"Parlan?"

"Hush a moment, lass."

His sudden tension began to make her nervous. Then she too tensed, feeling something, certain she had heard something yet unable to name it. When it became recognizeable, she stared at Parlan with growing horror.

"Get on your mount." Parlan leapt to his feet then yanked her up.

Aimil needed little prodding. Horsemen were riding their way and fast. She only felt that that meant trouble.

To her dismay, their alertness to the danger had come too late. They were barely ready to mount when the horsemen came into view. Her fear grew in leaps and bounds when she recognized Rory.

"Kill him! Kill the Black Parlan!"

The frantic scream chilled Aimil, but she had no time to think about it. Parlan grabbed her hand and raced for the wood, giving up on trying to flee on their mounts who had become panicked over the sudden intrusion of armed men. She heard Parlan grunt then curse as they entered the thick wood but she gave little thought to it until they stopped. Parlan tugged her down beside him as he sprawled behind a fallen tree thickly surrounded by brush. Looking to him for some further instruction, she saw that an arrow had pierced his leg.

"Nay." He stopped her when she reached to extract the arrow. "T'will bleed too freely and we havenae the time to tend it. We must elude that swine for an hour or so, mayhaps less."

"Someone will come?"

"Aye. I had to make a bargain with my men. My time without them hanging about was limited. Mayhaps we can circle back to the horses."

That did prove to be a possibility, but Aimil was not certain they could accomplish it. It seemed that they crept through the wood for hours while a ranting, cursing Rory and his sullen men searched for them. With each passing moment and each step taken, Parlan grew visibly weaker. She felt sure he could not hold out much longer, and if he became too weak or unconscious, Rory would have them. It was not really necessary to listen to the threats echoing through the wood to know that Rory would not take Parlan prisoner, that the man intended nothing less than murder. Rory was clearly after revenge for wrongs he felt had been done him.

By the time they reached the place where they had dined and loved such a short time ago, Aimil had to support Parlan. Her fear was replaced by concern for him. He needed his wound tended to and quickly. So too was she certain that, although she loathed the idea of falling into Rory's hands, her life was not in danger. It was, therefore, more important to get Parlan out of Rory's reach.

"Leave me, lass," Parlan rasped when they came into sight of where they had left the horses to find that a nervous Elfking alone remained.

"Nay. I have little desire to aid Rory in murdering ye."

"And I have little desire to see that hellhound get his hands upon ye. Leave me here and flee while ye can."

She ignored him and called softly to Elfking. The fact that Parlan had no strength to enforce his command added to her concern for him. It made it all too clear that his condition was worsening. When Elfking reached them, she helped a complaining Parlan onto the horse's back.

"The reins, lass. I cannae reach them."

"I will get them in a moment. Are ye secure?"

"Aye."

Hearing Rory's men, she smiled faintly. Parlan was going to be furious, but she had no choice. His life was at risk. She only wished her time with Parlan did not need to end but she doubted that he would try to fetch her back once she was gone.

"Elfking, go home." She slapped her horse on his rear flank, and Elfking bolted. "Home, Elfking. Ride!"

"Aimil!"

Ignoring Parlan's angry bellow, she turned to face Rory and his men who were closing in on her. She knew that if she could give Elfking a few moments lead there would be no catching him. To keep Rory and his men occupied for that few moments, she let them see her then bolted.

Her way back into the cover of the wood was quickly blocked. For a moment she kept the mounted men in a confused knot as they tried to follow her nimble, elusive moves.

Then several men dismounted to chase her. She was not really surprised when she was neatly tackled an instant later. She was roughly pulled to her feet and dragged before Rory. The look in his eyes made her heartily wish she had found a way to go with Parlan.

"Ye dress like a whore." Rory studied her lad's attire with scorn.

"Ye ken their style of dress weel, do ye?" Aimil wished she felt as calm as she sounded then bit back a cry when he back-handed her, causing her teeth to score the inside of her mouth, drawing blood.

"Where is your lover, that whoreson, the Black Parlan?"

"On Elfking and halfway to Dubhglenn by now. Out of your reach."

He knew she was right, that he had lost part of the prize he had sought. "Ye will pay dearly for that, ye slut."

With a detachment that seemed odd to her, she watched his fist come at her. Not surprised by his brutality, the blow to her jaw caused pain to explode in her head. As she slipped into unconsciousness, she prayed that Parlan was able to stay on Elfking, that he would reach Dubhglenn and safety.

Parlan heartily swore at the mount he clung to, but there was no stopping or turning the animal. The reins swung out of his reach, nearly impossible to get ahold of even if he had not been weakened by his wound. He was enraged by Aimil's trick yet understood why she had done it. Most of his anger came from the knowledge that he had failed in protecting her from Rory.

Left with no choice, he clung to Elfking and resigned himself to being taken back to Dubhglenn. He could only hope that there would still be time to snatch Aimil from Rory before the man reached the security of his keep. Parlan tried not to think about what Rory would do to her, but the knowledge refused to be ignored, tormenting him as he rode.

When Elfking finally reached Dubhglenn, Parlan was barely conscious. As he was lifted from Elfking's back, he noticed that his men were readying themselves to ride out. Espying his horse, he realized that his riderless mount had alerted his men to the trouble. He then found himself confronted by Leith.

"Where is my sister?"

"Rory holds her. Ride quickly. Mayhaps luck will be with us and we can intercept them." He started to move toward Raven only to have Malcolm and Lagan restrain him. "I must . . ."

"Ye must get that wound seen to." Lagan urged him toward the keep. "The men can ride without ye this once."

The truth of that was ascertained even as Parlan was pulled toward the keep. With Leith at the fore, Parlan saw his men ride out. He ached to be with them but knew that Lagan was right, that he had to have his wound tended. In his present state he would have been a hindrance, and speed was vital if his men were to catch up with Rory and rescue Aimil. For now he would have to swallow his pride and let others do what was necessary. He could only pray that they would be successful.

It did not take long for Parlan to realize that his wound was far more serious than he had thought. The removal of the arrow was an agony, but he grimly clung to consciousness. What worried him, and the ones nursing him, was how difficult it was to stop the bleeding. It was not its affect upon his own well-being that worried him the most but how it would affect his ability to try and rescue Aimil if his men failed to stop Rory.

"What happened?"

Revived a little by a strong drink after Old Meg had stitched and tightly bound his thigh, Parlan told Lagan all he could recall. Parlan realized that he had noticed less than he usually did in such a situation. In the past, even the smallest detail of a battle or an attack had not escaped his attention. He realized that he had been too concerned with trying to save Aimil from Rory for Parlan to exercise his usual alertness. It troubled him because he feared he may have missed some important detail.

"There is no way he could have kenned where ye would be. T'wasnae a habit of yours to go there. Nay, nor Aimil's."

"That occurred to me. I fear we have a traitor in our midst. Someone told him where we would be and when. For Rory to find us, that low traitor must have crept to Rory last night. I want the whoreson found."

"He will be, Parlan." Lagan was not sure it would be easy to find the traitor for the confusion caused by Leith's and Aimil's attempt to escape would have provided a very good diversion, insuring that few noticed any mysterious comings and goings.

At that moment Catarine burst into the room. Artair, a little stiff from his healing lash wounds, followed at a more discreet pace. Catarine put on a show of great distress until Parlan crossly told her to shut her mouth and stop pestering him.

Hiding her anger, she stood quietly while Parlan told Artair what had happened. She bitterly cursed Rory Fergueson for it was clear that the man had never meant to honor his part of the bargain, had intended Parlan's murder from the start. When mention was made of a traitor, she felt an alarm of fear but pushed it aside. Her man-at-arms would never betray her and the only other one who knew of her betrayal was Rory, who, if he ever came face to face with Parlan, would undoubtedly be dead before he could expose her. She relaxed as she decided that she had little to fear. What she needed to concentrate upon was ingratiating herself with Parlan by helping to tend to his wounds, to nurse him until he healed. By then she was certain she would have him snared.

When Leith entered the room, Parlan did not have to hear the younger man say that they had failed, he could read in it the man's face. With a raging roar, Parlan struggled to his feet. He did not need Old Meg's furious babble to tell him that had been a mistake. The pain that ripped through him and the sudden rush of warmth pouring down his leg told him that all he had succeeded in doing was opening his wound, which would only delay him more.

He cursed everybody and everything as he was pushed back down upon his bed. The restitching and rebandaging of his leg severely strained his hold on consciousness. When Old Meg handed him something to drink, he groggily did so only to realize too late what she had given him. With a foul oath, he threw the goblet across the room.

"Ye old corbie, I dinnae want to sleep."

Not in the least quailed by his anger, Old Meg retorted sharply, "Ye may not want it, ye young fool, but 'tis what ye need."

"I need to go after Aimil."

"Ye need to give that great hole in your leg time to close. Ye have just seen what happens when ye move."

"I dinnae have time." Frustration and despair gnawed at Parlan as he felt the potion Old Meg had given him start to cloud his mind, pulling him toward a sleep he did not want. "I must free Aimil from that hellhound."

"He willnae kill her, Parlan."

"Nay, he willnae, Leith." Parlan's eyes closed as blackness began to overcome him. "Nay, I dinnae think he will kill her, but I ken weel that he will soon have the poor lass wishing that he would."

Chapter Fourteen

Groaning softly, Aimil made the final struggle toward consciousness with reluctance. Her whole body ached. It took her a few moments to discern that one pain amongst the many was greater than the others. Muttering a curse, she gingerly touched her throbbing jaw. After another few minutes she recalled why her jaw hurt, and a sudden panic forced her that last step into awareness. Her eyes wide, she glanced around fearfully and with a sigh of relief, saw that she was alone.

Realizing her thoughts were clouded by her discomfort, she slowly sat up, fighting dizziness as she did so. Carefully, she eased herself off the crude bed. With slow steps she walked to a basin and pitcher that stood upon a rough table. After washing her face in the cold water, she leaned wearily against the wall and dabbed herself dry with the coarse cloth left by the bowl.

Looking around the ill-lit room, she felt the small hope of all that had happened being a nightmare falter and die. She recalled the room from the last brief stay at Rory's earlier in the year. Glancing up at the cobweb-strewn ceiling, she decided that she recognized them as well. If there were any maids about, they were clearly not made to do any cleaning, she mused. Considering the extreme care Rory took with his personal appearance, she was surprised that he would tolerate living amongst such filth.

Espying a decanter of wine and a goblet on a scarred table by the bed, she quickly moved toward it. A drink of wine would help her to think, she mused, and wash the dryness of a lingering fear from her mouth. She took a hearty swallow and nearly gagged. After the wine at Dubhglenn, what she drank now tasted little better than vinegar. Rory clearly spent very little money on wine either. Or, she thought crossly, it was purposely chosen to make her sick. She decided that Rory did not know her very well at all if he thought a little sour wine could accomplish that. Sitting on the bed, she sipped from the goblet and tried to think of what to do next.

A few moments passed before she decided that she was not going to talk herself out of trying to escape. She did not want to stay near Rory any longer than she was forced to. Neither did she think she could calmly wait for her father to arrive for he would either hand her back to Rory or lock her up firmly until the wedding. The only way she would see Parlan again was if she escaped. It would be dangerous but it was the only choice that gave her any chance of having what she wanted and that was to be with Parlan.

Moving to look out of the window, she glanced down and cursed softly. She had forgotten how high up the room was from the ground, but she suspected that Rory had chosen this room for that reason. Even though she searched, she was not surprised to find that there was nothing in the room that would make an adequate rope. The bedclothes were not only too few but too worn and frayed to be safe.

The door proved to be securely bolted from the outside. Aimil frowned because she could not remember noticing that the last time she had been at Rory's. It was as if he had been prepared to hold her prisoner which meant that Rory's appearance at the copse had been planned.

There was very little chance that he had accidently come upon her and Parlan in a remote corner of MacGuin land. Someone had told Rory where and when to find her and Parlan. She wondered if that traitor had intended Parlan's death or her capture or both. If she knew that, she would know better who the traitor was. The reasons for the betrayal would point the way to the betrayer.

The first person she thought of was Catarine, but she knew some of her readiness to suspect the woman was because she loathed Catarine and would like nothing better than to have a good reason to have the wretch banned from Dubhglenn. She also preferred it to be Catarine rather than the other suspect who came to mind—Artair. It would devastate Parlan to discover that his own brother had betrayed him. Aimil was not sure she would have the heart to tell Parlan if the traitor did prove to be Artair.

Her troubled thoughts were abruptly interrupted when Rory entered the room. Standing firmly between her and the door, she decided yet again that his physical beauty lacked a certain quality that made him moving to look at. It occurred to her that it could be the coldness in his eyes that stole the beauty from his face. She wondered if Rory ever smiled, then was not sure she wanted to know what might make him smile.

"And when does my father arrive?"

"He willnae arrive for I havenae sent for him."

"Nay? Weel, I suggest ye set about doing it."

"Nay, I think not."

"Ye cannae hold me here without at least telling my father where I am." Aimil did not like the way he studied her.

"But I can. Ye are my betrothed, my bride."

"Aye, but not yet your wife."

"That matters not. Your father gave me rights over ye when he agreed to the betrothal."

"Ye should at least tell him that he neednae keep collecting the ransom." She was suddenly desperate to let her father know where she was even if it meant facing his indifference and confinement to her chambers until the wedding.

"I will in time. I willnae let him pay that whoreson MacGuin. I have uses for your dowry and dinnae wish it depleted."

Inwardly, she cursed. She should have known about his need for her dowry. Everything she had seen in the few times she had been at his keep told her that he suffered from a lack of coin. It also explained why he had been so firm about staying betrothed to her despite knowing that she shared the Black Parlan's bed. She then wondered if she could make a bargain with him. If his only interest was in her dowry, she would give him as much as she could get her hands on.

"Has my father given ye my dowry yet?"

"Nay, he willnae even let me borrow on it. I cannae touch it 'til we wed."

That was clearly a sore point with him, and she felt her hopes for a mutually satisfying bargain rise. "Mayhaps I can get ye the coin."

"And how would ye do that, my pretty, aside from wedding me whereupon I get it anyway?"

"I can get it and then ye would have the coin ye need but wouldnae need to marry me."

"Mayhaps I wish to wed ye."

"Why should ye? We dinnae suit, never have. If 'tis the coin ye need, then I will get it for ye. There isnae any need for us to wed."

"Ye would leave unhonored my dead uncle's last wish, one your father swore to honor?"

She suddenly realized that he toyed with her. He was interested in hearing her bargain but only to be amused by how desperately she would try to get him to agree with it. It was hard to control her fury, but she fought to for she knew that raging at him would gain her nothing. She did not doubt that he would find that amusing, too.

"What game do ye play?" she asked with a calm she did not feel. "Ye dinnae wish to wed me yet hold to the betrothal."

"But I do wish to wed ye." He stepped closer to her and stroked her cheek with his knuckles.

His touch made her stomach knot, but she hid it. So too did she resist the impulse to pull away. It was a fairly innocent gesture, and she had no real reason to resist it. She suspected that to do so would make him very angry. Nevertheless, it troubled her to have him so close, to have that cold, emotionless gaze fixed so steadily upon her face.

What she had to do was convince him that he did not want to marry her. She also had to convince him that she had no wish and no intention of wedding him without insulting him and provoking his anger. Recognizing that her own temper was only loosely reined, she decided that it was going to be very difficult to do either.

"'Tis not necessary to tie yourself to a lass ye dinnae really want for a promise made to a dead man."

"Did I not just say that I wish to wed ye?" He stroked her neck.

"But why? I ken weel that there is much about me that ye dinnae like."

"Because ye are a lovely whore—just like your mother."

She slapped his hand away. "My mother was no whore."

"Aye, she was. She wasted her beauty upon that fool Lachlan. I could have given her youth and an equal beauty. We would have been a pairing to make the world sick with envy."

"And what do ye ken of my mother?"

"Enough. Ye are just like her. Aye, just like her. Ye too could have had me but ye turned to that whoreson MacGuin, turned to him and made me look the fool."

Each step he took nearer to her, she retreated in kind. There was something fearfully unsettling about the way he talked. Aimil sensed that he did not really see her or, at least, see her as Aimil Mengue. What really troubled her was all this talk about her mother. She had not realized that Rory had even known the woman.

"I was a captive, a prisoner for ransom."

"Ye were Parlan MacGuin's lover, his whore. All these months ye have wallowed in the mud with him." His hand darted forward and he grasped her tightly by the throat. "Ye have soiled yourself, cast away whatever honor ye had between his sheets."

Desperately Aimil tried to ease his grip, a grip so tight it was cutting off her air. She tried to pry his fingers loose, but they were like bands of steel. He seemed oblivious to the way her long nails scored his skin. Aimil suddenly realized that she was the captive of a madman. In thinking he would not kill her, she had made a serious error in judgment.

"Here now, ye dinnae want to kill the lass."

The breath-robbing grip on her throat was suddenly eased, and Aimil fell to her knees. As she massaged her bruised neck and gasped for air, she looked to see who had saved her. Her brief hope that it might be someone she could make an appeal to quickly died. She recognized the burly, sour-faced man calming Rory. Geordie would help no one save for Rory and perhaps himself. She could only think that Geordie had decided that killing her now was not good for Rory. The man did not act out of mercy.

Seeing that Geordie had left the door open, she glanced at the two men. They seemed too engrossed in their whispers to notice her. Cautiously, careful not to make a sound, she edged toward the door.

Suddenly, Geordie moved with a speed that was awe-inspiring. He slammed the door and latched it securely. Then he looked down at her with an expression that, in any other man, would be seen as pity, but Aimil doubted that Geordie suffered from that weakness. He had been Rory's faithful hound for too long.

"Ye arenae going anywhere, lass. Ye will set right here 'til Master Rory says otherwise."

"Then ye will be a party to my murder."

"Oh, he isnae going to murder ye. Not yet, leastwise. Ye need to be alive for the wedding."

"Then let us not waste time. He may as weel kill me now for I will never wed him."

"I shouldnae be so sure, Mistress Mengue. Our Rory has a way with the lasses, a way to turn 'em to his hand, ye might say. I would be verra surprised if he cannae change your way of thinking."

Before she could reply, she was painfully yanked to her feet. As she watched Rory's fist hurtle toward her face, she saw his expression. Now she knew what made him smile and she had been right. It was not something she had really wanted to know. Rory Fergueson found joy in inflicting pain.

His blow sent her flying back against the bed. Although groggy and one eye blinded by the pain of his blow, she managed to elude him when he grabbed for her again. While Geordie did nothing to help her, she was relieved that he was not going to assist Rory either. Twice more she eluded Rory before he landed another punch that sent her reeling.

She knew she was no match for Rory, but she refused to give up. However, when she tried to gain hold of something to use as a weapon, Geordie was there to stop her. Finally she grew too weak to break free then try to evade Rory. He delivered a blow that sent her slamming into the wall. As blackness overtook her, she wondered if Geordie had misjudged matters for, if Rory kept at her, she was sure she would never survive the night.

Rory stood over her supine body and watched as Geordie checked her over. "Dead?"

"Nay, she be a strong lass. Ye best temper your hand some though if ye mean to wed her before ye kill her."

"I have learned that lesson, Geordie. Ye dinnae need to keep carping on it. Get those cursed clothes off her and tie her to the bed post."

Even as he did as he was ordered, Geordie said, "Mayhaps ye ought to let her recover a wee bit."

"She needs her spirit broken, Geordie, and swiftly. I must have her wed to me before she is rescued or her kin comes after her." He watched closely as Geordie undressed the unconscious Aimil. "She is as fine a piece as her cursed mother ever was. We shall have us a fine time with her."

"Now?" Geordie lashed her hands to the bed posts.

"Nay, let her fash herself over it. She will suspect it, and the wondering about when it might happen will sorely torment her. First she must be punished for letting the Black Parlan between her thighs. Fetch my whip. The wee one. As ye say, I cannae let her die on me yet. There is a wedding she must attend. Move quickly. I want it in my hand before she wakes."

Aimil cursed as she awoke. The pain she felt reminded her where she was and what was happening to her. The last thing she wanted was to return to consciousness. There was some measure of safety in unconsciousness only because, if Rory continued to abuse her, she would be unaware. Awake, she would know all too well the pain he dealt her.

A coolness on her body made her frown then gasp in shock. One horrified glance at her body confirmed her suspicion that she was naked. When she instinctively moved to try and cover her nakedness with her hands, she received another shock. She looked up at her hands in stunned disbelief to see that her wrists were securely bound to the bed post at the foot of the bed. A brief frantic struggle to free her wrists was abruptly stopped when she heard a soft chuckle. At that moment, Rory moved to stand before her.

"I wouldnae waste what strength ye have left, my sweet whore. Geordie ties a fine secure knot."

She forced herself not to look at the small whip he idly slapped against his leg. "Ye will surely die for this, Rory Fergueson."

"Shall I? And who shall be your avenger? Your dear father? He cannae even bear to look at ye. The gallant Leith mayhaps? He is still a child and, if your father doesnae stop him from taking up a sword against me, I shall cut him down with ease. Your lover, that whoreson the Black Parlan, mayhaps? I think not. He is most likely dead."

"Nay, t'wasnae a fatal wound." She tried not to let his words weaken her, refused to listen to the part of her that agreed with him.

"Come, my pretty slut. He had an arrow pierce his thigh. Even a child such as ye has seen enough of war to ken the danger of such a wound. They bleed so freely and, ofttimes, naught can stem the flow." He shrugged. "And if he lives? What matter? Why should he trouble himself with ye? He has whores aplenty to choose from. He is careful with the lives of his men and willnae risk them simply to return some Lowland slut to his bed. Nay, no matter how good ye were, and ye were good, were ye not? Aye, ye must have been for the Black Parlan to keep ye in his bed for so long. Ye shall have to show me all he taught ye but not yet. Nay, not just yet. As your betrothed and master in the eyes of the law, I have decided to punish ye for your whorish ways."

He struck so swiftly that she was barely able to stifle her cry. She braced herself for the second bite of the lash, but it did not come. Instead, he stood staring at her back. The way he held the whip, caressed it lovingly, chilled her.

"Ah, so like your mother," he murmured, touching the

mark upon her back. "So like Kirstie. Her skin turned livid at the merest violent touch as weel. It took so verra little to bring forth the colors of pain. She too had to be punished for her whorish ways, but I punished her too virulently. She died. Howbeit, I do learn from my errors. Ye will live for a verra long time."

His murmured words, the talk of violence and death sounding like idle chatter, made her blood run cold but also confused her. "My mother died from a sickness caught on childbed."

"Aye, so your father said. He was too weak, too soft of heart to tell ye the truth. I believe 'tis past time that ye kenned it. Aye, t'will aid ye to understand what ye must do, to see the wisdom of bending to my will."

"Ye will never be my master, Rory Fergueson."

"Just as stubborn and foolish as Kirstie but ye will learn. She died defying me, but ye will live long enough to bend. She too scorned me. She too refused to wed me, and I was too young to see what I had to do in time to stop her from wedding another." He grasped her painfully by the chin and brought his face close to hers. "I waited years for ye to finish growing, to finish becoming like your mother, as I kenned ye would from the moment ye came squalling into this world. I have waited years to correct the mistakes I made with Kirstie. Although I have lost the chance to spill your virgin's blood, I can still make ye crawl to me. I will have ye begging my forgiveness for spreading your thighs for Parlan MacGuin."

"Nay. I will spread my legs for every pox-ridden beggar in Scotland before I would do that." She spat in his face.

That enraged him and soon she almost regretted her defiance. It took Geordie's interference to bring him back under control. From the curses and furious words Rory had spat at her, she realized she was acting so much like her mother that he was becoming confused, his twisted mind blending the past with the present.

So too did she finally believe that he had murdered her mother, that her father had lied to them all. What she wished she knew was whether her father knew who was guilty, if he had knowingly promised her to the man whose hands were stained with her mother's blood.

She was sure, however, that she did not want to hear any more about how Rory had killed her mother. While a small part of her demanded the truth, a greater part of herself knew that the truth might well be far more than she could bear. Rory, though, seemed intent upon confession. She suspected that he, knowing how hearing the tale would torment her, was using it as yet another means of inflicting pain, one as expedient and successful as his whip. It simply left no marks upon her body.

"Ah, Geordie, she tries to drive me past reason just as Kirstie did." Again he grasped her by the chin and forced her to look at him, but he did not draw near enough for her to be able to spit upon him again. "Ye think to escape me by dying but ye willnae. Nay, ye willnae die until I am ready to let ye. I did too much too quickly with Kirstie. I shall pace myself with ye. First the punishment then the possession. I think ye should hear about how I possessed your mother, my sweet whore. T'will do ye good to ken what lies ahead. Mayhaps t'will make ye see the wisdom of giving up this defiance, this contrariness, all the sooner. The first thing ye must do is to agree to our marriage."

"I would rather become the bride of Satan himself and spend my wedding night amongst hell's tormented souls."

Aimil began to think that she would make that wish come true if she agreed to wed Rory. If he was not the Devil himself, he was surely one of Satan's closest minions. With each stroke of the lash, Rory revealed another sickening detail of the murder of her mother. Inwardly, she wept bitter tears. Nothing her mother could have ever done had warranted such a horrible fate. Aimil began to think that even Satan would balk at accepting such an evil, twisted soul as Rory's.

She struggled against letting her pain, fear, and grief weaken her spirit. Thinking about how she must live to tell the truth about Rory helped. Someone had to see that he paid dearly for the vicious murder of her mother, and she was the only one, besides Geordie, who knew of his guilt, the only one who could see that he was brought to justice. That thought alone kept her spirit strong.

Finally Geordie stopped Rory. Geordie was, Aimil realized, the only rein upon Rory's madness. Without Geordie, Rory's evil would undoubtedly have come to light a long time ago. She deemed him as guilty as Rory, his calloused hands as soaked in blood as his master's. By helping Rory to hide his sickness, Geordie had undoubtedly insured more deaths than she cared to think upon. As she waited for the merciful oblivion of unconsciousness, she listened to the two men talk, their voices distorted as they came to her through ears ringing with pain.

"She will need to rest some before ye set upon her again, or ye will be killing this one too quickly as weel."

"And that I must never do. I will have from her what I couldnae gain from her mother. I have waited too long for it to lose it now." Rory grasped Aimil by the chin and shook her head until she opened her eyes a bit to glare at him. "Aye, ye curse me just as she did. She damned me as she lay there dying. She told me that if I hurt ye the Devil would rise up and drag me into hell. Weel? Where is he?"

"He will come for you yet, Rory Fergueson, though I am thinking even he will find ye too foul." She closed her eyes again, refusing to look into his soulless eyes.

"I dinnae think t'was wise to tell her about her mother. What if she tells someone?"

"She willnae."

"How can ye be so certain of that?"

"Because soon she willnae have the strength nor the will to betray me. I will break this lass. Soon, aye, soon, she will crawl to me and think only of what she can do to please me."

"And then what will ye do to her?"

As Aimil finally sank into blackness, she heard Rory softly reply, "I will let her die and with her will go the truth about Kirstie Mengue's death."

Chapter Fifteen

Aimil woke to more pain than she thought any body should have to bear. If this was to be her treatment at Rory's hands, she knew she would not last long. That he had not yet raped her seemed small consolation. One more hurt would hardly have mattered.

Through her swollen eyes, she saw the door open. If Rory tried to beat her anymore, she knew he would kill her. Panic seized her, but she was unable to move her battered body. Instead of Rory, it was a buxom, young maid and Aimil's terror receded. For now, at least, she would have a respite from that madman's attentions.

"Who are ye?" she rasped as the young woman set a bowl of water down on the table near the bed.

"Maggie. He did ye weel, didnae he? I am here to try and mend ye."

"So that he may have at me again?" She grit her teeth against a scream when the girl began to wash her back.

"Aye. He wants ye to last awhile yet."

Noticing the faintly discolored skin around Maggie's eyes, Aimil said, "He has had at ye as weel."

"There isnae a wench here that hasnae been done. He is a madman, a bastard."

Hearing the hate in Maggie's voice, Aimil sensed a possible ally and asked, "Help me?"

"I can give ye a potion that will take ye out of his hands."

"Nay, I dinnae mean that." Aimil was shocked that the girl would offer something so cowardly and sinful. "Help me escape."

"I will be slain the instant 'tis found that ye are gone."

"Then come with me. Black Parlan or my family will take ye in gladly if ye aid me." She saw that the young woman was pondering the move, knew that such an offer would be a sore temptation for the girl. "He will kill me if I stay here. 'Tis my life I am asking of ye, my life ye will save."

"Nay doubt he will kill me soon as weel. His sort of loving does that. I could be saving me own life, too."

"Will ye help me then?"

"Aye, I be willing since ye offer what I have always lacked, a place to go, but I dinnae ken how."

"If I can get into the bailey, can ye get us out without us being spotted?"

"That isnae any trouble. 'Tis the getting out of this room that will be difficult."

"Nay, it willnae. Just get me a sturdy rope to reach the court below this window."

"Ye mean to go out the windy? Ye are daft," Maggie gasped, her hazel eyes wide.

Although she was unable to change Maggie's attitude concerning the sanity of such a venture, Aimil was finally able to get the girl to fetch what was needed. Aimil tried not to think of how weak she was now. Knowing what faced her if she stayed had to be enough to give her the strength to escape. If she was to die, she would much rather do it in an attempt to save herself than in cowering beneath the blows of a madman.

As she rested, trying to recoup the strength the beating had stolen from her, she thought on Maggie. The girl was young and very attractive with her chestnut curls and large hazel eyes. It was no surprise that Rory had taken notice of her. All Aimil could hope was that the girl was as sincere as she was pretty, that her hatred of Rory was real. A betrayal now would cost Aimil dearly.

When Maggie crept back into the room with a set of clothes and a rope concealed under her voluminous skirts, Aimil felt almost guilty about her lack of trust. The girl watched in amazed admiration as Aimil dressed in lad's clothing without a blink and then secured the rope. It was quite possible, Aimil mused, that the girl was thinking that all the gentry were at least slightly mad.

"Where is Rory?" Aimil asked as she tested the knot she had made.

"Drinking in the hall. He willnae be moving this night."

"That is one thing in our favor then. T'will be a long while before he knows that we are gone." She straddled the window ledge. "Weel, off ye go. I will meet ye below in but a moment." When Maggie frowned, she smiled reassuringly. "I have done this often. Dinnae fash yourself. If I do fall, better to die quickly this way than slowly by Rory's hand and giving him pleasure by doing so."

That made great sense to Maggie despite her continued opinion that to lower oneself out of a window so high from the ground was madness. "Shall I steal us a horse? I cannae ride but ye can, cannae ye?"

"Aye. If ye can, that would do us weel indeed but dinnae risk much for it, dinnae chance discovery."

After Maggie left, Aimil sent up a brief prayer that the girl would be successful in stealing a mount. Her pain sapped her strength. She knew they would both have a better chance of succeeding in their escape if she rode than if she tried to walk.

The climb down the wall was sheer agony. It seemed as if every muscle she used caused a fiery pain in her back. Her body trembled with the effort to remain conscious, her skin clammy with the sweat her efforts squeezed from her. She hardly gave a thought to the chances of being caught in her descent. All of her concentration was on reaching the ground. When she reached it, she collapsed there for a long while, afraid that what strength she had had was now used up. Her body shook and felt about as solid as water.

"Are ye all right, mistress?" hissed Maggie from where she lurked in the shadows. "Did ye fall? I got us a horse."

"Nay, I didnae fall." Aimil struggled to her feet, using the wall she had just descended as support. "I but collapsed with weakness for a wee while. Ye must help me onto the horse."

Maggie's strong arms proved more than adequate for that chore. She then led the horse out a side entrance in the outer wall. It was not until they reached the trees to the east of the Fergueson tower house that Maggie mounted with a great lack of skill and grace. By then Aimil had recovered enough to lend a hand and then take control of the reins.

"We are riding to the Highlands," ventured Maggie after a short while of riding.

"Aye. I go to the Black Parlan. Thinking on it, I realized that Rory would seek me at my kin's first. 'Tis closer."

"They be a fearsome lot I hear." A fear prompted by dark rumor could be heard in Maggie's voice.

"No more than any other, Maggie. On the border as we are, we are more akin to them than to Lowland folk."

"The Black Parlan roasts wee babes and picks his teeth with their wee bones," Maggie whispered tremulously.

Aimil giggled weakly. "Poor Parlan. Nay, Maggie, he does-nae. The man can look fearsome as the Devil but he has a gentleness in him. His men are beaten if they abuse a woman." She heard Maggie gasp softly in disbelief. "He doesnae hold with the brutal handling of the weaker such as children and women. Trust me, I have been as close to the man as any, and ye will find no cruelty at Dubhglenn. Now, heed me weel. I will tell ye how to handle the horse. I am verra weak, and ye may yet need to take the reins before we reach Dubhglenn. We dinnae want to lose after having come so far because I faint and ye cannae prod the horse onwards."

To Aimil's relief, Maggie revealed a natural aptitude for horse-riding that with training could become an admirable skill. So too was the horse a gentle, easily-ruled beast. Maggie could manage nothing too intricate, but she could get them to Dubhglenn if the need arose. It took a great weight from Aimil's abused shoulders.

The need for Maggie to take over came far sooner than Aimil would have liked. By the time the sun rose, Aimil's eyes had swollen shut, her head swam with exhaustion, and her stomach churned. At Maggie's urging, they dismounted for a while. Aimil promptly emptied her stomach, then her bladder, and then passed out. She awoke to a cool cloth across her eyes and to the sure knowledge that many hours had passed, hours they had not had to lose. Groaning, she sat up slowly, finding that she still could not see.

"Ye should have tossed me over the saddle and kept riding, Maggie," she said weakly but with no real censure in her voice.

"Ye needed to rest, mistress. I had hoped that your eyes would get better but they havenae. They are still swelled tight shut."

"Aye, using them all the night has finished what Rory started. I can see but a slight line of light and that hurts. Where is the sun?"

"Straight overhead, mistress. Is it far yet that we must travel?"

"T'will be dark before we near the place if we ride without

ceasing at a walk as we have been. Rory will ken I have slipped away by now."

"Mayhaps. T'will depend upon how urgent the one who discovers your escape feels it is. The laird isnae one ye like to wake. Nay, especially not with news ye ken weel he doesnae want to hear."

"Let us pray that the one who discovers us gone is a thorough coward then. We must ride east. Help me onto the horse."

"Ye had best stay before me on the beast. T'will be easier to catch ye if ye feel weak again."

Even getting up on the back of the horse drained Aimil but she fought it. It was a relief, however, to feel Maggie's strong, young body behind her, her arms reaching around so that she could take the reins and acting as a secure cage. Falling from the horse would surely finish her, Aimil mused.

"I would give my father's fortune to ken who betrayed us," Aimil muttered as they started out.

"T'was a woman," Maggie replied. "I saw her. Aye, and heard her tell Rory how to find ye."

"Who was it? What was her name?" Aimil had a very good idea who it was but fearing jealousy tempered her view wanted it confirmed.

"I didnae hear the name but I can tell ye of her looks. She was lovely with rich brown hair. Said she wanted ye out of the Black Parlan's bed so that she could crawl back into it. She was staying at Dubhglenn. Felt that once ye were gone she could have the man."

"Catarine. It could be no other. Nay doubt the bitch is nursing Parlan's wound so that she can then nurse something else."

Catarine decided that she was not receiving the gratitude that she felt she deserved for her tender ministrations to the

Black Parlan's leg. Between the Black Parlan's rage at being wounded and having lost Aimil and Old Meg's constant interference, Catarine was very near to losing her facade of gentle, patient nurse. Only the thought of what Aimil would be suffering at the hands of Rory Fergueson kept Catarine in a good humor. She felt certain that Rory would put the girl firmly in her place if he did not kill her first. After savoring that vision for a moment, she turned her attention back to a foul-tempered Parlan.

Twice Parlan had risen from his bed only to set the wound in his leg to bleeding freely again. Common sense and the threat of being bound and drugged finally held him to his bed. It was hell to lie there knowing what might be happening to Aimil, and he made life miserable for all those around him, his sense of helpless fury causing him to lash out at all who ventured near.

"Railing at friend and kin willnae help the lass at all," snapped Old Meg as she dressed his wound after curtly ordering Catarine from the room so that she and Parlan were alone.

Parlan sighed. "I am sorry, Meg. 'Tis just that I ken weel how the bastard can hurt her but I am stuck here abed, helpless."

"Send your men out. Malcolm and Lagan can plot and plan near as weel as ye. Aye, ye can plot as weel. Your head and mouth work just fine."

"I should go. 'Tis I that gain if she returns."

"That docsnac matter to your men. They will gladly take up sword against a Fergueson nay matter what the cause."

"Ye are right, as always. I must swallow my pride and let others fight for me. Fetch me Lagan. Aye, and Leith if the lad still lingers here. 'Tis past time to fetch Aimil back."

* * *

A force left Dubhglenn riding hard for Fergueson land but a few hours later, aiming to arrive under the cover of nightfall. Volunteers for the venture had been so numerous that some had had to be turned away. Leith rode between Malcolm and Lagan, smiling grimly as he wondered what his father would think about his joining a MacGuin raid. He found that he cared little about that. Aimil was far more important to him than his father's approval. He only hoped that they had not waited too long.

Maggie sat staring sadly at the girl upon the ground. She was surprised that they had gotten as far as they had. For a while after Aimil had fallen unconscious, Maggie had continued to ride. Aimil's dead weight had become too much, however, forcing her to stop.

She had dressed Aimil's injuries then sat down to wait for the girl to wake. There was nothing else she could do. She could not go home, did not even want to. Neither could she move on, leaving Aimil behind. Her future, if there was one, was tied to the girl lying at her side.

When she heard the horses, Maggie's first thought was to run away. Then she realized that the hoofbeats headed toward Fergueson land. Keeping to the shadowy cover of the trees, she moved closer to the path they rode. When she recognized the colors the men wore as those of the MacGuin clan, she leapt from her cover, waving her arms, and shouting without thought of danger to herself.

There was a moment's hectic confusion as the force of hard-riding men reined to an abrupt halt then Malcolm dismounted, bellowing, "What are ye about, ye fool lass? We near raced over ye. Have ye nae an ounce of sense in your wee head?"

"Ye are from Dubhglenn? Ye are MacGuin men?" she asked urgently.

"Aye," replied Lagan. "Who are ye?"

"Maggie Robinson. Ye neednae ride any further. I have what ye seek, I be thinking. Aimil Mengue?"

"Where?" Leith was dismounted and at her side in an instant.

"Through here." Maggie adroitly avoided the men as she led them to Aimil, Rory's attentions having left her terrified of a man's touch.

"Oh, my sweet God," groaned Leith as he fell to his knees by Aimil's side, followed by Malcolm and Lagan. "Did he rape her as weel?"

"Nay. I dinnae ken why unless he meant to fash her by making her wait for it to happen. He is a madman."

"Och, the poor wee lassie," Malcolm mourned, his light brown eyes awash with tears.

"Dinnae touch her back," Maggie warned when Malcolm moved to pick Aimil up. "She be sore beaten there."

As a way to carry Aimil with the least pain to her was sorted out, Maggie told how they had escaped Rory. She never mentioned Aimil's promise of a place but was given the same promise by the men who fretted over the unconscious girl. With those assurances warming her, Maggie remounted her horse with equanimity, politely refusing all offers to ride with one of the men.

Some of the MacGuin men stayed behind as the rest began the return to Dubhglenn. Those who remained would check to see if any Fergusons trailed the women and, if they did, that they got no further.

The trip back to Dubhglenn was taken easily in deference to Aimil's injuries. None wanted to cause her any more pain than they knew she must already be suffering. They ached to avenge her but knew it was more important to get her to the care and safety of Dubhglenn. So too did they know that Parlan would wish the pleasure of seeking vengeance.

"Malcolm, that lass is falling behind again. See if ye cannae get her to ride with one of us," said Lagan after a while.

Aimil, waking to find herself in Leith's arms, heard the order and said, "She willnae. She cannae bear the touch of a man."

"Aye, I could see the fading bruises." Malcolm's square face darkened with anger. "Fergueson's had at the poor lass." He started to turn back toward the faltering Maggie. "I will take her reins. T'will be enough to keep her with us."

"How do ye feel, Aimil?" Leith asked, each look at her battered face increasing his hatred of Rory Fergueson.

"Like the verra Devil." She sighed. "I wouldnae have made it as far as I did without Maggie's aid. We must find a place for her."

"We will, m'eudail. Never fear of that. I ken by looking at ye that I owe her your life."

"How fares Parlan?"

"Weel," replied Lagan, "now that we have threatened him into staying in bed. He sore ached to ride with us."

A little smile touched her bruised mouth. She could just picture Parlan tied to his bed by his wound and making life a misery for all. As the blackness overtook her again, she recalled that there was something she needed to tell Leith, but it would have to wait.

Parlan's roar could easily be heard even before the raiding party had entered the tower house. He had heard the men returning far earlier than they should have and was anxious to know why. Catarine's pleas for him to lie still earned her only curses. She wished she had obeyed her desire to leave when the men entered with Malcolm carefully carrying the girl Catarine had thought dead.

Maggie espied Catarine trying to slip out of the room. "'Tis her. 'Tis the one who told Rory where to find mistress Aimil."

Catarine fled, and Lagan moved to pursue her, but Parlan stayed him. "She willnae show her lying face about here again or elsewhere we go to. She willnae dare. She will be in fear for what remains of her natural life. So too will her treachery become weel known thus closing many a door to her. 'Tis enough. Tell me what happened."

Maggie was urged to retell her story as Old Meg tended to Aimil who was placed beside Parlan in his huge bed at his insistence. His dark gaze never left Aimil as Maggie spoke. The extent of the beating Aimil had endured became evident as Old Meg stripped her. Even though he was filled with a blind rage against Rory Fergueson, Parlan felt like joining young Leith in weeping over his sister's injuries.

"Poor, poor wee lassie," Old Meg crooned then fixed her keen gaze upon Parlan. "Could have been worse. She could have lost the bairn."

"What?" Parlan's question was but a soft croak in the silence of the room.

"The bairn, ye great gowk. Ye certainly have been working at one hard enough. 'Tis weel past time, too."

"Aimil carries my child?" His stunned gaze was fixed upon Aimil's slim waist, the covers drawn up only to her hips.

"Aye. 'Tis time ye stopped tossing good seed to the four winds. I ken what ye planted at the verra first took root or near to. She will be rounding before long now. 'Tis set in there good and tight. Fergueson couldnae shake this fruit from the tree for all he tried to."

"Why did she tell me naught?" Parlan's unsteady hand brushed the hair from Aimil's bruised face.

"I dinnae think she kenned it," spoke up Maggie. "She was sick a time or twa, and I guessed it, but she thought t'was from the beating. I noted a thing or twa whilst I tended to her as weel. Nay, I be fair certain that she doesnae ken it."

"Ye must wed her now," said Leith. "Ransom be damned."

"Aye, I must wed her. Recall that I had set my mind to it before Rory took her." Leith nodded and Parlan's big hands suddenly clenched into fists. "I wish to God that I could kill that bastard Fergueson more than once. By faith, he will beg for death before I finish with him."

Aimil heard that familiar, if muted, roar through the receding haze of unconsciousness and was comforted by it despite how the voice trembled with fury. "Parlan?"

He caught the small hand that reached out to him. "Aye, little one. Ye are safe at Dubhglenn now. Tucked up in my bed again."

"T'was Catarine, Parlan. She betrayed ye."

"Aye, we ken that now. She will never give us any further trouble. The bitch will keep herself weel out of sight."

She nodded wishing that she could see him. "Are ye still angry about the trick I played on ye? He would have killed ye."

"Aye, he would have for all he promised Catarine he wouldnae. Nay, I am not angry though 'tis furious I was at the time."

She managed a little smile. "I didnae think he would try to kill me so it seemed the thing to do at the time."

"Aye. I should have told ye about him, but I didnae want to frighten ye and I thought ye safe here." He looked at Lagan and Malcolm. "I can hear the other men returning. See if there was any incident. Old Meg, show Maggie to a room."

"Humph," Old Meg grumbled as she ushered Maggie out of the room, "sitting in that lewd bed, barking out orders like some king."

"Is Leith still here?"

"Right here, Aimil." Leith immediately turned from leaving and returned to her side.

"I must speak to Papa." She shivered as she recalled the tales Rory had related as he had beaten her.

"Aye, Leith," growled Parlan, "fetch your father. Best he sees how the man he chose to wed Aimil treats a lass." He shook his head. "Here is the proof we sought of the man's madness though I wish to God it hadnae come into our hands this way."

Leith was gone before Aimil could say anymore. He was anxious to show his father that the dark, whispered tales about Rory Fergueson were not rumors. There would be no wedding now. Even Lachlan Mengue could not send his daughter to such a man.

"Aimil? Did he rape ye?" Parlan asked, realizing that no one had mentioned that and he feared the worst.

"Nay, Parlan. He kenned that, for all my brave talk, I feared that, and he planned to torture me by nae letting me ken when he would do it."

"It wouldnae have mattered to me save that it would be one more hurt to make him pay for." He lightly traced her bruised cheek. "He will pay for each and every bruise he put on ye. I swear to it."

"He isnae one to fight fair, Parlan. Ye mustnae think he will face ye square like an honorable man."

"Och, I ken that weel enough. Fear not for me, little one. I have fought snakes like Rory Fergueson before. I ken their ways weel."

"Dinnae go," she cried when he tried to draw his hand from her grasp.

"Now where would I be going with a great hole in my leg?" he teased gently. "Ye rest, Aimil. 'Tis the surest cure."

"I cannae seem to do aught else," she murmured even as blackness yet again embraced her.

While she slept, he studied her closely. It seemed a miracle that she was still alive let alone had been able to get free of her prison. Carefully, so as not to touch any of her wounds, he ran his fingers over her waist, tracing the side of the area that held his growing seed. So too was it a miracle that all she had been through had not robbed them of that precious gift. Their child clung to life with all the stubbornness his or her parents had. If Rory had known of the child or had held Aimil any longer, Parlan was sure the child would have been lost.

"Is it right for her to sleep so often, Meg?" he asked when the old woman returned with a cold meal for both of them.

"'Tis a natural sleep," she reported after a careful look at Aimil. "'Tis the wee lass's way of healing. The bairn could have a wee bit to do with it."

"Ye mean 'tis hurt in some way? I thought ye said the bairn was fine." Parlan wondered how he could panic so over a creature he had not even known existed until only a few hours ago.

Old Meg rolled her eyes in disgust. "Keep still. 'Tis natural for a woman to sleep a fair bit at the start." She set a plate of bread and meat before him and pushed a tankard of ale into his hand. "Eat up, laddie. I think ye will need your strength."

"'Tisnae a matter of jest," he grumbled. "Do ye think she will be all right? Such a wee lass to be beaten so badly."

"Aye, she will be fine and bear ye a bonnie bairn. The lass is a wee one, but there is steel in her bone and sinew. This has lain her low for now, and there will be a scar or twa upon her fair back, but she will be hale before too long. That be when ye will have a great deal of trouble."

Parlan chuckled. "Aye, keeping her from carrying on as ever. And what do ye think of my choice of wife?"

"As if ye care what this old woman thinks. Aye, but I will tell ye despite that. She be a good lass and she willnae cower before your every scowl. Ye couldnae abide a weak woman.

More important, she has the approval of your people. They have all asked after the lass, fashing themselves over her."

That left Parlan feeling quite content. He did not let his clan rule his life to the extent where they could choose his wife, but their approval of Aimil meant a lot. It would, if nothing else, make life much easier for her. She would have no trouble finding a place for herself at Dubhglenn.

Lying beside her, lightly holding her hand, Parlan contemplated the step he planned to take. With marriage and fatherhood staring him in the face, he was surprised to feel no qualms. He was, in fact, quite content. It seemed natural to picture the future with Aimil in each scene.

Aimil stirred restlessly, reliving the recent horror of being Rory's captive in her dreams and calling out fretfully, "Parlan! Parlan, where are ye?"

He spent several moments easing her fright with murmured words of reassurance that finally penetrated to her sleeping mind then, glaring at the ceiling, hissed, "Ye will pay for putting the darkness in her dreams, Rory Fergueson. I swear it. Ye will pay dearly."

Chapter Sixteen

A grin broke out upon Lagan's face as he entered Parlan's chambers. The two invalids were playing dice, and Parlan's grumbling told him that Aimil's good luck at the game was holding true. He then recalled what he was there to announce and frowned slightly.

"Lachlan Mengue is in the hall and ready to see Aimil."

Parlan saw Aimil shiver as the shadow he had seen several times before passed over her face again. He had wondered what troubled her but, with uncharacteristic patience, had held off asking her about it. That it would be revealed in time had been enough to restrain him.

"Weel, send the man up. Ye best disarm him." Parlan propped himself up on his pillow to await the visitor.

"Ye arenae intending to stay here, are ye?" Aimil gasped as a chuckling Lagan left and Parlan gave no indication that he would also leave or even get dressed.

"'Tis my bed and do ye forget that I am sorely wounded? My leg, ye recall."

"As if I could forget that tree stump. Parlan, ye cannae stay here. What will my father think?"

"That we are twa invalids sharing a bed so as to ease the work of our nurses?"

She thought his innocent look far too overdone. "Ye ken verra weel what he will think when he sees us abed together and naked."

"Aye, he might think that especially"—he lifted the covers and peered beneath them—"if he catches a glimpse of this poor fellow what's a mere shadow of his former mighty self."

Aimil could not resist a peek and rolled her eyes. "Some shadow. 'Tis plain to see that your wound hasnae dimmed your appetite."

"I begin to think that my appetite for ye will never be dimmed."

Her gaze flew to his and widened slightly for there was no twinkle in his eyes. His obsidian eyes were warm and serious. As she was about to inquire just how serious he was, a choking sound reached her ears. She looked toward the door, and her eyes grew even wider but with horror as her gaze locked with her father's. Seeing how his face was turning a choleric red, she buried her face in the pillow with a soft moan. It was cowardly but she could not help herself.

"I ken now why I was disarmed," Lachlan bellowed, his hands curling into fists. "Ye bastard! Ye swore ye wouldnae harm her."

"I havenae, have I, Aimil?" Parlan asked, his voice soft as he ran his hand through her hair.

"Then ye deal in a rough wooing, ye bastard," Lachlan snarled as he neared the bed.

"Papa," Aimil gasped, forgetting her cowardice and looking at her father, suddenly realizing that his fury had not been due to her place in Parlan's bed but her wounds. "These marks werenae made by Parlan." Without thought, her hand sought Parlan's in a gesture meant to soothe the sting of her father's assumptions. "T'was Rory Fergueson who left me so."

Lachlan's expression changed with alarming speed from anger to a fearful disbelief. He moved to Aimil's side of the bed. Leith, who had arrived with him and Lagan, hastily produced a chair. Lachlan sat down heavily, suddenly showing his age.

"Ye dinnae mean it, lass," he rasped, but his knowledge of her honesty weighted his words with doubt.

"I do. T'was Rory not Parlan. Parlan has never hurt me, never raised a hand against me even when he was in a fury spurred by my tongue which often runs too free and with a sharp edge." She swallowed nervously. "Papa, how did Mama die?"

Tensing at her soft question, Lachlan replied, "Birthing Shane, as I told ye."

His reaction made her fear that all Rory had told her was true. "Is that true or a tale to ease our pain for the truth would have been too great a horror for a child to bear?"

"What have ye heard, lassie, and who has told ye the tale?"

"Did ye not tell him what happened, Leith?"

"Nay, Aimil. It never occurred to me that he would think your wounds were delivered by Parlan. I thought to speak before he saw ye."

"I will tell that part, sweeting," Parlan said, his anger over Lachlan's assumption gone as he realized the man had made it due to a lack of information. "Save your strength for the telling of what has been troubling ye. I ken it will cost ye dearly to tell all that has made your dreams so dark and frightening."

In a voice that revealed his simmering fury, Parlan told of the treachery that had resulted in Aimil's capture by Rory. Parlan left out nothing including her rescue of him and then herself with Maggie's aid. By the time he had finished, it was clear that Lachlan shared his rage. Parlan mused that it would take Rory Fergueson a great deal of running to escape death.

"What is it that ye must tell me, lass?" Lachlan asked in a voice hoarse with anger at Rory.

"Rory Fergueson told me a tale of my mother's death that doesnae match yours," she answered quietly.

Rising slowly, Lachlan went to the window, turning his back to her, and clenching his fists at his side. "Tell me. Do ye remember it all?"

"I cannae forget. He told me as he beat me. With each stroke, he released another sickening detail. She was murdered."

"Aye," Lachlan murmured. "Go on, lass. Tell it all. Dinnae think to spare me."

"He said I would die in the same way, but t'would take longer for he kenned how to make the pain last now. I would survive long enough to give him the vengeance he felt his right. His revenge for her spurning of him."

Lachlan nodded heavily. "'Tis right so far. She did spurn him. I always felt I had wronged the man by taking her from him. That was foolish for he was five years younger than she, barely grown. T'was a lad's first love. She didnae return it."

"He seems to think she would have. He said he found her alone that day. She refused his offer of love, told him she loved only ye. He said he meant to change her mind, to show her how much more a man he was than ye." Aimil began to shiver, the tale Rory had tortured her with spilling from her lips uncontrollably.

By the end of her tale she was so choked with tears she found speech almost impossible. "She never stopped calling for ye, Papa. He told Mama that he would finish avenging himself upon me, for she was dying. He said she damned him with her dying breath, told him that if he hurt me the Devil would rise up and drag him into hell. He said he left her there, in the wood, dead and no longer beautiful."

Parlan held her face against his shoulder for she began to weep. His gaze rested upon Lachlan whose hands gripped the window frame and whose head was bent. He was sure that the man wept as well. Remembering the nightmare Aimil had suffered, Parlan wished he had heeded it more closely.

"Papa?" Leith rasped. "Is that the true tale? Did our mother die that way and not of a sickness of the birthing bed?"

"Aye," Lachlan answered in a choked voice, his back still to them. I couldnae tell ye, ye were all so young. T'was a tale that would have badly frightened a child. I never suspected Rory. He wept like a bairn at her burying. We never found the one who did it. He searched with us, didnae he?" He gave a shakey, harsh laugh. "Her slaughterer rode amongst us."

"Her killer was to wed her child come the summer," Leith cried out. "Ye were to hand her over to him like a sacrificial lamb."

"I didnae ken he had killed Kirstie." Lachlan finally turned to face his son. "God forgive me my blindness, I didnae ken that it was Rory."

"But ye were aware of all that has been said about the man."

"Many a man has a rumor spread about him, an evil word or twa said. I had no proof, son. T'was a marriage contracted at cradleside. My old friend, a man that was as a brother to me, asked for the match. Even as a bairn, Aimil bid fair to look as her mother did. He thought t'would soothe the hurt Rory had felt when Kirstie had chosen me.

"She did look like Kirstie," he continued softly, his gaze fixing upon Aimil, "even to her nature. When she walked in that night all gowned and budding, looking the woman she was becoming, I couldnae bear to look upon her. She was Kirstie reborn and this time Rory would have her."

"So ye have ignored her," Parlan said as he felt Aimil stiffen in his arms.

"Aye. T'was easiest. I kenned she didnae care for Rory even then. She could have turned me against my word so verra easily. I also thought t'would make it easier to give her up. T'would not be like losing Kirstie all over again." He looked at Parlan, his eyes narrowing as his mind began to take in the fact that his daughter shared the man's bed and both appeared to be naked. "When this rogue got his hands on her, I found myself hoping that Rory would break the betrothal. Many another man would have. I wouldnae break my word over rumors but they did haunt me."

"But he wouldnae withdraw," Parlan said, his voice cold.

"Nay. He said only that someone would pay if she were no longer a maid. I ken now that he meant for Aimil to pay." He reached out his hand to touch Aimil's hair lightly, hair exactly like that of the wife he had loved so dearly and had lost. "How much did he make ye pay?"

"He didnae rape me, Papa," she replied, looking at him with her mother's eyes. "He wanted me to fear and fash myself over when he would."

Looking at her delicate features, bruised and swollen by Rory Fergueson, Lachlan saw his wife as he had found her that day. The image still churned his stomach and tore at his soul. He felt like weeping knowing that he had nearly given the man another Kirstie to kill.

"I will clear all trace of the man from the face of this earth."

"Nae alone, Mengue. I have a debt or twa to extract from the bastard myself," Parlan growled. "My cousin's life for one. This," he nodded at Aimil, "for another."

"I am to ride against my wife's murderer with my daughter's debaucher at my side?"

Aimil stiffened, her swollen eye widening. "He didnae debauch me."

"Nay? Ye lie naked at his side, lassie."

She blushed deeply even as she puzzled over her father's apparent lack of anger. "I came here willingly."

"T'was him or Rory?"

"Weel, in a way, Papa. Actually, t'was me or Elfking. T'was a bargain." She prayed her father would not question it.

"That cursed horse," Lachlan drawled. "I kenned t'was a mistake to give him to ye, but I sought to ease the guilt I felt over the way I treated ye."

Parlan's eyes narrowed. He began to grow very suspicious of Lachlan Mengue. The man should be ablaze with righteous anger. Some demand or sword-rattling should occur under the circumstances. Instead, Lachlan looked calm and considering.

"I think I have been playing your game and not my own," he said quietly.

"Mayhaps our games merely collided." Lachlan made no attempt to deny Parlan's suspicions.

"Ye were that confident?"

"I was wed to one like her. Aye, that confident. Was I wrong to be so?"

"Nay. Ye have won the game." Parlan could not help but return the man's grin. "Do ye wish to finish playing?"

"Aye. Allow an old man his fun."

Confusion was a mild word for what she felt, Aimil decided, as she looked from Parlan to her father and back again. Even Leith and Lagan knew what was going on, judging by the grins on their faces. That it was something to do with her that caused their amusement was all Aimil was sure of and it irritated her. They were playing some male game and leaving her out of it. She scowled at them even as she continued to struggle at guessing what was going on.

"So ye gave him your innocence in exchange for your horse?"

"Aye, Papa." She tried to search his gaze for a clue to what game he was playing, but there was only amusement to be read there which was so unexpected that it left her even more confused.

"I think ye have paid more than the beast is worth."

Again she blushed furiously and stared at him helplessly, unable to think of any reply. The ones that did come to mind would tell Parlan far more than she wanted him to know. She had the sinking feeling that her father knew the state of her heart.

"Elfking's a verra fine mount," she said, and grimaced when her father smiled.

"I think the debt is now MacGuin's."

"Aye, Mengue, it is and I mean to pay it in full. T'will only be by a priest."

"My thoughts exactly. Handfast isnae firm enough."

"Papa," Aimil gasped, realizing that they spoke of marriage. "Ye cannae make the man wed me. I willnae stand for it."

Callously, if gently, Parlan pressed her face into the pillow so that she could not speak. "How soon can we find a priest?"

"As soon as it takes to bring him from my keep where he has suffered my hospitality for this past month," replied Lachlan.

"Ready for the wedding that was to take place between Aimil and Rory?" asked Parlan idly, not believing it for a moment.

"Of course," Lachlan replied smoothly, and started toward the door.

"I ask a boon for this sacrifice I make." Parlan grinned at Aimil's clearly outraged, if muffled, squeal.

"And what is that?"

"That ye hold seeking revenge against Rory Fergueson until I can ride at your side."

"Agreed. Coming, Leith?"

"The old rogue," Parlan murmured with admiration after Lachlan and Leith had left.

Released from the silencing folds of the pillow, Aimil snapped, "Ye didnae let me have my say."

"Nay. 'Tis a matter between men, lassie. Now that your father has seen what a beast parades as Rory Fergueson ye are left no maid and with no husband. Ye came to my bed a virgin, and he calls upon my sense of honor to see things set right."

She consigned his honor to a dark and uncomfortable place. When he simply chuckled and kissed her forehead, she cursed and turned her face into the pillow. To talk a man like Parlan out of what he saw as the honorable thing to do was impossible, but she struggled to think of a way to do it. She wanted to be his wife but not for honor's sake. It was his heart she ached for, his love, not simply his good name.

"Come, Lagan, help me up. I must test this leg. I willnae take my vows before a priest whilst on my back."

Startled out of her sulk by her concern for him, she cried, "Ye will open the wound, ye great ox."

Gritting his teeth as Lagan helped him stand, he said, "I willnae push it that far, sweeting. Walk me to my dressing room, Lagan. Even if I must be in bed when I marry, I will be dressed fine. I will send Old Meg to ye, lass. Ye too will be done up as fine as possible." He frowned and glanced at her back. "There must be something ye can don that willnae hurt your back."

By the time he reached the chair in his dressing chambers, Parlan was awash with sweat but his wound stayed closed. That showed him that, despite his weakness, he was on the mend. He collapsed into his chair and made quick work of the drink Lagan passed to him. When he saw Lagan frowning, he raised his brows in query.

"Some sweet words might have soothed her," Lagan offered quietly.

"When I give her sweet words, t'willnae be simply to soothe the lass. Let me see what clothes I possess."

Picking out the best of Parlan's attire and laying it on the bed, Lagan mused, "She wants a husband who cares for her."

"Ye think I dinnae? Aye, the black and silver will do verra nicely. I will have it freshened."

"Aye, I think ye do and mayhaps she suspects that ye do, but a woman needs words. She darenst guess at what her man feels. Can ye not give her a few?"

Parlan shrugged. "I willnae tell her sweet lies. When I speak love words, t'will be because I feel them. I dinnae now."

Recalling the man's frenzy when he thought Aimil lost to him, Lagan asked, "Are ye certain of that?"

"Nay, but when or if the words ever leave my lips, I will be. For now 'tis enough that I like and trust her."

"I wonder what Rory will do when he kens that ye have wed Aimil?"

"If he is wise, he has found a great hole, crawled into it, and pulled the earth over him. T'will do him no good though. As soon as I am weel, I will dig the adder out of his nest."

"He isnae sane, Parlan. Ye ken as weel as I that his sort willnae act as ye think they will."

"Aye, ye can never tell how a mad dog will jump. A watch must be kept on Aimil at all times. She is never to be left alone."

"'Tis wise. His madness is strongest there. 'Tis a strange thing. I wonder if his madness started with Lachlan's wife?"

"Nay, t'was simply unearthed. That he sees Aimil as her mother is the danger. She must never fall into his hands. She will never escape him a second time and with her would go our child. That she carries my child could make it worse if he kens it."

"Dinnae fash yourself. She will be watched. The lass willnae be able to turn round for the guard that will be set on her."

Aimil noticed her increased guard even before the priest arrived but, for the moment, had too many other concerns to be worried about it. She too wanted to be dressed and on her feet when she was wed. That she would be wed despite any objections she might have grew quickly evident. The marriage was going to be performed no matter what she said or wanted.

She could not even get anyone who mattered to heed her objections. Lagan, her brother, and her father all kept their distance. So did Parlan. Though he was still weak from his wound, he managed to disappear with remarkable speed any time she even thought of bringing up her objections. Her strange continual exhaustion helped every one of them in their avoidance of her.

The priest arrived and was made comfortable, but the wedding did not come about immediately. Parlan wanted all the paraphernalia that went with a chief's wedding or as much of it as could be organized at such short notice. Dubhglenn became a hive of activity as a grand feast was prepared, and word was sent to any who might take offense if not invited.

So too was the wedding delayed so that the bride and groom could heal enough to endure the festivities. Aimil watched her bruises fade and felt her back heal more each day. What she could not understand was why she continued to suffer from sickness and tiredness. The sickness came and went swiftly, but it worried her and she finally mentioned it to Old Meg.

"'Tis often the way of a woman who is with bairn," the old woman replied tartly, shaking her head over Aimil's apparent ignorance.

Aimil hated to do so but she knew she was revealing that she was far more ignorant than Old Meg hinted at as she asked, "What has that to do with me?"

"I told ye she didnae ken it," muttered Maggie, who sat working on Aimil's wedding dress, one with a loose bodice that would not irritate Aimil's rapidly healing back yet look as fashionable and lovely as possible. "Told ye all that from the verra start."

"Do ye mean to say that that great gowk hasnae told ye?" squawked Old Meg, her thin arms flailing like boney wings.

"Told me what?" asked Aimil in a weak voice for she was beginning to suspect exactly what ailed her.

"What all of Dubhglenn kens and then some. That ye carry the laird's bairn. Ye carry the heir we have all waited for."

"I am with child," Aimil repeated, her voice flat. "That is why he rushes to wed me. 'Tisnae all his honor but his need of an heir."

"Ye are a foolish lass. The laird kens weel how to keep from seeding a woman. He has nary a bastard that I ken of for all his wanton ways." Old Meg shook her grizzled head. "What do ye fash yourself about? Why does any man take a wife? To get a child. 'Tis the way of the world, lass. Ye cannae change it. Be glad ye have got yourself such a braw laddie with a brave heart and a full purse."

"I wouldnae care if his purse held naught and he were weak and sickly," Aimil snapped. "I want to be loved."

Old Meg shook her head again. "Ye are foolish. Few wives find themselves loved. Be thankful for what ye have. 'Tis a great deal."

She knew the old woman was right, but it did not make Aimil feel all that much better. Her heart and soul had been put into Parlan's large hands, and she wanted a little return for all she had given. Honor, strength, and wealth were indeed fine attributes in a husband, and Parlan had many other fine qualities as well, but she craved his love. It seemed the worst of calamities to be wed to a man she loved as much as life itself but who did not return her love. A lifetime of unrequited love seemed little to be happy about. Even a stern scolding about not indulging in useless self-pity did not really change her feelings about that.

"Aimil?" Maggie ventured carefully after Old Meg left the room. "Do ye wish to run away?"

Briefly Aimil contemplated such a move then shook her head. "Nay. Where would I go? I must wed Parlan."

"He isnae as fearsome as I had thought he would be for all he is so dark. Aye, even his eyes. Like black pools. He seems a good man."

"Oh, aye, he is, Maggie. 'Tis just that I love him but he doesnae love me. It could be a verra large problem, could give me a lot of pain."

"Mayhaps not." Maggie's gaze fell to Aimil's stomach. "Ye will feel the bairn soon. I long for a bairn, but it will never be."

"Maggie, it doesnae hurt," Aimil said gently. "The loving, I mean. With a good, kind, and gentle man, it can be verra fine indeed. A man like Malcolm?"

A blush suffused Maggie's face. Malcolm had been very attentive to her, and she had felt some lessening of her fears. Despite that, she still feared lovemaking, its possible good points overshadowed by Rory's brutal handling. He had left her badly scarred in her mind.

"I dinnae think I could bear it. I see Rory whenever Malcolm tries to kiss me, see him behind my eyelids."

"Then leave your eyes open and the candle lit. Dinnae let Malcolm's image ever leave your sight. Even once with him will cure your fears. I am verra sure of that. That is, if ye have a mind to and 'tis marriage Malcolm offers."

"Aye, 'tis wedding me he wants, but I feared to fail him as a wife." Maggie's eyes were wide as she reviewed Aimil's advice, and her hopes rose. "May I go now?" Aimil nodded, and Maggie raced from the room in the hope of finding Malcolm before her courage failed her.

"Weel, that may be one problem sorted out but 'tis little done for me." Aimil sighed as she struggled to sit up.

"Here, sweeting, let me help you," said a deep voice that had lately been absent from the room. Parlan came to her bedside. Aimil stared at her husband-to-be as he helped her, his gaze studying the loosely-fitting shift she wore. "Ye could have told me I was carrying your bairn. That is why ye want to be wed, isnae it, because I might be carrying the heir to Dubhglenn?"

"Aye," Parlan agreed, and lightly kissed her sulking mouth, "ye are carrying my heir. 'Tis a good reason to wed ye."

She wondered how such a simple statement could hurt so much but fought to hide it. "Is it true that ye have no bairns?"

He saw something flicker in her eyes but could not read it and decided that Lagan was wrong, that Aimil was a practical girl and did not need sweet words. "None that I ken."

"If ye were always so careful, why werenae ye with me?"

"Because I didnae want to be. I wanted the full pleasure of ye. I trust ye. Aye, and like ye. I didnae care if my seed took root."

She sighed inwardly. That was apparently all she was going to get. It did please her, but she still wanted more. Telling herself she was being quite foolish did not ease the wanting. She told herself that she would be wise to accept what he said as enough and set her mind to being happy.

Chapter Seventeen

In a gesture she admitted to herself was childish, Aimil stuck her tongue out at Parlan's departing figure. She then met Old Meg's stern frown with a sweet smile. Even though no one else seemed to agree, she felt she had a right to be annoyed about the way she was being rushed into the marriage. Little heed was given to her objections, of which she honestly admitted there were one or two, or fears, of which she regretfully admitted there were far too many. With a sigh, she got out of bed and let Old Meg assist her in bathing and washing her hair. She decided it was probably petty of her to be so irritated by Parlan's calm confidence.

Parlan cursed as he glared at the scar on his leg. It seemed twice as livid and unsightly as it had the day before. He took a walk around the room and swore some more. The stiffness in his leg made him limp. He had sorely wanted to be at his best when he stood with Aimil before the priest, but that was clearly not to be. Cursing was not going to change that but he decided, as he limped around the room, that it soothed his disappointment to indulge in a few hearty rounds of it.

A soft sound distracted him from his annoyance. He looked up to see that Artair had quietly entered the room. Artair had only made a few fleeting visits since the time he had delivered his warning about Catarine, something Parlan still cursed himself for not acting upon immediately. The expression on his brother's face told Parlan that this visit was not going to be a fleeting one.

"Such cursing." Artair moved closer to Parlan. "Doubts about the step ye take? Mayhaps ye should wait."

"Nay, I have no doubts. I but curse this scarred and still useless leg. 'Tis a poor thing to show a bride."

"I dinnae think the lass will mind but, if it troubles ye so, wait some more. It should be better before long."

"Aye, it should but I willnae wait any longer. Her sweet little belly already starts to round. Last eve I felt the bairn move. I mean to set the name MacGuin on that bairn as quickly as possible."

"The bairn isnae due for several months yet."

"I ken it. I also ken how swiftly life can be ended, snuffed out in a winking like some tallow candle. What happened with Rory reminded me of that. I repeat, I will set the name MacGuin on that bairn as soon as can be. I have hesitated long enough." He sat down on his bed and frowned at Artair. "Is that why ye are here? Have ye come to try and talk me out of wedding her?"

"Nay. 'Tis your choice. If ye wish to wed the lass, do so. She seems a good lass."

"Aye, she is and 'tis my wish to wed her. So, why are ye here? I ken that something weighs heavily upon ye. Have out with it."

"'Tisnae easy." Artair nervously paced. "I finally took heed of what ye said. That eve of Rory's attack?" Parlan nodded. "Oh, I listened when ye spoke and heeded for the moment, as I have always done. Then I walked away and set aside your words. Something else I have always done. They wouldnae leave me be this time. They kept preying upon my mind forcing me to think and think again. I found it an uncomfortable process, this thinking. I have done little of it in my time. Then I saw what Rory Fergueson had done to Aimil, heard what he had done to the lass's mother, and it frightened me."

"'Tis naught to fash yourself over. It frightened me."

"Ye dinnae understand. I saw myself in him, saw what I could become."

"Nay, laddie. Ye are but misguided. Rory Fergueson is mad, totally mad and thoroughly evil."

"Aye, but when did he turn so? When did he stop but slapping a lass now and again and take to beating them, enjoying the pain he could inflict? When did he stop taking unwilling lasses because he let his lust rule him and begin to enjoy their unwillingness, their shame, and their hurt? I take unwilling lasses, let my lust rule me, and use my strength against them. When does that stop being the act of a drink-besotted, unthinking lad and become the sickness that infects Rory Fergueson?"

Parlan frowned. He wanted to ease the fear he read in his brother's face but could not find the right words. While he did not believe that the evil which tainted Rory could have the humble beginning Artair described, neither could he ignore the logic of Artair's words. He simply did not know enough about such madness to give Artair the firm denial to his fears that he sought. However, neither could he believe that his brother held the seed of such evil.

"I dinnae ken what turned Fergueson into the filth he has become or when he turned so. I cannae believe that ye could become like him. Ye do no more than many other men yet there are few Rory Ferguesons about. As I have said, there is a brutal side to every man. 'Tis but something we must learn to control. The beast in Rory cannae be controlled; it just grows stronger. Rory cannae change what he is. The rot is too strong. I dinnae really think ye are so afflicted. Ye can change."

Seeing that the fear in Artair's expression was only mildly lessened, Parlan desperately sought some other tact. "Here now, Artair, ye havenae coldly murdered some innocent have ye?"

"Nay." There was a hint of outrage in Artair's voice.

"Aye, and ye have no thought to do so. Rory has. He was younger than ye when he murdered Kirstie Mengue. I would-nae be surprised to find that there were other deaths or near ones before that. I ken weel there were others after that. His kin or his man, Geordie, kept the truth weel hid. I would wager there were other signs of his madness, things to indi-cate the seed of it and more as the seed flowered. Aye, ye have been a woe at times, but there has never been any real mean-ness in ye."

"But ye said that to ignore a lass's nays and to strike a woman is wrong."

"Aye, wrong and I heavily disapprove, but as I said ye do no more than many another man. 'Tis legal for a man to beat his wife yet I think one who does try to rule his woman with his fist isnae much of a man. There is no honor in beating one who cannae really stop ye though they might try. And, I dinnae see it as my right to take a woman as I please or where I please. So too have I seen what rape and brutality can do to a lass and 'tisnae right. Ye willnae find a lot that agree with me though."

"Nay, but I begin to. I have"—he took a deep breath and faced Parlan squarely—"weel, I have recognized the folly of wallowing in drink and the stews. There is naught there for me but the pox or death. I dinnae want to say I have had some sense beaten into me but, in a way, I have. I couldnae drink, ye ken, and being without it made me think a lot on what I have been doing."

"'Tis glad I am to hear this though, I dinnae quite understand why ye say ye couldnae drink. There is plenty about."

"Aye, but it wasnae brought anywhere near my chambers.
Malcolm and Lagan, aye, even Leith, felt it best if I suffered
a clear head for a wee while. I wasnae too pleased at first
but I ken they intended only good. I sorely wanted to drown
in it too when I began to think too clearly and too much, when
I began to see what a useless fool I have been acting."

He shrugged and attempted a smile. "I but came to say that
I mean to change. T'will take some time, I ken, if only to gain
some respect from the people here. I ken that I lost whatever
I had by my own actions so I must win it back on my own."

Deeply moved and feeling hopeful for the first time in far
too long, Parlan heartily embraced his brother. "Ye ken that I
am willing to help in any way that I can."

"Aye, but I also ken that this is mostly my own fight.
Weel," Artair said, smiling faintly as Parlan released him,
"that is that chore done. Now I have but one more to do." Grimacing, he jested weakly, "Best I see to it whilst I still feel
ready to be humble and to confess to fault and errors."

Parlan grinned briefly, then asked, "What is it?"

"I must yet seek Aimil's forgiveness."

Aimil sighed and stared into the flames of the fire. She found
it tedious to sit alone, waiting for the heat of the fire to dry her
newly-washed hair. When a rap came at the door of her chambers, she eagerly bade the visitor enter only to frown slightly
when she saw that it was Artair. There had been whispers of a
change in him, but she was not sure she wished to be alone with
the young man. Although, for Parlan's sake, she had tried to
dismiss it she could not forget that he had intended, at one
point, to beat and to rape her. To have him near when she was
alone and wearing only a robe unsettled her.

"I am quite sober," he murmured as he approached her, "and I swear I willnae touch ye."

Determined to give him a chance since he was Parlan's only close kin, she indicated the other stool before the fire. "Sit down."

Somewhat stiffly he did so. "I have come to ask forgiveness for my attack upon ye."

"Ye were drunk, verra fou, in truth."

"Aye, but I cannae hide behind that any longer. I will confess that it took me some time to see what I had done as wrong. To me, ye were naught but some captive, and I could do as I wished. Beyond that, ye were also just a lass. I believed the ones who called Parlan a soft-hearted fool for his beliefs about how women should be treated. Few think as he does. Weel, now I see the right of his thinking. A lass has a right to say nay, and 'tis naught but a weakness in a man to use his greater strength over the weaker to bend them to his will. 'Tis a strong man who kens when not to use his fists."

"Then ye have learned a great deal and, aye, ye have my forgiveness. I give it fully and easily."

"Ye say that because 'tis what ye think will please Parlan."

"In part, aye. What I did because ye are Parlan's only brother, his nearest kin, was to let ye speak to me at all. 'Tis for Parlan that ye even got inside the door. The rest is my own doing. I wasnae but mouthing words for Parlan's ears but from the heart."

"Then I thank ye—from the heart. 'Tis a comfort to ken that I willnae be starting this change in my ways with what little kin I do have set against me. I think t'will be quite hard enough as it is."

"Change is never easy. Ye have seen your weaknesses and your errors. That is the hardest step to take. Have ye spoken to Parlan?"

"Aye, and it proved a two-edged sword. I was pleased to

make him happy yet to see how happy simply speaking of changing made him caused me to see how unhappy I have made him in the past. I was keenly aware of how I had failed him."

"Weel, he is happy now and that is what matters most. Ye cannae brood too long upon the past. 'Tis the future ye must look to. To think too long on what ye could have done or should have done will take time better used to see what ye must do now."

Before he could make any reply, a rap came at the chamber door. When Aimil bid the person to enter, she had to bite back a smile. Giorsal entered with a big smile on her face only to stop and glare at Artair who smiled crookedly.

"Ye told her."

"Aye, Artair, I did and now I will tell her that all is forgiven." She looked sternly at Giorsal.

"And I am to fall into step with that?" Giorsal moved to stand next to Aimil.

"Aye, t'would be nice."

"Oh, verra weel then."

"A most grudging forgiveness but sincere for all that." She met Giorsal's glare with a smile.

Artair laughed softly as he stood to leave. "The time for the wedding must draw near. I will go to see if I can be of any help."

"Ye forgive verra easily," Giorsal said as soon as Artair was gone. "I dinnae think I would do so."

"He means to change and now sees that he acted wrongly. I couldnae reward that by refusing to understand and to forgive. If naught else, I couldnae bear to be the one to hinder his changing. If he returned to the alehouses and whorehouses to wallow in that filth, I would always wonder if t'was my inability to forgive that caused him to stumble. Right now he needs the strength friendship can give."

"Aye, ye are right in that. Come now, 'tis time to dress for your wedding." She took Aimil by the hand and urged her to her feet.

"Ah, so the time does indeed draw near."

"Ye dinnae look as happy as I thought ye would be. Dinnae ye wish to wed Parlan?"

"Aye, I do but I do not. There shines a contrary nature, eh?" She tried to smile but felt sure it was a miserable effort.

"A troubled nature to be certain. Come, ye can tell me all that frets ye as I help ye dress, and I shall tell ye what a foolish, wee lass ye are."

"I think I have been told that quite enough, thank ye kindly." Aimil shed her robe.

"Clearly ye havenae been listening or ye wouldnae be so dowie when ye are soon to get what I ken weel ye want."

"Does my back look verra unsightly?"

"Nay, it doesnae as I am certain ye ken weel. Dinnae try to divert me. Talk, child. 'Tis the best way."

Aimil knew that was true. She simply was not sure of how to explain all that troubled her. As Giorsal helped her dress, she struggled to find the right words, words that would make Giorsal understand her worries and fears.

"I do want to be Parlan's wife. 'Tis something I have wanted for a verra long time. 'Tis just that I wished him to ask me for reasons other than what sets in my womb. He weds me because I carry his heir."

"To get an heir is the reason most men wed. If t'was allowed, I wouldnae be surprised if most of them waited to stand before a priest until their seed took root in some woman's belly."

"Most likely that is true, but 'tis not why I wish to be stood before a priest."

"Did Parlan say t'was naught but the bairn that he was wedding ye for?"

"Weel, nay."

"What did he say?"

"He said I was the first to carry his bairn, that he was always careful in the past to keep his seed from taking root. He said he didnae want to take such care with me, that he liked and trusted me. No lover's vows those."

"Mayhaps not in your eyes but 'tis no small thing for a man to feel so for a woman. Some wives never gain as much."

"I ken it. It doesnae stop me from wanting more though. I am friend and lover to him and weel I ken the value of that. Though I curse myself for a greedy, ungrateful wretch, I still want more."

"Ye want him to love ye, love ye as ye love him and that is a lot, isnae it, Aimil?" Giorsal gently bade Aimil to sit down and began to brush out her hair.

"I never said so."

"Nay, not plainly but it shone through each word whenever ye spoke of Parlan. I kenned it from the first."

"Do ye think Parlan has seen it?" Aimil was dismayed by the thought that her feelings could be so easily read.

"Most likely not. Men can be verra blind about such things. Och, listen to me. So can women. Look at me. I ken now that Iain has loved me from the start, but I never heeded it. I see only now, after all the years we have been together, what he has shown me so clearly in all he did. I had to discover my own love for him before I saw his love for me, before he even dared speak it aloud."

Shaking her head, Giorsal continued, "When I first realized ye had fallen in love with the man, I was sore worried for ye. There were some verra dark things said about him, and he looked dark and fierce enough for them to be true. I soon realized that he had been sorely slandered by rumor, but I still worried over ye for he is, weel, as Iain says, 'such a great lad.'" She smiled faintly when Aimil laughed. "It took awhile before I saw that ye arenae troubled or afeard, that ye can manage what seems to be a great deal of man."

"Aye, manage him, but can I hold him? Can I keep his hungers sated so that he doesnae answer the lure of others?"

"Has he been unfaithful to ye?" Finished with Aimil's hair, Giorsal sat down to face her sister.

"I think not. Nay, I ken he hasnae been. He didnae even tumble Catarine though she did all in her power to draw him to her bed. He did travel to the Dunmore keep, but even in that short while he was out of my sight, I dinnae feel he turned elsewhere."

"Then why do ye fash yourself over it? He has been faithful when he wasnae bound by any oath or vow to be."

"Aye, but the passion between us is still hot and new. What happens when that wanes as it will do, if only in some ways? 'Tis love that keeps one person trying to stay faithful to another. He hasnae given me any words to make me even think he loves me.

"Ah, Giorsal, I love him so much that, at times, it frightens me. I daren't even think of him with another. I fear it would tear me to pieces if he began to seek his pleasures elsewhere, if he decided that my being his lover, his friend, and the mother of his bairns was not enough to satisfy all his needs. Worse, I fear I would tear us apart in my pain."

Taking Aimil's hand in hers, Giorsal sought words to soothe her sister's worries. "Aye, he could turn to other women, but then what he already feels for ye could turn to love. Look again at what happened in my marriage. Iain loved me but I didnae love him at all. For five long years he was patient, quietly loved me, and has gained what he sought. I now love him back and dearly so. I am loath to admit it, but I was not even a good friend and lover to him though he tried to be to me.

"Could not the same happen with ye and Parlan? Ye already have a firm place for yourself here, already are so important to him though I do understand why it isnae quite enough. He trusts ye, likes ye, and soon ye will share a child. Build upon that, child. Give him all your love, and the chances are verra good that ye can draw the same from him. Ye have already gained a lot."

Staring at their joined hands, Aimil thought upon all Giorsal had said. There was a great deal of sense to it. While it might be easier for a good, kind man like Iain MacVern to make Giorsal love him than for her to make a man like Parlan love her, that did not mean that it was impossible. She certainly had a greater chance of doing so than any other woman in his life had ever had.

"Aye, I see the sense of what ye say. I must cease using time and strength to bemoan what I dinnae have and use it to try and gain what I want. Aye, to gain what I need."

After briefly hugging Aimil, Giorsal stood and tugged Aimil to her feet. "And be patient, dinnae lose heart."

"I will try verra hard not to, but 'tis a thing far easier to speak of than to do."

"True enough, but I think ye can do most anything ye set your mind to. Come, now, there is a wedding to attend."

Parlan scowled toward the door of the hall. "Where is the lass?"

Doing a poor job of hiding a smile, Lagan shook his head. "Takes a lass time to ready herself for her wedding."

"Weel, if she isnae here soon, I will go and fetch her down. The priest grows impatient," Parlan added a little pompously.

"Och, aye. 'Tis why he sets there sipping his mead and quietly talking to Lachlan. A sure sign of displeasure."

After glaring at Leith, Malcolm, and Artair who snickered, Parlan frowned at Lagan. "I will concede that I grow a wee bit restless."

"Quite. Just a wee bit."

"Ye can sore try a man's good humor, Lagan Dunmore."
He swore softly when Lagan just laughed.

Parlan was about to complain that it should not take any
woman so long to don a gown when Aimil finally entered the
hall. He caught his breath at the sight of her. Her gown was
loose and flowing, not only to keep anything from aggravat-
ing her nearly-healed wounds but because he and Old Meg
were firm believers that no tight clothing should restrict the
growth of his child in Aimil's womb. The rich blue of her
gown made her eyes seem even bluer. What truly caught his
admiration was her long, bright hair, its thick length glisten-
ing and festooned with blue and gold ribbons. He had never
seen her look lovelier.

"Ah, Parlan, ye rogue, ye are gaining a fair, wee lass."

"Aye, Lagan, that I am." Parlan immediately strode toward
Aimil.

Aimil was a little taken aback by her first sight of Parlan.
She had never seen him dressed in such finery, in clothes
worthy of an appearance at the king's court. The black and
silver seemed to heighten the imposing cast of his dark looks.
She felt in awe of him and decided it was not a feeling she
was particularly fond of. It certainly shook what little confidence she had.

How could she expect to hold such a man? She was but a
small Lowland lass with a short temper and a sharp tongue.
At the moment, Parlan looked every inch the fierce Highland
laird, a man to make women far prettier than her pursue him.
He looked a man no woman could hold for long. Inwardly,
she sighed as he took her by the hand and raised her fingers
to his lips.

"Ye are lovely beyond words, Aimil Mengue." He was puzzled by the hint of sadness in her eyes. "Can ye nae add to it
with a wee smile?"

She tried but suspected that it was a poor, weak one that finally shaped her mouth. "I am a wee bit nervous, 'tis all, Parlan."

He did not really believe that was all of it but did not press her. It was neither the time nor the place. So too was there an urgency within him to get the vows said and done, to claim her and the child she carried as his. There would be plenty of time later to sort out her various moods and understand what lay behind them he decided. With a smile he hoped would soothe her, he tugged her toward the priest who was now ready to perform the marriage service.

As he knelt before the priest holding her faintly trembling hand in his, Parlan searched his heart one last time for any doubts or regrets about the step he was about to take. It did not really surprise him to find none for he had expected that, having found none since the moment he had decided to take her as his wife. There was a concern or two, even a few things that could be termed fears, but he pushed them aside. He did not really understand them but knew that they made no difference to what he did now. Instinct told him that they would be somewhat eased once Aimil was legally his.

Mine, he thought with a sense of pride and possession that nearly made him smile. It was not something he had ever felt toward a woman before. With Aimil, however, it was important that he tie her to him in any and every way he could. It troubled him deeply that she did not seem to feel the same way as was indicated by the way she was hesitating to repeat the vows that would finalize their marriage. Looking at her, he tried desperately, yet fruitlessly, to read in her expression the reason that she faltered.

Although she parted her lips to begin repeating the vows that would make her legally Parlan's, a sudden rush of doubt stilled her tongue. What lay ahead could be the answer to all her dreams or a long painful nightmare. She loved him beyond what was probably sensible, but there was no guarantee that he would ever return that love. To spend a lifetime caught in the painful hold of unrequited love seemed more than anyone should be forced to bear.

Glancing at him, she felt common sense return. There really was no choice for her. If she humiliated him now by suddenly refusing to wed him, she would undoubtedly lose all chance of gaining his love. So too there was the child. He had a right to his child, as much right as she did, and she was certain that it was not a right he would relinquish. Even if she did not wed him, she would still be tied to him through the child. Far better to take her chances, she decided. Taking a deep breath, she repeated the vows that made her forever his, something her heart had done months ago.

Chapter Eighteen

"Are ye happy, child?"

Aimil looked up at her father and smiled. It gladdened her heart considerably to be on good terms with her father again, but she suffered from a touch of wariness, even disbelief. At any moment she expected to see him turn away from her as he had in the past. Knowing how that could hurt her, she found herself trying to keep a distance between them. She could only hope that with time and a lessening of her wariness her distrust would vanish. The last thing she wished to do was spoil the renewal of her relationship with him.

"Aye, Papa. He is a good man." She thought that sounded a little trite but could not think of anything else to say.

"Of course, ye are happy. Your voice fairly trembles with joy."

Grimacing, Aimil admitted to herself that it had been foolish of her to think that she could divert him by mouthing platitudes. "I am happy. He is the man I want. Aye, there are a few pebbles in our path, but they can be cleared away."

"That is the way to think on it. Ye are the one he wanted too, lass."

"Aye, because of the bairn."

"Wheesht, fool lass. Do ye think a man like the Black Parlan would be made to wed a lass simply because his seed had set root in her? He would stand firm and tell me to do as I will, and weel ye ken it."

"But honor demands . . ."

"Not when ye are but a captive. Aye, if ye were the daughter of some ally he had seduced but, nay, not for a captive."

She was still thinking on her father's words when Giorsal and Maggie took her up to Parlan's chambers. His words had made a greater impression upon her than nearly anything anyone else had said. Her father saw it as only another man could have and had succinctly explained that elusive concept to her. The more she looked at it the more she wondered why she had not seen it before. She began to suspect that she had purposely avoided any logic that might inspire hope, possibly a fruitless hope.

Whether Parlan wanted the child or not, and she was sure he did, he would not tie himself to her for life because the child rested in her womb. In her case, honor only demanded that he give her back alive when the ransom was paid. If she happened to have lost her chastity while captive and her belly swelled with his child, most would shrug. They would see it as one of the costs of being caught, perhaps even as part of the ransom. Parlan really had done what he had wanted to.

Still mulling that over, she somewhat absently said goodnight to her sister, and it was a moment before she realized that Maggie was lingering. "Is there something wrong, Maggie?"

"Nay, everything couldnae be finer." Maggie smiled almost radiantly. "I have been trying to talk to ye since yester morn." She blushed faintly. "I heeded all ye said about how to go on with Malcolm. Aye, heeded it and acted upon it."

"And it worked, aye? Weel, that is a foolish question for 'tis clear to see that it did by your face."

"Aye, it worked though leaving the candles lit and keeping

my eyes open caused my poor man a blush or twa." She giggled along with Aimil. "I willnae have to do it again. I found I didnae really need to do it the first time for I never thought it was any but my Malcolm loving me. Howbeit, the lit candle took the fear from me so that I had the courage to try the first time."

"I am so glad for ye, Maggie." She kissed the maid's cheek. "Aye, and for Malcolm. He is a good man. When are ye to be wed then?"

"The priest said he would wed us before he left Dubhglenn. I wished to thank ye, m'lady. Thank ye with all my heart."

"Thank me? Whatever for? T'was Malcolm's doing."

"Aye, once I was set in his arms, but t'was ye that set me there, gave me the heart to try."

"Weel, I think ye would have found it on your own in time, but ye are verra welcome."

Maggie smiled then hurried toward the door. "I will leave ye be then. 'Tis certain I am that your man will be here soon."

Aimil was certain of that, too. As soon as Maggie left, Aimil nervously went to check on her appearance in the mirror. It seemed far too long since Parlan had held her. She had sensed his growing hunger as they were healing from their wounds, but he had abstained from satisfying it, even to moving her to a separate room. He had clearly felt that now that they were to be wed, now that she was no longer his hostage, and now that her family came and went from Dubhglenn as they pleased, it was time to act with a little discretion.

It was probably for the best, but she had not liked it much and not simply because, as she had healed, she had begun to feel as eager for a taste of the passion they shared as he seemed to be. Rory had scarred her with a fear she could not seem to shake. It haunted her dreams, bringing nightmares. Although Parlan had often appeared at her bedside to ease those fears when she had come awake shaking and cold, he had been absent enough for her to know how much she needed him there, needed to be able to reach out and touch him to assure herself that she was safe, that Rory was only a chimera in her mind. Although she cursed her weakness, she could not deny it and reluctantly accepted the fact that it would be awhile before she would be free of it, that time was needed for her body, mind, and heart to forget those hours of terror and pain.

Slipping into bed, she propped up the pillows then leaned against them to wait for Parlan. Because they had been lovers for so long and she was carrying his child, there would be no bedding ceremony. She was not at all regretful, recalling how coarse and embarrassing it could get from her sisters' weddings. All she had to do was wait for Parlan to arrive so that they could begin the arrangement that Rory's attack had so brutally interrupted. Suddenly yawning, she hoped Parlan did not linger in the hall too long with ale and friends or he would find his new bride sound asleep.

Parlan took a deep breath, squared his shoulders, and entered his chambers. He did not understand why he felt so uncertain, even nervous. Aimil was not a woman new to his bed, nor a virgin bride that he had to move cautiously and tenderly around. Nevertheless, he could not dislodge the feeling that he was taking a very important first step.

Catching her yawning, he had to smile, especially when she looked so guilty. "I can see I am eagerly awaited."

"Sorry. It has been a long day, and I do seem to weary more easily." She watched him undress and idly mused that she might find it easier to feel confident about him if he was not such a handsome rogue. "'Tis the bairn I am told."

"Ye dinnae feel ill or unduly weak?" He briefly washed up, mostly out of habit for he had bathed before the wedding.

"Nay, nay. There is naught that feels wrong. I just tire with more ease than I have ever done. I need to rest more often but I ken weel that that is surely for the best." Seeing that he was already aroused as he walked to the bed and slid in beside her, she murmured, "Mayhaps I should rest now."

Tugging her into his arms, he met her impish smile with a fraudulent scowl. "Ye shouldnae do that."

"Nay? Ye have something that might interest me enough to keep me awake?"

Hastily removing her nightgown, he held her silken body close and sighed with pleasured relief over the return of something that had been gone too long, something he had missed far more than he could have imagined. "I think I may have a thing or twa to hold your interest for a wee while." He cupped her shapely derriere in his hands and pressed her closer.

Feeling a familiar, delightful warmth curl through her loins, she murmured her appreciation. "I think ye just might at that, m'lord."

When he kissed her, she slid her arms around his neck and reveled in it. This time he would not be cutting the kiss short, leaving them both wanting more. Even as she began to succumb to her hunger for him, she was a little unsettled by the strength of it. She was not sure it was good or even wise to want him so much. That worry was soon drowned in a flood of passion, however, as his hands began to move over her in a way that revealed his own hunger.

After being so long deprived, they needed little to bring them to the point where the joining of their bodies was a necessity. Aimil was fleetingly surprised that he seemed as lacking in control as she was. She cried out with relief when he entered her and equaled his ferocity as he lifted them both to desire's apex. As she began to slip down from the heights his lovemaking sent her to, she clung to him, unwilling to end the unity too soon. Sensing him staring at her, she opened her eyes and smiled lazily.

"Weel, ye were right. That did hold my interest for a wee while." She met his grin with her own.

"Ye are an impertinent wretch." He withdrew from her slightly. "I was a wee bit rough. Too long without a taste of the sweetness of ye. I havenae hurt ye, have I?" His hand covered her abdomen.

"Nay. Think of all we did before I even kenned I was with child. The bairn still grows and thrives. Aye, think of all Rory did to me yet, as Old Meg says, he couldnae shake this fruit from the tree. Ye cannae hurt the bairn with a wee bit of love-making. I think ye see it as rougher than it truly is. I dinnae feel as if it t'was verra rough at all." She smiled crookedly. "So ye neednae fear that the reason for this fine wedding has been banished."

"Ah, I kenned that something was gnawing at ye." He gently brushed a few wisps of hair from her face.

"There is naught gnawing at me as ye put it." She did not exactly wish to get into a discussion about feelings.

"Aye, there is and there has been. Ye hesitated before ye would say the vows."

"Weel, 'tis a big step to be wedded. Ye cannae tell me ye had no pause, didnae hesitate a wee bit."

"I didnae." He smiled when she frowned and watched him through narrowed eyes. "Nay, truly, I didnae. I have been thinking on wedding ye from the verra first time I held ye in this bed."

"Ye never said a word to me about it." She felt a spasm of doubt, yet knew that Parlan was not a man to say something simply because he thought it might please her to hear it, to give her lies to ease a worry he only sensed she had.

"Of course I said naught to ye. I was but pondering it. My pondering might have led me to decide I didnae want ye for a wife. Then I would have had to tell ye that. Much better to say naught until I was certain."

Although she was not sure she liked the idea that for all the time they had been together, he had been more or less testing her, she could easily understand why he had done such a thing. A marriage was forever, and the woman he chose would be the one to bear his children, his heirs. Such a weighty matter should be well thought on. Handfast marriages were little more than a test of the suitability and fruitfulness of a match. Nevertheless, she mused a little sourly, he had taken his sweet time in deciding whether she suited him. That did seem insulting.

"Ye find that less than flattering, do ye? T'was never my intent to deliver any insult."

"I ken it. I can see the sense of being certain about such an important thing."

"Aye, but?"

"I didnae say but."

"T'was there to hear in your voice, sweeting. But?" Although he had no intention of telling her anything he did not feel, he was determined to ease the uncertainties he knew she felt.

"Oh, God's toenails, did ye have to take so long in deciding?" She hoped her question reflected only hurt pride.

He forcibly restrained a laugh, knowing that would only add to her injured pride, mild as it seemed. "I didnae take as long as ye might think, dearling. Nay, truly, I didnae." Smiling at the doubt he could read in her expression, he lightly kissed her pouting mouth. "I was but slow in telling ye. I realized I best hurry and speak before I went to the Dunmores."

"And returned to find I was set to escape." She realized that had undoubtedly added to that air of wounded pride she had felt in him that night.

"Weel, set to drown, leastwise."

"It was a good plan. It just went a wee bit awry."

"Oh, aye, just a wee bit. Dinnae divert me." He grinned when she shot him a look of mild annoyance. "That fine feast I set before ye the day Rory attacked had a purpose."

"Aye, seducing me. Ye accomplished that."

"Weel, I willnae deny that I had thought to have me some of that as weel. I had planned the moment to ask ye to wed me."

She felt sorely disappointed that that opportunity had been lost even though she knew it would not have given her the words of love she craved. "Oh, and that cursed Rory ruined it."

"Aye, but I did speak once ye were returned to Dubhglenn."

"True enough, but t'was in such a manner that I was left to think that t'was naught but the bairn that prompted ye."

"Come now, I did tell ye there was more to it than that."

"Aye, in a way, but"—she put her arms about his neck and kissed him— "but kenning that ye had planned to ask me to be your wife before either of us kenned that there was a bairn soothes the sting even more. I didnae want to become a bride because ye felt a duty to wed me or because honor demanded it. Aye, or because your seed decided to take root in me." She smiled faintly. "I didnae want ye to do something ye didnae truly wish to do for I kenned the trouble that could bring."

"I am not a man to do what he doesnae really wish to, m'eudail."

"Aye, so Papa said."

"Did he now?"

"Aye, and the way he said it eased some of my worries though 'tis a greater comfort to hear ye say it."

"Ah, lass, I cannae deny that I sorely want the bairn, but 'tis a feeling stirred in most part because 'tis ye that helped create him. I want the bairn because he is part of ye.

"Lass, I hold a score and eight years. For more than half of those I have kenned the pleasures of the flesh. Aye, I have had more women than I should have. 'Tisnae a boast for I ken that 'tis naught to be verra proud of, but 'tis a fact. Not once, with any of them, did I think of children. Aye, my only thought was, ''Ware, lad, ye dinnae wish your seed to root here.' I have been as careful as a man can be and near as any man can be sure, I ken that I have no bastards.

"Now, with ye, I never once gave a thought to being wary, not since the first moment we made love. I didnae see the need of it, didnae want to take care. It didnae worry me when I kenned there was a chance ye could get with child. In truth, the few times I gave it any thought I felt naught but pleasure. T'was a pleasing thought.

"Aye, I want this bairn, but it didnae force me to wed ye. Nay, it but gave me the means to set ye before a priest even if ye didnae feel like being set there. If anyone was forced to wed, t'was ye, Aimil, never me. Ye were the one who was given no choice nor chance."

She was touched by his words. It was not what she ached to hear, but it did ease some of the sting she had felt over the way the marriage had been arranged. So too did it ease some of her fears. Since he had really wanted to wed her, there was a very good chance that he was nearly as willing and as ready as she was to make the marriage a good one, firm and happy.

"Ye cannae truly say I was forced. Aye, ye and my father decided it, but ye didnae hear me put up too much of a wail."

"Nay, true enough. Why didnae ye, Aimil?"

The very last thing she wanted to tell him was exactly why she had gone along with his and her father's dictates with little protest. "'Cause I didnae really have any complaint. I have been happy here. Ye ken it. I was never too happy with the idea of leaving and not just because Rory awaited me for I didnae ken what Rory was. I wanted to stay. Now I can."

He felt somewhat disappointed yet could not really say why. Love was what he sought from her yet he knew that it was unfair to demand it of her when he was not willing to give it, at least not yet. He told himself he was being contrary as he held her close. She had admitted to being happy at Dubhglenn and happy to stay. That should be enough. It was something that even being deeply in love did not necessarily promise.

His hand returned to rest upon her slightly-swollen stomach.

It was still a little difficult to believe that he would soon be a father. He also found the waiting trying. He wanted to know if he would have a son or a daughter. He wanted to know if the child would be fair like Aimil or dark as he was. He wanted to hold his child, a feeling that intensified a great deal when he felt the flutter of movement within.

"T'will be verra difficult to wait."

"Aye, though"—she smiled a little—"I think t'will be a little harder for me than for any others for I shall have to tote the wee one around as I wait. Aye, and the wee one will make me a lot less wee."

"Ye will grow round and beautiful." He smiled at her disgusted look.

"A lady who is round isnae beautiful. Nay, nor when she waddles like some fat duck."

"Ah, ye plan to waddle, do ye?"

"Nay, I dinnae plan to but I ken that I will. My sisters did and so has any woman far gone with child that I have ever seen. Aye, I will waddle and if ye laugh, I will strike you."

"I shall keep that warning in mind."

"Aye, best that ye do."

For a while they lay quietly in each other's arms, idly caressing each other and enjoying the closeness they had both sorely missed. Parlan knew Aimil shared those feelings by the way she touched him and sighed with something more than passion when he touched her. No matter how puzzled he might get over what else she might feel or think, he knew he could trust in her passion. That was always honest and open, given forth without hesitation or any attempt at subterfuge. He knew that a lot of husbands would pay a king's ransom to find that in their wives.

One small problem pricked at his current contentment, however. Aimil had said nothing about Artair. Neither had Artair said a word about his meeting with Aimil. Although Parlan knew there had been no time to enter into such a conversation, he could not relinquish the fear that things had not gone well between the two. He knew Aimil had a right to be angry, especially since any memory of the time Artair had attacked her still caused him a twinge of fury, but he wanted his wife and his brother to get along, to be friends. It was especially important now that Artair seemed sincere in his wish to change and there was the chance of a better relationship between them.

Although he was not sure he wanted to hear that their meeting had gone terribly wrong, Parlan finally gave into his need to know. "Aimil, Artair said he was going to talk with ye today."

"Oh, aye, he did. Just before the wedding."

When she said no more about it, he became impatient despite the fact that her soft, gentle caresses were heating his blood. "So? What happened between the pair of you? He still lives is all I ken at the moment."

Wondering why he was so interested in the subject now when her interests were somewhere else entirely, she looked at him with a mixture of puzzlement and mild annoyance. "He apologized for what he had done to me and asked my forgiveness. I gave it."

"Just like that?" He could not believe that what could have been a real problem had been solved so easily.

"Aye, what did ye think had happened?"

"I wasnae sure. Neither of ye said a word so I began to think . . ." He shrugged. "Ye were quick to forgive."

"Nay, not truly. Weel, after Rory, what Artair had done seemed little or naught. Then too, Artair didnae accomplish what he had intended. He was then shamed by a public lashing. What truly, or mostly, prompted my forgiveness was that he kenned he had done wrong, was shamed by his actions. He wasnae mouthing words he didnae feel to make us all happy."

"He says he intends to change."

"Aye, so he told me. Dinnae ye think he can?" She trailed her fingers up his inner thigh, and felt him tremble slightly.

"I daren't. He has disappointed me far too often. I will help him all I can though, not just sit back to see if he falters. Aimil, are ye listening to me?"

"Oh, aye, I cling to your every word."

Since her small, clever hand was stroking him in a way that made thinking very difficult, Parlan rather doubted the veracity of her claim. His grin faded into a soft groan of enjoyment as her tongue gently lathed his nipples. He decided that there were a lot better things to do on one's wedding night than talk. Closing his eyes, he reveled in the way she could make him feel and knew that she shared that feeling, a thought that both comforted and stirred him.

He grimaced when her caresses moved over the rough scar on his leg, the pinch of his vanity causing him to be concerned over how she saw it. "Nay, come away from that ugliness, dearling. I had hoped that t'would be faded more before now."

Although she moved so that she was held tightly in his arms and could kiss his cheek, she had to smile. She heard his concern about his scar in his voice. It amused her to think that a man like Parlan should be troubled about his appearance.

"A wee scar doesnae trouble me."

"'Tis hardly a wee scar."

"Wheesht, wee enough when it sits upon a man as strong and fine of line as ye are, Parlan MacGuin."

Unsettled by her flattery, he muttered, "Fine of line? Ye speak of me as ye would your stallion."

"Ye mean the horse ye married me for?"

"Married ye for Elfking, did I?"

"Aye. Ye can admit the truth. I ken how weel ye like to ride him."

"Aye, I do, but there is something I fancy more than riding Elfking."

"Oh? And what is that?"

Gently pushing her onto her back, he growled, "Riding Elfking's lady."

"Ye are a crude man, husband."

"Be quiet and kiss me, wife."

Aimil decided that it was a very good time to practice a little wifely obedience.

Chapter Nineteen

"Must I go?"

Parlan looked at Aimil who wore only a shift and was sprawled upon her stomach on their bed. "Ye would send me off alone?"

Looking at the crestfallen face he made, she giggled. "Poor, wee laddie." She grimaced and sat up as her child moved within her, making lying upon her stomach very uncomfortable. "Ye truly wish me to come along?" Placing a hand over her rounding stomach, she delighted in the feel of her child's life and idly wondered how unattractively noticeable the changes in her shape were.

"I wouldnae ask ye otherwise. Why are ye reluctant to go?" He moved to stand by the bed as he finished donning his doublet.

"Weel, I would prefer to be looking my best when I meet your closest allies."

Biting back a smile, he bent down and kissed her then started out of the room. "Ye look bonnie enough to turn any man's head. Get your clothes on, lass, and I will send Maggie to help ye with the packing. We must leave Dubhglenn before the noon of the day arrives."

Sighing, she got off the bed. He did not understand and she doubted that she could make him. While she was delighted to be carrying his child, the way it was swiftly changing the shape of her body did not please her at all. She often felt awkward, even misshapen and knew that the feeling would only grow stronger as she grew rounder. Although he showed no lessening of his passion for her, she was not feeling her prettiest nor too capable of inspiring and holding onto his passion.

That, she mused, was not the feeling she wished to hold when she came face to face with his past. She knew there would be women at the Dunmore keep who had shared Parlan's bed in the past. There was also a good chance that at least one of those women would be sure to remind her of that fact and even intend to repeat it despite the presence of a wife. Even at her most confident, Aimil knew she would find that difficult to deal with. She did not want to face it when her waistline was little more than a memory.

Giving a soft, self-derisive laugh, she admitted that, waist or no waist, a part of her also wished to go. Worse, it was for the same reason she did not want to go. His former lovers were there, and she did not want him to go without her. The presence of his wife, rounding with child or not, would help push aside most temptation. And that, she decided wryly as Maggie entered, was why she would be riding at Parlan's side when he left Dubhglenn.

"Do ye need a rest, sweeting?" Parlan asked when they had been riding for an hour.

"Nay, I am fine. 'Tis a good brisk day for riding, and I feel little discomfort when on Elfking's back." She patted her mount's neck. "I thought, mayhaps, that ye would be riding him."

"Nay, not this time. Ye look grand on the beast. When I rode into the Dunmores that last time, I thought on how it would

look if ye rode in on Elfking and I upon Raven. T'will be a
fine show."

Although she laughed, she saw the truth of his words when
they rode into the Dunmore bailey a few hours later. The admiration on so many faces was embarrassing to endure. Aimil
noticed that Parlan had little trouble with it, and had to smile.
He did like to put on a fine show as he called it.

After being led to their chambers, she joined Parlan in washing away some of the dust of the journey. The way the maids
who brought them their heated water ignored her and greedily
eyed a half-naked Parlan annoyed her. Parlan seemed oblivious
to it and she tried very hard to follow his example. It was not
easy, however, and she found it even less so as the evening wore
on. Even Lord Dunmore's fulsome daughter, Janet, seemed
more flirtatious and inviting than was appropriate.

When they retired for the night, she held Parlan close and
knew there was a hint of desperation in her lovemaking. That
he sensed it as well was proven by his quizzical glances but
he asked nothing and she offered no hints. She did not want
him to know that she battled with a gut-twisting jealousy for
he had done nothing to deserve the poison such emotion
could arouse. She held him tightly and prayed that she could
continue to control her jealousy.

By the next afternoon she was beginning to think that an
impossible task. Needing some time alone, she wandered out
to the stables. As she brushed down Elfking, she began to
calm the emotions that knotted her stomach only to glance up
and see Janet sauntering toward her. Aimil mused ruefully
that peace would clearly not be something she could enjoy
until they were back at Dubhglenn. Wherever she turned at
the Dunmores, there seemed to be someone only too eager to
remind her that her husband was once a man of healthy appetites who had never hesitated to satisfy them.

"I cannae believe that the Black Parlan would wed some Lowland wench."

And there, Aimil thought crossly, *is another source of annoyance, something else that gnaws at my temper threatening to break my weak control over it.* There were several of the Dunmore clan who held only contempt for anyone not of the Highlands and they made little or no attempt to hide it. Janet added to that with her constant throwing of lures at Parlan. She was twice the annoyance, Aimil mused, as she got ready to answer the woman's slurs yet try to prevent any trouble.

"Ah, weel, life has always been strewn with surprises." Judging by the look upon Janet's face, Aimil decided that she had kept her voice as calm and amiable as she had hoped to, that she had succeeded in keeping her seething anger out of her voice.

"How verra amusing." Janet moved closer to Elfking's stall. "I would never have thought Parlan a man to be caught by a bairn."

"The bairn didnae catch him."

"Nay? 'Tis why he wed ye. Ye somehow tricked him into letting his seed take root. I never would have thought some Lowland slut to be that canny as to get Parlan to err as he never has before."

"That, of course, is assuming that it was an error."

"Of course it was. A MacGuin would never taint his line with the blood of some Lowlander."

It was very hard but Aimil continued to try to control her temper over Janet's continuous slurs. Her pride was rebelling against taking such blows. She knew many an insult about Highlanders with which to battle Janet's cuts but she refused to use them. Not only did she find that sort of thing distasteful but she could not bring herself to insult what was also Parlan's heritage. She certainly did not want him to hear that she had and she knew that Janet would not hesitate to tell him. She also wished that she would not be pushed to trading insults with the woman. It lacked a certain amount of dignity and maturity—both of which she wanted to maintain in this confrontation with one of Parlan's past lovers.

"Taint? Nay, rather strengthen. It can never hurt to bring in fresh blood."

"If ye hadnae come along, it would have been Dunmore blood, my blood, that would have run in his heir's veins."

"Ye are certain of that, are ye?"

"Aye, verra certain. Even if my father hadnae spoken of it so often, I had the heat of Parlan's love words against my skin to tell me. A man doesnae speak to a woman as he did to me whilst we pleasured each other unless he intends more than a night's pleasure."

Aimil sternly told herself not to listen but her mind drew pictures of Janet and Parlan together, locked in an intimate embrace. It cut her badly, fueling her jealousy to a fever pitch. The only thing that kept her from flying at the woman was a loathing of letting Janet know how jealous she was. She suspected that jealousy was what Janet wanted to provoke in her although, for what reasons beyond self-satisfaction, Aimil was not sure. *Probably to make me appear a shrew to Parlan,* Aimil thought crossly, *or even to turn him from my bed whereupon she will so graciously offer him hers.* Aimil felt strongly inclined to hit the woman.

"Any woman is a fool to believe what a man says when he is but trying to part her thighs."

"T'was more than that," Janet hissed.

"Was it?" Aimil looked at the woman coldly. "Then why is it that I am wed to the Black Parlan and not ye?"

Deciding that retreat was her wisest option, Aimil started out of the stable, but Janet grabbed her by the arm. The woman yanked her back then slapped her across the face. Aimil decided that that was not something she would silently endure or walk away from. Moving swiftly, she got a good grip upon Janet, dragged the cursing woman toward the muck pile and tossed her in. Ignoring Janet's screams and curses, Aimil then strode out of the stable and headed straight for her chambers. She did not want to be around when Janet's state became more widely known which she was certain it would be as soon as Janet pulled herself from the mire.

Parlan gaped along with everyone else in the hall when a muck-covered Janet staggered in. An overpowering stench of the stables preceded the clearly enraged woman as she approached the table. Even before the woman spoke, Parlan began to suspect that Aimil was involved. He had sensed that Janet was testing Aimil's patience but he had hoped that Aimil would prove to have more control, would understand the importance of keeping things amiable.

"God's teeth, lass," grumbled Lord Dunmore, "why are ye in such a state?"

"She did this to me, that Lowland slut."

"'Ware, lass." Lord Dunmore cast a wary glance at Parlan. "'Tis Lord MacGuin's wife ye speak of."

"I dinnae care who she wed. She had no right to do this to me."

Parlan held his temper as she ranted on. He hoped that Lord Dunmore would calm her down and get her to leave quickly as he was so evidently trying to do. Then something Janet said drew his full attention.

"Ye hit my wife?" He spoke softly but coldly as he slowly rose to his feet in the suddenly quiet hall.

Paling slightly, Janet strove to defend her actions. "She insulted me."

"She is with child. Ye dinnae strike a woman with child. She could have fallen or been hurt in other ways. And if she did insult ye, 'tis but fair payment for all the ones ye have flung at her head since we arrived." He bowed slightly to Lord Dunmore. "If ye will excuse me, m'lord, I must see how my wife fares." He strode out of the hall.

Lord Dunmore glared at his daughter. "Ye fool lass. If ye werenae so covered in muck, I would slap you."

"For hitting some Lowland slut?"

"For hitting the Black Parlan's woman. 'Tis clear that he prizes the lass. Aye, and I prize the alliance too much to risk it for your folly. Ye will stay to your chambers until he leaves and best ye pray that he doesnae decide to pay this back with far more than one cold smile."

Aimil sighed when Parlan entered their chambers. She knew it was him by the sound of his footsteps but she did not move from where she lay on her back on the bed. Neither did she open her eyes even when he grasped her gently by the chin. She was feeling very weary of conflict and did not wish to face the anger he must surely feel.

"So, she did strike you." Parlan lightly touched her bruised cheek with his fingertips.

Surprised, she finally looked at him. "'Tis bruising?"

"Aye, as always. So too did Janet let slip that she had struck you. How do ye feel?"

"It barely stings. I am certain that the bruise looks worse than it is."

"Nay, I didnae mean your cheek though 'tis glad I am that ye suffer little from it." He gently placed his hand over her abdomen. "Ye didnae stumble or grow too upset, did ye?"

Realizing that his concern was for the child, she felt a bit hurt. "Nay, 'tis fine. Your heir rests secure."

"Good, for any trouble with the bairn now could surely harm ye."

"It wouldnae do the bairn much good either."

"Nay, and t'would sore grieve me if aught happened to him, but 'tis ye I feared for. Ye should have just turned away from her." He sat down beside her on the bed.

"I did but she pulled me back. Have I caused a great deal of trouble?" She was not sorry for what she had done to Janet, felt the woman deserved that and more, but did not wish to be the cause of difficulties between Parlan and his closest allies.

"Nothing worth fashing yourself over." He kissed her then sprawled at her side.

"Ye didnae need to leave your business, did ye?"

"Weel, nay, and I had just as soon wait until the stench of the muck heap has left the hall." He grinned when she grimaced.

Before she could stop herself, she murmured, "Ye were betrothed to Janet?"

"What?" He sat up straight and stared at her in surprise. "What did ye say?"

"Nothing," she mumbled weakly, surprised by his violent reaction and hoping vainly that she could act as if the question had never been asked. "Mayhaps the hall smells better now."

"Aimil, did Janet tell ye that she and I were betrothed?"

"Did I say that?"

He leaned over her, one hand palm down on either side of her head. "Aye, nearly. Did she say that?"

Parlan had known that Janet was pinching at Aimil but he admitted to himself that he had given little thought to the possible content of the woman's words. Although he knew, to his increasing regret, that there were women in the keep who could rightfully claim to have known him very well indeed, he felt he had made Aimil understand that the women he had bedded in the past meant nothing to him and, if reassurance was needed, he could give it again. He did not, however, want any woman filling Aimil's head with lies about promises never made or feelings never felt.

Aimil grimaced as she met his stare. She knew he would press her until she told him everything. She was not sure why it was of any importance to him, why he did not simply say no and leave the matter at that, but he clearly was not going to. Reluctantly, she decided that she might as well tell him the whole of it and save them both a great deal of annoyance.

"She said that, if I hadnae come along, your heir would have carried Dunmore blood, that her father spoke of such a match and"—she took a deep breath and watched him closely as she finished—"that ye said as much yourself." Her eyes widened at the curse he spat.

"And no doubt I whispered these sweet words into her fair ears during some embrace."

"Against her skin, she said. 'Heated love words against her skin' to quote her more exactly." Aimil found the words bitter.

"And that is when ye came to blows?" He kissed her bruised cheek.

"Nay. I swear, Parlan, I sorely tried to rein in my temper. I swallowed her insults about me and about Lowlanders. I even swallowed the insults about why ye married me at all. I ken ye were no monk before we wed so I was willing to ignore all talk of what ye had done in the past and with whom but, when she struck me . . ." Aimil shrugged. "I couldnae stand still for that no matter how strongly I reminded myself that ye wanted no trouble nor upset."

"And ye were within your rights, dearling. She had no call to strike ye, none at all."

"Weel, I ken that my tongue can be sharp though I did try to temper my words." She sighed. "I was fair pressed to control my temper too, there isnae any denying it, which is why I was leaving. I kenned that I would hear of lasses ye had bedded but I wasnae ready to hear that there had been more than that with any of them."

"There wasnae, especially not with Janet Dunmore. Neither was there any 'heated words of love.' I have never even glimpsed Janet Dunmore's skin though she has always been eager to show it to me. I have never bedded the fool woman. Not once."

"Not even once?" She had never doubted that Parlan had

bedded Janet just what feelings had been or had not been involved in the act.

"Nay. If naught else, I kenned weel that Lord Dunmore would cry for marriage if he discovered it."

"And Janet would be sure that he did."

"Aye, before we had caught our breath. Aimil"—he caught her face between his hands and kissed her gently—"I was never her lover and I never spoke love words to the silly woman. I have never been betrothed, or even near to it, with any lass.

"I kenned that Lord Dunmore would have liked such a mating but I never hinted that I would agree to it. Now, if ye hadnae come along, I may weel have ended wedded to the lass for a man has to wed sometime. I never even hinted that much to her.

"I kenned she was pinching at ye but felt it wouldnae help to meddle. I wish I had now for I dinnae want ye worried with these lies. They were lies, Aimil. I swear to that. I am also verra sorry that I didnae realize what sort of insults she would fling at your head."

She sighed and shook her head. "I hadnae realized that the Highlanders hated the Lowlanders so much."

"Not all of us, lass. There are some of us with the wisdom to like or to hate a man according to what sets in his heart not by the place he calls home." He smiled crookedly and winked. "Though 'tis a trial to be so fair toward a Sassanach." His smile grew wider when she laughed softly; then he kissed her again before nimbly getting off the bed. "Enough of that, lass. I have work to do."

Before she could gasp out her outraged reply, he was gone. She shook her head, half-smiling over his nonsense then decided to rest until they all had to gather in the hall for a meal. It annoyed her that the incident with Janet should be enough to make her feel so weary, but she decided it was best for the child to heed her body's urgings to rest. So too would a good rest make it a little easier to face Janet later.

To Aimil's surprise, Janet never appeared for the meal. Since she was sure she had not really hurt the woman, Aimil found it difficult to understand Janet's absence. To her added consternation, Lord Dunmore kept glancing toward her bruised cheek, and scowling. Aimil suspected that the powder and paint she had applied had not hidden the bruising as well as she had hoped. She decided it might be best to avoid the man only to be confronted by him as she started to retire for the night, leaving the men to discuss past glories and their hopes for more in the future.

"M'lady, I wish ye to accept my most humble apologies." Lord Dunmore took her hand in his and raised it briefly to his lips.

A little confused, Aimil asked softly, "For what, m'lord?"

"For my daughter's actions this afternoon. T'was inexcuseable."

"Oh. Weel, t'was but a wee squabble, m'lord. Dinnae fash yourself."

"Ye are too generous."

It took her a few more minutes to convince him that she was neither hurt nor deeply offended. As she finally made her way to her chambers, she shook her head. Lord Dunmore clearly wished the alliance to remain firm as much as Parlan did. Even his plainly cherished daughter took second place to it.

Upon entering her chambers, she found no maid nor had the fire been tended to. It did not really surprise her for such small discourtesies had become common. *Dunmore might be the laird*, she mused as she lit a candle, *but he doesnae rule as completely as he might think he does*. She was certain that he would not approve of the lack of courtesy but she was not going to tell him. Aimil felt sure that such tale-bearing would, in the end, only add to her problems.

She was tending to the fire when Parlan strode in. Glancing briefly at him, she continued to work but cursed to herself. She had hoped to be done before he came. The look upon his face as he strode toward her to take over the chore of the fire told her that he was as furious as she had expected him to be. It was going to take a lot to calm him down.

"Where are the cursed maids? Ye shouldnae be doing this work. Did ye dismiss them?"

"Aye." She had answered too quickly and she knew it so was not surprised when he turned to eye her suspiciously.

"They were never here, were they?"

Sighing, she shook her head, seeing no point in lying to him. The laxity and often the absence of any assistance to her was something she had been expecting him to notice. She was surprised, in fact, that it had taken him so long.

"I will speak to Lord Dunmore in the morning."

"I wish ye wouldnae, Parlan." She shed her robe and climbed into bed, watching as he washed up.

"They break the rules of common courtesy, loving. I cannae believe Dunmore would order it so."

"Oh, nay, I dinnae think he has aught to do with it. I doubt he even kens what games are played."

"And the ones who play them should be punished," he said flatly as he finished undressing. "If only because they could be making a lot of trouble for their laird. 'Tis also that they shirk the work given them and that shouldnae be tolerated."

"Nay, it shouldnae." When he slid into bed beside her, she quickly cuddled up to him when he reached for her. "Cannae ye ignore it?"

"Why, lass? Ye cannae like coming into an unreadied bed-chamber. Aye, ye can do for yourself but ye shouldnae have to. Dunmore has more than enough lasses to see to your needs. Aye, and since ye are with child, they should tend ye even more vigilantly."

"Ye are right in all ye say but, I beg ye, Parlan, leave it be. They must think they have good reason for what they do."

"There is no reason, no pardon, for treating a guest of their laird so discourteously."

"Nay, 'tis true enough." She sighed, wondering how she could explain her feelings to him. "But some of the women might resent me for I keep ye from seeking them out this visit."

"Ye kept me from seeking them out the last time, too," he murmured.

That delighted her, but she pushed on with her explanation. "So, Parlan, there could weel be jealousy at work here. T'will work itself out in time like the festering splinter it can be. As ye said, no promises were made so they will soon cease to pout and turn their interests elsewhere." *Or so I hope*, she added silently.

"Then there is the fact that I am a Lowlander." She placed a finger over his lips to silence him when he began to protest. "Nay, dinnae say it. I ken that many a man can be fair but the ill feeling is there. There is no ignoring it. No doubt there has been a Dunmore man or twa who has died at the hands of a Lowlander and the circumstances wouldnae matter much to one who had lost a loved one.

"What I am trying to say is that 'tis best that ye leave it be, that ye let me sort it out upon my own. Bearing tales to the laird will do little else but harden what ill feeling there is. I must push it aside without aid, prove myself if ye will."

"Ye are my wife, the mistress of Dubhglenn. That should be enough to settle this matter, to end all troubles."

"Not when it may be the verra reason the troubles began. Parlan, abide with me in this. I must settle it myself, win or lose upon my own merit, or, for however long I abide in this land, I willnae be welcome."

"For now I will let ye have your way." He held her close and nuzzled her neck, flicking his tongue over the soft skin at the base of her throat. "And what do ye mean by 'however long I abide in this land?'"

"Weel, I didnae want to speak too firmly of the uncertain future."

"Where ye will abide isnae uncertain. 'Tis with me—forever."

As she succumbed to the passion of his kiss, she decided not to quibble since it was what she hoped for anyway.

Chapter Twenty

Sighing heavily, Aimil tossed aside her needlework petulantly. She was tired of sitting, tired of doing little or nothing. Glancing at her well-rounded figure with a hint of disgust, she reluctantly admitted that she was, perhaps, a little hindered in what she could do. To her dismay, she did waddle when she walked, but Parlan valiantly managed not to laugh, something he found difficult when he had to help her get out of bed in the mornings.

Still, she thought crossly as she struggled to stand up, there had to be something she could do that would satisfy the sudden extreme restlessness that had lately afflicted her. Plying her needle was certainly not enough. Suddenly, she knew what she wanted to do and, she mused as she started out of the hall, without Parlan about, she just might be able to accomplish it.

Partway to the stables she had to fight the impulse to giggle. She had been trying to be secretive, to slip away unseen. The whole idea was ludicrous, and she suddenly saw it that way. She was far too pregnant to move about stealthily. Everyone was keeping a close watch upon her as well, far too close for her to elude it completely. She was the laird's wife, carrying his first child which was now past due and Rory was still alive, had even been spotted a time or two far too close to her for anyone's comfort. Finally, chuckling over how she could have ever thought that she could sneak about Dubhglenn, she stepped into the stables and moved toward Elfking.

"What do ye think ye are doing?"

Gasping and pressing a hand over her rapidly beating heart, Aimil whirled around. "Artair, dinnae frighten me so."

"I didnae mean to." He eyed her very protuberant belly warily as he stepped closer. "Do ye feel all right?"

"Aye, I willnae have the bairn here and now, though, if ye scare me so again, t'wouldnae surprise me if I did."

"Then I shall be verra careful not to frighten ye again. Now, answer me. What are ye doing?"

"I intend to go for a wee ride."

"Are ye mad?"

"Aye, with boredom."

"Now, Aimil, I ken how ye must feel . . ."

"Nay, ye dinnae. Ye could never ken. 'Tis as if I am a prisoner again. Nay, 'tis worse. I had more freedom when all I carried was ransom value. I cannae abide sitting still, doing needlework and just waiting for another moment. I must do something."

"Fine, but that doesnae mean going for a ride."

"Aye, it does."

"Ye could hurt yourself or the bairn."

"Aye, and just mayhaps I will shake this wee one into recalling that a bairn is supposed to come out sometime."

"Exactly, and he could decide to do so whilst ye are out there somewhere, nowhere near the women ready to aid you."

The way he was standing before her, his arms crossed and looking down at her as if she were some errant child reminded her a great deal of Parlan at his most overbearing. It annoyed her just as much. However, she hid her annoyance for she knew that, unlike Parlan, Artair could be persuaded to change his mind. The younger MacGuin was susceptible to subtle pleading.

"Artair"—she laid a hand upon his arm—"a wee ride, a gentle wee one, cannae hurt the bairn. I have been riding all my life. T'willnae hurt me to do something I have been doing all my life. Aye, and whilst I carried the bairn, right up until I grew too round to mount with ease. Ye can help me mount. I can do it. I just need a wee bit of help."

"If ye need help to get into the saddle, then ye shouldnae be riding."

"Nonsense. There are a lot of ladies that willnae even try to mount a horse without aid yet they are never told not to go riding."

"They arenae big and round with Parlan MacGuin's heir. I am certain Parlan has told ye to do no more riding."

"Weel, ye are wrong in that. He hasnae ordered me at all, never said I couldnae go riding." She decided that was not really a lie for Parlan had never told her not to, even if he had made it clear that he was about to when she had ceased her rides all on her own. "I stopped because I was beginning to feel verra silly and awkward atop Elfking, looking as I do."

"Then why do ye suddenly need to ride now?"

"Because I cannae abide another moment of doing naught!" she snapped then sighed, honestly sorry to be so short-tempered with him. "Sorry. 'Tis just hard to be so verra big and so verra restless. The twa dinnae go together weel at all." She smiled hopefully at Artair. "Can ye help me with the saddle?"

"Aye, I can," he grumbled even as he did so, "though I ken weel I will be sorely regretting this. I should make ye wait until Parlan returns."

"Parlan willnae be back until 'tis far too late for me to go riding."

"I ken it. I just pray he comes back late enough for me to have got ye back safe from this folly."

"Ye arenae heeding what is said at all, Parlan." Lagan exchanged a grin with Leith before nudging Parlan.

Parlan grimaced as he silently acknowledged the truth of that. He had come to a meeting of the Mengues and their allies not only to assure the lot of them that he considered his marriage to Aimil Mengue a treaty of sorts with all of them but to hear whatever news had been gathered on the elusive Rory Fergueson. While he felt sure he had done the former, his intention to listen was sadly wavering. He could not keep his mind on the business at hand. His mind wished to busy itself thinking of Aimil and the child she carried.

"I dinnae like leaving Aimil when she is so near to her time."

"She has been near her time for almost a month. I begin to think the bairn plans to wait until he can walk out."

Chuckling over Lagan's remark, Parlan nodded in amused agreement. "Aimil has puzzled over that as weel."

"Here, heed what old Simon Broth is saying," hissed Leith, urgency tightening his voice.

"I tell ye I am certain it was him, that whoreson, Rory. I dinnae mean to bring ye pain, Lachlan, old friend, by stirring up the painful memories of the past, but the lass they found was murdered in the same manner your wife was. Who else could it have been? The killing held his mark. T'was clear for even an old man like me to see."

"Do they ken who the lass was?"

"Nay, Leith. None had seen her before, not until she arrived a few weeks past," Simon Broth answered.

"They must have had some knowledge of her." Parlan knew that few people ignored a stranger in their midst. "Some information that might lead us to ken who she was or someone who did ken."

"Do ye think it is important?" Simon asked.

"It could be."

"Weel, 'tis said she was a fair and fulsome brown-haired lass, twenty years of age or older. They couldnae say exactly. What little she had to do with the plain folk, even the ones at the inn where she stayed, didnae make them feel she was the friendly sort. Haughty and shrewish, they said, though she did favor the innkeeper's son who be a braw, handsome laddie."

"That could be any of a thousand lasses. Was there naught else? Naught upon the body to give any clue?"

"Ooh, aye, aye. I meant to show it before I had finished my tale." Simon dug a ring from a pocket in his pourpoint and held it up for all to see. "I dinnae hold much hope for it to help. I couldnae place it and I ken most all about here who would wear such as this."

"Lagan," Parlan whispered, his gaze fixed upon the ring he suddenly recognized.

"Aye, I fear so." Lagan rose and slowly moved to take the ring from Simon. "She wasnae from about here, old man. That is why ye couldnae recognize her or this. She was Catarine Dunmore, a cousin of mine. What was done with the body?"

"T'was buried proper. Any in the village can tell her kin where to find her. What was the lass doing 'round here, with him?"

"After betraying Aimil and Parlan to Rory, she had no place to go and no one else to go to. Did none see anything or hear anything where she was murdered?" Lagan was not surprised to find Parlan and Leith flanking him for the village where Catarine had been murdered was very near the border of the Highlands and the Lowlands, placing Rory uncomfortably close to Dubhglenn.

"Little of worth. They do feel it was the man who came to visit her from time to time but they couldnae say what he looked like for he and the short one, as they called his constant companion, slipped about like shadows, never letting any get a good look at them. The lass was bound to the bed and gagged so she wasnae able to alert any to the danger she was in. The inn was quite raucous that night as weel. They ken when the man came but none saw him leave. She was found in the morning. As I said, the manner of her death tells me she died by that whoreson's hand," Simon insisted.

"Aye, it tells me that as weel. Where she died tells me that Rory draws too near to Aimil. I am returning to Dubhglenn now. Do ye come with me, Lagan?"

"I ache to, Parlan, but duty commands me to ride and tell Catarine's kin of her death."

"Aye, I understand." He briefly clasped Lagan by the shoulder. "My condolences."

"Weel, I dinnae grieve for her even though she was kin. 'Tis the manner of her death that troubles me. Nay, Catarine wasnae one to leave many grieving for her passing but she didnae deserve what must have been a hard, long death."

"Nay, no one does save for the ones who deal in such. Ye will be returning to Dubhglenn?"

"Aye, as soon as I have accomplished my sad chore."

"I will come with ye now."

Glancing at Leith, Parlan nodded. "That little surprises me." He looked at Lachlan who was already standing up. "Ye as weel? Do ye doubt my ability to keep Aimil safe?"

"Nay, lad, and weel ye ken it if ye but think a moment, so smooth down those ruffled feathers. I dinnae mean to go along for that reason. Ye have been searching about your lands and I have been searching about mine because we didnae ken where that adder had slipped away to. Now we have an idea. Until that changes, t'would serve better if we search together."

"Aye, verra wise. Let us hurry then before that sheep dung named Geordie talks a moment's sense into the madman he serves and all hint of Rory fades again." Parlan turned sharply and left the hall of Lachlan's keep, the others hurrying to follow.

They were halfway to Dubhglenn, moving slowly for a change as they tried to pace their mounts, when Leith moved next to Parlan, and struggled to find the words to ease the increasing worry he could see in the man's face. "Aimil is weel guarded."

"Aye." Lachlan moved up on Parlan's other side. "The man cannae get to her within the walls of Dubhglenn."

"Nay, not if she stays there." Parlan could not find the words to explain the fear that had begun to grip him and continued to grow.

"Weel, where would the fool lass go? She must be verra large with child by now."

"Aye, Father, verra large." Leith smiled faintly. "I saw her but days ago, and she needs a hand to but rise from her seat."

"Verra true." Parlan too fleetingly smiled, but his grim mood returned quickly. "Another lass would be kept still by such a thing. They wouldnae even think on going far when the bairn weighs upon them so heavily. I cannae be certain Aimil would act so."

"Nay, and I cannae tell ye she would either." Lachlan grimaced. "She has never been as other lasses. A bairn coming wouldnae change that."

"Nay, it wouldnae. She has been growing restless of late and it now has me worried. I cannae say what it is but I feel that something has gone wrong. That feeling gnaws at me now and grows stronger each moment that passes."

"Weel, then, we best gain some speed." Even as Lachlan spoke, he gently urged his mount to a swifter pace.

Doing the same, Parlan muttered, "If she isnae setting quietly in the keep, I shall beat the wench, I swear it."

"I will hold her steady so that ye can," Lachlan offered.

"I think we shall find her in childbed. She is past due and that may be all that eats at you."

"I hope ye prove right, Leith. Though I have my own worries about the birthing, I would far prefer that than to find her outside Dubhglenn and mayhaps within Rory's foul reach."

Aimil took a deep breath and smiled at a frowning Artair. They had paused for a moment so that she could enjoy the feeling of being outside of walls for the first time in many days. It was far more wonderful to be in the glorious weather than to acknowledge it while standing behind thick stone walls. Artair, however, was proving a less than enjoyable companion for he made no secret of his continuing disapproval of the ride.

"Come, Artair, can ye not enjoy such a fine day? They are a pleasure that is too rare."

"I would enjoy it more if I kenned that ye were safe back in Dubhglenn with your feet back on the ground."

"I am nearly as safe as that on Elfking's back." She patted her mount's strong neck. "He would never harm me in any way."

"True. Ye have spoiled that beast to your hand. Still, 'tis not that which truly troubles me." He frowned darkly as he looked around. "I have a bad feeling about our being out here. Parlan wouldnae like it."

That was true but Aimil had no intention of admitting it. "We are taking it most carefully. In truth, we go along as if we ride old weary nags instead of the fine, swift mounts we have. What harm in that? If Parlan decides he must rage about it, I shall take all the blame. After all, I did talk ye into it against your better judgment."

"Aye, ye did and I dinnae ken why I let ye do it." He shook his head.

"'Tis because ye are sweet."

"Am I or am I but stupid? Aimil, 'tis undoubtedly mad to let a woman so far gone with child go for a ride. But ye forget that Rory Fergueson has yet to be found and brought to justice?"

"I am not about to forget such a thing. Surely he wouldnae come so close to Dubhglenn and Parlan's sword?"

"Who can say? The man isnae right in his mind. T'would seem foolhardy indeed to come so close to a place where so many ache to kill him but it was foolhardy for him to take ye and do as he did. He couldnae have hidden ye there and carried on so for verra long. Then too, a man who suffers madness can be verra clever."

"Ah, but Geordie, Rory's man, is clever. He wouldnae let Rory come near here."

"T'would be fine if that is how it goes but"—Artair shrugged—"in such cases, who can tell? Geordie may seem to lead Rory at times but that doesnae mean that Rory isnae the master still."

Aimil shivered and could not stop herself from looking all around her. She told herself her fear was nonsense. Pure nonsense. Rory had always been very careful about keeping himself safe and coming so close to Dubhglenn was not.

Despite that reassurance, she felt a chill ripple up her spine. She could not stop herself from thinking about how totally helpless she was in her present state nor about how any threat to her was also a threat to her child. Her hand instinctively went to her abdomen as she thought on that. No matter how sternly she told herself not to let her fears rule nor to let Artair's dour words upset her, she felt as if Rory did indeed lurk nearby, as if he watched her. The fear she could not dismiss annoyed her, and she glared at Artair.

Artair eyed her warily. They were slowly working toward being friends, but he could not yet claim to know her well. He wondered if Parlan really knew her or ever would. Never had he met a woman who seemed to so delight in acting contrary. He had hoped to evoke a little common sense in her by voicing his honest concerns but she seemed to be annoyed.

"Ye were trying to frighten me, werenae ye, Artair MacGuin?" She scowled when a fleeting look of guilt crossed his face, confirming her suspicions.

"I was but trying to stir a wee bit of common sense in you."

"Your idea of common sense."

"It should be yours as weel. I wasnae feeding ye lies. I spoke of my honest worries I hold about all of this."

She sighed, reined in her annoyance and nodded. "Fair enough. I rather wish ye hadnae though."

"Weel, I didnae really mean to frighten ye badly. Do ye feel all right?" He warily eyed her bulging stomach.

"Ye didnae scare the bairn out of me if that is what ye fear." She could not restrain a laugh when he flushed. "Artair, a bairn doesnae come out with such speed. Nay, especially not a first one. Even had ye scared me into labor, t'would be hours before Parlan's heir arrived. Dinnae fash yourself over it so."

"Weel, ye are a wee bit late."

"Aye, mayhaps, but being late doesnae mean the bairn will come any faster when it does decide to leave me."

"I think I would still feel more at ease if ye were back at Dubhglenn nearer to your bed and the women to help you."

"I begin to think I would too. Try as I may, I cannae ignore your warnings about Rory. The taste of fear he left me with is still too strong. Your words have made me feel that eyes watch us from every bush and tree."

He grimaced and reached out to squeeze her hand briefly. "I am sorry. That really wasnae my intent."

"I ken it. Your intent has succeeded. We will return to Dubhglenn in a moment."

"Why hesitate?"

"Because when I return to Dubhglenn, I ken weel that

t'will be a long time before I can leave again. As ye say, the bairn is late. He will bring me to my bed verra soon, and I shall be tied to it for a while. Aye, and then to him and his hunger. For just a moment longer I wish to sit here, breathing the fine, crisp air and seeing no walls about me." She smiled crookedly. "Ye can busy yourself looking to find all those eyes I now think are peering at us."

"Aimil, I dinnae think he is that close."

"Now, dinnae back down. 'Tis only wise to be cautious. I let myself forget that for a moment. That is something I cannae do. Nay, I cannae relax my guard until Rory Fergueson is dead."

Rory glared at the pair in the clearing. "T'will be a long time before that happens, my pretty slut. Look at her, Geordie. Do ye see her?"

Hate poured through Rory's veins with a heat as strong as any passion he had ever tasted. Aimil Mengue sat there proud and beautifully clothed as if she were some fine lady but he knew better. She was no better than a base whore.

His gaze fell to her bulging abdomen, and his hands clenched so tightly they hurt. As Kirstie had done, Aimil had allowed her body to take and to nurture the seed of another. Worse than Kirstie, however, Aimil had let one of the MacGuins he so loathed to possess her and to round her lithe shape with child.

With Kirstie, he had gained only the satisfaction of avenging her scorn with her death. In killing Aimil, he could accomplish so much more. He could avenge her scorning of him, repay them all for the ruin they had brought him, hurt Lachlan Mengue by depriving him of the clearest memory of Kirstie the man had ever had, and bring the great Black Parlan to his knees for, in one stroke, he could deprive the man of his wife and his heir.

From where he lay at Rory's side, Geordie peered through the bracken. "Aye, I see her. Now can we leave this place?"

"When she is so close I need but reach out and take her? Dinnae be a fool."

"I begin to think a fool is just what I am. 'Tisnae wise our being so nigh to Dubhglenn without even a horse to flee on. The land crawls with men aching to spit us on their swords. Aye, and now there will be more since ye killed that Dunmore wench."

"She deserved to die. She was naught but a whore who never let a moment pass wherein she didnae complain or whine. I doubt there is any who will miss the ill-tempered slattern."

"True, but even if every Dunmore alive hated the wench, she was kin and they will demand blood for blood."

"Let them demand. They willnae catch me. None has in all these months. Do ye expect me to crawl away like some whipped cur? I have lost everything. I am hunted and haunted at every turning. Someone must pay for that."

"Aye, but there isnae any need to set yourself in their hands. Look, 'tis Artair MacGuin himself who rides with the lass. Do ye think he will let ye take the lass without a fight? She is his laird's, his brother's, wife and she carries the heir to Dubhglenn. If he even catches scent of ye, he will seek ye out, howling for your blood."

"Let him seek. Let him howl. He is naught but a drunken boy. I neednae fear him."

"'Tis said he changes. Aye, for the better, growing stronger and more like the Black Parlan every day. He looks verra sober now."

"Ye fret as badly as any old woman, Geordie. Look at the slut. She sets there with her belly swollen by that whoreson's bastard, and smiles at his brother. T'wouldnae surprise me to learn that she services them both. Just like her mother. Kirstie turned from me to another, let that fool Lachlan fill her belly with his spawn over and over. Weel, she paid for her slighting of me. Now I shall make her daughter pay as weel, and t'will be a double victory for me. I will take the Black Parlan's woman and his child in one stroke."

"Aye, if the Black Parlan doesnae arrive to take ye in one stroke."

Geordie heartily wished that he had deserted Rory Fergueson years ago. The man was too mad to heed sense or to be controlled now. Rory would lead them both to the slaughter, but it was far too late for Geordie to turn away now and he knew it. He may not have struck the death blow to the women, and some men, that Rory had murdered but he had aided the man so that his own hands were as bloodstained as Rory's. The men now hunting them knew that and would not allow him to escape. His fate was irretrievably tied to Rory's. Geordie simply wished the man was not so set on making that fate a swift, bloody death.

"Let that whoreson come. Aye, let him come. He shallnae find me to cut down. Nay, if the Black Parlan comes here, he will find only corpses, only grief and blood. God willnae deny me my rightful vengeance upon that whoreson and the bride that scorned me." Rory unsheathed his sword and left his hiding place, his gaze fixed upon the couple in the clearing.

Thinking to himself that God had long ago denied Rory, Geordie reluctantly followed the man. He really had no wish to kill Aimil for he dreaded the thought of how firmly that would set the Black Parlan upon their trail. The man would never relinquish the hunt. Nevertheless, he made no attempt to stop Rory nor stop himself. He was no longer sure that he knew how.

Aimil stretched and then smiled at Artair. He was trying very hard to be patient with her. His eagerness to quit the

place and hie back to Dubhglenn was evident in every line of
his body. She decided it was probably past time for her to
consider his point of view and position with more sympathy.
He had given her her brief taste of freedom and so it was only
fair that she return to him his peace of mind.

She smiled, acknowledging that she was not acting self-
lessly. She was very weary of sitting on Elfking. It was no
longer comfortable for her body was too awkwardly shaped.
So too was she still unable to shake the feeling that they were
being watched. Pleasant as the place was, she could no longer
feel safe in it.

"All right, Artair, I am done with freedom. We may return
now." She smiled when he breathed an audible sigh of relief.

"Are ye sure? We could linger another moment or twa if ye
wish."

"Nay, there is naught here for me now."

"Ah, but there is where ye are wrong, my pretty slut. Death
is here for ye now. Aye, death is here."

Chapter Twenty-One

Aimil sat as if frozen and stared at the ragged, dirty man before her. Despite the loss of his finery, she had no trouble recognizing Rory. His was a face that would never leave her nightmares. He was the cause of the fear that had never left her since the day he had taken her from Parlan and revealed the monster that lay beneath his beauty. His words seemed neither fanciful nor mad to her. In her eyes, he was death in all its horror and pain.

"Get behind me, Aimil," hissed Artair as he drew his sword and prepared himself to face the rather poor odds of two against one.

Shaking free of her fear, she moved to obey Artair. They could flee, she thought. They had horses. Then she realized that Geordie lurked to the rear of them. Artair stood his ground for fear that Geordie would block the horses, startle them and probably unseat her. If she were not so large with child, they would have no fear of such things. Her condition stole their chance of bolting for freedom. Even as she thought that they ought to try it anyway, Geordie moved with a speed that was astounding and, with only a few moves, had knocked

Artair from his horse, wounding him and forcing the younger man to fight for his life.

"So quickly does your gallant knight fall." Rory lunged to grab for Elfking's reins.

Cursing, Aimil kicked at him, but her foot barely grazed his face. She then found herself clinging for dear life to Elfking. The horse, sensing the danger to her, reared and struck out at Rory. The man dodged the first strike, but the second caught him on the side of the face. As he screamed and tried to scramble out of reach of Elfking's deadly hooves, the horse struck him again, Aimil felt sickened by the sound of hooves striking flesh.

Each time Elfking came down before rearing again, Aimil felt the jarring throughout her body. She knew that Elfking was accomplishing what Artair had feared from many another source. Her labor had begun. She made no attempt to halt the horse's attack, however. It was undoubtedly keeping her, her child, and Artair alive.

She finally dared a glance Artair's way. Geordie was deserting the battle to race to Rory's side. Artair sank to his knees, clutching his side which bled far too freely for Aimil's liking. She had to get him away before Geordie could renew his attack. The wound might not be fatal but the weakening from the loss of blood made Artair easy prey. Since his horse had fled, she had to stop Elfking's attack at the safest moment to allow Artair to mount. She could only pray that Artair would be strong enough.

"Look at my face! Look what that Devil's spawn did to my face!"

Despite a voice that warned her not to, Aimil looked. As she glanced Rory's way, he removed his hand from his face to show Geordie the results of Elfking's attack. Even though she wondered how a stomach gripped by contractions could do so, hers heaved, sickened by the sight of Rory's ruined face.

Elfking had not struck Rory squarely. The horse's hooves had dragged along the side of Rory's face, taking the skin with them. Nothing could restore Rory's face to its former beauty. If the wound healed without infection, the scar would be large and ragged. Despite her loathing of the man, Aimil found no joy in the sight.

Since Geordie was busy trying to calm Rory and to tend to the wound as well as avoid Elfking, Aimil decided the time was right to flee. "Artair, can ye mount?" She kept her gaze fixed upon the enemy as she fought to quiet Elfking.

"Aye, I think so though, God's tears, I feel close to death." Artair struggled to his feet.

"Ye will be far closer than ye wish to be if ye dinnae mount and quickly. Their attention will again turn our way verra soon."

Keeping a watch on Geordie and Rory, she felt Artair falter twice in trying to pull himself up behind her. Although Elfking was steady, the horse was still agitated and could flare up at any moment. Nevertheless, she knew she had to chance it when Artair faltered a third time. Releasing one arm from its firm grip around Elfking, she grasped Artair by the arm when he made his next attempt to mount. To her relief Elfking did not rear, and the extra pull she exerted upon Artair was enough to get him up behind her. She then cautiously retrieved the reins she had dropped when Elfking had begun to rear and she had held tightly to his neck.

"Here is the chance to kill that filth yet I must tuck tail and run."

"Ye could do none of us any good dead, Artair. Hold tightly. I cannae catch ye or lift ye if ye fall."

As soon as she felt him grip her tightly, she spurred Elfking into a gallop. The frustrated cries and curses of Geordie and Rory were like music to her ears. It meant she had gotten away from them. Now all she had to concern herself with was getting to Dubhglenn before she had the child or Artair fell off Elfking.

She mused a little wryly that that would undoubtedly prove enough concern to last her for a lifetime. Then some of Rory's screaming rage reached her ears, and she thought of nothing save escaping the madman, of reaching the safety of Dubhglenn.

"Ye have lost the chance," Geordie finally screamed at the raging Rory. "Let us leave here before ye lose your life, too."

It was another moment before Rory gained enough control to speak in a normal voice. "Are ye telling me to give up?"

"I am asking ye to flee now, before she has a chance to tell anyone where ye are. 'Tisnae the same at all." Geordie sensed that Rory's madness had reached the point where even his life was at risk. "Ye willnae have another chance if ye linger here for there is sure to be someone along soon and they willnae let ye live."

"Aye, aye. Ye are right. I must never risk my chance to seek vengeance." He lightly touched the wound on his face that Geordie had awkwardly bandaged. "Here is but another crime to add to the ones that slut must pay for."

"And she will," Geordie soothed but, as he silently urged Rory on, he felt it would be a very long time, if ever, before Aimil left Dubhglenn so lightly guarded and he knew that the hunt for Rory would now become even more determined, especially if Artair died from his wound.

It was a long while before Aimil felt safe enough to slow Elfking's pace. Artair rested so heavily against her back that it worried her. Her contractions too were growing stronger. She feared she had erred in telling Artair that even a baby startled into birth did not come very speedily. Her child felt very determined to be set free.

"Artair? How fare ye?" She felt him stir and sighed with relief. "Can ye hold on until we reach Dubhglenn?"

"By my teeth if I must." He frowned as, beneath his hands which rested upon her belly, he sensed something. "How do ye fare? Has the bairn been hurt? I dinnae mean to be indelicate but your belly feels strange."

"It seems the bairn's memory has been shaken."

"Eh?"

"He has recalled that he cannae always abide in there."

"Now? The bairn comes now?"

"Aye. Now."

"Jesu. What do we do now?"

"Go on."

"But, ye must be feeling verra uncomfortable."

"Aye, I am but I have no choice, do I?" She was not surprised when he gave no reply but was rather disappointed that he could offer no other choices.

"Doesnae this hurt the bairn?"

"Nay. Artair, he willnae come for a while yet though it would be fitting for a child of mine and Parlan's to be born in the saddle, dinnae ye think so?"

"I may think it fitting but I dinnae want to see it. Does . . . does it pain ye much?"

She almost smiled over the hesitant question. He sounded shy and decidedly nervous. It had never ceased to amaze her that men who so vigorously went about the business of creating children knew so little about childbirth, what to do, what should be done, or most anything else. His ignorance was simply another reason to get back to Dubhglenn as quickly as possible. Aimil did not want to ask Artair to deliver her child and she was confident that he did not want that either.

"Aye, it hurts, but not as bad as it will. Nae as much as your wound, I wager."

"Oh, that isnae so bad. I have tied my shirt about my waist, and the bleeding has eased."

It was not only the pain-ridden tone to his hoarse voice that suggested he lied. He still rested too heavily against her, and his breathing was irregular. While the suggestion that she was close to birthing her child had roused him some, Aimil suspected that he was periously close to unconsciousness. He was fighting that blackness, however. She only hoped that he continued to win the battle against it until they reached Dubhglenn. If he fainted and fell from Elfking, she would have to leave him—for she could never move him—and that was not something she really wished to do. Rory and Geordie may not have fled and could find the helpless Artair.

Gritting her teeth, she kept Elfking at a steady pace. Even his smooth gait was a torture, however. She could not give into the pain, stop, and concern herself with the birthing of her child. It was tempting but she fought that temptation, using the spectre of Rory to drive her onward.

"Would ye like to stop?" Despite his own pain and weakness, Artair was aware of Aimil's increasing difficulties.

"If I stop, Artair, I shall never continue until the child is born. I fear to stop for neither of us ken much about birthing a bairn. Neither can we be sure that Rory has left, has run for his life. We thought t'would be foolish for him to come so near to Dubhglenn yet he did. We cannae think that he will now become wise. I dinnae think I have to tell ye how it would be if he caught us off Elfking, me giving birth." She gasped as a fierce contraction ripped through her.

"Nay, there would be no chance for us. No chance at all. 'Tis just that ye seem to be growing worse."

"Aye, I am, but we are also drawing nearer to Dubhglenn. Dinnae fash yourself. I have hours to go yet."

"If ye say so." He laughed weakly, the sound drained by his pain. "Parlan will come home to find himself a father."

Parlan knew he was not going to like what he found at Dubhglenn the moment he rode through its gates. The people gathered in the bailey looked too guilty and fretful for his liking. Even Malcolm was hesitant to respond when Parlan dismounted and signaled to him. He felt his worry for Aimil become a hard knot in his stomach. A glance at Leith and Lachlan did nothing to ease his concern. They too looked worried. Malcolm's feeble attempts at a cheerful greeting made Parlan scowl.

"Where is Aimil?"

"Ye cannae expect a lass so heavy with bairn to rush out to greet ye."

"Malcolm, dinnae trouble yourself with playing that game. It willnae work. Where is my wife? I want the truth."

"Weel, ye willnae like it."

"That much I have discerned for myself."

"She isnae here."

"Aye? So, where is she?"

"I fear no one is too sure. She isnae alone. Artair is with her," Malcolm hurried to say when Parlan's anger reflected in his face. "No one would ever let her go off on her own."

"She isnae within Dubhglenn?"

"Nay." Malcolm cringed slightly as Parlan hissed out a stream of vicious curses. "She is out riding with Artair."

"Out riding?" Parlan's bellow made several men nearby jump nervously. "The fool lass is overdue upon her childbed and she goes out riding? How could ye let her do such a fool thing? How could Artair? Is there not an ounce of wit left within the walls of Dubhglenn?"

"Calm yourself, laddie." Lachlan placed a hand on Parlan's arm. "I am as worried as ye are but be fair. Ye ken as weel as I do that Aimil can be verra clever in getting her way. Why should they watch for such a thing? As ye said, the lass is overdue to take to her childbed. No one would ever think she would get upon Elfking and go for a ride now."

With much effort, Parlan reined in his fury. "Has anyone gone to look for that pair of fools?"

"Nay. We decided to give them another hour to return. Even if the lass has had some difficulties, Artair would soon come for help."

"If he was able to. Malcolm, 'tisnae just that she has gone riding when she should be carefully awaiting the birth. Aye, I can even understand what might have driven her to such a rash act. She has been kept much fettered. We have strong proof that Rory and his hellhound, Geordie, are lurking near. Catarine Dunmore has been found."

"Dead?"

"Quite dead. He did to Catarine as he did to my cousin and Lachlan's wife. Aye, and as he tried to do to Aimil. That is why I am back so soon. Old Simon Broth was the one called when Catarine was found. I left as soon as the man told the tale."

Malcolm grasped him by the arm when Parlan made to remount. "'Tis still wisest to wait. No one even kens which way the pair rode when they left here."

"He is right."

"Lachlan," Parlan protested even as he stopped trying to mount.

"Aye, he is. When ye dinnae ken whether they be south, east, north or west, ye can do naught more than run about blind. We only ken that Rory lurks at the border. Give it a wee bit more time. They could yet return on their own and safely."

Although he hated doing it, Parlan had to agree with Lachlan. It would be a fool's errand to charge out to search when no one even knew where to begin looking, an errand that should not be made use of unless all else had failed. Cursing, he turned from his mount toward the gates, and stared blindly out at the empty landscape.

"I will wait one more hour."

"That is what we thought to do," murmured Malcolm. "Then t'will be too long she and Artair have been gone, considering that she, weel, she isnae really fit for a long ride."

"She isnae really fit for a short one either." He strode to the gates and halted inside of them. "I could use some ale to wash the dust from my throat, Malcolm. I mean to wait here until she returns so that I may beat her or until the search begins."

As Malcolm hurried to fetch some drink and the others dispersed, Leith moved to Parlan's side. "She isnae a helpless lass."

"Nay, not for the most part but she is now, and ye ken it as weel as I do. She cannae even rise from her bed in the morn without aid she has grown so full. Artair is all that would stand between her and Rory if the man set upon them."

"Artair isnae without skill. Nay, in truth, he has a fine skill with a sword and his fists."

"Aye, I meant him no slur. I mean that he would be one against twa and with a helpless Aimil to protect as he could. Those arenae odds I feel good about. For all they are but murdering cowards, Geordie and Rory possess a fine skill, too."

"And Rory wouldnae hesitate to harm Aimil just because she is large with child," Leith said softly, voicing their fears.

"Nay, God's beard. He could easily see it as but another reason to do her harm."

"Come, let us not weary ourselves thinking of all the worst that can happen. Aye, there is a chance that Rory could have come upon the pair but there is also a verra good chance that she and Artair will soon come riding back, safe and untouched."

"Aye, and then all I need concern myself with is which one shall I beat first." His words were harsh and cold but, when he looked back out over the empty land, the lines on his face were those of worry not fury, and he prayed that he would soon see his errant wife riding toward him unharmed and concerned only that he had caught her in her foolish act.

* * *

"Artair," Aimil cried hoarsely, relief momentarily diverting her from her discomfort. "I see Dubhglenn. We are nearly there." When he did not reply, she grew worried. "Artair?"

"Aye, little mother, I am still amongst the living. 'Tis good to hear that we are so close for I fear I cannae hold onto ye verra much longer. T'would be verra fine indeed if to this success we could add Parlan's not finding out about this folly."

Easily recognizing the tall figure that stood at the gate watching them, Aimil sighed. "I fear our luck isnae that good."

"Nay, even if the wound I suffer could be kept a secret, we must tell him how close Rory has come."

"Verra true but I wasnae meaning that. I fear 'tisnae only Rory lurking at Dubhglenn. Parlan has returned early."

Rousing himself to look over Aimil's shoulder, Artair groaned. "And here he comes looking as black as he ever has."

"Ye could always give into that faint ye have fought so weel until now."

"And leave ye to face his wrath alone?"

"If 'tis too bad, I have my own retreat I can make. By the time I bring his child into the world, he should have calmed some."

The alarm Parlan had felt upon seeing the pair return upon only Elfking had turned mostly to anger by the time he reached their side. "How could ye be so thoughtless, so foolish? What has happened?" Even as he bellowed at her, his gaze swept over her as he carefully searched her for some sign of injury and, despite her paleness, found none. "I begin to think ye witless."

Exhausted and in increasing pain, Aimil felt very inclined to bellow right back at Parlan. Artair diverted her, however. Although she had made the suggestion in jest and knew Artair had not seen it as serious, she knew he was about to faint. She clung very tightly to Elfking so that she would not be dragged out of the saddle when Artair finally fell.

"I think ye best catch Artair. He has stayed conscious as long as he was able."

Startled, Parlan moved quickly to catch the falling Artair. Leith helped him carry the unconscious, young man back into Dubhglenn. Parlan silently cursed himself for not seeing what Artair's condition was because he had been too concerned for Aimil.

Aimil followed them into Dubhglenn on Elfking. Her father quickly moved to help her dismount so that she could go after Parlan who was already inside of the keep, shouting orders that would swiftly bring all Artair might need. A look upon her father's face told Aimil that he knew what ailed her, but she curtly shook her head. A shrug was his only reply, but she knew it meant he would not say anything for the moment. She needed to see that Artair was fine before she gave into her own needs for she felt responsible for his wound.

She entered Artair's chambers, faintly aware of her father closely following her. Parlan and Old Meg, with Leith and Malcolm aiding as they could, were already busy caring for Artair. Aimil stood to the side, out of the way. Her hope that she would also be out of mind was quickly shattered by Parlan.

In the one look he shot her way, Aimil saw how angry he was. She had not really anticipated such fury but she supposed she should have. So too did she reluctantly admit that he had some right to that anger. In one innocent bid for a moment's freedom in the sun, she had put three lives at risk, one not even really begun. She suspected it was risking the child's life which angered him the most. That tweaked at her only slightly for she could easily understand it. It was a substantial part of the annoyance she felt with herself.

Parlan fought desperately to control his anger. He knew it

was bred by his fear for Aimil more than by anything she had done. She looked pale and weary, not able to deal with his ire at the moment. Knowing that she had undoubtedly already been through enough and that, in her condition, she should not be pushed too far or too hard, he was determined not to unleash that anger on her. Despite his efforts, it came through in his voice, making it clipped and cold.

"What happened and no evasions."

The chill in his voice only hurt her fleetingly, and she realized she was simply too burdened with other worries and too weary to get upset by the fact that he seemed to hate her. "Ye will get no evasions nor half-truths for this is too important. T'was Rory."

"Aye, I ken it."

"'Tis why ye came back early."

"Aye, t'was said he was on the border and I feared he would be mad enough to come near Dubhglenn. I had but hoped that ye wouldnae be foolish enough to place yourself within his grasp." He winced for that was argumentative and he did not wish to carry on like that, especially not when he needed information.

Aimil knew she was poorly when she did not immediately bristle in response to that prod. "Quite." She hurriedly described where she and Artair had been attacked, and Parlan immediately sent Malcolm to begin a search. "He was mildly wounded, Malcolm, if that is of any help to ye," she called after him and he acknowledged her comment with little hesitation in carrying out his orders from Parlan. "I would think the man would be far away by now but then I would never have thought he would come so close to here."

"Nay, neither would I but he wants ye."

"Aye, he does and I fear I may have given him yet another reason to hunt me."

"The bairn?" Parlan felt sure that the sight of a very pregnant Aimil must have enraged Rory.

"Well, I cannae say how he feels about that though I do ken that it wouldnae have stopped him from doing whatever he wished to. Nay, 'tis his face. Elfking has destroyed Rory's fine face."

"Elfking has?"

Nodding, Aimil hesitated a moment before replying for Old Meg was stitching Artair's wound and Parlan had to hold his brother for, although still unconscious, Artair could still move dangerously in reaction to the pain Old Meg had to inflict. Aimil also relaxed at the way Old Meg kept glancing her way. The woman had clearly guessed her condition but, as with her father, had decided to let her be the one to speak. Aimil decided that was going to be soon if only because she was passing the point where she could suffer in silence, could hide the forces tearing through her body.

"It seems Elfking doesnae appreciate my being attacked or mayhaps 'tis Rory Fergueson he doesnae like. He attacked the man. One of his strikes tore the flesh from the side of Rory's face. T'will never heal right. He will be horribly scarred. The left side. It may aid ye in finding him. Although, I would have thought a man like Rory would have been easily noticed anywhere he went. Oh, he is also looking poorly. Dirty and ragged, I mean. None of his fine elegance left for him."

"A man running for his life cannae afford the time nor the coin to make himself pretty."

"Nay, I suppose not." Seeing that the tending of Artair was finished, she asked, "How does he fare?"

"He has lost a lot of blood," replied Old Meg, "but I ken that the laddie will heal."

"Thank God. I thought his wound didnae look a mortal one but t'was only a fleeting look I got before he was mounted behind me and we were racing for Dubhglenn. Weel, I will seek my bed now."

"'Tis about time," muttered Lachlan.

"I needed to ken how Artair fared. I couldnae bear to think my idea had cost him too dearly."

"Your folly, ye mean," Parlan growled as he strode over to her, already plotting the stern lecture he would give her.

She almost felt sorry that she was going to deprive him of the argument he so clearly intended. "Not now, Parlan."

He was startled by her tart response then grew angry. "What do ye mean—'not now'? We are going to talk, lass, and now."

"I am afraid this really has to wait, Parlan"—she grit her teeth as a contraction tore through her—"until after I have the bairn."

Chapter Twenty-Two

"What is taking so long?"

Artair, awake and sitting up in his bed, nearly grinned as he watched his brother pace the room. Never had he seen Parlan in such a state. If he did not sympathize, did not have a few worries himself concerning how Aimil fared, he knew he would find Parlan's agitation a source of amusement. It was also interesting to watch his brother for Parlan was yet again revealing that Aimil meant more to him than perhaps even he realized.

"Bairns take awhile to enter the world."

"And when did ye become so knowledgeable about bairns and the having of them?"

"Quite recently actually. I feared Aimil would have the bairn in the saddle, that t'would appear with the first pain. Aimil told me what little I do ken now."

"She was in labor when she was riding?"

"Weel, whilst returning to Dubhglenn. Didnae she tell ye?"

"Nay, I have had little time to speak to her since then."

"Oh, weel, t'was Elfking's rearing whilst attacking Rory. She wasnae thrown but t'was the rough ride that, as she said, jolted the bairn into recalling that he must come out sometime. She was laboring the whole way back to Dubhglenn, poor lass."

Parlan resumed his pacing, sipping at the ale Malcolm had brought him earlier. He felt like drinking far more heavily but did not wish to be drunk when his child finally arrived, and considering the time it was taking, that would have been assured. It was a decision he almost regretted making, however, for he felt that a good wallow in drink might ease the fear that gnawed at him. So tempting was the thought of it that he had finally left the company of Leith and Lachlan who were indulging heavily as they waited. They were drowning their concerns for Aimil as he heartily wished he could.

"Mayhaps I should return to her side. At least then I would ken what is happening."

"Aye, and ye would get underfoot again which is why Old Meg told ye to leave. She also said ye fret too much and that that isnae good for the lass. She has her own fears to battle without ye looming over her and adding to them."

"True enough. 'Tis the pain she is in. I keep wishing to put an end to it." Parlan sprawled on a bench by the window.

"Only the bairn's birth can put an end to it and weel ye ken it. Come, she is in good hands, and her pain will soon end."

"Aye, I ken it. 'Tis that I never took much notice of the whole matter, of childbirth or," he added softly, giving voice to some of his fears, "the dangers it holds. Suddenly I can recall too many women who never rose from their childbeds. Aimil is such a wee, delicate lass and she has grown so large with this bairn. It seemed too much for her to carry yet alone birth."

"Aye, a wee lass and delicate-looking but nae delicate. Dinnae sit there thinking only of that for it feeds your fear for her. Think instead on how she suffered at Rory's hands yet escaped and returned here all the while carrying the bairn. Think instead on how she rode back here, bringing me along, and was in labor yet wasnae harmed by it. Aye, think on the spirit and strength I ken weel were the reasons ye wed her. 'Tisnae a weak, faint-hearted lass birthing your bairn now."

"Nay, 'tisnae. Ye are right. I must keep that in mind. Howbeit, I wish there was another way to beget children."

Aimil panted and wondered why God could not have found another way for a woman to become a mother. Putting the bairn into her womb was exceedingly enjoyable but it seemed unfair that she should do all the suffering in payment for that pleasure for Parlan had quite enjoyed himself as well. She knew the church had a vast list of reasons for her suffering but she had never believed them and, she thought crossly as another contraction gripped, if they were true, it was still unfair.

"I think I am glad now that ye made Parlan leave, Old Meg. I ken weel that I must look verra poorly."

"Aye, ye arenae verra bonnie at the moment. Ye are near to done. It willnae be long."

"It seems like years." She glanced at Maggie who gently bathed her face and who was now gently rounded with Malcolm's child. "Mayhaps ye shouldnae be here. Ye cannae like seeing it take so long."

"I have seen many a birth, and ye arenae really taking so long. Aye, and 'tis going weel. I hope mine does as weel."

"If ye say so." Aimil's doubt was clear to hear in her voice. "I still say it feels like years."

"Weel, 'tis a big bairn, I am thinking." Old Meg nodded vigorously. "Aye, 'tis a fine braw son ye will give my laddie."

"Mayhaps t'will be a fine braw daughter." Aimil managed a faint smile when Maggie giggled.

"Nay, the MacGuins always have a son first. Aye, for as far back as any can tell ye. Ye will have a son, lass."

Something told Aimil she would too but she was suddenly too busy to say so. Her child had finally decided to make his final push for the freedom of her body, and her body worked furiously to grant him that wish. For most of her labor, she had made little sound, pride making her determined not to scream and wail as some women did but when her child finally broke free of her body, she could not restrain a scream that left her throat sore and which she suspected they had heard in Aberdeen.

"Aimil!" Parlan leapt to his feet and stared fearfully at the door.

Even Artair was alarmed. "And she has been so verra quiet 'til now."

"Aye, she has. Something must be wrong," Parlan said even as he bolted from Artair's chambers, leaving his brother to curse his inability to follow.

When Parlan reached his chambers, he found the door barred. As he pounded on it to demand entry, Leith and Lachlan joined him. The wail of an infant made Parlan hesitate a moment as emotion assailed him, but he quickly renewed his pounding on the door. His sole concern at the moment was to know how Aimil fared.

"Be still, ye great fool," Old Meg yelled as she worked to clean off the baby. "I will open the door in a moment."

"I want to see Aimil now."

"In a minute, Parlan." Aimil struggled to help Maggie all she could as the woman cleaned her.

The testiness in Aimil's voice caused Parlan to sag against the wall in relief. Her voice had been hoarse and heavy with weariness, but he felt sure that no woman on the brink of death could sound so naturally cross. The way Leith and Lachlan were smiling told him that they felt the same. He was not pleased to be kept waiting, however.

"He sounds a healthy lad," Leith finally said. "A fine strong voice."

"A lad? God's beard, I didnae ask what the bairn was."

Old Meg opened the door at that moment. "Ye have a son. A braw laddie to be your heir."

Parlan suddenly felt hesitant as he entered the room. Something had happened that would change his whole life. Becoming a husband had not seemed so great a change after months of having Aimil at his side. Now he was a father and he knew that was going to seem a far greater step to take. There would be someone expecting him to teach, to lead, and to train. Parlan suddenly felt unsure of himself, unsure that he could do all that was needed to raise a son and do it right.

He forced his attention to Aimil. She looked very small, wan, and tired. Yet, as he drew nearer to her, he realized that beneath the exhaustion shone joy and excitement. He bent to kiss her lightly.

"Ye are all right?"

"Aye, just tired. Look at your son, Parlan. Ye said a son was what ye would get and, though it galls me to say it, ye were right."

A shaky laugh escaped him before he was caught up in looking at his son, held in Aimil's arms with an ease he envied. He especially envied it when a chuckling Leith urged him to hold the infant for a moment, Lachlan seconding the notion. Aimil offered no escape for she quickly ceased suckling the child and held him out to be taken.

Gingerly, obeying Aimil's soft instructions, Parlan took his new son in his hands. With one hand beneath the infant's tiny head and another cupping the equally small bottom, Parlan stared at his child. He was oblivious to Leith and Lachlan poking and peering at the baby, commenting upon how well-formed the child was. All he knew was that he held his son, his first child. Emotion choked Parlan, and his first thought after picking the child up was that he wished everyone would leave.

"He is so small, such a wee thing," he managed to say at last but made no move to relinquish the child.

"Wee?" Aimil was finding it hard to fight her weariness. "Weel, mayhaps he seems so to a great brute like ye. He didnae feel so wee a few moments ago." She smiled faintly when Maggie gasped and blushed but felt no embarrassment about speaking so bluntly before Parlan, her brother, and her father.

"He is a braw laddie," Old Meg declared. "I have seen a lot of bairns and I ken weel that he be both verra strong and a good size for a bairn. Aye, even his color is good, equal to that of a bairn days older."

"Aye, I thought he looked fair for a newborn," agreed Lachlan. "Some can be so red, so shriveled, they are naught but ugly and the father is left to wonder what he has bred."

"Ye must take him and show him to the clan. They have long awaited this moment."

Looking to Aimil for her opinion of Old Meg's sugges-tion, Parlan found her lying very still, her eyes closed. "What ails her?"

"Naught, ye great gowk." Old Meg ignored the glare he sent her for that disrespectful mode of address and gently tucked the covers more securely around Aimil. "She is but asleep. Having a bairn is a wearying business. Aye, and the lass likes a good sleep."

Parlan laughed as much with relief as over the blithe way Old Meg uttered such an understatement. "Oh, aye, she does that."

Realizing that he was not going to get to visit with Aimil, to talk to her, for a while yet, Parlan went to show his son to his clan. He went first to Artair to ease the worry he knew he had left his brother suffering. Then he went to the hall where a great many had gathered, having heard in the usual if sometimes apparently miraculous way such news of import was spread, of the laird's child.

Unwrapping the baby with the help of a maid, Parlan held his son up. This not only let his people see that he did indeed have a son but that there were no apparent deformities that could possibly impede the child taking his place as laird. He then loudly proclaimed the child his son and heir, a statement the ones gathered showed no hesitation in agreeing to with several loud cheers. Wrapping his son back up in his swaddling, Parlan handed him to the maid, instructing her to take him back to Old Meg, when the celebration of the long-awaited heir began in earnest.

For a while Parlan drank with them, accepting praise and congratulations. He could not completely join in, however as his heart and mind were with Aimil. She was the one with whom he wished to share the joy of the birth. Finally, he gave into that desire and left the hall, smiling faintly when he saw that his absence would do little to stem the celebration.

When he reached his chambers, he thanked Old Meg and Maggie, then sent them on their way. He had the feeling that Old Meg was training Maggie to take her place eventually. No other woman had shown much skill or interest in the arts of healing, and Parlan was glad that someone had finally been found. It would be a great loss when Old Meg died, but Parlan felt sure that he could now cease worrying that the loss would be even greater, that all of Old Meg's knowledge and skill would die with her.

Sitting on a bench by the window, he observed his sleeping son and wife. He had been doubly blessed, for it seemed certain that both had survived the dangers of birth. So too had Rory Fergueson failed to harm them. Parlan did not care to think of all he could have lost if Rory had been able to get ahold of Aimil.

He prepared himself for what could be a long wait but found that he had a lot of patience for once. Watching his small family sleep filled him with contentment. So too did he have a great need to talk to Aimil and not only about the child they shared. He had to convince Aimil to understand that, until Rory Fergueson was dead, she and the child would have to be closely watched, more closely than they had been, and that meant that there would be some restrictions she might not like. The difficulty there might be in doing so was the only thing he did not look forward to when Aimil finally woke up.

Aimil winced as she slowly struggled out of a deep sleep. For a moment she was confused, not sure why she felt so battered, then she remembered. Her hand went to her belly, and she looked around for her son. As she located the baby's cradle, the child sleeping peacefully within, she saw Parlan step from the shadows near the cradle.

"Awake at last," he murmured as he sat on the edge of the bed.

"Have I been asleep long?"

"Long enough."

When he kissed her and she felt a flicker of desire, she nearly smiled. Nothing could have shown her more completely how much she needed him. The last thing she should feel while still aching from childbirth was desire, even the faint taste of which his kiss had inspired. She decided it was better to laugh at her weakness than to bemoan it.

"Have ye finally decided upon a name for our son?" Aimil asked.

"Aye. Lyolf. I decided it might suit him far more than the others we had talked on."

"Aye, 'tis a fine name, a strong one," she agreed.

"Aye, and ye have made me a proud man, sweeting. He is a bonnie, braw laddie."

"He isnae all of my making," she protested softly but felt warmed by his words.

"I ken it but ye had the hardest part."

"I think he will look most like his father." She smiled at Parlan. "Already he has a thick head of raven hair."

"Poor laddie," he jested but was pleased by the thought that something of himself would be seen in the boy.

"Poor lasses in a few years when he reaches an age to be interested in them. I shall be begging forgiveness for birthing a rogue."

He laughed softly then grew serious, taking one of her hands in his. "We have to talk, Aimil. About Rory Fergueson."

She grimaced but knew she had to confront the matter and Parlan. He did not look as angry as he had earlier, but she sensed his intensity. There would no doubt be some demands made of her that she would not like but she decided she would make no complaint. She, Artair, and her child could have died. Aimil needed no other reminder of the danger that still threatened.

"Aimil, I am no longer angry about the ride that ye took. My anger was spurred by my fears for ye. Ye see, I kenned that Rory might be near. Simon Broth was the one who had word of him though none had truly espied the man. There was a murder."

"Oh, Parlan, did he kill another poor lass?" She shuddered as she thought on the way Rory did his killing.

"Weel, poor lass isnae the way to describe the one he murdered but no one should die so, with such pain and fear as she must have suffered. T'was no better than torture. He has murdered Catarine Dunmore. Lagan has traveled to tell her kin."

"Are ye certain?" Although she had never liked the woman, she had to agree with Parlan that Rory's way of killing was a horror no woman deserved.

"Aye. There was a ring. Lagan kens that it was hers. 'Tis no surprise that she was with him either. So too did the descriptions of the woman match Catarine's. Nay, I have no doubts that t'was her nor did Lagan."

Although part of her shrank from the knowedge, Aimil had to ask, "As was done to my mother?"

"Ah, sweeting." He sighed and nodded, kissing her palm then her cheek when she shuddered with revulsion and horror. "Even though she put me into that beast's hands and near got ye killed, I would never have wished such a fate upon her."

"I ken it, lass. Therein lies the difference between ye and her. She wouldnae have cared how ye were treated. She erred in staying near Rory, didnae see the danger in it. Appalled though we are, she set her own fate. Ye must not fret so over it."

"Aye, ye are right and I am getting cursed sick of saying that." She smiled weakly when he laughed.

"And now I must say what I ken weel ye dinnae wish to hear but ye will heed this, Aimil. Heed it and obey it. I ken why ye had to take that ride, ken weel how the walls of even a place ye favor can close in about ye, choking ye. Ye are just going to have to grit your pretty teeth and endure, lass.

"There will be no more rides with only one man to watch over ye. If ye must travel somewhere, t'will be with an escort of a half-dozen or more strong well-armed men. Ye will be watched at all times. I must see that there is no way for Rory to reach ye, no way at all, and if that means ye are kept close, that I must make a prisoner of ye again, then so be it."

"Ye dinnae make me a prisoner, Parlan. Rory does. His hate and madness lock me inside these walls, not ye."

"So, ye mean to obey me, eh?" Although he knew she had common sense, he had not expected her to comply so easily.

"Aye. When he attacked me today, I kenned that he would not hesitate to kill the child I carried. Because the bairn is no longer within me willnae make any difference. The bairn and I will be close until he is weaned. If I am in danger, then the chance grows that the bairn is too. In truth, I fear Rory's simply kenning a bairn exists."

"Nay, I cannae like it either. He was enraged that ye shared my bed. I think he would hate any bairn we had made together."

"He would. He also hates me. More so now than he ever did. He frightens me more than I can say. I have no wish to face him. I ken too weel what he wishes to do to me. I was a fool today not to think of him before I set out."

"Not a fool. T'was not wrong to think yourself more or less safe. So many swords are searching him out that in the midst of the enemy t'was the last place to expect him. Howbeit, that shows us that he can and will get close if we are not exceedingly vigilant."

"He has made us prisoners." She sighed then looked at him with narrowed eyes. "Or has he? Ye dinnae intend to just sit behind these walls, do ye?"

"Aimil, the man must be found."

"And ye must do the searching."

"Mayhaps I could stay here and send others yet not be cried a coward but I willnae do that."

"Nay, I didnae think so."

"Aimil, Rory must be found and killed. He is a threat to all of us. What matters to me is that he is a threat to ye and our child. I mean to hunt him in every corner of this land. Aye, and elsewhere if the whoreson slips free of Scotland's boundaries. It must be done for, until he rots in hell as he deserves, ye and the bairn arenae safe. 'Tis my duty as your husband. My duty as a father. Aye, as a man."

She wrapped her arms around him, tugged him closer, and laid her head against his chest. "Ye will be verra careful?"

"Aye, sweeting. More careful than I have ever been in my life." Kissing the top of her head, he glanced at his sleeping son. "I have more of a reason to be careful now." He smiled down at her when she glanced up at him. "A wee wife that gives me bonnie, braw sons and a son I wish to see as a man, to see what mistakes I have made with him."

His words hurt even as they flattered. He was clearly pleased to have her as his wife, but she ached to be more than the wife who gave him strong sons. It was, however, a beginning. She was not foolish enough to scoff at the bond the tiny infant had created between her and Parlan. What she needed to do was make it stronger and all-encompassing.

"Ye willnae make mistakes." She gave him no resistance when he silently and gently urged her to lie back down.

He smiled faintly when she yawned then grew serious as he looked at his son. "I will. 'Tis something I wager cannae be avoided. Ah, Aimil, though I rejoice in the gift ye have given me, I tremble when I think of the responsibility that comes with it."

Although she felt weary and wanted to rest, she brought his hand to her mouth and kissed his palm. "'Tis a heavy one but I dinnae fear that ye cannae carry it. Aye, ye will carry it weel with few stumbles."

"Such trust ye have in me."

"I have seen ye with Artair."

"Ah, ye mean the brother I had beaten."

"As ye had to."

"I was angry."

"But 'tisnae the only thing that prodded ye and t'was an honest fury, one that had cause. Do ye think he would be as he is now if he didnae ken that? Ye couldnae treat him different from all the rest. That would have hurt him more than the lash. Ye have never deserted him. That is what has stayed in his heart. In all his follies, he kenned ye were there for him if the need arose. That is how ye raise a child.

"Love your son, Parlan. Let him ken it. Aye, he will falter and ye will have to punish him be it with strength or word. Teach him honor and right from wrong. 'Tis all any can do for a child. If he still turns out bad"—she shrugged—"'tis God's will and no fault of yours. I have never seen a child who was loved and kenned it turn bad, however. Nay, not when 'tis a love tempered with guidance and strength."

"Such wisdom from a lass who has but born her first child."

She colored slightly with pleasure at his sincere words. "I may be wrong."

"I think not. Such sensible advice could never be wrong. If followed, I cannae see how one could err. I dinnae believe in bad seeds either for I have seen good come from rot. Aye, and I ken that t'was because they found the guidance and love they needed elsewhere."

"Ye raised Artair, Parlan, and, though he faltered some, he is a good man and tries to be better. Find strength in that." She tried and failed to smother a yawn. "Ye dinnae think Rory is a bad seed? I cannae believe my father could befriend a man who could raise such a monster yet my father loved Rory's father as a brother."

"Rory isnae a child turned bad. He is ill. We ken naught of how he was raised. A man who is a good friend for another man neednae be a good father. Aye, and there is other kin to consider, others that could have turned Rory, even his mother. Even so, with a madness such as Rory's, it could have been there at birth, a deformity no eye could see. Thank God men like Rory are the exception to the rule."

Seeing her yawn again, he smiled and lightly kissed her. "Rest, dearling."

"'Tis an order I shall have no trouble obeying," she murmured even as her eyes drifted closed.

He sat for a long time, holding her hand and watching her sleep. The contentment he felt made him smile for it seemed to be fed by such simple things. A pretty wife and a son were fine things but not so difficult to gain. There was far more to it than that and he knew it. Soon he would have to give more careful thought to it all.

For the moment, however, there was little time for soul-searching. Aimil and his son were in danger. What was of the greatest importance at the moment was to find Rory Fergue-son and kill him. Until that was done, whatever happiness and contentment he or Aimil could find would only be fleeting.

Chapter Twenty-Three

Even as the door to his chambers was still swinging open, Parlan was on his feet, his sword in his hand. A small part of him acknowledged that it was highly unlikely that any attacker could reach his chambers with no other warning sounded but weeks of fruitlessly searching for Rory had left him tense. He noted fleetingly that his wife slept peacefully on.

"Here now, Parlan, 'tis Artair. No need for that."

Setting his sword aside, Parlan lit a candle. "Surprising a man can get ye killed. What is it? 'Tisnae yet dawn."

"Weel, I didnae think ye would wish to wait for this news." He frowned at Aimil. "Shouldnae we go elsewhere to talk so that we dinnae wake her?"

"There is little that will wake her yet. The bairn was fretful most of the night, and she is exhausted. When Aimil is tired, she can sleep though a battle of thousands raged around her. What news?"

"We may have found Rory."

Parlan immediately began to get dressed. "Where?"

"But twa hours ride from here."

"So close?"

"Aye, but, if this is the whoreson, ye neednae worry. He is dead. 'Tis a corpse we must go to view."

Although keenly disappointed that he was not about to come to swordpoint with Rory, Parlan also felt hopeful. He ached to take revenge against the man but, more than that, he ached for an end to the constant watchfulness and fear. It would be a shame if Rory had died by any other than his hand but it would also be a cause for celebration.

"Tell me about it."

"A fire it was, in a small house outside of a wee village. From what little the folk say about the twa men who were there it sounds like Rory and his faithful dog, Geordie. They have both died. Lagan and I feel certain 'tis them, but ye ought to have a look."

"Aye, and Leith for he kens the man better. 'Tis why he lingered here after his father left. Rouse him and I will join ye in the hall."

The sun was beginning to rise when they set out for the village. With each new detail Lagan and Artair supplied, Parlan's hopes were raised yet he tried to rein them in. That Rory's threat could be ended so conveniently seemed too good to be true. Parlan had expected it to cost him far more than an early-morning ride to view a corpse.

An acrid smell tainted the air as they reined in before the ruined cottage. Two blanket-shrouded shapes were on the ground, and three of Parlan's men lingered nearby, coming alert when he arrived. Since the house was little more than ashes, Parlan was not sure the bodies would be recognizable. Artair and Lagan had said the corpses were burnt, but only now did Parlan see that there was a chance that they were burned beyond any hope of recognition. Hesitantly, he started toward the bodies.

"I ken I willnae enjoy this," muttered Leith as he fell into step beside Parlan. "They willnae be a pretty sight."

"Nay, they willnae. Nevertheless, we have to be certain 'tis the pair we search for."

"Aye, ye dinnae want to ease your guard before ye are verra certain indeed. That could be a deadly folly." Leith took a deep breath and reached for the blanket. "I have always detested fires and their consequences."

When Leith pulled the blanket back, he paled and gagged softly, something Parlan sympathized with. He had been right. There was not much left that was recognizable. Steadying himself, he helped Leith closely examine each body then joined the younger man in making a hasty retreat from the scene. When they were several yards away, Parlan silently offered Leith a drink from the wineskin he had snatched from his saddle.

After taking a long drink, Leith handed the wineskin back to Parlan. "Weel, ye cannae tell much by looking at them save that one was tall and slim and one was short and burly. What little remains of the clothing and hair indicate that the tall one was fair and dressed fine. I have made my judgment on what few belongings survived the fire with them."

"The ring?"

"Aye, 'tis Rory's. So was the dagger and the sword. Rory often displayed them for he was proud of them."

"And the other man is Geordie?" Parlan rinsed his mouth with wine to wash the acrid taste of smoke and death from it and then took another long drink.

"Aye. Strange but I feel no doubt about that."

"Without Rory he wouldnae be a danger. Rory would always be. Kenning that ye are wary. 'Tis all."

"Aye. A lot weighs upon my word. I cannae think of any way a man would get Rory's possessions and be with Geordie as weel. It must be Rory."

"T'would seem so," Parlan agreed.

"So your worries are at an end. Ye seem little pleased."

"I am pleased yet, at the moment, I am both angry and regretful. The whoreson has slipped beyond my reach again and this time to a place where none can hunt him down." He smiled crookedly. "I have no wish to ride into hell before my time is due."

"Ye wished to send Rory there by your own hand. 'Tis verra easy to understand. Father shares that wish. I ken he will share your torn feelings about this—glad the swine is dead but verra sorry t'wasnae by his hand. This lacks the satisfaction revenge craves."

"Aye. Mayhaps that is why I am slow to accept the ending. I didnae see it or cause it."

"So ye suspect it." When Parlan nodded, Leith sighed. "Cut down by sword or fire, dead is dead. Do we bury them?" He finally turned to look back at the bodies.

"T'would be fitting and just to leave them for the carrion but I have ne'er done so, so why begin now. Aye, we bury them."

Although he cursed himself for a fool, knowing Rory would never have honored his remains if the situations had been reversed, Parlan saw to the burials. He could not leave a body, any body, for the carrion. The thought turned his stomach. In a way, he also hoped that the act of burying the pair would make him accept their deaths which he still had some difficulty doing.

"T'was a waste of our time and sweat but 'tis done," Artair said as he shared the water Parlan had drawn from the well and joined his brother, Leith, and Lagan in washing off. "I wouldnae be surprised to see the ground spit them out."

Parlan laughed softly. "Aye, neither would I. Mark the graves, Wallace," he called to one of his men.

"Why trouble with it? There cannae be any who will care where they rest. Weel, except, mayhaps to spit upon the bones."

"There are those who wished that pair dead yet arenae here to see it. Marked graves might do as weel, Artair."

"Aimil?"

"Mayhaps her. My word on it might be enough. Then again the man bred a deep fear in her, one that haunts her dreams. My word might not be enough to still that. Sometimes the sight of a grave is needed to make one really believe in a death, especially in one like this, one that she needs to ken is true. Poor lass hasnae liked wishing for Rory's death but she also kenned that t'was the only way we would be free of the threat of him."

"Aye, and I think my father may need to see it."

"True, Leith. His need to see Rory Fergueson dead might even have been greater than mine. Do ye travel now to tell him?"

"Aye, I shall leave from here. Tell Aimil I shall visit again soon," Leith called as he strode toward his horse.

"I never thought we would be kin and friends with Lowlanders." Artair shook his head as he watched Leith ride off.

"Weel, there hasnae been much blood spilt between our clans." Parlan walked toward his mount and the others fell into step with him. "That eases the way. Being so near to the border of the Highlands, I think ones such as the Mengues are more akin to us than the true Lowlanders. There is much that they do that follows our way. Ye can see that in the way that Leith goes too and fro so easily."

"Aye, but I begin to think that Leith Mengue is a man who can fit any boot he slips on."

"I think ye might be right in that, Artair, and 'tis a gift that could serve him verra weel one day." Parlan mounted and sat staring back at the burned-out cottage as the others did the same.

"Second thoughts or a few doubts mayhaps?"

"Nay, just wondering over the ease of it, Lagan. Weel, best we hie on back to Dubhglenn. Aimil has surely roused by now and shall wonder where I slipped away to with nary a word to anyone."

By the time Parlan rode into Dubhglenn the relief, even the

joy, over the ending of Rory's threat to him and his family had conquered all his regrets and doubts. He jovially greeted each person he met as he took his mount to the stables. On his way to the keep, he met Old Meg who greeted his happiness with a severe frown.

"And what have ye been up to, me fine rogue? Creeping off before dawn like some thief? Eh?"

He kissed her cheek. "I had to go view a body, a corpse I have long hoped to see."

"The hellhound is dead?"

"Aye, verra dead. How is Aimil?"

"Gnashing her teeth. Best ye hie on up to your chambers. She is suckling that greedy son of yours, but I doubt that has stopped her from watching for ye. If ye dinnae get up there quick, she will be down here to greet ye with the bairn still dangling from her breast."

Aimil heard the increased activity in Dubhglenn and tensed. Idly patting her nursing child's back, she listened more closely, trying to hear something that would tell her it was Parlan's return that had stirred things up. She had just decided to go and see for herself, detaching her son who immediately began to wail with fury, when Parlan strode into the room.

"Where did ye slip away to?"

Staring at his screaming son in mild astonishment, Parlan replied, "Eh? I cannae hear ye over the din. What ails him?"

"He wasnae done but I stopped him for I meant to come see if ye had returned." She frowned at her son whom she held at a distance.

Sitting on the bed, Parlan gently pushed the baby back toward Aimil. "I beg of ye, let him have his fill before he deafens us all."

She put the child back to her breast, and after a few convulsive sobs, he quieted down. As she was about to question Parlan again, something about the way Lyolf nursed distracted her. Curious, she looked down at her son and saw that he was not nestled against her breast in the usual way. His small hands clung tightly to her bodice, and his eyes, the color matching hers to a shade, were open. His gaze was fixed upon her face, and his brows, so like Parlan's, met in a vee over his tiny nose. Diverted, she tried to loosen the grip of one of his small hands only to have him grunt, frown even more, and cling more tightly. It was clear that he did not intend to be moved again until he was finished.

"Your son looks verra much like ye at this moment, Parlan."

Leaning over to look at Lyolf, Parlan drawled, "I have never looked so discontented when savoring that sweetness." He bent forward to kiss the curve of her breast only to jerk back with an oath when a small fist struck his nose.

Aimil tried not to laugh. She looked at Parlan who scowled and rubbed his nose. Then she looked at Lyolf who scowled in exactly the same way as he clung tenatiously to her bodice. Despite her best efforts not to, she began to giggle. When that only deepened the scowls on her husband's and son's dark faces, she laughed harder.

"Wheesht, ye are equally bad-tempered."

Lying on his side next to her, he glanced at his son. The child's gaze followed him, and the fierce expression remained on the tiny face. Slowly, Parlan started to grin. Along with amusement, he felt pride. Even though so young, the boy already showed spirit. He laughed softly.

"'Tis a good thing he is still a wee bairn or I might be in a lot of trouble."

"Aye, ye might at that." Aimil's eyes narrowed as she looked at him. "Ye might be anyway. Why did ye creep away without a word?"

"Ah, back to that, are we?"

"Aye, back to that. 'Tis that ye left no word, not with anyone. Ye were simply gone."

"Och, lass, I didnae mean to worry ye. Artair burst in shortly before dawn. He will enter more carefully now."

"Nearly skewered him, did ye?" She was well aware of his increased watchfulness, of how his sword was ever at hand as they slept.

"If he hadnae stopped inside the door, aye, I might have. 'Tis not something I care to think on."

"Nay, of course not. I didnae even hear him."

"This ill-tempered child had exhausted ye with his fretting half the night away."

She grimaced and nodded knowing that it would take far more than a sudden rude intrusion into their chambers to wake her when she was exhausted. "What did he want that couldnae wait 'til a more reasonable hour?" She tensed as she realized the only thing it could have been since Dubhglenn had neither been raided nor attacked. "T'was Rory."

He took her hand in his. "Aye, sweeting, but ye have naught to fear. He cannae hurt ye any longer. Nay, never again."

"Ye have slain him?"

"I fear it wásnae I who had that pleasure. Artair had heard of twa men that sounded much akin to Rory and Geordie at a village but twa hours ride from here. He tracked them down only to find that they had perished in a fire. He sought me out thinking I could better vouch that t'was truly Rory Fergueson and his faithful hound, Geordie."

"And it was them?"

"Aye, though t'was Leith who determined it. I could do no more than agree that the shapes matched those of the ones I sought. Leith was certain t'was Geordie and he recognized Rory by a few of his belongings that werenae destroyed in the fire. He has gone to tell your father, and I ken that the man will be sore grieved that he wasnae the one to end Rory's murdering life."

"He will but I cannae help but think that 'tis the best way.

Father isnae a cruel man yet, if he reached Rory, I think he would have acted verra cruelly. There was so much anger in him, so much hate. When it left him, he would have suffered. I fear he would have seen himself as little better than Rory and, aye, if he had gained hold of the man, I think my father would have gone a little mad."

"T'would be easy to understand."

"For we who didnae do it but mayhaps not so easy for the one who did. He would have to face the beast within himself and that cannae be easy. Nay, 'tis best this way though my father may be some time in seeing that."

"Aye, it took me a wee while to see it. I felt as if something had been stolen from me, as if he had escaped me."

"I am just as glad that no one had to face him. He was a snake." She smiled faintly at Lyolf who was finally done and held him at her shoulder, rubbing his back to release any air he may have swallowed. "I feared he would play some loathesome trick that would cost one of ye your life. Fair fighting wasnae Rory Fergueson's way. A man cannae always watch his back or all the shadows."

"Mayhaps not. We will never ken now. The man is dead."

"Are ye verra sure of that, Parlan?"

"As sure as any can be. Do ye have some doubt of it, dearling?" He reached out to stroke her cheek. "I had a few myself but they have faded away."

"As mine will, no doubt. 'Tis that the end came so abruptly, so unexpectedly. I had never thought it would be this way."

"Nay, nor did I. It was a surprise and I did fear the way of it would leave ye still afraid, still uncertain."

"A wee bit but I shall get over it."

The baby was falling asleep so she reclined more on the bed, settling Lyolf more comfortably against her chest. She suspected that being a mother made her less able to shrug off her fears, to accept an end to the danger. There was so much more at risk if it proved to be a false safety. The child might not become a victim, but she dreaded the thought of being parted from him. She wanted to see him grow into a man.

Lying there quietly, the baby sleeping on her chest and Parlan stroking her hair, she felt drowsy and content. At times like this, it was nearly impossible to recall all her fears and worries. It seemed that nothing would intrude to shatter her peace but she knew that was foolish. Rory had done so before. What she had to do now was believe that he could not do it again.

"Are ye sure he is dead, Parlan?" She hated herself for the fear that prompted her repeating of the question, for needing the reassurance.

"Aye, loving." He kissed her forehead, smiling faintly when her eyes closed. "We will celebrate on the morrow. T'will be a fine day."

She smiled but did not open her eyes. "Angus says so, does he?"

"Aye. He promises sun to bask in."

"It seems wrong somehow to celebrate a man's death."

"If it troubles you, we can find something else to celebrate. Weel, if Old Meg says what I wish her to, that is. Tomorrow makes near to twa months since this wee rogue was born."

Knowing what he referred to, she forced herself not to blush and not to look at him. "My, my, he is growing apace, isnae he?"

"Aye, and ye will be running apace if Old Meg says ye are healed from the birth."

"Mean to chase me, do ye?"

"Until we fall. Preferably with ye on your back but I am nae too particular after near to three months."

"Near to three months of what?"

"Of naught, and therein lies the trouble. I thought ye paid the highest price for bearing our son but I begin to wonder."

She lazily opened one eye to peek at him. "Regrets?"

Gently touching the thick raven curls decorating his son's small head, Parlan said quietly, "Nary a one but I do have an itch that screams to be scratched."

"And ye mean to do some scratching on the morrow?"

"Aye, a lot of it so"—he kissed her cheek—"ye best get some rest, lass. Ye will be sore pressed to keep pace with me."

She doubted that for she was as hungry for some lovemaking as he was but she was not inclined to tell him. He would discover it quickly enough on his own. Once Old Meg deemed her healed from the birth, Aimil knew she would probably be running after him. The image that invoked made her smile and lingered in her mind as she finally gave in to sleep.

As soon as he was certain that she was asleep, Parlan gently took the baby from her lax hold, causing a murmur of protest from both of them. Smiling faintly, he put the child back into his cradle. For a moment he crouched there, watching his tiny son sleep, and feeling unabashedly proud. It was going to be easy to love the boy, as easy as it was to love his mother.

Startled, Parlan rose and went to stand by the bed to look down upon a sleeping Aimil. He did love her. It was the only explanation there was for so many of the things he had done and felt. He wondered when it had happened then decided that it did not really matter.

Reaching out to take a lock of her hair between his fingers, he then wondered when and if he should tell her. She still spoke no words of love to him yet some instinct told him that she cared, could quite possibly love him. There was the possibility that she did not speak because he had not. Aimil had more than her share of pride. So too did he, he admitted with a crooked smile, and it was making him reluctant to be the first to bare his soul, to take the chance of revealing how he felt when it might not be returned.

Shaking his head over the uncertainty she could stir in him, he left the room and met Lagan in the hall. "I thought ye would be resting after such a long night."

"Aye, I am weary but I need to fill my belly first."

"That is where I head to." Parlan started on his way.

Falling into step beside Parlan, Lagan asked, "How did Aimil take the news?"

"With a touch of doubt as we all did but she means to be rid of it. It cannae be easy to dismiss the fear that Devil bred in her heart."

"And yours," Lagan murmured.

"I didnae fear him." Parlan bristled, hearing the insult of cowardice in Lagan's words. "I was ready to fight that hell-hound."

"Ye mishear me. I didnae speak of the fear that makes a man run from a fight but of your fear for Aimil and your child. T'was that fear that has driven ye so hard these last weeks and that fear was stirred and heightened by something I begin to think ye will never see."

"Is that so? Mayhaps I am not as blind as ye think, old friend. Tell me, do ye still think Aimil would like to hear a few sweet words?" He smiled over his friend's obvious surprise. "Even more important, do ye think she will give a few back?"

"If ye cannae tell that for yourself, mayhaps ye are blind. Aye, she must be thinking the sweet words will never come. I should be sure to speak them in the right place at the right time or the shock might kill her."

Parlan ignored Lagan's sarcasm. "I have an idea for both. Aye, and mayhaps t'will serve to ease her fears. The last time we were there Rory set upon us. This time we can have our time alone in peace, and I mean to make the most of it."

"Are ye sure ye ought to act so free so soon? Mayhaps ye ought to wait to, weel, be sure."

"If I followed that advice, I would never feel safe nor free. Nay, Rory is dead and I mean to act accordingly."

* * *

Wildflowers drifted down to scatter over the fresh mounds of dirt. Their soft colors gentled the stark, barren look of the burial rises. The wind gently tugged at the full cloak of the figure who stood before the graves. A sigh broke the quiet.

"Weel, old friend, how is hell? At least I ken that ye will-nae be lonely. We ken many who have settled there. I will join ye there eventually.

"Ah, old friend, I hope ye understand. I had to do it. They were too close, yapping at my heels until I couldnae do aught but hide and I need to do more. I must have the freedom to move or I will never get the revenge my soul craves.

"Ye do understand, dinnae ye, Geordie, my friend. Your sacrifice willnae be wasted. If I cannae survive to kill Aimil and the man she plays the whore for, I will drag them down into hell with me. Ye willnae be alone for long, Geordie."

Chapter Twenty-Four

"Dig him up."

Leith stared at his father in shock. Such a request was the last thing he had expected when he had brought his father to view Rory's and Geordie's graves. Neither could he understand why his father requested such a gruesome thing. There seemed no reason for it.

"Ye cannae mean it. I told ye he was dead. What purpose can be served by digging up his corpse?"

"Do ye fash yourself over some fear of desecrating the dead? This dead was desecrated before he was set into the ground. Dig him up."

"But why? I looked at him and t'was a sickening sight but I recognized his things. Why do you do this?"

"To be sure. Ye saw a ring, a dagger, and a sword. I wish to see more." He signaled to the two men with him. "Dig him up. There isnae any need to hesitate as I argue with my son." He looked back at Leith as the men began to dig. "Who put the flowers on the grave?"

Staring at the withering blooms his father held out to him, Leith shook his head. "I ken of no one who would. Dung, mayhaps. Flowers, nay."

"Another part of a puzzle."

"What puzzle save for these flowers?" Leith tossed them aside and scowled at the graves.

"Mayhaps the only puzzle is that he was taken before we who had a right to vengeance could extract it."

"Weel, digging him up to stare at his corpse willnae ease that."

"Nay, but t'will ease my mind of worrying that it isnae his corpse." Lachlan sighed, his gaze fixed upon the men digging. "When ye first told me of his death, I was angry. I felt something had been stolen from me. Then the anger began to ease and I began to think."

When his father said no more for several moments, Leith finally swore softly in exasperation. "Began to think what?"

"Ah, that t'was all so neat. Too neat. Aye, we hadnae caught him yet, but he was cornered. He couldnae move freely, couldnae even try to get near his quarry. We ken how badly he wished to reach Aimil. I began to think he may have found a way."

Suddenly understanding what his father meant, Leith swore. "He made it look as if he was dead. I was wrong."

"Mayhaps not and I wouldnae lash myself with guilt if ye are. Ye saw what ye were meant to see—Rory and Geordie dead."

"Odd, though I had a doubt or twa about Rory, I had none at all that it was Geordie I saw. I would still swear to it."

"It could weel be Geordie. T'was no doubt part of why ye believed ye saw Rory. Do ye really think a man like Rory would hesitate to kill what might have been his only friend if it served his purpose?"

"Nay, not for a moment. He would do it without regret."

"Weel, if I am right, he may have a regret or twa. There are the flowers and they were mostly upon the grave ye said was Geordie's."

Leith absently nodded. His attention was upon the shrouded body the men pulled from the grave. Despite his father's advice about not feeling guilty, Leith knew he would if he proved to be wrong. He knew he would also be afraid, afraid that his error could prove very costly.

With tension knotting his insides, Leith stood by as his father carefully examined the body. He knew Lachlan needed time to be certain but his impatience grew. If he had been wrong, time was not something they had too much of. When his father stood, signaled the men to reinter the body, yet said nothing, Leith gave up being patient.

"Is it him?"

"Nay."

That one soft word struck Leith to the heart. "Sweet God, I was wrong."

"Dinnae take it to heart. I too would have thought it him. He chose weel. Aye, and there is damage to the face from what little I could see amongst the ravages and wounds caused by fire. Nay, this was verra nearly perfect."

"But not perfect and I missed the error that whoreson made. What was it?"

"I kenned something about Rory that ye didnae, something I learned of years ago. He has a mark. T'was there at birth."

"I never noticed one upon him."

"Ye wouldnae unless ye had seen him naked and looked verra closely. The body beneath the charred clothes wasnae so ruined as the rest. Rory had a mole, a small dark one, below the curve of his left buttock. T'was hidden by the bend of his body most times, even when he was a bairn. I never would have kenned the mark was there save that his father showed me. He feared t'was the mark of the Devil."

"He had a right to worry on it."

"Nay, not over a wee spot upon the skin. Such a simple,

innocent mar couldnae cut to the soul to rot it as Rory's soul is rotted."

"I told Parlan that that was Rory."

"Ye said he doubted."

"He did then but he felt it foolish, meant to cease doubting."

"Then we best hie to Dubhglenn. He may believe it by now and act as if there is naught to fear. That is just what Rory wants."

As she reined to a halt beside Parlan, Aimil looked around and then shook her head. "Here again?"

"'Tis a fine place." He dismounted then helped her to do the same. "I have always favored it, finding peace here. I mean to do so again." As he spread a blanket upon the ground, he glanced her way. "Mayhaps after a peaceful day here, ye will lose a few of your doubts."

Cautiously, she approached the blanket and sat down. She told herself it was foolish to still fret and fear but she could not stop herself. The last time she had come to this place with Parlan their time together had ended with Rory attacking them, badly wounding Parlan, and taking her away to suffer a time she wished never to suffer again. Despite the beauty of the day and the place, the memories of that time remained clear.

Glancing at the food Parlan set out, she then surreptitiously studied him. He looked very cheerful, and there was an eager, hungry look in his eyes. Old Meg had neatly evaded her, but Aimil felt increasingly sure that the woman had declared her healed from the birth. She did wonder why he played the game of secrecy then decided not to complain. There could be a great deal of enjoyment in relaxing and letting him play his game for she was sure that it would lead to something they both wanted. She also knew she would enjoy every step as he led her along.

When she took a quick look at herself, she sighed. She was not dressed as fine as she would have liked for such an occasion. The plain outfit, given to her for she had had no gowns, was clean and comfortable but not beautiful so as to enchant Parlan, something which she would really like to do just once. He did not seem to mind but she did wish that she could show him that she could be as elegant and as finely bedecked as any lady he had ever known. Biting into a chunk of bread with more force than necessary, she thought crossly that that would be easier if he had not known quite so many ladies.

Parlan finally noticed that his wife was looking less than pleased with the arrangements he had made. "Something troubling ye, dearling?"

"Is this the celebration ye spoke of?"

"Aye, meager as it is."

"Weel, I wish ye had warned me. I would have done myself up a lot finer."

"Ye look as beautiful as any man needs." He gently let her hair down. "Why do ye put it up? 'Tis a crime to chain it, hide it."

"I am a wedded lass now, a mother. T'would be unseemly to leave it loose like a maiden."

"Even if your husband commands it?" He enjoyed the feel of her thick, silken hair in his hands, combing his fingers through it.

"Are ye going to command it then?" She nearly laughed at how such a simple action as he was performing had her breathless and eager.

"I think I might. Unbound and glorious when I am near but bound and kept from tempting others when I am away."

He brushed his lips over her cheeks and lightly teased her mouth with his but found that he lacked the patience for such play. Having her near and knowing that he could make love to her had his blood running so hot it made him feel feverish.

He kissed her hungrily, and the hunger he sensed in her return kiss severed what little control he had. It had been too long since he had loved her.

Pushing her down onto the blanket, he quickly began to loosen her clothing. Need controlled him, a need only she could fulfill. When he finally freed her breasts, he pressed his face against their fullness and vainly tried to slow himself down. Over the sound of his own harsh breathing, he could hear hers and realized that she suffered as he did, making all his efforts at control useless.

"I thought ye were going to chase me." Aimil finished baring his chest and smoothed her hands over its strong expanse.

"Havenae I yet? I feel as if I have run miles."

He cupped her breast in his hand and gently suckled the hard tip, relishing the flavor his child so often demanded. When she cried out softly and arched against him, he shuddered. He felt dangerously close to release already.

"Old Meg said I was healed from the birthing, did she?" Since he was already pushing up her skirts and somewhat roughly tugging off her braies, she decided that that was probably a foolish question.

Placing his hand between her thighs and feeling her warmth, he needed a moment before he could speak. "Aye. What do ye say?"

Starting to unlace his hose, she whispered, "I say hurry. If ye wish it, I could also say please." She smoothed her hands over his taut backside, pushing the loosened hose down as she did so.

"Just say aye."

"Aye, Parlan. Aye."

She cried out in surprise and relief as he plunged into her. Wrapping her limbs around him, she held him tightly. His heated breath came fast against her neck as he blindly carried them to the heights of passion. It was fast, fierce, and a little rough but, as her release seized her in its blinding grip, she decided that it was also glorious. Even as she cried out, arching to draw him deeper within her, she heard him say her name, felt him clutch her hips, and hold her closer as he sought to bury himself as deeply as possible within her eager body.

Holding her close and making no move to break the intimacy of their embrace, Parlan savored the lingering effects of the pleasure only she could give him. She could have been as ugly as sin, he mused, and he still would have kept her close for the pleasure she gave him, to revel in the passion they shared. *I simply would have kept the candle snuffed more often*, he thought, and laughed softly.

Not ceasing her languid caress, Aimil looked at him curiously as he propped himself up on his elbows to look at her. "And what so amuses ye?" She decided she must have grown more confident of him for she felt only curiosity about his laughter.

"I had intended a seduction but I think that was more of a ravishment."

"Weel, I have no objection to being ravished now and again." She smiled faintly and kissed his nose.

"Ye shouldnae make your poor husband suffer so many long weeks without a wee taste of you."

"I didnae make ye suffer, t'was your son, but I thank ye for suffering."

Slightly easing from their embrace, he gently brushed a few stray wisps of hair from her face. "Why thank me?"

"Other men would have turned elsewhere when their needs were so long denied."

"Now, that wouldnae have been quite fair, seeing as ye too were being denied of something ye favor, too. Oof!" He caught the small fist that had punched him in the side and kissed it. "Besides, lass, why should I seek out something common when I kenned that waiting awhile would give me the best?"

"The best?" She whispered the words, his seriousness making her nervous.

"Aye, the verra best. I think I have told ye that before. Do ye doubt me?"

"Weel, what begins as the best could become common after a while. The fire wanes, and the newness of it all fades."

"True, and I ken that that will happen to us in some ways but it cannae stop it being the best. Time and familiarity cannae change that. 'Tisnae a thing I like to keep reminding ye of but I have had enough women to ken a thing or twa about this. I was no innocent as ye are."

"Mayhaps I should taste me another man or twa so I can judge with such surety."

"Weel, best ye choose a man ye care naught about, for he will be dead before the sweetness of ye has left his tongue."

She nearly gaped at him. Though he spoke quietly and without any apparent ire, the very coolness of his voice and the look in his eyes told her he was completely serious. Her testy remark had been an empty threat, but Parlan's was chillingly real. She sought a way to ease the sudden tension between them, not only troubled by it but disliking it.

"Ye mean I cannae leave a trail of broken hearts behind me?"

Fighting to quiet the sudden fierce jealousy that seized him, and not doing too well, he tried to smile but could tell by the look upon her face that it probably resembled a baring of teeth. "Not unless ye wish to leave a trail of bodies behind ye as weel."

"Ye are proving to be a verra possessive husband." Even though she found that pleasing, she was unsettled by the ferocity of it.

He traced the delicate lines of her face with his fingers and brushed a kiss over her lips. "Aye, I am. I kenned that when I was so eager to have the priest deliver our vows. I wanted ye marked as mine, only mine. I dinnae plan to let any man change that."

"Och, weel, plans are made for changing."

Before Aimil could accept that she had heard another voice, Parlan leapt to his feet. One hand hastily, if very loosely, tied his breeches as the other hand grabbed his sword. She did not think she had ever seen anyone move so fast.

Without thinking, she sprang to her feet and darted behind Parlan. She stared at Rory in disbelief and horror. Not only the realization that he was not dead shocked her but his face. A gruesome sight, the whole left side was little more than one great scar. Ragged and filthy, there was nothing left of the Rory Fergueson she had once known. Not even his eyes were the same. His gaze burned with the strength of his madness.

She did not understand why he had not struck them down as they had been oblivious to all around them. Rory had never wanted to face Parlan on equal terms before yet, by announcing himself, he had insured that he would. In the grip of his madness and hate, he suddenly seemed to want to do battle. She was not sure that that boded well for Parlan and her, even though Parlan looked ready and eager to fight.

Parlan felt like screaming out his rage. He had been caught off-guard. Telling himself that he could not know that a man declared dead would suddenly appear to threaten him and Aimil again did not lessen his fury. The first advantage, that of surprise, had gone to Rory. Parlan was determined that he would give the man no other.

He then almost laughed. One purpose for returning to the spot near the Banshee's Well was to try to erase the bad memory Aimil had of the place. Instead, that memory seemed intent upon reliving itself. This time, however, Parlan was determined not to let Rory get his hands on Aimil.

"Get out of here, Aimil."

She turned to obey even as she thought that she could not leave Parlan alone with Rory. For a moment she considered riding for help, and wished she had brought Elfking. It was then that she realized that she was staring at empty space where the horses should have been.

"The horses are gone." She wondered why she should feel so disappointed and afraid when she had never intended to flee anyway.

"Aye, ye were so busy ye didnae notice that the beasts, er, wandered away."

The soft giggle that escaped Rory chilled Aimil. Pressed against his back, she felt Parlan shiver. In the flat small sound, one could clearly hear Rory's madness. She knew that Parlan also heard it and tasted the fear such madness could inspire.

"Let her go, Rory." Parlan was not surprised when the man laughed but he had seen no harm in trying for Aimil's release.

"And they say I am mad."

"They also say ye are dead. Did the Devil spit ye up from hell then because he couldnae stomach ye?"

"Ye mean to goad me but t'willnae work. That was a clever ploy, wasnae it? It worked just as I had thought it would."

"What poor innocent soul did ye murder to play out your game?" Parlan demanded.

"Some fool from the local tavern. A few coins and the hint of more and he followed me like some faithful puppy."

"And died for his error in faith just as Geordie did."

"Geordie's blood stains your hands. 'Tis your fault I had to kill him," Rory snarled.

That broke Aimil's stunned silence. "Ye cannae blame us for that murder. Ye took his life with your own hands."

"Because of ye!" he screamed then forcibly restrained himself. "I couldnae move, couldnae act, because ye hunted me. I had to put an end to that. T'was the only way. Ye had to think me dead. Geordie understands. He kens that I must have my vengeance, that ye must pay for all ye have done—both of ye.

"Ye were to be mine, Aimil, but ye chose this Highland rogue instead. Aye, rutting with him without a care or shame. So like your mother. Then ye had that Devil of a horse ruin my face. There is so much ye must pay for, my pretty whore."

"I would be wary of what ye say, Rory, or I may need to cut your tongue from your mouth before I kill you," Parlan challenged him.

"Such boasting. Killing ye will be no more trouble for me than swatting some bothersome fly."

"'Ware, Parlan." Aimil lightly touched his taut arm. "He means to dull your skill by blinding ye with fury."

"I ken it." He spoke softly through gritted teeth as he tried to speak to her without Rory hearing as well as fight the anger the man stirred in him. "Ye are to flee the moment the battle begins and I hold his attention."

"Nay, I willnae leave you."

"Ye will flee, woman. Curse ye, how can I fight my best if I must worry about ye? Run to Dubhglenn and get help."

"By the time I could reach Dubhglenn, even if I were a swift runner, ye would be thrice dead. Aye, he could have buried ye and brought the pope himself from Rome to pray over your grave."

"So be it but at least ye will still be alive."

"Mayhaps living without ye isnae something I can view with any ease," she said softly.

Despite their desperate situation, he felt his heart give an odd skip at her words. It was the first time she had put any hint of her feelings into words. He mused, a little crossly, that she had chosen the worst possible time for doing it. He wanted to hold her close, to make love to her, and to drag even more such declarations from her. Instead he faced a man

who could attack at any moment and who meant to see him
and Aimil dead. When they were both safe again, he would
find a way to make her pay some penance for her ill-timing.

"Then do it for the bairn. He deserves better than to be left
an orphan."

That tender statement cut her to the heart. For a moment,
seeing Parlan in such danger, she had forgotten their son and
his needs. She had to think of their child. Although she knew
Lyolf would be well cared for and loved, no one could replace
his true parents.

"Aye, our son. He needs us both, Parlan."

"I intend for him to have us both for many a year yet to come.
Ye will run, Aimil, for my peace of mind, if naught else."

She made no reply, and he took that to mean that she would
obey him. He turned his full attention upon Rory. Rory did
have skill and, if madness had finally given him courage,
the man could prove a formidable opponent. Parlan was confident of his own skill but did not give into a false cockiness. Skill did not always determine the outcome of a fight.
He also knew that, if Rory proved to be his equal, even the
smallest of errors could prove fatal.

"Come, Parlan MacGuin, are ye ready to meet your fate?"

"Do ye think ye are man enough to deal it out to me?"

"As easily as I did to your foolish cousin. What was her
name? Margaret? Aye, aye, that was it. A weak, puling lass."

That nearly broke Parlan's control. He could see poor
Morna's body in his mind's eye, knew that Aimil's mother and
Catarine had undoubtedly looked the same, and ached to put
an end to the life of the man standing before him. A soft word
from Aimil stopped him when he would have charged at Rory,
a mistake that could have cost him and Aimil dearly. He
wished he knew Rory well enough to force the man into acting
foolishly but his knowledge concerned Rory's crimes and he
doubted that the man could be angered by mentioning them.

"If she was puling, t'was most like for the lack of a man." Aimil saw Rory flush and knew she had found his weak spot. "That is why she was going to leave ye, wasnae it? She had discovered that your skill as a lover didnae match your beauty. Fine to look at but boring to bed."

She was startled by the swiftness and ferocity of his response. For a moment she feared Parlan had also been caught off-guard, but he met Rory's attack without hesitation. Parlan's only other move besides joining in the battle with apparent eagerness was to push her away. He then turned over even that fragment of his attention to the fight.

Aimil knew that Parlan assumed she would now obey his order to flee. She had more or less agreed to. It was something she realized she could not do, not even when she thought of their child. She did run, however, but only to the edge of the clearing to hide there, out of sight yet able to watch. Parlan would be soothed by the thought that she was safe or soon would be, and she would be able to stay close in case he should need her.

To flee and not to know how he fared until it was all over was not something she could do. If Parlan should lose, a thought she dreaded, and she had fled, she knew she would then spend her whole life tormented by the thought that she could have helped him, might have been able to do something that would have saved him. Although it was an agony to watch him fighting for his life, she stayed, her fists pressed to her mouth to stop herself from screaming.

Parlan fought coolly, with a strained detachment he was finding harder to maintain. Rory was good, very good. Parlan wondered if the madness the man suffered honed his skills. There certainly seemed to be more strength in Rory than any man should possess. For the first time since his youth, Parlan was not sure that he would win.

"Why do ye struggle so against the inevitable? Ye will die, Parlan MacGuin, and then I shall go after Aimil."

"She has fled you, Rory. Ye willnae get your filthy hands upon the lass." Parlan hissed a curse when Rory's sword nicked his side.

"The lass will be easy enough to catch. She is on foot, and I ken where there is a horse."

Fear for Aimil gnawed at him but Parlan fought it. It could steal his skill and he needed all he had. Although he had inflicted as many small wounds upon Rory as Rory had upon him, Rory seemed far less troubled by them. Parlan could feel himself losing strength as he bled. Rory's smile told Parlan that the man had guessed at his growing weakness.

A new fear suddenly seized him as he felt the ground crumble beneath his heels. So intent had he been on the battle, he had let himself be driven to the very edge of the Banshee's Well. Even as he struggled to elude that new danger, Rory laughed and then lunged. Knowing he would not be able to parry the sword headed straight for his vitals, Parlan sidestepped. The ground gave way beneath his feet, and he fell into the hole, barely managing to latch onto the less than firm earth around the edge. Cursing viciously, he tried to pull himself up before Rory could act but knew it was fruitless even before Rory laughed again. He cried out as Rory's foot caught him full in the face, sending Parlan plummeting down the hole. As he fell, Parlan thought he heard Aimil cry out then knew only blackness.

Chapter Twenty-Five

"Parlan! Nay!"

Aimil thought of nothing save that Parlan had plunged to his death. She bolted from her hiding place and raced to the Banshee's Well even though a part of her mind kept screaming that there was nothing she could do. The sensible side of her urged her to flee to Dubhglenn but she was not feeling very sensible after watching Parlan swallowed up by the earth.

Her headlong flight toward the hole was abruptly stopped by Rory. He grabbed her by the arm and yanked her to a halt. The pain of nearly having her arm wrenched from its socket as well as being flung to the ground dimmed the hysteria by which she had been seized. Now she could see her error very clearly. She had put herself into Rory's hands, and Parlan had died trying to save her from this very fate.

Thinking of Parlan's death, her fear turned to fury. The loathing she felt for the man laughing at her seemed a living thing inside her. A small part of her feared that she could easily turn as mad as Rory but she was too furious to care about that.

"Whoreson," she hissed as she got to her feet. "Ye will rot in hell for this."

"Oh? And do ye mean to send me there, my fair slut?" He struck her across the face.

Stumbling backward, Aimil fought against screaming. The warm salty taste in her mouth told her she had cut it, but she simply spit the blood out. This time she had plenty of room to move in, and there was no Geordie to stop her from grasping some weapon. Rory would find it not so easy to brutalize her this time, and if she was lucky, she might even strike a blow or two for Parlan.

Parlan stared up at the small circle of light. It took him a few moments to recall where he was and how he had gotten there. Then he recalled the scream he had heard as Rory had kicked him into the hole, a sound that told him that Aimil had not run away as he had told her to. That could easily mean that Rory now held her. If that madman got his hands on Aimil, she was as good as dead. That thought was enough to make Parlan try to struggle to his feet, something his body was loath to do.

As he had fought dizziness and pain, he had heard Aimil's cry as he had fallen. There had been such a heartrending agony in that cry that he had almost responded to it. He then knew that he could not shake it from his mind because it told him something that was very important to him. Aimil did care for him, quite possibly loved him. No woman could produce such a sound unless she did.

Deciding that it was a poor time to ponder such things, he grit his teeth and started to make his way out of the hole. Although the rocky sides of the hole were not smooth, they were not rough enough either to make for an easy climb. A place to grip onto was hard to find. Parlan cursed his slow progress and his pain as he inched his way back to the surface. *If Aimil and*

I live through this, he thought furiously, *I will most assuredly beat her for her gross disobedience.*

His hands were quickly skinned and oozing blood which made his climb even more difficult. As he got nearer to the top, he heard Aimil fighting Rory and that gave him the strength to force himself onward. He only prayed that he reached the top in time to save her from any and all of the cruelty Rory wished to inflict upon her.

Aimil bit down hard on Rory's hand which tried to shackle her wrists. With a bellowed oath, he released her to clutch at his hand. She quickly scrambled to her feet and backed away from where he had tried to pin her to the ground.

She sensed that the Banshee's Well was but a step or two behind her. In one quick move she could enter that pit and join Parlan in death but she could not do it. In that first frantic moment after watching him die, she could easily have hurled herself after him but her will to survive had reasserted itself. Despite the grief that ate away at her, yet had not been given any release, she could not repress the need to try to stay alive.

"Ye will pay dearly for that, my pretty whore."

"Ye are forever trying to make others pay for what ye bring upon yourself."

"Bring upon myself?" He touched his mutilated cheek. "Do ye think I would bring such as this upon myself? Ye did this to me. Ye and that hellborn stallion of yours!" His voice rose with every word until he screamed at her.

"Nay, ye attacked us and got all ye deserved. Now the outside of ye is as loathsome as the inside. Now all can see your ugliness."

She was not surprised by his attack when he bellowed with rage and lunged at her. What she had hoped for did not happen, however. When she neatly eluded him, he was able to halt himself before he plummeted down the hole. He turned on her far more quickly than she had planned for as well. Her attempt to escape his second lunge failed, and she was badly winded when he tackled her to the ground. Before she could regain it and the strength to fight him, he had her pinned beneath him.

"Did ye really think ye could escape me again, Kirstie?"

A shiver ran down Aimil's spine. She had known that Rory had seen her mother in her, that his twisted mind had seen a chance to avenge her mother's imagined slights upon him. It was chilling, however, to know that he no longer even saw her, that he saw only Kirstie Mengue—a woman he had brutally murdered years ago. Rory's madness was truly complete now.

It also made Aimil angry that he thought she was Kirstie whom he intended to abuse then kill. Somehow it seemed almost an insult and unfair that he no longer even knew whom he was going to murder. She wanted him to know who fought him and whose blood was on his already blood-soaked hands but knew that was impossible. There was no reasoning with a madman.

"Ye willnae find this murder such an easy one, Rory Fergueson." She struggled to shake him off her but he resisted her efforts with apparent ease, which caused her to feel a dangerous sense of resignation.

"Ye brought this upon yourself." He began to undo her clothing. "Ye turned from my love."

"Ye dinnae ken what love is. Ye ken only hate and pain." Her squirming to thwart his efforts to strip her was briefly halted when he struck her hard across the face with an indifference that was chilling.

"Oh, but I do ken what love is. I love ye, Kirstie. I could have made it so beautiful between us but ye wouldnae let me. Ye gave all I craved to Lachlan, parted your sweet thighs for him when ye wouldnae even part your lips for me. That must be punished. It must be."

"Ye cannae punish someone for going where their heart commands."

"Your heart should have chosen me. Me! I could have given ye everything. We could have been the envy of the world. Nowhere would there have been a pair as fair to the eyes as we. Instead ye chose that fool who never treated ye as ye should have been treated. He took ye nowhere, simply kept ye in that heap of stone, and filled your belly with bairns. Ye should have been laughing, gay, and admired at courts over the world not sweating upon a childbed for that fool." He roughly bared her breasts. "These were made to be admired by a lover not tugged at by greedy bairns."

When his hand moved over her breasts, she gagged. It seemed her rape was inevitable. Unless he made some error soon that she could take advantage of, there was no way she saw of breaking free of him and evading that abuse. Although she hated it, she resigned herself to it, waiting for that moment when his release would weaken him. If she could keep her mind clear, despite the horror he would inflict, she might make good use of that weakness.

Suddenly she realized that he had stopped, even though his hand still rested upon her breast. He sat upon her and stared at something behind her head, something she could not see no matter how hard she tried to turn round. Whatever it was, she thought, it horrified Rory. His face was the color of parchment, his mouth was agape, and his eyes were open so wide they bulged.

Parlan found the added strength to pull himself up and out when he saw Rory on top of Aimil. The sight of Rory's hand touching her breast enraged Parlan and this time he made no effort to fight that. He needed the strength it gave him. Rory had nearly defeated him when he had been at his full strength, but now he was battered, bruised, and bleeding. Rage might lend him a fleeting, if false, strength that would not last long, but he would take what he could get.

It puzzled him that Rory made no move to stop him. He stared at Parlan in horror, but said and did nothing. Watching him carefully for the attack he was sure would come, Parlan collected his sword which lay where he had dropped it when he had fallen. *Mayhaps the mad fool thinks I am a ghost*, he mused, and liked the idea of proving to Rory that he was very much alive.

"Release her, Rory, and prepare to die."

"The Devil," Rory whispered as he scrambled off Aimil and away from Parlan. "'Tis the Devil himself."

Aimil paid little heed to Rory. She rolled out of his reach and quickly stood up to stare at Parlan. The sight of him battered but still alive made her weak with emotion. It took all her strength to stop herself from running to him and clinging to him, touching him to assure herself that he really was standing there.

"Ye are alive. Sweet God, Parlan, I had thought ye dead."

"Wheesht, lass, a wee tumble cannae send me to my Maker. Now, get out of the way as ye should have done before." He scowled at Rory. "What ails this fool? Ye cannae run this time, Rory Fergueson."

Turning at last to look at Rory, Aimil frowned. He was trembling, visibly shaking as if he had lost all control over his body. Then she heard the words he muttered as he backed away, his hands held out as if to ward off something. "The Devil. 'Tis the Devil come out of hell."

"'The Devil will rise up from hell and pull ye down with him,'" Aimil murmured, repeating her mother's curse.

"What is that?" Parlan demanded.

"He thinks ye are the Devil come to drag him into hell. 'Tis what my mother's dying curse was—that the Devil would rise up out of the earth and drag him down into hell. Ye rose up out of the earth, Parlan. In his madness, he thinks the curse has come true."

"Weel, I surely mean to send him to hell." He grimaced as he stared at the quivering man. "Though, I find it hard to strike at a man who is drooling like some brainless fool and has soiled his braies in his fear."

"Think of the blood that fair drips from his hands and it may come easier."

He nodded slowly and advanced upon Rory.

As if some higher power had relayed to Rory Parlan's reluctance to kill him, Rory began to shake free of terror's grip. Instead of surrendering meekly and whimpering to the Devil he had thought had come for him, Rory decided to fight. Even as Parlan struck him, Rory found the strength and the will to raise his sword and deflect the blow.

While Aimil felt pleased that Parlan would not have to cut Rory down coldbloodedly, she hated to see Rory fight back. Parlan was hurt. She saw it in the way he moved and by the ominous dark stains upon his clothing. She clasped her hands tightly and prayed harder than she ever had before. While she could not bring herself to pray outright for a man's death, even Rory's, she did pray strenuously for Parlan to win, to live.

She moved out of the way, even ready to flee if the need arose. This time she would obey Parlan although she continued to pray that she would not have to. She knew now, however, that even though she would grieve until the day she died if Parlan was taken from her, her need to live was so strong that she could not willingly join him in death nor did she think he would even want her to. In fact, she knew he would be furious if he thought she had even contemplated such a thing.

When a frantically battling Rory managed to add to Parlan's

wounds with a dangerous slash to Parlan's side, Aimil nearly screamed. Watching Parlan fight for his life, she decided, was the surest way to drive herself mad. She saw every swing of Rory's sword as a mortal threat even though she knew Parlan was a very skilled fighter.

Then she tensed, her gaze fixed intently upon Rory. He was very close to the edge of the gorge. If he fell down there, he would have no chance of survival. Parlan was pressing him hard, and she began to think that Rory's fall was inevitable.

"Your murdering days are over, Rory Fergueson. Ye willnae send another lass into the grave."

"Nay, I willnae let her curse come true. I will come to hell in my own sweet time."

"The sweet time is now, Rory. If I die doing it, ye will pay for all the horror ye have done."

"I gave none of them any less than what they asked for. Whores, the lot of them."

"Even the lowest of whores doesnae deserve what ye do to a lass. The ghosts of those ye have slaughtered cry out for vengeance."

"Let them cry, Satan. I willnae be taken before I am ready."

"No one can choose their time, Rory, especially not filth like you."

Parlan saw how close to the edge Rory was. For a brief moment he hesitated in pushing the man any further. A part of him strongly objected to the battle ending that way, wanted to end Rory's life himself. Good sense prevailed, and Parlan regretfully knew that he was not sure he could fight any longer. He was stiff and sore from his fall and had several wounds that bled and weakened him. No matter how it occurred, the battle had to be ended as quickly as possible. Sighing, Parlan lunged, forcing Rory back that final step.

Rory hovered on the brink of the ravine for an instant, his arms waving frantically as he sought to regain his balance.

With a scream of denial, he fell, his cry abruptly cut off as his body smashed upon the rocks below.

Aimil immediately rushed toward Parlan. He looked unsteady, and she feared he might follow Rory into the ravine. Upon reaching him, she tugged him back from the edge. He began to collapse, and, when she tried to help him stay upright, she was pulled down with him until they both knelt upon the ground. She was frightened by the weakness he displayed.

"Parlan?"

"Is he dead? I was unable to see." He fought to regain some strength but realized that, for now, he had none left.

Although she did not want to, she cautiously moved to the edge of the ravine and looked down. Her stomach was turned by what she saw, despite the knowledge that the threat to her and those she loved was now ended. Rory lay upon the rocks below, his body broken, twisted grotesquely, his blood staining the stones. Hastily, she moved back to Parlan's side.

"Aye, quite dead. Broken beyond repair. How is it that your fall didnae do much the same to ye?"

"There were no rocks at the bottom." He smiled crookedly. "I near to broke more than I care to think on though."

"Are ye sure ye havenae broken anything?"

"Nay, not fully sure. I may have cracked a rib or twa. 'Tis naught. But let me catch my breath and we will head back to Dubhglenn."

"On foot? Ye will never make it."

Before he could argue, she left him. He gave in to the need to lie down as he watched her collect up a few things to tend to his wounds. After a few moments of thought, he decided she was right. He would not be able to walk to Dubhglenn. He was fairly sure he would not have been able to ride either, even if they could find their mounts. What he was not really sure of was what to do next.

The moment Aimil returned and started to do what little she could to tend his wounds, he stopped puzzling over the problem. Pain combined with curiosity about what wounds he had suffered diverted him. He soon saw that he was a lot worse off than he had thought. It had indeed been mostly his fear for Aimil, his need to try and save her, that had been all, that had carried him on.

"Ye will have to go back to Dubhglenn and get help, Aimil." He watched her closely as she knelt by his side.

Tossing aside the scrap of cloth she had used to bathe his wounds and sitting back on her heels, she grimaced. She had been afraid that he would say that. Leaving him here alone was the last thing she wanted to do but she could see no other course open to her. He needed more help than she could give him. So too there was no way to get him back to Dubhglenn without aid or, at least, a mount, both of which were at Dubhglenn.

"I hate to leave ye here alone."

"The weather is fine and the dark is hours away, sweeting. I think 'tis the least dangerous course for me."

She hated to admit it but she nodded. "I certainly cannae carry ye back to Dubhglenn."

"Nay, and I fear ye would have to but a few steps down the road." He reached out to touch her cheek, the bruises Rory had inflicted becoming livid. "Are ye sure ye are able? He didnae hurt ye more than I can see or ye have told me?"

"Nay. He but slapped me about, was rough. Ye rose up like some avenging angel before he had a chance to do his worst."

"I feel it was a fine show. A shame I couldnae see it myself. Go on, dearling. Hie to Dubhglenn but dinnae push yourself too hard. I will be safe enough here." He patted the sword she had placed at his side.

Bending forward, she kissed him then got to her feet. There were not that many dangers about, especially now that Rory was dead, yet it worried her to leave him alone when he was so weak. The unexpected could always happen and, for now, Parlan could put up little defense against anything. After tending his wounds, she was surprised he had faced Rory that final time and won. The only way to end her worry was to get help as fast as she could. As she started out for Dubhglenn, she prayed that someone had been given reason enough to come and look for her and Parlan.

"Not dead? Are ye sure?" Lagan stared at Lachlan in horror. "But, Parlan buried the man." Malcolm and Artair, who flanked him, nodded agreement.

"Someone was buried, but it wasnae Rory Fergueson. I couldnae believe t'would end so simply, so bloodlessly. I had them dig up the body." He smiled grimly at the shocked surprise of the three younger men. "There was enough left for me to be certain that it wasnae Rory. Aye, t'was Geordie but not Rory.

"He has played us a fine trick. Even killed the only friend he has ever had to make it work. We hunted him too weel. He had to shake us off his heels."

"And he did." Artair cursed viciously. "Parlan set aside his doubts as foolishness."

"So I had feared. Where is he? Where is my daughter?" Lachlan asked worriedly.

"They have traveled to a secluded spot to be alone for a wee while, the same spot where Rory found them before."

"Then I suggest that we ride there as swiftly as we can. He could weel find them there again and, since a man usually has but one reason to get his woman alone, they may be less than alert."

In but moments, Lagan, Artair, and Malcolm were riding out of Dubhglenn with Lachlan, Leith, and their men. Artair found some grim amusement in riding with men he had raided so often in the past. He also felt a deep fear for Parlan and Aimil. In bettering his relationship with Parlan and coming to know Aimil, he had gained a sense of family he had no wish to lose.

Aimil heard the approach of several mounts and nearly panicked, so strained were her nerves. She realized that they came from the direction of Dubhglenn but decided some caution would be wise. Seeking cover behind a tree, she watched as they drew into view and felt weak with relief when she recognized them. The instant they had passed, she darted out of her hiding place and called to them, almost able to smile when they reined in and turned back with a little confusion and a lot of swearing.

"He found you," Lachlan stated flatly as he saw his daughter's bruises.

"Aye, but I am not too sorely hurt. Parlan remains back at the Banshee's Well for he didnae fare as weel."

Artair helped her mount behind him, a little astounded at the depth of the relief he felt and suspecting that he was a little bit in love with his brother's tiny wife. "He lives? He won?"

"Aye, he won. Rory lies dead and shattered at the bottom of the ravine. Parlan needs tending to though."

"Then we best hie to the big fool and fetch him back to Old Meg's less than tender mercies," Lagan said, even as they all spurred their mounts into a gallop.

Parlan half sat up with surprise when the horsemen came into view. His grip on his sword was instantly released when he recognized Lagan in the lead. He not only wondered how help had arrived so soon but why Aimil had brought back so many men.

"Ye must have flown to Dubhglenn, lass," he said with a weak smile when she hurried to his side.

"Nay, I have never been that swift. I met them hieing here. It seems my father insisted upon viewing what we all thought was Rory, and he kenned that it wasnae." She glanced at the men peering into the ravine. "He is dead for certain this time?"

"Aye, lass," her father replied then he looked at Parlan. "If ye can wait but a moment, Leith will go down to be sure."

"I can wait for that. For that and the burying. Aye, buried with a lot of rock piled atop his bones so he cannae rise again."

Shivering at the mere thought of a resurrection of such evil, Aimil moved so that Parlan could rest his head in her lap. "Are ye certain, Parlan? Ye are looking somewhat wan." She placed her hand upon his forehead but could detect no hint of fever.

"I am but weary, dearling. A good rest and I will be much improved. Aye, and that rest will come easier when I have seen Rory Fergueson set deep in the ground, closer to the reach of the Devil whom he will reside with now."

She did not try to argue with him but was relieved when the men worked quickly to bring Rory's body up and bury it. Parlan's weakness troubled her greatly. He could have hurt himself more in the fall he had suffered than he knew, and she was not skilled enough in the art of healing to judge the extent of his injuries, injuries she knew might easily be fatal in the end.

Her fears were not eased until they had Parlan back at Dubhglenn. In truth, the journey had only added to them for Parlan had needed help to stay in the saddle and was parchment-white by the time they put him into Old Meg's capable hands. However, Aimil fought to hide her fear from Parlan as she lent Old Meg a hand. Not until she got a moment alone with the woman in the hall outside of Parlan's chambers did Aimil give voice to her fear.

"Will he die?"

"I dinnae think so, lass. I could find naught wrong with him that I couldnae fix. I will speak true though. I am no judge of whether he has done his innards a real hurt. We can only wait and pray."

Chapter Twenty-Six

"What are ye doing out of bed, ye great fool?"

Aimil stared at her husband with a mixture of amazement and amusement. It had been nearly a month since they had fought Rory and finally beaten him. Parlan had taken a long time to recover. She did not think he ought to be up and prancing about the room. Her eyes narrowed as she decided that prancing was the only way to describe it.

"Preparing to take a wee trip, loving." He walked over and kissed her on the nose.

"A wee trip? Are ye daft? Ye were near to death not a month back."

"Weel, not that near." He decided that she was adorable when she was trying to be stern.

"And when did ye start getting out of bed and stomping about?"

"As soon as my nursemaids werenae hanging about me night and day." He turned her toward the door and patted her backside. "Go ready yourself. Ye are coming with me." He smiled at her when she turned round to glare at him.

"I dinnae think ye ought to go anywhere—with or without me. Ye are still on the mend."

He tugged her into his arms, lifting her off her feet. Although it strained his control, he gave her a kiss that revealed all the hunger nearly a month without her had brewed in him. When he slowly released her, he was hard pressed not to pick her up, toss her onto the bed, and make love to her immediately but he forced himself to smile at her.

"There now, sweeting. Was that the kiss of a man still on the mend or one who is fair mended and past cosseting?"

She stared at him dazedly. What she felt inclined to do was to push him back into bed and make love to him, but he seemed set upon doing something else, despite the heat of his kiss. With great effort she pulled herself together and frowned at him.

"Ye have been playing us all for fools then, have ye?"

"Nay, lass, I but wished to surprise ye. Now, ye go and ready yourself to ride with me for I plan for us to celebrate my return to good health." He opened the door and nudged her out. "And, ye tell Maggie to bring your things back in here. The bairn too. Since I am healed, there is no longer a reason to worry that I might have my night's sleep disturbed."

That was something she did not mind doing, she decided, as she finally left. She hated sleeping alone but, in the beginning, Parlan had been so easily awakened that she and the baby had left his chambers. He had needed his sleep. Even he had not protested too much at the start. It had bothered her that he had done little complaining as he had grown stronger. To have him order her back into his bed was almost a relief no matter how high-handed it was.

What she was not sure of was whether she should let him have his way in the matter of going out. He had been as battered as any man could be without breaking any bones. Although his wounds had quickly begun to close and had remained free of infection, he had lost a lot of blood, leaving him very weak. He had looked strong and healthy, but she was not sure she could trust in that. Unfortunately, she could not find anyone to talk to about Parlan's health, Artair, Lagan, Malcolm, and Old Meg having strangely disappeared, and without an ally, she could not see any chance of changing Parlan's mind. Even Maggie seemed to have found some place to go. It made Aimil very suspicious about Parlan's part in it all.

Parlan whistled jauntily as he saddled his and Aimil's horses. For several days he had planned the little trip they were about to make. At any moment he expected her to join him, looking none too pleased for she would have discovered that there was no one about to gain as an ally to stop him.

"How much longer do we have to hide up here?"

Glancing up at Artair and Lagan who peered down at him from the hayloft, Parlan smiled. "Not much longer, Artair."

"Dinnae see why we have to carry this game so far."

"Because, if she found any of you, ye ken weel that she would soon have ye convinced to help her keep me confined, being so near death as I have been." He grinned when the two younger men made derisive sounds.

"Ye arenae really taking her back to the Banshee's Well, are ye?" Artair asked, surprised.

"Aye, I am. 'Tis a fine spot and I willnae let bad memories spoil it. This time we will have no trouble or grief there."

"With so many MacGuins and Mengues encircling the place, I would be surprised if even Rory's spirit could slip through the net. She will be sore embarrassed if she ever kens that the men are about, even if it is at a respectable distance," Lagan added.

"Then I best be sure she doesnae find out. Hide, for here she comes and she has a face near as dark as mine."

Aimil met Parlan's cheerful, welcoming smile with a frown.

"I still dinnae think this is a good idea but I couldnae find a soul to agree with me. In truth, I couldnae find a soul at all. I dinnae suppose that ye ken why that should be."

"'Tis a fine day, lass. I expect many a lad or lassie has slipped free of work to enjoy it."

"Aye, near to half of Dubhglenn if my eyes dinnae deceive me." Knowing very well she was being played with, Aimil was torn between amusement and annoyance.

"And such lovely eyes they are too."

She rolled her eyes in disgust over that blatant flattery intended to divert her. "Ye arenae going to explain it all, are ye?"

"T'will all be clear in a moment," he said brightly as he picked her up and set her upon her horse.

Starting to get down she said, "Now, wait a moment. I think I have a right to ken what game is being played here."

"Ah, ye intend to be troublesome, do ye? Weel, I am prepared for that."

A near screech of annoyance and surprise escaped her when he grasped her by the wrists and gently, but firmly, secured them with a soft binding. He then blindfolded her. In the midst of her sense of outrage was the feeling that he had intended to do this right from the beginning unless she had been totally and blissfully accepting.

"Are ye mad?" she ground out as he set her back upon her horse.

"Not at all, dearling. Best hold on," he advised cheerfully as he mounted and took up her reins.

Aimil barely got a good grip upon Elfking when Parlan started them on their way. She wished she knew where they were going. In fact, she had a lot of complaints about how he was acting and what he was doing. As they rode, she informed him of each and every one of them, and grew increasingly exasperated at the pleasant way he refuted or ignored each of them. When they finally came to a halt and he took her down from her horse, she waited impatiently for him to unbind her so that she could hit him.

Warily, Parlan took the binding from her wrists then slipped the blindfold from her eyes. He knew she was not going to be pleased about where he had brought her. It was necessary to him, however, to erase all the bad memories of the place. He did not want there to be any part of his lands where she did not feel safe, or as safe as anyone could feel in such troubled times.

"Weel, here we are, love."

Before he had uncovered her eyes, she had heard the now familiar soft wail, and forgetting about her intentions of hitting him, she stared around her in near horror. "Oh, nay, Parlan, not here."

"Aye, here." He thrust the basket of food into her arms then collected the blanket. "'Tis a fine spot."

"Weel, aye, 'tis pretty." She reluctantly followed him as he went to the same spot they had gone each time before and spread out the blanket. "'Tis just that I dinnae really like it any longer, foolish as that may seem to ye."

Sitting down and tugging her down beside him, he lightly kissed her mouth. "I willnae have ye fearing a place on my land—our land. I willnae have there be a place that holds naught but bad memories and bad feeling. 'Tis true that none can think themselves perfectly safe wherever they go, but I mean to have ye feel as much so as possible while ye are upon MacGuin land. There is also the fact that, from the first time I brought ye here, I thought it would be a fine spot for our special place and, being a stubborn man, I dinnae mean to let aught change that." He served her some wine, smiling at her when she sipped from her tankard.

"Our special place?"

"Aye, all couples should have one. A place to go to to

mark the special moments in their lives, like having a new, healthy bairn."

She smiled, her mood improving quickly. Although a part of her remained wary, expecting something to go wrong at any moment, she tried to relax and enjoy the time they had together. Parlan was indeed recovered and that was certainly something to celebrate. He was also acting his most charming and it was nearly impossible to be anything but happy when he did so.

After he was finished eating, Parlan cleaned his mouth and hands with a dampened cloth. He then leaned closer to Aimil to do the same for her, kissing each spot he washed clean. Seeing how her breathing grew swift and erratic, and her lovely eyes darkened with passion increased his ever-present hunger for her. He smiled crookedly as he tossed aside the cloth and pulled her into his arms for he knew that their first bout of lovemaking was going to be swift and fierce, their need for each other demanding it.

Some time later, Aimil slowly opened her eyes and looked at the man collapsed atop her. Neither of them had managed to shed much of their clothing, their bodies too eager to join for them to be bothered by undressing. She felt deliciously ravished and smiled as she slipped her arms more securely around him. Despite the pleasant feelings that surrounded her, however, she could not stop from glancing around a little warily, looking for a danger her common sense said was not there.

"Ye are safe, Aimil," Parlan murmured as he raised his head and brushed his lips over hers. "This time we will have no rude interruptions. All will go as I planned." He eased their embrace but stayed close to her.

"Ye planned something else, did ye?" She tried to take his assurances of safety to heart and ignore her fears.

"Weel, aside from a less hasty tussle with ye"—he grinned

when she blushed—"I thought we would have ourselves a wee talk."

"A talk? About what?"

"Us." He wondered why a brief look of fear crossed her face.

Even though she told herself not to be foolish, she could not suppress a tremor of fear. He looked so serious and never before had he wished to discuss their relationship. When he had never given her any real hint of his feelings, she could not help but view a talk on them as a couple somewhat ominously. Even telling herself that Parlan would never be so cruel as to make love to her then tell her that he no longer desired her as a wife did not stop the taint of fear from possessing her.

"What about us?" she asked in a whisper.

"Aimil, I wish ye wouldnae look as if I am about to say something ye have no wish at all to hear."

"I beg your pardon?"

He sighed, feeling his courage and determination waver. She did not look ready or willing to hear him speak his heart. Then he recalled the way she had cried out when she had seen him fall, quite possibly to his death. The emotion he had recognized in that cry gave him the strength to go on with his plan to be honest.

"Dearling, I dinnae ken what ye think I mean to say but it willnae be so bad." He smiled when she briefly looked guilty. "Dinnae ye think 'tis far past time that we talk on us?"

"Aye, I do." She wondered if he meant to pull truths from her that she was not sure she was ready to reveal.

"We have gone along for over a year with few words about how we might feel or what we might wish from each other. We talk on near to everything beneath God's sun, but when it comes to speaking of what we feel, 'tis only to talk of the passion we share. That is glorious, loving, but 'tis not all that binds us and I think 'tis past time for us to look at what does and what we truly wish to give or to get from each other." She still looked nervous to him, and he smiled, kissing her gently. "Come, Aimil, can it be so hard?"

"Aye, it can. I cannae think that there are many who can speak freely of all they hold in their heart. 'Tis not easy to reveal oneself so fully."

"True. I planned that as the second thing I meant to do whilst we were alone here."

"The second?"

"Aye, I have already done the first thing I wished to, what I was sore pressed to do when I kissed you back at Dubhglenn."

She smiled and ran her finger along the strong line of his chin. "I was briefly thinking of pushing ye back into bed but nae to rest."

"Ah, so I didnae have to chase ye after all."

"Ye never have," she murmured, and grimaced. "I didnae even fight ye at the start though all I have always learned and believe in told me I should, bargain made or nay. I tumble back for ye with the ease of any whore espying the glint of gold."

"And that troubles ye, does it? Do ye think 'tis different for me? Ye can have me any time ye even think ye might want me."

"'Tis not the same for a man. A man is always ready to tussle with a lass."

"Aye, in most ways but 'tis only lusting that brings that about." He took her hand in his and kissed her fingers. "Ye but crook one of these wee fingers and I am like a stag in rut. That isnae the usual way. It never has been with me at least."

It was not such a really big thing but his admission of sharing her weakness for making love sent her heart soaring. She thought wryly that she was easily pleased. There was so much more she hungered for yet she found delight in crumbs.

"Should I crook my finger now?" she whispered.

"Nay, still it for the moment. We arenae done talking, lass, and weel ye ken it. All we have talked upon is our passion for each other and that has always been acknowledged between us. I wish to speak on things we have held within us, kept silent about."

"Who goes first?"

"Now, there is a puzzle, eh? 'Tis often what stills one's tongue. No one wishes to be the first to bare one's soul."

"Because then the other need not do the same but then holds all the power, especially the power to hurt," she added softly.

"Aimil, my wife, I would never hurt ye on purpose. I swear that. I cannae swear I never would for a man can be an unthinking creature at times but I never want to cause ye pain. What hurts ye, hurts me." He lightly touched her mouth with his finger. "Tell me what ye want from me, Aimil. Ye have never asked a thing of me. I dinnae truly ken what ye want or need."

"Faithfulness. I fear I am a verra jealous sort."

"I noticed," he murmured, and grinned.

"'Tisnae verra funny, Parlan." She sighed. "It isnae a verra nice feeling."

"I ken it. I suffer the same ailment myself."

"Aye?"

"Aye. It gnaws at my innards whenever ye smile at any man. What troubles me about it is that I sometimes fear what I might do to ye if I thought ye had turned to another."

Recalling that coldness that had been in his voice whenever he responded to her occasional threats to find another man, she realized that he spoke the truth. He did get jealous, fiercely jealous. She knew it was not the best of emotions but was pleased that he suffered from it.

"Why do ye think I grew so angry with Artair that day he assaulted ye? Aye, I dinnae hold with such things but it wasnae his breaking of my rules that spurred that rage. It was because he had struck ye. I saw it even then, kenned it as the source of my fury. It became the reason I sought Rory's death as weel. I forgot most all the evil he had done, only remembered what he had done to ye.

"As to being faithful, I have been and I mean to do my best to stay faithful. I have no true interest in the wenches who smile so welcomingly. They cannae give me what I can find in your arms, and none of them are worth spoiling what we have. A man can be a weak creature though, dearling. The right touch, a weak moment . . ." He shrugged. "I can but swear that I never intend to break your trust in me."

She caressed his cheek, deeply moved by his words. Each thing he said seemed to indicate that he did care for her. So too did she know that his promise of faithfulness was no small thing. Few men gave it or felt it necessary, did, in truth, feel it their right to bed a woman, any woman, as the need took them. His promise, though qualified with an admission of a man's weakness, eased the fears she had never successfully fought.

"And I have no want or need for another. I had such fears," she whispered.

"Of what, Aimil?" He knew he was close to pulling some confession of the heart from her, and felt himself tense.

"That I couldnae hold a man such as ye, that I would wake one morn to find that I couldnae give ye all ye needed and ye had gone elsewhere. I feared to find that I no longer even held your passion." She bit her tongue to stop her confessions.

Seeing her reluctance, he decided he could be excused for using underhanded methods. It was past time for them to be honest with each other. He knew that, if he got her passion running hot, she would not be able to guard her words so well, so he proceeded to do his best, albeit subtly, to get her into a fever. With a touch of self-derision, he admitted that he wanted at least a strong sign of deep feelings on her part before he bared his soul. He wanted her to go first, fair or not.

"Aimil, ye worry over naught." He eased open the bodice of her gown and brushed soft kisses over the swells of her breasts. "I have had no wish for another since I first set eyes upon ye. The first time I held ye, I lost all interest in holding others, an interest that had already begun to wane. There was a need in me that they werenae feeding, lass, and ye touched it. When I left your arms that first night, I thought on keeping ye, but I am a cautious man and wished to wait to be certain. As Lagan said, being the first man with a lass can stir something in him. I needed to be sure I wasnae seeing what wasnae truly there. It can make a lass be fooled as weel," he murmured.

"Not this lass." She sighed with pleasure as his tongue stroked the hardened tips of her breasts. "My first clear thought was that, since my maidenhead was gone, it didnae matter if ye did it again, and then I hoped ye would."

"'Tis glad I am that I didnae disappoint ye."

Her soft laugh turned to a purr of delight as he drew the tip of one breast into his mouth, drawing upon it slowly as if he relished the taste of her. "Ye have never disappointed me, Parlan. I thought ye wished to talk."

"We are talking. Did ye ever have hopes that I would come to wish ye to stay at my side?"

Finding it difficult to think clearly as he eased off her clothing and kissed each newly-exposed patch of skin, she buried her hands deep in his thick hair and nodded. "Aye. I did. All the time. I never wanted the ransom paid but"—she had to catch her breath as his kisses burned the inside of her thighs—"I feared staying until ye grew tired of me and set me aside."

"I have never once thought of setting ye aside." He rose up onto his knees and hastily shed the last of his clothing.

She stared at him, savoring the way the sun's light enhanced the warmth of his dark skin. "Ye are beautiful."

"A great brute like me?" He laughed softly as he returned to her welcoming arms.

Her answer never came for he smoothed kisses over her stomach then took the warmth of his lips lower. A protest was only half-made as searing waves of pleasure made her forget such things as the fact that she was allowing these intimacies in the full light of day. The next coherent thing she was able to say was to cry out for him to join her as her release drew near. A soft moan that was a mixture of delight and frustration escaped her as he entered her ever so slowly then remained still. She looked up at him in dazed confusion.

"I want ye to love me, Aimil," he whispered as he brushed his lips across hers. "Love me, Aimil."

As he began to move, she sighed with pleasure and clung to him. "Oh, I do, Parlan. God's beard, I do."

"With your heart not just your body, sweeting."

"With every part of me. God help me, I love ye past thought, past reason."

A part of her cried out in dismay but she was too caught up in her passion to heed it. Parlan's movements grew fierce, and she succumbed completely to her need for him. It was not until they lay sated in each other's arms that she realized the full extent of the confession she had made as well as of how he had pulled it from her. Sensing him staring at her, she slowly opened her eyes. He was looking at her with a warmth and tenderness that made her heart skip a beat.

"Ye are a verra sneaky man, Parlan MacGuin."

"Aye, I ken it. I wanted ye to go first." He smiled faintly when her eyes widened.

"Go first?" she whispered.

"Aye, t'was unfair but there it is." He lightly brushed a few stray wisps of hair from her face. "I wasnae doing weel in spitting out the words so I thought t'would help if ye said them first. Ye arenae alone, Aimil. The same madness holds me tight in its grip. Aye, I love ye." He laughed when she hugged him tightly.

"When did ye first ken it?"

"I surprised myself with it when ye had the bairn but I ken it was there already. I but put the words to it. And ye?"

She laughed shakily. "When Catarine arrived that day and kissed you. Leith wasnae surprised so I ken it was there already. I didnae want to see it though, for I saw what we shared as being fleeting, doomed to end."

"Nay, t'will never end, lass. I havenae hesitated so long for naught. I ken weel that we are a pair 'til our bones are naught but dust. I just wasnae sure ye saw it as I did. Nay, not until I heard ye cry out my name when I went tumbling down that hole. There I was, in the midst of a struggle just to keep us alive and all I could think on was how ye must care for me, that no woman could make such a sound unless it was driven out by a heart's pain. I decided t'was past time we spoke on such things, far past time."

"I nearly hurled myself after ye," she whispered, and hugged him tightly, a hug that was heartily returned.

"Weel, 'tis glad I am that ye didnae. I never want ye to even think I want ye to join me in death. A man doesnae fight as hard as I have done these last months to keep his lass alive just to have her toss that life away. I want ye to live."

She kissed his cheek. "I fear I discovered quickly that I wanted to live too, for all I kenned that a part of me had died with ye." Holding him close, she asked, "Tell me again, Parlan."

"Ye need not beg the words of me, sweeting. They will come most freely now." He kissed her. "I love ye. Ye are what makes each day worth waking up to."

"And I love ye. There are no words full or sweet enough to say it." She smiled faintly. "Ye should have guessed it when I let ye get your handsome backside on my horse."

"I thought it but I found that I needed the words."

"I see. Ye had the horse and now ye wanted his lady," she teased. "What a greedy rogue."

"Ye can keep your fine stallion, dearling. I have all I will ever want or need—Elfking's fine lady."

Please turn the page for an exciting sneak peek of
Hannah Howell's newest historical romance,
HIGHLAND SINNER,
coming in December 2008!

Chapter One

Scotland, early summer 1478

What was that smell?

Tormand Murray struggled to wake up at least enough to move away from the odor assaulting his nose. He groaned as he started to turn on his side and the ache in his head became a piercing agony. Flopping onto his side, he cautiously ran his hand over his head and found the source of that pain. There was a very tender swelling at the back of his head. The damp matted hair around the swelling told him that it had bled but he could feel no continued blood flow. That indicated that he had been unconscious for more than a few minutes, possibly for even more than a few hours.

As he lay there trying to will away the pain in his head, Tormand tried to open his eyes. A sharp pinch halted his attempt and he cursed. He had definitely been unconscious for quite a while and something beside a knock on the head had been done to him for his eyes were crusted shut. He had a fleeting, hazy memory of something being thrown into his eyes before all went black, but it was not enough to give him any firm idea of what had happened to him. Although he ruefully admitted to himself that it was as much vanity as a reluctance to inflict pain upon himself that caused him to fear he would tear out his eyelashes if he just forced his eyes open, Tormand proceeded very carefully. He gently brushed aside the crust on his eyes until he could open them, even if only enough to see if there was any water close at hand to wash his eyes with.

And, he hoped, enough water to wash himself if he proved to be the source of the stench. To his shame there had been a few times he had woken to find himself stinking, drunk, and a few stumbles into some foul muck upon the street being the cause. He had never been this foul before, he mused, as the smell began to turn his stomach.

Then his whole body tensed as he suddenly recognized the odor. It was death. Beneath the rank odor of an unclean garderobe was the scent of blood—a lot of blood. Far too much to have come from his own head wound.

The very next thing Tormand became aware of was that he was naked. For one brief moment panic seized him. Had he been thrown into some open grave with other bodies? He quickly shook aside that fear. It was not dirt or cold flesh he felt beneath him but the cool linen of a soft bed. Rousing from unconsciousness to that odor had obviously disordered his mind, he thought, disgusted with himself.

Easing his eyes open at last, he grunted in pain as the light stung his eyes and made his head throb even more. Everything was a little blurry, but he could make out enough to see that he was in a rather opulent bedchamber, one that looked vaguely familiar. His blood ran cold and he was suddenly even more reluctant to seek out the source of that smell. It certainly could not be from some battle if only because the part of the bed-chamber he was looking at showed no signs of one.

If there is a dead body in this room, laddie, best ye learn about it quick. Ye might be needing to run, said a voice in his

head that sounded remarkably like his squire, Walter, and
Tormand had to agree with it. He forced down all the reluctance he felt and, since he could see no sign of the dead in the
part of the room he studied, turned over to look in the other direction. The sight that greeted his watering eyes had him
making a sound that all too closely resembled the one his niece
Anna made whenever she saw a spider. Death shared his bed.

He scrambled away from the corpse so quickly he nearly
fell out of the bed. Struggling for calm, he eased his way off
the bed and then sought out some water to cleanse his eyes so
that he could see more clearly. It took several awkward
bathings of his eyes before the sting in them eased and the
blurring faded. One of the first things he saw after he dried
his face was his clothing folded neatly on a chair, as if he had
come to this bedchamber as a guest, willingly. Tormand
wasted no time in putting on his clothes and searching the
room for any other signs of his presence, collecting up his
weapons and his cloak.

Knowing he could not avoid looking at the body in the bed
any longer, he stiffened his spine and walked back to the bed.
Tormand felt the sting of bile in the back of his throat as he
looked upon what had once been a beautiful woman. So mutilated was the body that it took him several moments to realize that he was looking at what was left of Lady Clara
Sinclair. The ragged clumps of golden blond hair left upon
her head and the wide, staring blue eyes told him that, as did
the heart-shaped birthmark above the open wound where her
left breast had been. The rest of the woman's face was so
badly cut up it would have been difficult for her own mother
to recognize her without those few clues.

The cold calm he had sought now filling his body and
mind, Tormand was able to look more closely. Despite the
mutilation there was an expression visible upon poor Clara's
face, one that hinted she had been alive during at least some

of the horrors inflicted upon her. A quick glance at her wrists and ankles revealed that she had once been bound and had fought those bindings, adding weight to Tormand's dark suspicion. Either poor Clara had had some information someone had tried to torture out of her or she had met up with someone who hated her with a cold, murderous fury.

And someone who hated him as well, he suddenly thought, and tensed. Tormand knew he would not have come to Clara's bedchamber for a night of sweaty bed play. Clara had once been his lover, but their affair had ended and he never returned to a woman once he had parted from her. He especially did not return to a woman who was now married and to a man as powerful and jealous as Sir Ranald Sinclair. That meant that someone had brought him here, someone who wanted him to see what had been done to a woman he had once bedded, and, mayhaps, take the blame for this butchery.

That thought shook him free of the shock and sorrow he felt. "Poor, foolish Clara," he murmured. "I pray ye didnae suffer this because of me. Ye may have been vain, a wee bit mean of spirit, witless, and lacking morals, but ye still didnae deserve this."

He crossed himself and said a prayer over her. A glance at the windows told him that dawn was fast approaching and he knew he had to leave quickly. "I wish I could tend to ye now, lass, but I believe I am meant to take the blame for your death and I cannae; I willnae. But, I vow, I *will* find out who did this to ye and they will pay dearly for it."

After one last careful check to be certain no sign of his presence remained in the bedchamber, Tormand slipped away. He had to be grateful that whoever had committed this heinous crime had done so in this house for he knew all the secretive ways in and out of it. His affair with Clara might have been short but it had been lively and he had slipped in and out of this house many, many times. Tormand doubted even Sir Ranald, who had claimed the fine house when he had married Clara, knew all of the stealthy approaches to his bride's bedchamber.

Once outside, Tormand swiftly moved into the lingering shadows of early dawn. He leaned against the outside of the rough stone wall surrounding Clara's house and wondered where he should go. A small part of him wanted to just go home and forget about it all, but he knew he would never heed it. Even if he had no real affection for Clara, one reason their lively affair had so quickly died, he could not simply forget that the woman had been brutally murdered. If he was right in suspecting that someone had wanted him to be found next to the body and be accused of Clara's murder then he definitely could not simply forget the whole thing.

Despite that, Tormand decided the first place he would go was his house. He could still smell the stench of death on his clothing. It might be just his imagination, but he knew he needed a bath and clean clothes to help him forget that smell. As he began his stealthy way home Tormand thought it was a real shame that a bath could not also wash away the images of poor Clara's butchered body.

"Are ye certain ye ought to say anything to anybody?"

Tormand nibbled on a thick piece of cheese as he studied his aging companion. Walter Burns had been his squire for twelve years and had no inclination to be anything more than a squire. His utter lack of ambition was why he had been handed over to Tormand by the man who had knighted him at the tender age of eighteen by the same. It had been a glorious battle and Walter had proven his worth. The man had simply refused to be knighted. Fed up with his squire's lack of interest in the glory, the honors, and the responsibility that went with knighthood Sir MacBain had sent the man to Tormand.

Walter had continued to prove his worth, his courage, and his contentment in remaining a lowly squire. At the moment, however, the man was openly upset and his courage was a little weak-kneed.

"I need to find out who did this," Tormand said and then sipped at his ale, hungry and thirsty but partaking of both food and drink cautiously for his stomach was still unsteady.

"Why?" Walter sat down at Tormand's right and poured himself some ale. "Ye got away from it. 'Tis near the middle of the day and no one has come here crying for vengeance so I be thinking ye got away clean, aye? Why let anyone e'en ken ye were near the woman? Are ye trying to put a rope about your neck? And, if I recall rightly, ye didnae find much to like about the woman once your lust dimmed so why fret o'er justice for her?"

"'Tis sadly true that I didnae like her, but she didnae deserve to be butchered like that."

Walter grimaced and idly scratched the ragged scar on his pockmarked left cheek. "True, but I still say if ye let anyone ken ye were there ye are just asking for trouble."

"I would like to think that verra few people would e'er believe I could do that to a woman e'en if I was found lying in her blood, dagger in hand."

"Of course ye wouldnae do such as that, and most folk ken it, but that doesnae always save a mon, does it? Ye dinnae ken everyone who has the power to cry ye a murderer and hang ye and they dinnae ken ye. Then there are the ones who are jealous of ye or your kinsmen and would like naught better than to strike out at one of ye. Aye, look at your brother James. Any fool who kenned the mon would have kenned he couldnae have killed his wife, but he still had to suffer years marked as an outlaw and a woman-killer, aye?"

"I kenned I kept ye about for a reason. Aye, t'was to raise

my spirits when they are low and to embolden me with hope and courage just when I need it the most."

"Wheesht, nay need to slap me with the sharp edge of your tongue. I but speak the truth and one ye would be wise to nay ignore."

Tormand nodded carefully, wary of moving his still-aching head too much. "I dinnae intend to ignore it. 'Tis why I have decided to speak only to Simon."

Walter cursed softly and took a deep drink of ale. "Aye, a king's mon nay less."

"Aye, and my friend. *And* a mon who worked hard to help James. He is a mon who has a true skill at solving such puzzles and hunting down the guilty. This isnae simply about justice for Clara. Someone wanted me to be blamed for her murder, Walter. I was put beside her body to be found and accused of the crime. And for such a crime I would be hanged so that means that someone wants me dead."

"Aye, true enough. Nay just dead either, but your good name weel blackened."

"Exactly. So I have sent word to Simon asking him to come here, stressing an urgent need to speak with him."

Tormand was pleased that he sounded far more confident of his decision than he felt. It had taken him several hours to actually write and send the request for a meeting to Simon. The voice in his head that told him to just turn his back on the whole matter, the same opinion that Walter offered, had grown almost too loud to ignore. Only the certainty that this had far more to do with him than with Clara had given him the strength to silence that cowardly voice.

He had the feeling that part of his stomach's unsteadiness was due to a growing fear that he was about to suffer as James had. It had taken his foster brother three long years to prove his innocence and wash away the stain to his honor. Three long, lonely years of running and hiding. Tormand dreaded the thought that he might be pulled into the same ugly quagmire. If nothing else, he was deeply concerned about how it would affect his mother who had already suffered too much grief and worry over her children. First his sister Sorcha had been beaten and raped, then his sister Gillyanne had been kidnapped— twice—the second time leading to a forced marriage, and then there had been the trouble that had sent James running for the shelter of the hills. His mother did not need to suffer through yet another one of her children mired in danger.

"If ye could find something the killer touched we could solve this puzzle right quick," said Walter.

Pulling free of his dark thoughts about the possibility that his family was cursed, Tormand frowned at his squire. "What are ye talking about?"

"Weel, if ye had something the killer touched we could take it to the Ross witch."

Tormand had heard of the Ross witch. The woman lived in a tiny cottage several miles outside of town. Although the townspeople had driven the woman away ten years ago, many still journeyed to her cottage for help, mostly for the herbal concoctions the woman made. Some claimed the woman had visions that had aided them in solving some problem. Despite having grown up surrounded by people who had special gifts like that, he doubted the woman was the miracle worker some claimed her to be. Most of the time such *witches* were simply aging women skilled with herbs and an ability to convince people that they had some great mysterious power.

"And why do ye think she could help if I brought her something touched by the killer?" he asked.

"Because she gets a vision of the truth when she touches something." Walter absently crossed himself as if he feared he risked his soul by even speaking of the woman. "Old George, the steward for the Gillespie house, told me that Lady Gillespie had some of her jewelry stolen. He said her ladyship took the box the jewels had been taken from to the Ross witch and the moment the woman held the box she had a vision about what had happened."

When Walter said no more, Tormand asked, "What did the vision tell the woman?"

"That Lady Gillespie's eldest son had taken the jewels. Crept into her ladyship's bedchamber whilst she was at court and helped himself to all the best pieces."

"It doesnae take a witch to ken that. Lady Gillespie's eldest son is weel kenned to spend too much coin on fine clothes, women, and the toss of the dice. Near everyone—mon, woman, and bairn—in town kens that." Tormand took a drink of ale to help him resist the urge to grin at the look of annoyance on Walter's homely face. "Now I ken why the fool was banished to his grandfather's keep far from all the temptation here near the court."

"Weel, it wouldnae hurt to try. Seems a lad like ye ought to have more faith in such things."

"Oh, I have ample faith in such things, enough to wish that ye wouldnae call the woman a witch. That is a word that can give some woman blessed with a gift from God a lot of trouble, deadly trouble."

"Ah, aye, aye, true enough. A gift from God, is it?"

"Do ye really think the Devil would give a woman the gift to heal or to see the truth or any other gift or skill that can be used to help people?"

"Nay, of course he wouldnae. So why do ye doubt the Ross woman?"

"Because there are too many women who are, at best, a wee bit skilled with herbs yet claim such things as visions or the healing touch in order to empty some fool's purse. They are frauds and ofttimes what they do makes life far more difficult for those women who have a true gift."

Walter frowned for a moment, obviously thinking that

over, and then grunted his agreement. "So ye willnae be trying to get any help from Mistress Ross?"

"Nay, I am nay so desperate for such as that."

"Oh, I am nay sure I would refuse any help just now," came a cool, hard voice from the doorway of Tormand's hall.

Tormand looked toward the door and started to smile at Simon. The expression died a swift death. Sir Simon Innes looked every inch the king's man at the moment. His face was pale and cold fury tightened its predatory lines. Tormand got the sinking feeling that Simon already knew why he had sent for him. Worse, he feared his friend had some suspicions about his guilt. That stung, but Tormand decided to smother his sense of insult until he and Simon had at least talked. The man was his friend and a strong believer in justice. He would listen before he acted.

Nevertheless, Tormand tensed with a growing alarm when Simon strode up to him. Every line of the man's tall, lean body was tense with fury. Out of the corner of his eye, Tormand saw Walter tense and place his hand on his sword, revealing that Tormand was not the only one who sensed danger. It was as he looked back at Simon that Tormand realized the man clutched something in his hand.

A heartbeat later, Simon tossed what he held onto the table in front of Tormand. Tormand stared down at a heavy gold ring embellished with blood-red garnets. Unable to believe what he was seeing, he looked at his hands, his unadorned hands, and then looked back at the ring. His first thought was to wonder how he could have left that room of death and not realized that he was no longer wearing his ring. His second thought was that the point of Simon's sword was dangerously sharp as it rested against his jugular.

"Nay! Dinnae kill him! He is innocent!"

Morainn Ross blinked in surprise as she looked around her.

She was at home sitting up in her own bed, not in a great hall watching a man press a sword point against the throat of another man. Ignoring the grumbling of her cats that had been disturbed from their comfortable slumber by her outburst, she flopped back down and stared up at the ceiling. It had only been a dream.

"Nay, no dream," she said after a moment of thought. "A vision."

Thinking about that a little longer she then nodded her head. It had definitely been a vision. The man who had sat there with a sword at his throat was no stranger to her. She had been seeing him in dreams and visions for months now. He had smelled of death, was surrounded by it, yet there had never been any blood upon his hands.

"Morainn? Are ye weel?"

Morainn looked toward the door to her small bedchamber and smiled at the young boy standing there. Walin was only six but he was rapidly becoming very helpful. He also worried about her a lot, but she supposed that was to be expected. Since she had found him upon her threshold when he was the tender age of two she was really the only parent he had ever known, had given him the only home he had ever known. She just wished it were a better one. He was also old enough now to understand that she was often called a witch as well as the danger that appellation brought with it. Unfortunately, with his black hair and blue eyes, he looked enough like her to have many believe he was her bastard child and that caused its own problems for both of them.

"I am fine, Walin," she said and began to ease her way out of bed around all the sleeping cats. "It must be verra late in the day."

"'Tis the middle of the day, but ye needed to sleep. Ye were verra late returning from helping at that birthing."

"Weel, set something out on the table for us to eat then, I will join ye in a few minutes."

Dressed and just finishing the braiding of her hair, Morainn joined Walin at the small table set out in the main room of the cottage. Seeing the bread, cheese, and apples upon the table, she smiled at Walin, acknowledging a job well done. She poured them each a tankard of cider and then sat down on the little bench facing his across the scarred wooden table.

"Did ye have a bad dream?" Walin asked as he handed Morainn an apple to cut up for him.

"At first I thought it was a dream but now I am certain it was a vision, another one about that mon with the mismatched eyes." She carefully set the apple on a wooden plate and sliced it for Walin.

"Ye have a lot about him, dinnae ye?"

"It seems so. 'Tis verra odd. I dinnae ken who he is and have ne'er seen such a mon. And, if this vision is true, I dinnae think I e'er will."

"Why?" Walin accepted the plate of sliced apple and immediately began to eat it.

"Because this time I saw a verra angry gray-eyed mon holding a sword to his throat."

"But didnae ye say that your visions are of things to come? Mayhaps he isnae dead yet. Mayhaps ye are supposed to find him and warn him."

Morainn considered that possibility for a moment and then shook her head. "Nay, I think not. Neither heart nor mind urges me to do that. If that were what I was meant to do, I would feel the urge to go out right now and hunt him down. And, I would have been given some clue as to where he is."

"Oh. So we will soon see the mon whose eyes dinnae match?"

"Aye, I do believe we will."

"Weel that will be interesting."

She smiled and turned her attention to the need to fill her very empty stomach. If the man with the mismatched eyes showed up at her door, it would indeed be interesting. It could also be dangerous. She could not allow herself to forget that death stalked him. Her visions told her he was innocent of those deaths but there was some connection between him and them. It was as if each thing he touched died in bleeding agony. She certainly did not wish to become a part of that swirling mass of blood she always saw around his feet. Unfortunately she did not believe that fate would give her any chance to avoid meeting the man. All she could do was pray that when he rapped upon her door he did not still have death seated upon his shoulder.

ABOUT THE AUTHOR

Hannah Howell is an award-winning author who lives with her family in Massachusetts. She is the author of twenty eight Zebra historical romances and is currently working on a new Highland historical romance, HIGHLAND SINNER, coming in December 2008! Hannah loves hearing from readers and you may visit her website: www.hannahhowell.com.

More by Bestselling Author
Hannah Howell

__Highland Sinner	978-0-8217-8001-5	$6.99US/$8.49CAN
__Highland Captive	978-0-8217-8003-9	$6.99US/$8.49CAN
__Wild Roses	978-0-8217-7976-7	$6.99US/$8.49CAN
__Highland Fire	978-0-8217-7429-8	$6.99US/$8.49CAN
__Silver Flame	978-1-4201-0107-2	$6.99US/$8.49CAN
__Highland Wolf	978-0-8217-8000-8	$6.99US/$9.99CAN
__Highland Wedding	978-0-8217-8002-2	$4.99US/$6.99CAN
__Highland Destiny	978-1-4201-0259-8	$4.99US/$6.99CAN
__Only for You	978-0-8217-8151-7	$6.99US/$9.99CAN
__Highland Promise	978-1-4201-0261-1	$4.99US/$6.99CAN
__Highland Vow	978-1-4201-0260-4	$4.99US/$6.99CAN
__Highland Savage	978-0-8217-7999-6	$6.99US/$9.99CAN
__Beauty and the Beast	978-0-8217-8004-6	$4.99US/$6.99CAN
__Unconquered	978-0-8217-8088-6	$4.99US/$6.99CAN
__Highland Barbarian	978-0-8217-7998-9	$6.99US/$9.99CAN
__Highland Conqueror	978-0-8217-8148-7	$6.99US/$9.99CAN
__Conqueror's Kiss	978-0-8217-8005-3	$4.99US/$6.99CAN
__A Stockingful of Joy	978-1-4201-0018-1	$4.99US/$6.99CAN
__Highland Bride	978-0-8217-7995-8	$4.99US/$6.99CAN
__Highland Lover	978-0-8217-7759-6	$6.99US/$9.99CAN
__Highland Warrior	978-0-8217-7985-9	$4.99US/$6.99CAN

Available Wherever Books Are Sold!

Check out our website at
http://www.kensingtonbooks.com